Feather

OLIVIA
WILDENSTEIN

FEATHER
Book 1 of the ANGELS OF ELYSIUM series

Copyright © 2020 by Olivia Wildenstein

For information contact:
OLIVIA WILDENSTEIN
http://oliviawildenstein.com

Cover design by *Daqri Bernardo*
Editing by *Kelly Hartigan & Katelyn Anderson*

Leigh and Jarod

ART BY SALOME TOTLADZE

ONLY *darkness* REVEALS
THE REACH OF A *light.*

ANGEL HIERARCHY

SERAPHIM

Also known as archangels. There are seven of them. Highest
ranking celestial being.
Verities (pure-blood angels).

MALAKIM

Soul collectors.
Verities.

ISHIM

Rankers. They establish sinner scores.
Verities.

ERELIM

Celestial sentinels.
Verities and hybrids.

OPHANIM

Guild workers: professors and supervisors.
Mostly hybrids but open to Verities.

FLETCHINGS

Young angels who haven't yet completed their wings.
Verities and hybrids.

NEPHILIM

Fallen angels. Disgraced. Wingless. Mortal.

FRENCH GLOSSARY

À la tienne. Cheers.
Absolument pas. Absolutely not.
Adieu. Farewell.
Allez-y. Go ahead.
Au revoir. Goodbye.
Bon, tu viens ou pas? Well, are you coming or not?
Bonjour. Good morning.
Bonsoir. Good evening.
Celle-là parle le Français. This one speaks French.
C'est elle, non. That's her, no?
Elle est mignonne, celle-là. She's cute, this one.
Elles sont peut-être des putes. They're probably whores.
Flûte. Shoot.
Hé-oh. Derrière. Hey. Get back in line.
Il y a bien trop de merde dans ce monde. There's way too much shit in this world.
Incroyable. Incredible.
Jamais de la vie. No way.
Je me la ferais bien, celle-là. I'd do her.
Je n'arrive pas à croire qu'elle a réussie. I can't believe she succeeded.
L'amie. (*in context*) The girlfriend.

La bouteille. The bottle.

La petite est un peu jeune pour se prostituer, non? The small one is a little young to prostitute herself, isn't she?

La Cour des Démons. The Court of Demons.

Le culot de celles-là. The gall of those two.

L'enculé. The asshole.

Les bons coups. Profitable business ventures *or* good lays.

Loge. Theater box.

Ma chérie. My darling.

Ma petite. Little one.

Ma plume. My feather.

Magnifique. Beautiful.

Merci. Thank you.

Mon amour. My love.

Mon argent. My money.

Non. No.

On va chez vous? We go to your house?

Où à Saint-Germain? Where in Saint-Germain?

Oui. Yes.

Pains au chocolat. Chocolate pastry. Similar to a chocolate croissant as it uses the same puff pastry dough, but instead of being rolled and folded into a triangle, it is a rectangle.

Pardon. Sorry.

Pardonne-moi. Forgive me.

Praliné. Praline (hazelnut spread)

Putain, lâches la meuf. Fuck, let the chick go.

Sablés. Shortbread.

Salaud. Bastard.

S'il vous plaît. Please (*formal*).

Suis-moi. Follow me.

T'es drôle. You're funny.

T'es un ange. You're an angel.

Tu peux aller lui chercher quelque chose à se mettre? Et un pansement. Can you find her something to wear? And a Band-Aid.

Tu t'occupes d'elle? Can you get her ready?

Une vraie merveille. Delicious (*though, literally, the words mean:* A real wonder)

Viens, ma chérie. Come, sweetheart.

Vous êtes perdue? Are you lost?

Vous êtes si beaux. You two are so handsome.

PROLOGUE

*S*now drifted from a steel-gray sky the day my mother was buried, powdering the grid of gravestones and mausoleums in the Montparnasse Cemetery. A few people had rolled out of bed to join us, but their reasons for standing by our side were selfish—they either worked for my family or hoped to ingratiate themselves with Uncle.

"Jarod."

I craned my neck at the sound of my name. Snowflakes hit my dry eyes, melting and coursing down my cheeks, substitutes for my absent tears.

Uncle nodded to the custodian holding a bowl under his arm. For a horrible second, I believed it contained my mother's ashes, and my limbs seized up.

"It's just dirt, son." The cold wind batted Uncle's words to me. "To toss into the crypt."

Mimi tightened her arms around my shoulders before pressing a kiss to the top of my head and releasing me to perform my filial duty for a person who'd forsaken her maternal one.

Steeling my spine, I advanced toward the officiant, took the spoon from his thick, hairy fingers, and studied the crumbly soil a long moment before scooping it out and heaving it into the dark pit my mother would never again rise from.

A pit I'd put her in even though Uncle insisted it was my father's death which had stopped Mother's heart and not the letter opener.

TODAY — LEIGH

I'd never shed a feather.

Which wasn't to say I was perfect. Perfect angels didn't have a devastating sweet tooth or an addiction to romance novels. I simply hadn't lost any feathers because none of my imperfections were true sins. Bless Elysium for that; otherwise, my wing bones would've been as bare as a cherub's bottom.

Over the unrelenting rain and incessant honks of cars stuck in after-work traffic, I caught Eve's dragging groan. "It's Ben again."

Although we weren't encouraged to date, my best friend and I were both a few months short of twenty-one, so boys were never far from our minds, thoughts of them wedged between helping humans and ascending to Elysium, our future home.

Somehow, a yellow cab found a way to speed down the bottle-necked road and splash gutter water over my navy dress and heeled booties. I gasped as cool ochre beads dribbled down my calves and into my shoes.

"It's not *that* shocking. He's been calling me nonstop since—" Eve raised her eyes off her cell phone. When she spotted the wet carnage, she whipped her head in the cabby's direction, her damp black hair smacking my arm, and yelled words that sounded like obscenities but weren't.

Unsavory words cost feathers, and although Eve had lost

some, she was so close to completing her wings she was extra careful about using angel-approved vocabulary.

"Seriously," she huffed, offering me the paper napkin we'd picked up in the ice cream shop on our way back to the guild.

We'd run in to take cover from the downpour, but the sweet milky scent had led me straight to the counter. Where Eve had ordered coffee—black—I'd gotten a thick, farm-fresh raspberry milkshake.

She glared at the cab's taillights. "Some humans are so inconsiderate."

Balancing precariously on one foot, I scrubbed a questionable brown glob off my ankle.

Eve growled as her phone started ringing anew. "I dance with this guy once at the guild's Spring Fling, and now he's calling me several times a day. *Ugh.*"

"Did you tell him you weren't interested?"

"Not in so many words."

"Maybe use more words? Honesty is the best policy," I added with a smile.

"Fine." She rammed her finger into her phone's screen, then mouthed "*I'll catch up in a sec*" before gushing, "Ben, hey." Her voice took on a breathy quality that made me roll my eyes.

If angels bet, I'd wager she'd have plans to hang out with Ben before the week's end. For all her annoyance with this poor guy, Eve enjoyed attention—especially male attention.

I crossed the road toward the building that housed my angelic home on Earth. The first year I'd been allowed to venture into the human world at the ripe old age of twelve, I would only enter it once the sidewalk was clear of passersby. Which was silly considering humans couldn't see the opulent quartz residence that sprawled behind the nondescript green door.

I tugged on the handle, feet squishing inside my boots. *So gross.*

Unlike the wet mess that was New York City, the guild was, as always, warm and sunny, because the sky looming beyond the domed skylights that sheltered every room and hallway was Elysium's and not Earth's, and it never rained in the land of angels.

As I skirted around the fountains in the Atrium, a rainbow-winged sparrow dove toward me, then veered right, probably put off by the reek of city rolling off me.

"I'd do the same," I sighed, just as someone squealed, "He's coming tonight."

As I turned down the hallway that led toward my dorm room, I caught the tip of orange feathers swishing around a corner and the squeak of rubber soles on the white quartz floor.

We didn't have many male visitors in our all-female guild, so who was this *he*?

I magicked my wings into existence, feeling like they, too, were waterlogged and deserved a little sunshine even though feathers were impermeable and weighed as much as powdered sugar. As I slurped down some of my milkshake, I dug through my bag for another napkin but came up with my dog-eared paperback instead.

"Watch where you're going, Fletchling!" a strident voice I knew oh so well from my endless celestial history classes, screeched right as I banged into a large body.

The contact ripped the paper straw filled with raspberry milkshake from between my teeth and sprayed the thick pink liquid onto the torso of . . .

Of a . . .

I gulped as my gaze climbed up a leather-clad chest that ended in a face chiseled to such perfection it seemed cast from metal instead of flesh.

Before milkshake could drool out of my mouth, I snapped my lips shut but then remembered I owed my victim an apology. I swallowed. "S-Sorry."

"Clumsy, clumsy girl. Here, let me get that off you, Seraph." Ophan Mira's entire hand ignited with golden flames, which she ran over the archangel's brown leather tunic, burning away the pale splatter before it stained the supple hide.

I blanched. *Seraph?* I was in the presence of one of the Seven? *Oh, holy baby demon.*

The fire must've thinned the amount of oxygen in the pale stone hallway, because breathing became supremely arduous.

"Thank you, Ophan." The archangel had the molten voice of all my imaginary book lovers. "What's your name, Fletchling?"

"M-my name?" I stuttered.

Archangels were at the top of the celestial food chain; Fletchings were at the bottom. I'd never known one to take an interest in us. Then again, they didn't come around to Earth all that often, too busy reigning over Elysium where a handful of new inhabitants arrived each second.

"This is Leigh," my history professor said, obviously deeming me incapable of stringing words together.

"Ley, not Lee," I corrected. How many times had I told Ophan Mira of my preference? Granted, she so rarely used my name, favoring the term Fletching.

"Leigh." As the archangel pronounced my name, which sounded like warmed honey dripping from his tongue, he inspected my wings.

Although my best feature, I tucked them into my back. Our lineage caused our kind to have two types of feathers: colorful—human-angel mix, colloquially called hybrids—or colorful and metallic—pure angel, otherwise known as Verities.

And then, there was me.

"Verity. *Pure* Verity," he murmured in awe. "How rare."

What my feathers lacked in pigment, they made up for in luster.

"I didn't even know pure Verities were still being born," he added, tracing my silver down with his eyes. "How many feathers are you from joining us in Elysium, Leigh?"

"Um . . ." I moistened my lips. "Uh." His stare was short-circuiting my brain.

I'd heard many stories of the golden boy of Elysium, most from Eve. Only a century and thirty-some-years old and he'd won one of the coveted seats on the Council of Seven after several acts of bravery—most in the human world, but one in the celestial world. That was the one that had landed him the promotion. We weren't given specifics as to what had happened, just that it had taken place in Abaddon, where he'd volunteered as a guard during his formative years even though most new angels kept away from the dark place infested with high-ranking sinners.

An elbow jammed into my ribs. "Leigh's missing eighty-one feathers, Seraph."

He arched an eyebrow in surprise. "Eighty-one?"

I scowled at Eve for volunteering my number. I couldn't have lied—lies cost feathers—but perhaps, I could've deflected the archangel's question with one of my own.

Anything to drag his focus off my lacking wings.

My friend's skin began pulsing with light, which thankfully stole his gaze away. Eve was shameless. I would've been mortified to display my attraction so publicly. I discreetly checked my bare arms, hoping I wasn't lit up like a glowworm. Thankfully, I was my usual, pallid self, only wetter.

The archangel crouched, his coppery-turquoise feathers catching every particle of celestial sun drizzling over us. I had the sudden urge to run my palm over his wings, but deliberately touching someone's wings was a big faux pas. Once you were wed, you could grope away at your partner's feathers.

When the archangel unfurled his muscled body, I trailed my eyes up to his—turquoise with a swirl of brown around the pupil. Although our feathers didn't usually match our irises, his did.

"I've already earned nine hundred and eighty-seven," Eve chirruped, even though he hadn't asked, probably because he'd noticed her wings were practically full. "Only thirteen to go."

"You're almost ready to ascend." He shot her a blinding smile before lowering his attention to what was clutched in his hand— my paperback. He studied it, then gave it back without comment. He probably thought it was trashy. Angels weren't big on romance, deeming it a human trait, in other words, a paltry flaw.

I dragged my hands through my peach-colored hair, cheeks blazing. Not literally. Angel-fire would only be bestowed upon me a few years after I ascended to Elysium and proved my worth.

Ophan Mira angled her thin body between us. "Excuse me, Seraph Asher, but the Ophanim are eagerly awaiting you."

I backed up because her red feathers tickled my nose.

"My apologies, Ophan," Asher said, winking at me beyond my professor's shoulder.

He extended his wings as though he were stretching, but angels only spread their wings when they were about to fly or in a show of dominance. Since his booted feet hadn't lifted off the quartz floor, I assumed it was to put me back in my place for not averting my gaze, which would've been the customary procedure to abide by in the presence of such a powerful being.

A small smile played on his lips as he tucked his wings back and walked past me, the tips of his feathers skimming over my forearm, lifting goose bumps.

Once they disappeared around the corner, Eve spun me to face her, hazel eyes so wide her lashes hit her brow bone. "I am *so* jealous of you right now, Leigh."

"Of me?"

"Um, hello, an archangel just winged you."

"*Winged* me?"

She rolled her eyes at my ignorance, then gripped my wrist, and towed me toward our dormitories. "If you paid half as much attention in Ophan Greer's etiquette class as you pay your mortal romances"—she tipped her pert nose toward my book—"you'd know that winging means a male is interested in courting you. We smolder; they wing."

"I thought he did that because I was being impolite."

Could he have been winging me? I'd never been winged before. Not even by another Fletching. Maybe he'd winged Ophan Mira.

Before Eve could spill more of my milkshake, I shrugged her vise-like fingers off my wrist. "Talking about smoldering, you were giving off a lot of light."

She smiled. "You dream about becoming a Malakim, I dream of becoming a Seraphim, but since all seven spots are presently occupied, I'll settle for being one's wife. If I need to char Seraph Asher's pupils off to make him notice me, then so be it. Did you see his eyes, by the way?"

As Eve gushed about his stunning irises, my heart picked up speed, resonating against my eardrums, muting the arias twittered by the sparrows swooping overhead and the rapid footfalls of my peers rushing to the dormitories to change before the evening festivities.

"I thought he came down here to acquaint himself with the guilds and meet the Ophanim," I said as Eve flung open the door of our double, which was one of the largest bedrooms in the guild, spanning fifty or so feet in every direction and entirely adorned in white quartz, except for the ceiling that was made of arched glass. In all that space, though, the furniture was sparse. Only two queen-sized beds, two nightstands, and a long silk-tufted bench had made the cut, angels favoring basic necessities over clutter.

"Are you sure he's in the market for a wife?"

"Leigh, Leigh, Leigh," she chided me as she pressed her palm against the wall to make her closet door pop open. She dragged it out to expose her rackful of jewel-toned silks, satins, and sequins.

"What?" I tossed my book on the bed.

"How did my father meet my mother?" Hangers clinked as she contemplated her choices.

I frowned until I understood what Eve was getting at. "When she visited the all-male guilds after she was instated as Archangel."

She clapped her hands together a tad dramatically. "She listens!"

Considering Eve had recounted the story a trillion times, of course, I'd heard it. I bet all the American guilds were aware of the courtship between the first female archangel and the Fletching known as sixty-five, because that was the number of feathers he'd been missing the day he'd met Eve's mother.

His ambition to be considered as a potential suitor drove him to complete his wings in a month, which was how long he'd had until the courtship period expired. This accomplishment made him a legend in his own right because no other Fletching had ever earned more than twenty feathers in that amount of time—my own average was around ten, and that had been a particularly hectic month.

Then again, rare were the Fletchings who picked Triples—sinners worth a hundred feathers. You had better luck teaching a ladybug to spirit away their spots than make a Triple atone for their sins.

Eve slid a lamé gown adorned with pearls harvested from Elysium's Nirvana Sea off a hanger, a birthday present from her mother. "You should wear the dress I got you."

I slurped down the rest of my shake, then went to throw it out in our bathroom's angel-fire incinerator before heading back into the bedroom. I popped open my own closet and dragged out my rack of clothes. The ivory dress Eve had bought me stuck out like a sore thumb amid my mostly gray, black, and navy outfits. The only burst of color in my wardrobe was my prized collection of stilettos.

I magicked away my wings and unzipped my sodden dress,

then removed my booties, and tossed everything in the hamper that suctioned closed before warming with the angel-fire that would char off the grime. At least, doing laundry was painless.

"I was thinking black," I said, making my way back to the bathroom and slipping into the shower where the water was always at the ideal temperature. Spending time in the human world had taught me never to take these perks for granted. After lathering up more than once, I dried my soap-scented body.

Eve popped into the bathroom, brandishing the cream dress. "You're always wearing black. Please wear this one?"

Sighing, I relented. As the cool silk settled over my curves, I glanced at my reflection in the bathroom mirror. The fabric matched my skin tone better than any foundation I'd ever bought. "You don't think it washes me out?"

Eve appeared behind me, tying a beaded sash around her tiny waist. "On the contrary. It makes your hair and eyes really pop."

My hair and eyes *always* popped. I finger-combed my long waves, settling them over one shoulder. Out of all colors, why had I been saddled with orange?

Eve plucked a black kohl pencil from her makeup stash to accent her hazel eyes. After artfully smudging the lines to create a smoky effect, she twirled toward me, the gold fabric of her dress swishing around her willowy form.

Jealousy pinged through me at how *un*angelic my full-figured body looked beside hers. Sure, my waist was defined, but my chest and hips were so . . . so, *ugh.*

An archangel winged you, Leigh, I reminded myself. Unless Eve was wrong, and he'd just been flaunting his wings.

She popped her lips together, evening out the red tint she'd applied. "Promise to fill out your wings quickly? I don't want us to be apart too long."

"I only have fourteen months left, so I better fill them out fast," I murmured.

If I failed . . .

I shuddered.

Failure wasn't an option.

2

*O*phan Mira's voice boomed through the guild, asking us all to make our way to the Atrium.

I debated whether to even attend the celebration since I wasn't eligible—I was missing way too many feathers. Besides, I didn't even want to be an archangel's wife . . . if that was in fact the reason for Seraph Asher's visit.

Although archangel consorts were key social figures in Elysium, the equivalent of First Ladies, they couldn't travel to Earth. My ambition was to enter the Malakim's ranks in order to shepherd souls from one body to the next.

Ophan Mira's voice reverberated again from the guild's intercom-system. "Fletchings who do not show up to greet our honored guest will lose a feather."

Groaning, I closed my book and rolled off my bed. I slid my feet into a pair of crimson stilettos, then strode through the starlit quartz maze. In the Atrium, I sidled against the vines of honeysuckle racing up the quartz walls. The veins of angel-fire irrigating the stone made the tiny blooms glow as brightly as the girls smoldering Asher.

Like moths to a flame.

"You think they're attracted to him because of his status or his looks?" The voice belonged to Celeste, a fifteen-year-old wisp of a girl with hair the same chestnut brown as her tipped eyes and spray of freckles.

I studied our guest of honor as he threw his head back and laughed at something one of my peers had just told him. "Power makes people more attractive, doesn't it?"

Although five years separated me and Celeste, I sometimes found I had more in common with her than I did with Eve.

"Leigh, why are you standing back here?"

"Same reason you are."

"I doubt that."

I frowned.

"I'm standing back here because of these." She tipped her head to her purple winglets.

Although she'd gotten her wing bones at ten, a year or two younger than most girls in the guild, only a hundred and some feathers graced them. Celeste usually magicked them away, hating the pitying stares they garnered from the other fifteen-year-olds with much fuller wings.

I returned my gaze to the glittering, twittering crowd of Fletchings. "I'm missing eighty-one feathers, Celeste. There's no way I'll earn them in time to be considered."

"You could pick a Triple."

I grunted. "First off, I'm not interested in spending time with a murderer." All Triples had blood on their hands. You didn't earn the worst sinner score by committing petty thefts. "And two, I want to be a Malakim, not archangel arm candy."

She heaved a sigh. "I wish I could also be a soul shepherdess. Or a ranker."

I bit my lip, saddened that becoming a Malakim or an Ishim was outside of Celeste's reach.

"You know, if you were archangel arm candy, you could have that stupid, archaic rule changed."

Both my eyebrows shot up before I realized it was more pipe dream than attainable ambition. "Four out of the Seven would have to rule in favor of letting hybrids become Malakim and Ishim. When was the last time a law was amended? Two centuries ago?"

"Three hundred and sixty-one years ago. The law allowing angels to give up their wings."

And thus, their immortality. Before the law was amended, angels who wanted to forfeit their immortality were punished with menial jobs or locked in Abaddon for entertaining such blasphemous ideas.

I sighed. "The odds of getting anything revised are pretty dismal."

"Dismal's better than impossible."

She was right, and yet, it was such a long shot. Besides, I didn't want to marry someone for political gain; I wanted to marry someone for love. Was that so outrageous?

"I heard he winged you earlier," Celeste said, dragging my attention off the iridescent fountain lilies that bloomed at nightfall and zippered shut at dawn.

My cheeks blazed as hot as the wall at my back. "I don't think that was his intent . . ."

She slanted me a look. "Did he show you his wingspan or not?"

I averted my eyes from her all-seeing ones and stared at the angel statue spouting water from a solemnly raised palm. "I don't remember."

She let out a snort before growing contemplative. After a moment, she said, "Be both."

"What?"

"His wife *and* a Malakim."

"I can't, Celeste. Consorts can't travel to Earth."

"Did you ever think it might be because they don't want to?"

"Why wouldn't they want to come back here?"

Celeste puffed air out the side of her mouth. "You think your bestie will return to Earth once she ascends?"

"No. But Eve doesn't like it here."

"Eve doesn't like humans. Hybrids either, for that matter."

I crossed my arms. "Eve has nothing against hybrids."

"I admire you, Leigh, because you're the kindest angel I know, but you're so blinded by that girl. She's a snake with wings."

"Celeste!" I chided her just as her face puckered and a purple feather fluttered to the ground.

She stared down at it for several heartbeats, then, scrunching up her small nose, she crouched, picked it up, and closed her eyes to relive how she'd earned it. After the downy barbs showed her the memory, they disintegrated into spangling dust.

"That dude was so freaking stubborn. Drove me up the wall," she said, her lids pulling up.

Holding my breath, I surveyed her small wings, praying her confession about her obdurate sinner wouldn't cost her another feather. When none fell, I sighed. "Can you please be a little more careful with your wings?"

"You mean, stop speaking my mind? My mind's pretty loud."

"Well, tell it to be quiet."

We had ten years from the moment our wing bones appeared to earn our feathers. If we failed, they fell away from our backs, and we turned mortal . . . worse than mortal . . . *Nephilim*. There was no afterlife in Elysium or Abaddon for Nephilim. No reincarnation either, because Nephilim were soulless.

Four sparrows swooped over our heads, twittering an aria so languid it seemed inspired by stars and darkness. Whenever they had an audience, the elysian birds filled the vaulted stone Atrium with celestial music, canceling the guilds' need for live bands and human sound systems.

Celeste shrugged one knobby shoulder. "Immortality is overrated."

"Don't say that."

She wedged her lips together.

"Besides, dying is selfish," I added. "Don't be selfish."

"Like anyone would care if I was gone."

"*I* would care, Celeste!"

"I would care, too," came a deep voice that had me whirling around.

Celeste's small chin jutted out as she cranked her neck to look Asher straight on. Her expression told me she didn't believe him.

He ran his long fingers through his shoulder-length blond hair. "Why are you two discussing death?"

"Because, like Leigh, I want to join the Malakim," Celeste said, "but I'm not a Verity."

Asher observed my slight friend. "You're right; it's unjust that hybrids aren't allowed to be Malakim."

"Unjust enough to bring it up to the oh-so-forward-thinking-and-almighty Council?" she taunted.

"Celeste," I hissed, arrowing my gaze toward her wings. Like I feared, a feather fell.

She didn't crouch to pick it up this time, but Asher did. His forehead furrowed as the feather's memory played out in his mind.

When it dematerialized, he said, "It would be a shame to lose someone with such a proclivity for empathy."

Her rigid stance slackened. My limbs, too, softened at Asher's words. It wasn't that I believed archangels were selfish beings, but I didn't think they were particularly concerned about us Fletchings.

"Leigh"—the way Asher sounded my name made my heart fire—"I failed to mention this earlier, but your wings are striking."

I swallowed back my disappointment. The compliment should've pleased me, but somehow, I wished he'd commended my personality—not that he was acquainted with it. "Thank you," I said in a voice so thin the sound of it was absorbed by the gurgle of all seven fountains.

His brows drew in. Had he expected me to smolder him because he'd praised my wings?

"Aren't they?" Eve, who must've just spotted me standing in the back of the room, parked herself between Asher and me. "I tell her this all the time, but since I'm her best friend, she thinks I'm lying."

My pulse slowed. Did she really think I didn't believe her?

"They're beautiful because they match her heart." Celeste gestured to me. "And the rest of her. Do you know that she stays in contact with all the humans she saves? Goes to their weddings. Gets them gifts for their birthdays. Gives them her allowance when they fall on hard times."

"That's not true," I said, flushing. "I spend a lot on books and shoes."

Celeste rolled her eyes. "You only buy novels from the bookshop manned by the guy you saved three years ago. Before that, you had a library card."

My lips parted. I'd told Celeste this in passing. I never imagined it would stick with her.

"Leigh does have quite the addiction to romance novels," Eve said.

Celeste took a step forward. "That sort of addiction isn't a sin."

Even though Eve's eyes glinted with annoyance, her ruby lips were arched in a wide smile. "I suppose it isn't."

"I'm parched. Anyone else thirsty?" Choking on the scent of the honeysuckle at my back, I pushed away from the wall, away from the three angels crowding me. I didn't like attention, and since I was pretty unremarkable, I didn't usually receive much. Especially when my wings weren't displayed.

My *beautiful* silver wings.

As I walked away to find water, I magicked them away and faded into the throng of svelte bodies.

"*As* you all may have heard," Asher's voice resounded over the babbling fountains and chanting sparrows, "my visit to the guilds isn't purely selfless. I've come seeking a consort." His gaze swept over his many admirers, giving them all an equal amount of attention. "You might be wondering why I didn't choose someone who's already ascended. Truthfully, I wanted to give all of you a fair chance, not because I consider myself a superior candidate for your attention, but because I want a spouse who shares the same beliefs that are dear to me, and I have yet to find that person in Elysium."

His lips quirked in a stunningly white smile. I tried to remember if this was a trait of the Seraphim, if their teeth somehow radiated angel-fire. The only other archangel I'd met was Eve's mother when she'd visited her daughter for her wing bone ceremony. I didn't remember Seraph Claire's smiles glowing. Then again, I didn't remember her smiling.

I glanced at Eve who was standing beside me, Celeste's insinuations twisting inside my mind. Eve wasn't vicious. We'd been roommates for the past fifteen years. If she'd been ill-intentioned toward me, she would've shed feathers—maliciousness is a sin— and I couldn't recall her losing any. As though she sensed me thinking about her wings, she flexed them, and the yellow, gold-tipped feathers pulsated.

"The Council has given me the customary month to finalize my engagement. I still have ten guilds to visit, so in ten days' time, the countdown will begin. Sadly, this means many of you will not qualify as the ceremony needs to take place in Elysium. However, being ineligible does not take away from the fact that I'd like to become acquainted with all of you." He gestured with a sweep of his arm to the seventy Fletchings before him.

Eve fluttered her golden wings again, which had Asher's lagoon-blue gaze zeroing in on them. Two girls, who were feathers away from completing their wings, gravitated closer to Eve. Out of the Fletchings with wing bones, only five could tenuously qualify to become Asher's wife, lacking thirty feathers or less. They would still have to hurry, but scaling the fabric between the realms was an achievable prospect.

Asher turned slowly to behold the others—those who had no chance of ascending, those with whom I should've been standing.

"When I was a Fletching, I longed for my voice to be heard in Elysium but found no one to listen. Thus, after being sworn in by the Seraphim Council, I stated that my intention was to become *your* voice, the link between this realm and ours."

I tipped my head to the side. Could a man be attractive, powerful, *and* compassionate? I'd never met one who ticked all the boxes, yet Asher seemed to tick all three, which not only surprised but also intrigued me.

"All of this to say that you will be seeing a lot of me." He tossed another beautiful smile our way. "You must all be tired of hearing me speak"—I doubted anyone *could* tire of listening to such a beguiling voice—"and desperate to dig into the marvelous offerings the Ophanim have provided for my visit, but I will add one last thing. One criteria that is dear to me. This is for my prospective consorts." He looked in Eve's direction again, since all the eligible Fletchings had crowded around her. "I want my partner to travel with me. To accompany me. To work alongside me. To join her voice to mine"—his gaze surfed over the assembly again—"and to all of yours."

I suddenly wished my wings were fuller or that Asher's nuptials were a year out instead of a month.

"Are you saying you'll cancel the century-long ban to travel back to Earth?" Celeste's voice rose over the silence.

Asher searched the crowd for my friend. And so did I. She was still standing at the back of the Atrium, leaning against the wall, one raised black boot stamping the honeysuckle.

"I meant after the customary century," Asher amended.

The courtyard filled with hushed whispers.

"Is he for real?" I heard Megan—one of the eligible angels—ask Eve. She'd clapped her hand over her heart, her skin as bright as a firefly's.

The three others had their wings displayed for all to see, although I suspected it was mostly to garner Asher's attention.

Asher who was still concentrated on little Celeste.

"I need to find my next sinner," Eve announced. "Want to help me pick who to save, Leigh?"

I turned to her. "I thought you didn't want to come back to Earth?"

Eve lifted her long black hair, tucked her wings in, then let go of the silky rope, which settled like ink over her gilt-tipped feathers. "I want to become an archangel's wife. If I need to go to Earth, then so be it."

An arm threaded through Eve's. "I'll go to the Ranking Room with you," Megan offered.

Eve turned so that Megan's arm fell away from hers. "No offense, Megan, but our interests are no longer aligned. Or rather, they're too much so. Same goes for the three of you." Her gaze narrowed on Phoebe. "I mean, the two of you since Phoebe can't compete."

Even though Phoebe's long blond bangs obscured half her face, I noticed her eyes growing larger. "Why can't I compete? I'm only missing twenty-one feathers."

"Honey, you're a hybrid," Eve said matter-of-factly. "The Seraphim Council don't accept hybrids. Neither as archangels nor as consorts."

Phoebe's orange feathers bristled. "Surely, Asher's more modern."

"*Seraph* Asher." Eve snapped her fingers under Phoebe's chin. "Show him some respect."

A blush mottled Phoebe's cheeks.

"Seraph Asher?" Eve's voice resounded over the hubbub of

conversations filling the star-flecked courtyard. "Is the position open to hybrids?"

Asher's brow furrowed. "The *position*?"

"Of consort," Eve added with the aplomb of someone meant for the highest tier of power.

"Unfortunately, only Verities are eligible."

Phoebe's smile wilted from her lips as well as my own. Why must our world be so strict?

Maybe, Celeste was right . . . maybe, I should attempt to qualify. Our eyes met and held over Eve's golden wingtips. I knew hybrids often incurred disdain and denigrations from Verities. I'd lost count of the times I'd told someone off for disparaging a hybrid's lackluster plumage or inferior calling.

"Leigh?" Eve's voice carried my attention away from Celeste. "Are you coming?"

I nodded.

Not only was I coming, but I was going to pick out my next sinner, because hybrids deserved the same respect and chances granted to Verities, and perhaps, *my* voice could obtain this for them.

4

*T*he holographic image of a pigtailed teen sucking on a lollipop illuminated Eve's profile. "She's perfect, isn't she?"

I stopped flicking through prospective sinners to read the description below the moving picture of the high schooler whose skirt was so short I was surprised it wasn't a sin unto itself.

PENELOPE MOREL (11 DAYS)
PRONE TO BULLYING.

2

Eve's gold dress glimmered as she spun on her stool. "Right up my alley."

Footsteps echoed on the pale stone floor, and then the curved glass doors of the Ranking Room slid open. Megan and Lana settled opposite us at the quartz bar that ran the length of the circular room, then pressed their palms into the panels of glass embedded in the stone to switch on their holo-rankers.

As rays of light burst from the square panes, Eve squashed her palm against her own. Penelope's shifting image stilled, and a hum whirred from the desk as Eve's hand was scanned. A second later, a beep dinged, and the words **ASSIGNED TO EVE FROM**

GUILD 24 materialized over the three-dimensional picture like a stamp.

Her breathing seemed to ease after that. She leaned toward me to look at the holographic profile I'd brought up. "Eww. Thanks, but no thanks."

"What?" I glanced back at the shifting picture of a muscled, tattooed convict who'd earned a score of eighty-six for having assaulted four women.

"*Never.*" She shuddered. "I'm leaving this type of sinner to the boys. They're better equipped than us to deal with them."

"I wasn't—he wasn't . . ." *For her.*

"Try to find me sinners who don't look like walking night-mares, okay?" Eve said.

It was silly—I was missing so many feathers still—but the desperation that had tinged Celeste's gaze had fanned my desire to compete.

"He wasn't for you," I admitted.

Truth was, he wasn't even for me. However frantic I was to complete my wings, I didn't have the backbone to help a human like the one before me lower his sinner score. Besides, deep down, I believed the truly terrible sinners merited Abaddon and the years of torture their heinous crimes netted them.

The system displayed his name, current address, and the length of time he'd been in the Ranking System: 124 months. It also displayed how many points he'd earned back in that time—1 —and how many Fletchings had signed up to help him—3. What it didn't display were the names of those Fletchings. Since the man's sinner score had gone down by a point, I imagined one of my peers had been successful.

I felt Eve's gaze swing to my face. "*You* wanted to take him on?"

I palmed my knees through my silky dress. "I don't know. Maybe."

She shifted on the pebbled leather stool. "I thought you wanted to be a Malakim, Leigh."

Although I was still holding out hope to become a soul messenger, my ambition was selfish. If I could help Celeste and other hybrids earn the same rights as Verities, then—

A beep resounded against the curved walls and domed glass ceiling. One of the girls had picked a sinner. I didn't look over my shoulder to see who'd found their next mission. I just kept staring into my friend's unblinking eyes.

Eve leaned forward. "Well, then, let me help you find someone who's not going to endanger your virginity."

My heart stilled.

She rested her hand on mine and squeezed my fingers. "I don't want you to get hurt."

Relief curled through me. Relief that Celeste had been wrong about Eve. That my friend truly cared about me.

She began to scroll through the feed but then sucked in a breath and sketched a name with her fingertip across my glass panel. "I have the *perfect* sinner for you!"

My holographic feed flickered, and the face of a man with a bladed jaw, unruly dark hair, and eyes so black they seemed made of sin and starlight appeared before me.

My stomach dipped and lifted, tightening at the sight of such a beautiful, dangerous face. I slashed my finger across the glass panel to scroll down to his description.

JAROD ADLER (201 months)
Leader of *La Cour des Démons*.

Two-hundred and one months? He'd been in the system *seventeen years*? How could that be when he didn't look much older than I was? I flicked my finger across the image to bring up his score.

100

My stomach paused its strange contortions. "He's a *Triple*?"

Eve's arched eyebrows slanted as she also studied him. Since she'd brought up his profile, I imagined it wasn't her first glimpse of the sinner.

"What is *La Cour des Démons*?"

"The Court of Demons," she translated.

"I understand French, Eve." Understanding every tongue was

an angelic prowess. "What I meant was, *what* does this demonic court do? Terrorism? Mass murders?"

As she studied the Triple's hooded eyes, she said, "It's just a prettier word for the Parisian Mafia."

My lips pulled apart. "He runs the mob? How is he safer than a rapist?"

"Because that's the one thing he's not."

"He's surely murdered people, Eve! Or ordered their deaths."

Gazes prickled the back of my neck.

Eve flashed a hard stare at the two Verities behind me. "Not innocents."

Forcing myself to calm down, I murmured, "How do you know so much about this guy anyway?"

"Because I met someone during one of my missions who took him on. So, I looked him up. He's a Triple because he runs the Court of Demons. All you have to do is get him to cancel *one* operation—like make him reconsider extorting some high-rolling businessman or get him to help one person—and you get a hundred feathers. How hard can that be?"

"All I have to do?" A snort scraped down my nostrils and made them flare. "Eve, he's been in the system seventeen years." I flung my hand toward the number of Fletchings below Jarod's sinner score, my fingers cutting through the three-dimensional projection. "One hundred and thirty-one people have tried to reform him. *One hundred and thirty-one*, Eve. And his score hasn't wavered once, which means that none of them succeeded. I've never seen a profile like this. There's obviously something very wrong with this man."

Unruffled by my outburst, Eve said, "If anyone can do it, it's you, Leigh. The Fletching who never fails."

I *had* never failed a sinner, but I'd also never taken on a Triple *one-hundred-and-thirty-one* others had been incapable of reforming.

I stared at the holographic portrait of Jarod Adler again, the dark eyes framed by lashes so thick and curled they seemed pasted on. Could I truly alter this man?

Eve's soft hand wrapped around mine again. "At least, try. If I have to lose Asher to anyone, I'd rather it be you"—she tipped her pointy chin toward the back of the room—"than any of them."

I pulled my lip into my mouth and slid it between my teeth.

"Besides, what do you have to lose, Leigh? If you can't reform him, just come back here and pick someone else. No harm done."

No harm done, but time wasted. Plus, he was in France. I'd need to move to the Parisian guild for the duration of my mission.

"If my dad did it, you can too," Eve said.

I side-eyed her.

"And France has the best food."

"I'd be going there to work, not to sample French cuisine."

"You'll need food to keep your energy up during your mission. Plus, have you ever been to Paris? It's gorgeous in the spring."

I frowned. "When did you go?"

Her gaze returned to Jarod's. "Two years ago. Around the time you were helping that crack addict get clean."

"That crack addict has a name: Abigail." She was a mother of two who sank so deep she lost her kids, her apartment, and her job. She was barely conscious the night I'd found her curled up on a sidewalk in Alphabet City.

It took months to get her clean, but she'd succeeded, and even though she hadn't gotten her children back, she'd found stable work that put a roof over her head.

Eve flicked her hand. "They all do."

Did she remember any of the names of the people she'd helped?

"If you don't want this guy, then let's scroll through other profiles."

Before common sense could slap me upside the head, I yanked my hand out of hers and flattened my palm against the panel. I'd give Jarod three days, and if I got nowhere with him, I'd abandon my mission and incur the forfeiting cost of two feathers.

The machine whirred to life, scanning my handprint before emitting a shrill beep and inscribing my name over Jarod's, cementing my fate with his.

The realization that I was taking on a Triple hit me like pounding rain, soaking into my marrow, making me shiver fiercely.

Eve hopped off the stool. "This calls for some Angel Bubbles."

Which was just a fancy term for sparkling orange-blossom water. Alcohol was forbidden on the premises and outside guilds as well. Consumption of substances that altered the brain or body's performance was majorly frowned upon and cost feathers.

I turned off my holo-ranker, then slid off my stool on legs that felt devoid of blood and bones. I stumbled, catching myself on the seat Eve had just vacated. Before I could remove my hand, the Ranking Room vanished, and I found myself standing in front of a little girl with tears streaming down her face.

I'll g-g-give it b-b-back, she stuttered.

You already took the slime kit out of its packaging, Amy. You can't give it back. I heard Eve's voice, which sounded different, younger, a bit nasal.

I was reliving one of her missions . . .

B-b-but she had sooo many p-presents.

Which were all hers. Not yours. Now, write that letter, and we'll go give it to her together.

She'll tell everyone in sc-school.

Should've thought of that sooner. As the little girl rubbed her streaming eyes, Eve let out an annoyed grunt. *Come on. I don't have all day.*

The image faded into another, this time a bustling primary school hallway. I watched Amy carry the letter to another girl her age, the sheet crinkling in her hands. After handing it over, Amy curled her fingers into fists and dashed away. I dashed after her. Or rather, Eve did. We found her locked in a bathroom stall.

No more stealing, okay? Or I'll have to come back. You don't want me to come back, now do you?

N-no. I'll never steal again.

Good girl.

The gray peeling paint on the bathroom wall crumbled away.

"Eve!" I gasped as I raised my hand off her disintegrating feather.

"What?"

I tipped my head to the sparkling dust. "You lost a feather."

She stared at the levitating dust until it spangled out of existence. "So I did."

"How? Why?"

She lifted her gaze to mine. "It's the first time I want something that might not become mine."

Guilt crimped my heart. I didn't want to lose my friend over a man, Seraphim or not. "I didn't realize jealousy was a sin," I found myself saying.

"That's because you've never truly been jealous."

I'd always disliked the orangey shade of my hair and envied Eve's elegant figure. Weren't longing and envy the same as jealousy?

*a*fter leaving the Ranking Room, I didn't return to the festivities for Angel Bubbles. I didn't feel in the mood to celebrate. If anything, my upcoming mission had my stomach so knotted I felt sick. Sensing my unrest, Eve walked me back to our bedroom and helped me fold three days' worth of clothing inside a roomy handbag.

"What's the name of the person who told you about him?"

The leather belt Eve was rolling unspooled. "Why?"

"I was hoping I could ask them why they didn't succeed."

She wound it back up, then slotted it inside my bag. "They said Jarod Adler was rude and unreceptive."

I frowned. "Most are at first. Can I still get the person's name?"

She shook her head. "Sorry, but it would be a breach of confidence. No one wants to parade around their failures."

I sank down on my bed next to my overflowing bag. "Am I crazy? I feel crazy."

Eve sat next to me and draped her arm around my shoulders. "You're ambitious, not crazy."

I rested my cheek against her shoulder. "Don't ascend before I get back, all right?"

"I'm missing thirteen—*fourteen*—feathers," she said. "I'll still be around a while."

"You're so good at this you'll get them before the week's even over."

"Unlikely." For a minute, neither of us spoke, then she said, "But if I do complete my wings before you get back, I promise to stop by the City of Lights before ascending."

"Or you could take on a French sinner next?"

"Or I could do that."

I filled myself with the scent of neroli that had fragranced her skin since she'd discovered the perfume her first year out into the human world. "A Triple . . ." I whispered, because it still didn't feel real.

After a quiet moment, she said, "Whatever happens, remember that I love you, okay?"

Whatever happens? "You mean, if you beat me?"

Her body went a little rigid. "Yeah."

Odds were, she would. I sent a tiny prayer to Elysium that Jarod would be cooperative. Or at the very least, not overly uncouth.

"You should get going," she said, standing.

Sucking in a lungful of courage, I speared my arm through my bag and rose. I'd changed into a purple dress that downplayed my curves. Outside the guilds, I felt normal, but within the celestial quartz walls, I felt like my body was too heavy, my breasts too large, my hips too wide, and my stomach too soft.

"Here goes nothing," I murmured as I trailed Eve out of our bedroom and back into the Atrium to find an Ophanim willing to take me through the Channel. Until my wings were complete, I couldn't travel through the guild portals without assistance.

Fletchings were still swanning about the courtyard, feasting and drinking from the banquet laid out in Asher's honor. Asher who was still conversing with the Ophanim. I'd assumed he wouldn't have hung around after delivering his message.

Flanked by Eve, I walked over to our winged superiors. "Sorry to interrupt your conversation, but I need transport to the guild in Paris."

"Greer?" Ophan Mira said. "Can you take Leigh through the Channel?"

"Of course." My etiquette professor smoothed a hand over her form-fitting gray dress.

Like me, she was on the heavier side of the angel spectrum. Eve once joked that she must pull muscles in her wings when she flies. Her remark had cost my friend a feather even though she insisted she hadn't meant it as an insult.

"I was just about to depart," Asher said. "I can take her."

Color flooded my cheeks. *Sweet cherubs,* an archangel was going to escort me through the Channel?

Greer's hands coasted off her frock. "Are you certain, Seraph?"

I shot my gaze to Eve whose wings seemed to take up a little more space. If only I could duck behind them.

"Yes." Asher's turquoise gaze slinked over my bag. "All packed up, I see."

I squeezed my bag against me, hoping I'd stashed my undergarments at the bottom. If they were sticking out on top, I would die. Especially considering I had a great fondness for lace and silk.

As Asher commended the Ophanim for their impressive work, Eve enfolded me in a bone-crushing hug. "Go get those hundred feathers."

I forgot all about my embarrassment then, my mind wholly focused on Jarod Adler and his Court of Demons. I reassured myself that no demons actually lurked there.

At least, no real ones.

Demons, the sort humans pictured in their minds, horned beasts who sucked out your soul with their fangs and clawed through your flesh with their talons, thankfully didn't exist.

"Shall we?" Asher asked.

Shaking the image of bloodied, sharp extremities from my mind, I pressed my friend away. "Love you, hon."

Her eyes sparkled like the waterlilies bobbing in the fountains. "Me too."

Was she about to cry?

"Hey." I picked up her hand which felt cold in spite of the angel-fire irrigating the Atrium's walls, maintaining the temperature at a pleasant seventy-two degrees year-round. "We're going to see each other in no time."

Her red lips wobbled with a smile.

I hugged her again and then I turned around and followed Asher toward the Channel.

He clasped his hands behind his back. "You two are very close?"

"We've been friends since we were five and were assigned the same bedroom. Believe it or not, we never switched roommates."

But that would change soon.

So much would change soon.

"So, Paris, huh?" Asher asked as we turned a corner into another pale hallway bathed in glittering night. "Who's your sinner, Leigh?"

I glanced up at him. "A man called Jarod Adler."

He halted so suddenly my heart jounced against my ribs.

"What is it, Seraph?"

Leather whispered over his tanned skin as his chest expanded. "He's a Triple."

Had he assumed I would earn the hundred feathers Eve had mentioned in increments? "He is."

He stared fixedly at me for so long that I heaved my bag further up my shoulder.

"Why did you take on a Triple?"

Heat replaced the chill that had swamped my veins. "Oh. Uh." I bit my lip. "Because I'm missing eighty-one feathers."

His expression softened, a smile tipping the corners of his mouth. "I'm flattered."

My fingers froze on my bag strap. "You are?"

"I am."

He didn't touch me, but the warm blood pumping underneath his skin did. It penetrated every fiber of my being, solidifying my resolve like cooling metal.

I backed up before I could do something reprehensible like stroke Asher's glorious wings, which were, again, on full display. The romantic in me hoped he'd deployed them in my honor; the realist sensed they were spread because we were approaching the Channel, and he would need them to fly me out of the guild.

"Don't spend too much time trying to reform a Triple," Asher finally said. "They are Triples for specific reasons."

I swallowed. "I know."

He dipped his chin into his neck as though he didn't quite believe I understood what I was getting myself into.

It was silly, but I bristled. "I've never failed a mission."

It wasn't like me to boast, but I wanted him to stop looking at me like I was the naivest angel in the human world. I strode ahead of him into the square room filled with bright white light. When he joined me, the space, which was no larger than an elevator shaft, suddenly felt snugger than a shoebox.

He held his palms out, and I glided mine on top. His skin bled fire into my hands, whisking away their clamminess and replacing it with a prickling burn.

He murmured words from the celestial tongue that made lilac smoke gather and twist around us. Tightening his grip, he snapped his wings, and we rocketed up into the beam of elysian light.

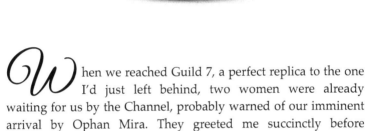

6

*W*hen we reached Guild 7, a perfect replica to the one I'd just left behind, two women were already waiting for us by the Channel, probably warned of our imminent arrival by Ophan Mira. They greeted me succinctly before lavishing Asher in attention. They were clearly there for the Seraph and not an insignificant Fletching.

Wait till I become his wife . . . Whoa. My snark made my even strides falter. Where had this confidence come from?

Asher glanced at me through the curtain of golden hair that framed his face. "Are you okay, Leigh?"

I stared at him wide-eyed, praying he couldn't discern my delirious thoughts. "I'm fine. Thank you, Seraph." And then I turned my attention toward the blonde with apple-green wings. "Ophan Pauline, could you show me to a free bedroom so I can put my things away, please?"

"*Biensûr. Suis-moi.*" Even though she spoke in French, my brain automatically translated her words. *Of course. Follow me.* "Don't forget to speak our language while you're here. It'll make Parisians a lot more accommodating."

I committed this to mind. Before leaving, I turned to Asher. "Thank you for the lift, Seraph."

"The pleasure was all mine, Leigh." His incandescent smile

replaced the concern that had wafted over his features at the mention of Jarod's name.

As I trailed Ophan Pauline down a grid of quiet hallways, I looked up at the strip of elysian sky burning with stars, the only other source of light beside the fire-veined quartz.

She led me into a bedroom similar in design to mine but smaller—four bare quartz walls, a domed skylight, an en suite bathroom, and two queen-sized beds made up with white linens. "How long do you think you'll be staying with us?"

"Depends how my mission goes."

She pressed on one of the walls, and a closet door popped open. "Myriam ascended last month, so this room is yours for as long as you need it."

"Thank you." As I walked over to the bed and set my bag on it, I felt her stare at me. I glanced over my shoulder wondering what warranted the attention, since my wings were magicked away.

"Your hair color is very . . . different."

Different was never a compliment. "Just like my wings," I sighed.

"What color are they?"

"Silver."

"And?"

"Just silver."

Her lids pulled up higher. "Can I see them?"

I magicked them into existence.

She circled around me taking them in. I hoped the color, or lack thereof, would keep her gaze away from my feather shortage. "*Incroyable*. I've never seen a Fletching with pure Verity wings before. You must be one heck of a pure-blood."

"Or the angels who made me used up all the color on my hair."

She smirked. "Do both your parents have pure Verity wings?"

"I don't know."

"You've never seen their wings?"

"I've never met them."

"They've never visited you?"

"No."

It wasn't completely unusual for parents not to seek out their children until they ascended. Some didn't want to get attached in case their progeny failed to reach the celestial city. Even though I was curious about them, there was pain mixed into that curiosity, and that pain dimmed my desire to meet them.

If I ever mothered, I'd live in the guild with my Fletching. Or at least, I'd try to. It wasn't allowed, but perhaps if I was a Seraphim's consort—There I went again, dreaming outsized dreams.

"I should get back to our honored guest, but it was a pleasure to meet you. Leigh, *correct*?"

"*Oui.*"

"If you need anything, come find me."

"Thank you, Ophan."

Once she was gone, I hung up my clothes, showered, then stood in front of my closet, debating whether to sleep or get dressed for the day ahead. Jarod's face flashed behind my pupils. Who was I kidding? There was no way I could sleep. I looked up at the lightening cobalt sky, estimating dawn was near. Jarod would probably not be awake yet, but leaving this early would give me time to study the lay of the land. I had no idea where the guild was compared to his house.

I donned a knee-length black skirt and a long-sleeved black top which had been cleaned so often the fabric had become a little droopy and fell off one of my shoulders. I tried to center it, but as I slid my feet into black heels and grabbed my bag, it slid askew again. *Oh well.* Perhaps, the French would find it stylish.

Careful about not making too much noise, I treaded lightly toward the sound of gushing water, my stilettos clicking on the stone. Just like in our guild, the walls of the Atrium were covered by rampant flowers. Instead of honeysuckle, pink roses bloomed here, which gave the space a slightly different aspect and smell to ours. A difference accentuated by the statues at the heart of the seven fountains. As I studied the quartz carvings of the celestial beings, the pungent fragrance coupled with my lack of sleep and firing adrenaline made my head spin. Meeting someone new and going on an adventure with them usually thrilled me, the same way starting a new book did. This morning, though, dread super-seded my excitement, because so much was at stake.

Borrowing courage from the statue of an angel brandishing a

golden shield, I strode through the Atrium and into the half-moon foyer where I unlocked a glass compartment from the wall of lockers by scanning my fingertip. Inside was a thin wad of bills that could be replenished as long as the sum demanded wasn't outrageous.

I stashed the money inside my handbag, and then, stealing one more breath of celestial air, I drew open the door and stepped into the unknown.

$\mathcal{A}$fter the door of the guild clanged shut, I pirouetted to take in my surroundings. The sky was dark, but the street wasn't. Smooth cobblestones framed by sidewalks too narrow for pedestrian use glistened underneath the row of antique cast-iron lanterns jutting from the limestone façade of two-storied houses.

A man sucking on a cigarette was hosing down the sidewalk in front of his bakery, seemingly the only other soul awake at—I checked the time on my phone—4:15 AM.

I smiled at him, which won me a *"Bonjour,* mademoiselle."

The scent of warmed butter wafted from inside the lit bakery where a woman with puffy red cheeks was rolling out a long strip of white dough.

My fascination made the man proclaim in rapid French, "We make the best croissants in all of Paris. They'll be ready in two hours."

My stomach rumbled. "I'll be back later then," I said, starting down the curved, cobbled street.

"We sell out before eight."

I glanced over my shoulder at him. "I'll be back before eight, then."

I brought up the map application on my phone to check where I was—Cour du Commerce Saint-André—and then I input where I needed to go—Place des Vosges. I discovered it was a half-hour walk through a neighborhood called Saint-Germain that reminded me of the East Village with its labyrinth of quaint streets.

When I burst out of the maze and onto a quay overlooking the river, my lips parted. Carved limestone ended in slate rooftops that glistened as wildly as the current sweeping through the city. I suddenly wished I wasn't in such a hurry to close my mission. The thought dampened the splendor around me, and then the sight of two homeless people cocooned in sleeping bags and panels of cardboard reminded me that not all was beautiful in the human world.

I crossed the bridge over the river that forked around l'Île de la Cité. The tiny island was even more quiet than the neighborhood I'd just left behind. Once I reached the other riverbank, though, there was noise. Not much at first—the occasional car or truck—but then I reached a larger street called Rivoli, and music spilled onto the sidewalk along with small groups of inebriated patrons. I sidestepped them, edging ever closer to a square dotted with lush trees. I scanned the buildings girdling the public garden until I located the stone mansion, which I'd flown from New York, in the middle of the night, to seek out. Although its entrance was shaded by an arcade that ran the length of the sleepy street, my digital map indicated this was Jarod's headquarters.

I crossed the road and dipped under the gothic archways toward enormous blood-red doors. If this weren't a mobster's domain, I might've found the color appealing. Instead, I found it ominous.

The porte-cochère clicked open, and two men dressed in tuxedos exited. I held perfectly still, trying to blend into the shade of a stone column, but both men noticed me. A lone girl out and about at this hour would surely draw anyone's eye.

Where one lost interest fast, the other kept looking. Although his hair was shot through with silver, his skin was smooth. "*Vous êtes perdue?*"

My mind translated his words: *Are you lost?* "*Non.*"

His pale blue gaze narrowed on me.

"Tristan!" his friend called out, drawing open the door of a black chauffeured sedan.

"I'm looking for Jarod Adler," I said quickly, hoping the blue-eyed man could somehow help me.

"What do you want with Jarod?" he asked in French.

"I'd like to discuss a . . . *project.*"

The man smirked. "What an interesting choice of word."

Was it? "Could you introduce me to Monsieur Adler?"

Tristan's friend grumbled. "*Bon, tu viens ou pas?*" *Are you coming?*

"*Non,*" Tristan responded, keeping his gaze on me. "I suppose I could introduce you."

When his gaze dipped to my breasts, I folded my arms.

"Well, I'm leaving," his friend said and shut the car door.

"Is Jarod awake?" I asked Tristan.

"Can't host a party asleep."

A party? I supposed that explained Tristan's fancy attire. "So, this isn't a bad time to speak with him?"

"Sweetheart, if Jarod doesn't want to talk to you, he won't." My eyes must've gone a little wide because Tristan added, "Relax. He'll definitely want to talk with you."

"What makes you so certain?"

"He likes pretty, soft things."

Was he talking about my cleavage, which he was still ogling, or me as a whole?

He winked at me. "Come. I'll take you into the devil's lair."

A chill slunk up my spine. What had I gotten myself into? "I'm not really dressed for the occasion."

"Don't fret about your outfit."

I raised an eyebrow.

"No one keeps their clothes on for very long beyond these doors."

I gulped, which made the man chuckle.

"I, uh . . ." I clutched my cell phone harder. "I probably should come back later—"

"Nonsense." Tristan swung his attention toward an unmarked silver plaque—not a plaque, a buzzer into which he pressed his finger.

Asher. Celeste. I repeated their names inside my mind until they ran together like watercolors and formed a single one. *Asherceleste.*

8

I stepped over the raised threshold and into an enormous paved courtyard centered around a fountain that held the statue of a woman, draped in a one-shouldered gown, spurting water. It was pretty, too pretty, for a mafioso haunt.

"You're not here to murder him, are you?" Tristan's voice made my gaze snap off the fountain.

"Of course not." A steady beat filled my ears. At first, I thought it was the sound of my heart, but then, a languid, high-pitched voice mingled with the thumping, and I realized it was music.

"Just checking. Don't want to get in trouble with the boss. Should've checked sooner but I was . . . *distracted.*"

I slid the palm that wasn't still wrapped around my cell phone over my skirt to rid my skin of its clamminess.

"You have a slight accent. American?"

Did I? "Yes."

He led the way toward yet another door. "Where in America?"

As I walked alongside him, I caught movement in my peripheral vision. A man dressed in a black suit detached himself from the shadows and threw a bladed glare our way. Tristan nodded to him, and the man ducked back into obscurity. Another black-clad figure prowled the opposite wall. I was suddenly incredibly thankful for my chance meeting. I wasn't sure how I would've gone about entering Jarod's domain if it weren't for the man beside me.

"New York," I finally said.

He knocked twice on a nondescript door. "And how old are you?"

"Old enough."

His lips quirked.

What had prompted me to answer *that*? Nerves. I was nervous.

A man clad in a bespoke suit filled the door frame. "Back so soon, Tristan?"

"Do I ever truly leave?" my escort answered good-naturedly.

"Unfortunately not."

Tristan chuckled.

"Who's the girl?" the big man asked.

"A friend," Tristan said slowly. "A friend who'd like an audience with the boss."

The man studied me a long moment before stepping back to let me through. He nodded to my bag, which I opened to prove no weapon was stashed inside.

He grunted. *"Elle est mignonne, celle-là."* She's cute, this one.

My spine tingled from the derogatory comment. *"Celle-là parle le Français."* This one speaks French, I shot back.

The man's lips flattened. "Your bag. It stays here. As well as your phone. Muriel!" he called out.

A woman sporting a fitted, knee-length dress and auburn hair coiled in a sleek twist parted a set of heavy curtains.

The guard nodded to my outfit. *"Tu t'occupes d'elle?"* Can you get her ready?

Muriel's heavily made-up eyes glinted in the dim lighting of the vestibule as she looked me up and down.

"See why you didn't have to worry about your outfit?" Tristan whispered into my ear, making goose bumps spring across my collarbone.

I almost took off running.

Almost.

Asherceleste.

I stashed my phone inside my bag before handing it over to the burly guard.

He didn't take it. "Muriel will put your belongings away. Follow her."

"I'll wait out here," Tristan promised.

I was about to tell him he didn't need to wait but thought better of getting rid of this man who seemed part of Jarod's inner circle.

Muriel ushered me through the burgundy velvet curtains and into what looked like a shop of oddities had exploded inside an old British parlor.

She pulled open a deep drawer. "You can leave your bag and clothes in here."

I dropped my bag in.

She looked me up and down. "You're what?"

"Excuse me?"

"Your clothing size."

"Oh. An eight."

She went toward a rack of clothes packed with women's clothing and pulled out a dress made of black leather and lace.

"Um." I cleared my throat. "Do you have anything . . . with more fabric?"

Muriel smiled, revealing a gap between her front teeth. "This is the most conservative one I have available."

"What sort of party is this?" I blurted out.

She lowered the hanger, smile waning. "*Ma chérie*, if you don't know what's happening inside, why in the world are you here?"

"Because I need to talk with Monsieur Adler."

She contemplated me almost a full minute before hooking the dress back on the rack and selecting a more modest one. The slit in the skirt would still hit mid-thigh, but at least, this dress wasn't made of leather—it was, unfortunately, the color of my eyes. In other words, very green. Where I didn't mind my irises being that shade, I minded my body being that shade.

"You don't have anything . . . else?" Something that wouldn't make me look like a houseplant.

Muriel shook her head.

Ugh. "Is there a changing room?"

Muriel turned around.

I guessed not.

"I won't look," she said.

She must've looked though, because she pushed my fumbling fingers off the zipper that ran the length of the dress's back, tugging it up before circling me to adjust the cap sleeves that fell off my shoulders.

Whose dress was I wearing? "Where do all these clothes come from?"

"Various boutiques. I'm in charge of buying them for Jarod's parties when his guests' attire don't meet his expectations." Her heavy black makeup had run into the wrinkles edging her ocean-colored eyes.

What sort of person cared so greatly about what others wore?

"It looks like it was made for you." Muriel gathered my hair and tucked it over my shoulder where it unraveled like spun copper, then glanced down at my feet. "Pretty shoes."

"Thank you." I smoothed the satin that felt spray-painted onto my skin. "Is he as horrible as everyone says he is?" When Muriel raised an eyebrow, I added, "Jarod Adler. I heard he wasn't very nice."

"I've been at his service for twenty-five years."

"Twenty-five?"

"Yes. Twenty-five. I was hired the day he was born." She stepped toward a basket sitting on a shelf. "People don't seek him out for his kindness."

Yet, that's what I'd come for.

Muriel fished out a black filigree mask, which she tied around my head before ushering me out of the weird closet. "Why don't you go make up your own mind about him?"

When I burst through the curtains, Tristan interrupted whatever discussion he was having with the surly guard. "Perhaps, bringing you inside isn't such a great idea."

"Why not?"

He slid a mask from the inside pocket of his jacket and pulled it on with the deftness of someone used to wearing them. "Because I'd much rather keep you to myself."

"Oh." I touched the base of my flushing neck, suddenly grateful for the mask ensconcing part of my face.

The brawny guard grunted as he walked to an ornate wooden door so thick that when he opened it the slow, sultry melody inside the room soared out. Tristan offered me his arm, which I was hesitant to take but reminded myself that he'd gotten me in.

And it was just an arm.

Latching on, I entered a room so dark it took my eyes a moment to distinguish anything. And when I did, I snapped my lids shut and lowered my head, certain that what I'd just seen would cost me feathers.

Perhaps, all of them.

*A*t some point, I opened my eyes so I didn't step into anything or *on* anyone. Although I kept my gaze cemented to the glossy parquet, I unfortunately couldn't shield my ears from the symphony of grunts and moans that overlapped the bewitching melody eddying through the room.

My heart struck my throat in time with the plucked harp strings accompanying the singer's chanting. Never in my wildest dreams did I imagine myself willingly attending a party where guests were in various states of undress and doing things to each other I'd never even read about in my wickedest romance novels.

It felt like I'd traveled an entire city block before Tristan stopped walking. A pair of shiny black dress shoes bumped into the pointy tips of my stilettos, reflecting my pale, masked face.

"Who's this?" The voice was deeply masculine and deeply blasé.

"Leigh," I supplied, still unwilling to look up.

"And you are here why?"

"She has a project for you," Tristan said.

A finger curled under my chin and tipped my head up. Although he was masked, I recognized his eyes—dark and rimmed with lashes so long they could curl all the way around my pinky.

My pulse hammered my veins as the twin pools of darkness

drank me in. Over the mixture of musk and spice swirling through the room, a new aroma reached my nostrils—mineral and green, like fig leaves after a rainstorm. I breathed in deeply, almost choking on Jarod Adler's scent.

He must've seemed certain I wouldn't look away, because he lowered his finger. "Who recommended my services?"

Bodies writhed in my peripheral vision. "Is there somewhere more private we could go to discuss this?"

A corner of his lips twitched. "I don't take payment in kind."

Revulsion surged through me. "I'm not a prostitute."

Although the mask hid his expression, it didn't conceal the curve of his lips which tempered at my fiery retort. "What's your last name?"

"It's not important." I didn't have one. "You wouldn't know my family anyway. They're all in America."

"I don't clean up messes outside my country's borders."

"The job isn't overseas."

He dipped his head, and a curl of dark hair fell over his mask and into his eyes. "What sort of job is it?"

"I told you. I don't want to discuss it in here."

He locked eyes with Tristan who suggested, "We could go into your study."

"You have five minutes of my time, *Leigh.*" He emphasized my name. Instead of *lay*, the single-syllable came out as *leh*, which meant ugly in French. Was that his intent? To cut me with my own name?

Tristan laid his palm on my forearm that was still speared through his. "Come."

"She surely doesn't need your assistance to walk, Tristan," Jarod said.

"*Surely*," he responded with a defiance and ease that had me pondering the nature of their relationship.

Cousins? Best friends? Did a man like Jarod have friends?

Jarod turned and took off at a clipped pace through the crowded room, sidestepping a couple eating each other's faces off. At least, that couple still had most of their clothes on.

As we trekked across the dark room, I focused on the line of Jarod's body, taut and lean. "Are you related?" I found myself inquiring.

"Do you find we look alike?"

"No, but everyone around here seems to know you. And the way you talk to him . . ."

Tristan's gaze settled on the back of Jarod's head. "We grew up together, but we're not related."

I was curious to know more, but we'd caught up with Jarod, so I stowed my questions for later. Jarod opened a set of doors that led to a black-and-white checkered marble hallway with a wide, curved staircase. Did he live on the floor above, or was this just his place of business?

A bodyguard stood beside the doors we'd just come through, and another guard stood by the ones Jarod was wrenching open.

He flicked a switch. Floor lamps and copper sconces flared to life in the markedly masculine space that smelled of antiquated vellum and wood varnish. Sculpted mahogany bookshelves lined every wall and forest-green velvet covered the four plush armchairs that stood at the center of the room with no coffee table to separate them.

Jarod dropped down into one of them, then gestured to the one across from him. I detached myself from Tristan to ease myself gracefully into the proffered seat, a feat considering my straitjacket of a dress.

"Take off your mask," he said.

Even though a *please* would've been nice, I removed it and placed it on my lap where my satin dress stretched so tight I worried the fabric might rip.

Jarod inspected me through his black mask. "Tristan, pour our guest a drink."

"I don't drink," I said.

"We're not going to drug you, Leigh," Jarod said, bruising my name again.

My fingers clenched around the ties of my mask. "Still, I don't drink."

Jarod stared at me again, his gaze seeming to harden behind his mask.

"And my name is pronounced *lay*."

"Wasn't that how I was saying it?"

"No, you were saying it differently."

The smile ghosting over his lips proved he knew full well how he'd been pronouncing it. "Tell me about your project."

I twirled the silk ribbon around my index finger. "Will you take off your mask? It's making me uncomfortable."

Jarod leaned back, his tuxedo sleeves straining, gleaming violet-black in the low lighting. "No."

I blinked.

"I don't care if it makes you uncomfortable. Right now, I don't care much about you, and you only have"—he checked a shiny, octagonal-faced watch that looked more expensive than the oil portrait of a frisky bay horse hung between two sets of curtained French doors—"three minutes left to make me care, so you better start explaining what it is you want me to do for you."

I wound the ribbon so snugly around my fingertip I cut off my own circulation. I let go, let it unravel. "I'm here because I'd like to understand what it is you do."

The slight jerk of his head told me he wasn't expecting that answer. "Understand what I do?" he all but choked out before his eyes became mere slits. "Who do you work for? The DGSI?"

"The DGSI? I'm not sure what that—"

Jarod swung around in his chair to look at Tristan who was pouring himself a glass of some transparent spirit. "Where did you pick this girl up?"

"On your doorstep."

Jarod wheeled back around and glared at me with a fierceness that made my vertebrae lock up. "What the fuck were you doing on my doorstep?"

I nibbled on my bottom lip, wondering how to phrase my intentions. "I came to help you."

"Ah. Help me." His expression eased back into contemptuous amusement.

I tried to square my shoulders, but my dress was so stiff I could hardly move.

"Let me guess. Your project is salvaging my soul."

My lips pulled apart.

Did he know what I was? I peeked over my shoulder to make sure my wings hadn't made an impromptu appearance. What was I doing? Humans couldn't see them even if our feathers were shoved in their noses.

"I'm not interested in what you're peddling. I'm perfectly content with the life I lead." He rose and strode back across the room. "Tristan, take the little zealot out of my house and make sure to inform my staff never to let her cross the threshold of *La Cour des Démons*."

I blinked. "But—"

"Get out."

Heat shot into my face. I got up and trounced over to him. "You are everything they said you were, Jarod Adler." My voice trembled. I hated how it trembled. "I just came here to help you."

"Liar." He took a step closer, looming over me like the monster in the children's stories Ophan Pippa used to tell us when we still lived in the nursery. Monsters made of sin and flesh. "You came here to help yourself."

I sucked in a breath. "I'm not a liar, but you're right. I did come here to help myself."

His eyebrows shot up behind his mask. "You're admitting to it?"

"I told you, I don't lie."

"Everyone lies."

"Not me." I held his hard stare, then plodded out into the silent marble foyer.

"How does helping me help you?" he said.

I glanced at him over my shoulder. "I can't tell you."

"Why not?"

"Because you wouldn't understand my reasons."

"Try me."

I shook my head, sealing my lips shut.

"To better your soul?"

"No."

"To get a promotion?"

"No."

"Tell. Me."

"Why should I? You just said you never wanted to see my face again."

He nodded to his bodyguards. "They won't let you out of this house until you do."

I balled my fingers. "You shouldn't use your power to trap people."

"Let me walk her out—" Tristan started, but Jarod clapped his friend's chest to hold him back.

"What should I use my power for then, *Leigh*?" There he was again, making my name sound so unpleasant.

"You should use it for good."

Jarod had the audacity to smirk. "Let me impart a little secret. When I make some people's lives worse, I make others' lives better. I restore the balance."

"Why don't you leave restoring the balance to people whose job it is?"

"Let me guess. This is when you tell me about God and how I should try to find him . . ."

"There is no God."

His eyes flashed behind his mask. "What is there then?"

"*Nothing*. There's nothing," I growled, not about to tell this human with a king-complex about us. Not that I was allowed to reveal our existence.

The feeling of something sharp nicking my shoulder blade made me wheel around. Grinding my molars, I readied to tell the guards to back off but found only empty air behind me.

*S*omething glimmered on the square of black marble underneath me. Although my lips parted again, no sound came out.

I'd lost a feather.

Shock washed over me.

My vehemence—or was it my lie?—had cost me a feather.

The silver barbs shivered and then began to blur as tears snaked behind my lids. The desire to retrieve it and clasp it against my chest surged, but four humans crowded me. Crouching to scoop up air would make me seem like the lunatic they already believed me to be.

I swallowed hard and lifted my stinging gaze off the floor. "I'd like to leave now," I murmured hoarsely, an unbidden tear rolling down my cheek. I wiped it away with my knuckles. I'd come to earn feathers, and here I was losing them.

Without taking his eyes off me, Jarod said, "Take her home, Tristan."

Tristan stared at the young mob boss before nodding and clasping my elbow gently, as though my meltdown had somehow reduced my trash status. Or perhaps, Tristan was gentle with me because he had the organ that was clearly missing from Jarod's system—a heart.

I whisked away another tear as I retreated into the dark, orgiastic den, tracking the lines between the floorboards.

I didn't utter a single word as Muriel escorted me inside the cloakroom and helped me out of my dress. If she was thinking anything, she didn't let on. I gave her a watery smile that made the wrinkles around her eyes crinkle with what resembled worry, but why would she worry about me? If she'd worked for the Adlers since Jarod's birth, her loyalties lay with him.

Tristan was tucking his mask into the breast pocket of his tux jacket when I emerged from the vestibule. "See you in a couple hours, Amir."

The guard grunted as he drew the door open.

I stepped glumly past him into the dawn-tinted courtyard, leveling one last look at the statue gracing the middle of the fountain. A discrepancy on the woman's shoulder made me circle her. Cracks and chips peppered her back, which was odd in comparison to how well preserved her front was.

"She used to have wings," Tristan said, coming up behind me, "but Jarod destroyed them the day his mother died. Took a hammer to the statue screaming that angels were assholes."

A chill seized me.

"He lost both his parents by the time he was eight, so you can imagine how it destroyed his faith in fantastical higher beings."

"What about you? Do you believe in higher beings?"

A kind smile tipped the corners of his mouth. "*Il y a bien trop de merde dans ce monde.*" There's too much shit in this world. "If anyone's looking out for us, they're doing a crap job of it. But, hey, if you believe in something, I'd be the last person to judge."

"Thank you."

"For what?"

For restoring my faith in humanity. "For being nice."

His smile turned a little brisker. "That's usually not the adjective associated to my person."

Beyond Tristan's shoulder, a set of heavy drapes rippled as though someone had parted them before letting them fall. Was that the window in Jarod's study or in the den infested with incubi?

"Our ride is outside." Tristan's voice stole my gaze from the house.

"*Our* ride?"

He started for the porte-cochère painted blood-red on the inside, too. "Jarod asked me to take you home, so I'm taking you home."

I hurried to catch up. "I can walk. I'd rather walk."

He opened the door. "I'm sorry, Leigh, but if I disregard Jarod's command, I'll pay for it."

I blanched. "Pay for it? How?"

"Don't you worry your pretty little head with how Jarod punishes insurgents."

"You can't say that sort of thing and expect me *not* to worry."

He walked over to a dark town car not unlike the one that had brought his friend home. Perhaps, it was the same one.

I trailed after him. "Tristan, do you fear for your life? I could help you get out—"

His brow furrowed, and then he burst out laughing. "I owe Jarod my life, Leigh. Besides, I enjoy what I do. Some might even say I'm good at it. If they were still around to speak about my feats."

He winked at me as though what he'd said was funny, but if the people were no longer around, then—I shuddered.

He nodded to the back seat. "Get in."

I wanted to refuse, especially after his last comment, but I swallowed my refusal and dipped into the car, incredibly grateful for being un-killable.

Once Tristan had settled in beside me, the white-haired driver glanced at me in the rearview mirror. "*On va chez vous,* Monsieur Tristan?" *We go to your house?*

"*Non.* We're going to drop off my companion. Saint-Germain, right?"

I gaped. "How—"

"That's where tourists usually stay."

Oh.

The driver pulled away from the curb. "*Où à Saint-Germain?*" *Where in Saint-Germain?*

"*Odéon,*" I answered, recalling the name from the map.

Tristan ran his fingers through his silvering black hair. "*Odéon* is a subway station, Leigh."

"It's close to where I'm going."

"It's five o'clock in the morning," Tristan said. "I'm not dropping you off in front of a subway station."

"I walked all the way here."

"I didn't know you then."

"Really, Tristan, it's fine."

"Leigh . . ."

Ugh. "Fine." It wasn't as though I would ever see him again after today. "Cour du Commerce Saint-André."

The thought dampened my already low spirits. No wonder no one had ever succeeded in reforming Jarod Adler. I mulled over every minute he'd allotted me. Could I have done something differently, or would he have tossed me out whatever I'd said? I was still contemplating this when the driver pulled up to the curb of the Boulevard Saint-Germain.

I got out, and so did Tristan.

"You're not planning on walking me to my door, are you now?" Our quartz residences only appeared to angel-bloods, so it wasn't as though he would see anything besides a normal human entryway if he peeked inside the guild, but still, I didn't think my fellow Fletchings and the Ophanim would appreciate sinners knowing where they lived.

He raised another brazen smile. "I pride myself on being thoroughly courteous."

His chivalry was beginning to weigh on me. "You're relentless."

"They don't call me the Pitbull for nothing."

Goose bumps rushed over me. "How did you earn that nickname?"

"Because I *never* let go."

I absorbed his answer slowly. "Is that because you're scared of where you'd land?"

His smile faltered. "What?"

"People usually hang on because they're terrified of falling."

I started down the narrow, winding street, hoping the analysis of his psyche had been so unwelcomed he wouldn't follow. But soon, the faint click of my heels wasn't the only sound echoing on the cobblestones.

"I'm not afraid of anything." Tristan trapped my shoulder and spun me around.

I inspected his face. "Everyone's scared of something whether consciously or not."

Wetting my lips, I thought of how I feared failing my angelic training in time—and I wasn't talking about Asher's nuptials. I was talking about the fourteen months I had left before my wing bones vanished from my undeserving back.

I sighed. *Eighty-two* . . . I'd only lost one feather, yet my wings felt ounces lighter. "But fear isn't inherently bad. Not if you use it as fuel for your goals."

He released me. "What is it *you* fear?"

"Not succeeding at what I was born to do."

"And what is that?"

How could I explain it without giving away any secrets? "Helping people become better versions of themselves."

He squeezed one of his eyes a little shut. "You were born to become a saint?"

"*Saintly.*"

"Well *Maman* hoped I'd be a cobbler, but I chose differently."

I had a brief flash of Tristan shaping stiff hide into shoes but blinked it away. "In my case, there's nothing I'd rather do."

"Are your parents missionaries?"

"I suppose you could call them that."

"So they're imposing their way of life on you?"

"No." I said this so quickly it made his slightly closed eye reopen. "It's a choice."

"Are you sure about that, Leigh?"

"Of course, I'm sure."

He made a sound like he wasn't convinced.

"What?"

"A choice is when you have more than one option. Do you have other options?"

My other option was becoming mortal and useless. "I'm not interested in another option."

"Then it isn't a choice."

"Geez, you really are a pit bull," I grumbled.

He grinned, clearly proud even though I hadn't meant it as a compliment.

"I'd love to explain my life to you, but I can't. Besides, after today, we'll never see each other again."

"Never say never."

"Let me rephrase myself then. It is *tremendously* unlikely that we'll run into each other again because I'll be leaving this city before the end of the day, and I won't seek you or Jarod out to say *adieu*."

The corners of his mouth kicked up higher. "I've heard that speech a thousand times, and yet women find their way back to me *all* the time."

I rolled my eyes. "Bye, Tristan."

I turned and started down the street. This time, he didn't follow, but I sensed him watching me until I disappeared inside my world of quartz and feathers.

*a*s I navigated through the Atrium toward the dormitory section, I crossed paths with two early risers. I said hi. After cocking their eyebrows, they returned my greeting. I didn't bother with introductions since I was about to pack up and leave. It dawned on me that before the day was out, I'd be another two feathers lighter. *Ugh.*

Pushing into my bedroom, I muttered, "Worst. Decision. Ever."

"What is?"

I screeched a little. "Celeste? What are you doing here?"

She folded a T-shirt, then rolled it up, and stashed it away inside a drawer. "Turns out, there are a lot of sinners in this town, and one of them needed some saving."

Once the shock of seeing my friend wore off and my pulse decreased to a somewhat normal rhythm, I asked, "You didn't pick a Triple, did you?"

"Nope. A fiver." She eyed me cautiously. "So, what was your worst decision ever?"

I walked over to my bed and flopped back onto it, arms outstretched. The mattress bounced twice before molding around my tired body. "Picking a Triple."

To think I'd done it to access Elysium quicker. Perhaps, this was why my mission had been fated to fail from the get-go. Because I hadn't come here for Jarod; I'd come here for myself.

"Didn't go so well?"

"I lost a feather."

Celeste's heart-shaped mouth popped open. "You've never lost a feather."

"My point exactly." I groaned at my stupidity or was it naivete? "To think I'm about to lose two more."

"You're quitting?" she exclaimed.

"He doesn't want to be changed."

"Since when do sinners want to be changed?"

"He was rude."

"Since when are they nice?"

"He made me lose a feather."

"How?"

"He angered me so much I lied about something."

"What did you lie about?"

"He asked if there was anything *up there*"—I set my gaze on the skylight that gave onto Elysium—"and I said no."

The mattress dipped, and then a soft hand set on my arm. "It's not as though you could've told him about us."

"No. But I didn't have to lie. I could've deflected his question by saying I believed in some higher being."

Celeste didn't speak for a while. Then, "So you're giving up because he made you angry?"

"He made me lose control. I've *never* lost control."

"Recover the control but don't give up."

I exhaled a short breath. "Did you miss the part about him not being interested in my services?"

"No, I got that, oh moody one, but the way I see it, you sign off now, and you lose two more feathers, which will make you . . ."

When she started ticking her fingers, I supplied, "Eighty-four feathers away from Elysium."

"He's a Triple, so he's still worth a hundred feathers."

"Great math skills, oh teeny one."

She flicked my rib cage. "So how about you give it another sixteen feathers before throwing in the towel?"

My eyes snapped wide. "You're encouraging me to lose sixteen more feathers?"

"I'm encouraging you not to be a complete coward." She shot to her feet and went back to unpacking her clothes that looked so small on the hangers, almost doll sized. Then again, Celeste was five feet nothing. "Did I ever mention how I looked up to you? And not because you're a foot taller." I wasn't six feet tall—only five seven. "It's because you don't give up. So, don't you start now." She side-eyed me. "And if you need extra motivation, everyone back home expects you to quit."

"What?" I sat up so fast my vision swam. "Who thinks I'm going to quit?"

"*Everyone.*"

Eve surely didn't think I'd quit, so it couldn't be everyone. Maybe, everyone minus Eve.

"I'm hungry. Want to go grab breakfast? I heard *pains au chocolat* are real tasty around here."

I ironed out my annoyance that everyone was betting against me.

"Did I make you mad? Your eyes just went Abaddon-black." There was a lilt to her tone that made me think she wasn't the least bit repentant for the anger she'd caused me.

My lips were squeezed too tight to allow words out. Jarod's stupidly-long lashed gaze zipped behind my lids. I couldn't go back there . . . Tristan would tease me, and Jarod would—What *would* he do if I showed up on his doorstep again? Have his huge-bouncer-slash-bodyguard Amir toss me in a landfill?

The corners of Celeste's eyes tipped in time with the ones of her mouth. "Will you have breakfast with me before you head back to New York?"

"What's with the look?"

"What look?" She feigned innocence.

"The 'cat who got the canary' look."

She blinked as though she had no clue what I was inferring. "Whatever do you mean?"

"You came out here to make sure I didn't quit."

She dropped the weird look. "Because I want *you* up there, not Eve, not any other Fletching. And from what I saw at the guild party, so does Seraph Asher. So please, please, *please* don't give up."

I twisted my lips, remembering my fallen feather glimmering atop the black marble.

"I know I'm pushy, Leigh, but I want to see you succeed. Which you will. You *always* succeed."

I was like a winged version of Tristan. As the image of a flying pit bull materialized in my mind, I almost cracked a smile.

"Promise to give your Triple another chance? Or sixteen chances?" Celeste watched me with such wide, hopeful eyes that I sighed.

I draped an arm over her narrow shoulders. "I won't sacrifice sixteen feathers, but I'll try one more time. Now, let's go hunt down those *pains au chocolat*. I'm going to need sustenance if I want to survive the coming day."

"By the way, I snore," Celeste said.

I laughed. "Good to know."

Her chestnut eyes sparkled. I didn't have siblings—at least, none that I knew about. We were tossed into guilds after our first celestial breath, so our true family wasn't the one we were born to but the one we forged during our formative years. Some Fletchings deemed these relationships simple friendships, but there was nothing simple about the bonds woven in the guilds.

At least, not for me.

My relationship with both Celeste and Eve was deep and intricate, glossed by tears and whittled by laughter, the sort of bonds that would last as long as we did.

An eternity.

I squeezed Celeste's small body against me. "Thank you for coming out here and kicking my butt."

Her freckles darkened.

"So, tell me about your mission now," I said.

As she touched on the thieving boy, I wondered if Eve would've come had she not been busy with her own mission. And then, I wondered if she'd already succeeded, but stopped wondering and focused on Celeste, who was the one here.

The one who'd come for me.

*a*fter wandering through the crooked streets of Paris for the better part of the morning, Celeste went to meet her sinner, and I took a nap that turned into hours of sleep. When I awoke, the elysian sky was purple with stars, which meant night had fallen over Paris, too.

I didn't get up right away, too busy contemplating the stars and the dire choice I'd made. Had I really signed up to take on a Triple? Had I really gone to his house and met him? Had I really lost a feather?

I turned onto my side, finding a small lump emitting soft snores and topped by a tangle of long brown hair in the bed next to mine—*Celeste*.

Sighing, I threw the sheets off my legs and tiptoed around the room as quietly as possible. As I ran a brush through my hair, which looked shot through with copper and gold in the angel-fire lighting, I popped open the two top buttons of my black dress because my breasts were straining the cotton. Had they grown again? I turned sideways, inspecting my body. The bodice was definitely too tight, but opening any more buttons would make me look like one of the women from Jarod's party, and although I wanted to be invited back into *La Cour des Démons*, I didn't want to be confused with one of his special guests.

I was there for business, not pleasure.

I set the brush down, grabbed my bag, and left the bedroom, closing the door gently behind me. Unlike this morning, many Fletchings were out and about. I got my fair share of stares again as I walked through the guild.

"*Bonsoir,* Leigh," Ophan Pauline said as I passed by her.

I smiled and wished her a pleasant night. I heard Fletchings ask her who I was—"a transfer from Guild 24"—and then I heard Asher's name fall from many sets of lips. He must've given his speech already. Was he still around or had he departed? And if he'd left, had he given anyone a lift? As I exited into the dusky night, jealousy coated me like a cobweb, barely there but present nonetheless.

I jerked to a stop.

Jealousy had cost Eve a feather. I prayed it wouldn't cost me one, too. I shut my eyes, waiting for the sting to come. Three pain-free lungfuls of oxygen later, I lifted my lids and pirouetted, checking the cobblestones around my bronzed heels.

I must not have been jealous enough to lose a feather. I took the subway this time, figuring it would be quicker than walking, but regretted my decision when I caught the reek of sweat rolling off the humans scurrying through the tunnels.

A woman with ripped clothes, dirt-stained cheeks, and a sleeping child cradled in her lap extended a paper cup filled with coins. "*Shivouplait,*" she said, jingling the cup.

It took me a couple of seconds to figure out she meant, "*S'il vous plaît.*" *Please.* I dug a blue bill from my bag and stuffed it inside her cup.

She blinked at the bill, then at me, but didn't say thank you. Hopefully, she'd use the money to feed her kid although I sadly doubted this. We had our fair share of beggars back in New York City, and most of them traded their cash for alcohol or gave it to their organization's boss.

I continued down the tunnel, hurrying when the grating sound of a train braking echoed against the tiled quay, and all but flew down a steep flight of stairs, lurching into the train right before the glass doors clasped shut.

Four stops later, I changed trains at an even busier station and then spent another ten minutes rocked sideways in a metal tube snaking under Paris. When I emerged above ground, I greedily gulped in air that didn't smell like a thousand bodies.

How I longed to fly.

I checked the navy plaque nailed to the building on the street corner to figure out where I was standing. Once I situated myself, I headed east toward the manicured square and the foreboding red doors. As I walked, I deliberated on the case I was about to plead to be allowed one more audience with the Demon Court's leader.

I shuddered at the idea of going back inside and facing Jarod, but when I reached the crimson entrance, I pressed the buzzer. Unlike yesterday, the door didn't click open. I waited before ringing again. Nothing. I supposed Jarod had passed around the order not to let me in.

He couldn't stay locked inside forever, though. And considering his line of work, he was bound to receive a visitor. I was good at waiting people out.

I took the book I'd brought along and settled against one of the arcade's stone pillars, angling the pages toward the lamppost. I'd wait all night if that's what it took.

An hour later, I shut the book, shocked by the final plot twist—the duke hadn't gotten the girl; the stable boy had. I wasn't sure how I felt about the turn of events. I'd been so certain the heroine would end up with the duke that I'd discarded the stable boy, and here he was besting his sovereign.

"I thought she was leaving the country," a gruff voice said.

I jerked my gaze off the cover, almost giving myself whiplash.

Tristan's light eyes sparked in the obscurity, and a smile flipped the corners of his mouth up.

Before he could say *I told you so*, I wet my lips. "Monsieur Adler, I know you didn't want to see me—"

"Jarod."

"What?"

He crossed his arms, stretching the sleeves of his fine navy suit. Skull-and-bones cufflinks gleamed on his white shirt cuffs. "Monsieur Adler was my uncle."

"*Oh.* Um, okay."

"Why are you here?"

"To explain my motivations." The only way he'd accept my

help was if I packaged it as something else entirely. "I bet my best friend I could get you to do *one* kind act, and I stand to lose a lot if I fail." I waited for a feather to loosen from my wings because I hadn't actually placed any wagers. Angels weren't allowed to gamble, not even if it wasn't for monetary gain. For some reason, perhaps because there was some truth in what I'd just said, no feather detached itself from my wings.

"Kind acts don't benefit me in any way."

"They benefit your soul."

His nostrils pulsed with a snort. "I like my soul just the way it is."

I gaped at him. *He's a Triple,* I reminded myself. *Triples don't care about their souls, the same way they don't care about anyone but themselves.* I glanced at the street that was empty of passersby and cars. What was I still doing here?

Right . . .

Celeste.

Asherceleste.

"You wouldn't like your soul the way it was if you knew what it meant," I said.

"What it meant?" Jarod dipped his stubble-coated chin into his neck. "What does it *mean*, Feather?"

I was about to feed him a basic explanation, the one we were allowed to share with humans, when my mind caught up with the word he'd just uttered. *Feather.* The pounding in my chest migrated to my temples. "Why did you call me that?"

"Why did I call you what?"

"You just called her Feather," Tristan supplied.

Time stretched on endlessly before Jarod said, "Because she looks soft and spineless. Like a feather."

I should've winced or balked at the use of the word soft—first Tristan, now Jarod . . . couldn't I be described any other way?— but the nickname struck too close to home. "Worms are spineless; feathers have shafts."

"Shafts aren't spines." A smile played on Jarod's lips. "But if you'd rather I call you Worm—"

"No! Feather's fine." I licked my lips. "Does this mean you'll give me a second chance?"

"Well, you're nicer to look at than Tristan."

"*Salaud*," Tristan cursed, but his chuckling told me he wasn't angry.

Jarod pivoted toward the porte-cochère. "This should be amusing."

This wouldn't be amusing. Not in the least. But if I could get him to amend just one of his terrible ways, then it would be worth it.

As he rang his own doorbell—did he not have a key to his house?—he turned back toward me, "How long before your bet expires?"

"A month."

Click.

He pressed his fingers into the lacquered wood. "You have twenty-four hours."

"What?" I squeaked.

"I'm yours for a day. Once your time's up, you'll never seek me out again, and you'll stop stalking me."

"I'm not stalking you."

He tipped his head to the pillar I'd been leaning against and the book still clutched in my hands. "What do you call frequenting my doorstep? Sightseeing?"

Okay, perhaps, I had been stalking him.

"In twenty-four hours, I want you gone from my life forever. Take it or leave it, Feather. Makes no difference to me."

My heart ticked like a bomb inside my chest. Could I reform this man in a day? "The hours you sleep don't count in my allotted time frame."

"She drives a hard bargain," Tristan mused.

"Fine," Jarod said.

Tristan sidled in close to me and murmured, "Well done, Leigh."

I turned wide eyes on him, wondering why he was congratulating me.

His hand landed on the small of my back. "Jarod isn't in the habit of giving second chances."

"The minutes you spend flirting with my staff count triple." Jarod's voice snapped my gaze and body away from Tristan.

"I wasn't flirting," I said, scrambling toward the door Jarod was holding open.

Tristan started to follow, but Jarod said, "Go home. I have everything under control."

A flicker of hesitation crossed Tristan's face, hesitation that made my stomach clench like a fist. I didn't really know Tristan any better than Jarod, but he felt like a buffer, and I sort of wanted a buffer. I kept my mouth shut, though. I wouldn't show weakness. This was my one shot. A hundred feathers could be mine before the day was even over.

Injecting as much courage as I could muster inside my spine, I squared my back and walked past Jarod. Would he give me a fair chance, or did he have nefarious plans for me?

"What's on your mind, Feather?"

"Are you going to call me that all the time now?"

"You mean for the next twenty-four hours we'll know each other? Yes. Unless you like *Leigh* better."

Why did he have to make my name sound so awful? "I don't like the way you say it."

"What's wrong with the way I say it?"

I narrowed my eyes to show him I wasn't buying his mock act of innocence.

He smirked. "Feather it'll stay, then."

When the heavy door clanged shut, I let out a muted gasp. Open air stretched over the courtyard, yet I had never felt so confined.

Jarod stared at my parted lips, then at my eyes, and then at my hair, which I tucked behind my ears nervously. He took a step forward and flicked a lock, holding it up to the thin light dripping from the iron and glass lantern above us.

I pushed his fingers away. "What are you doing?"

"Checking if the color's real."

"That's really none of your business."

"I like to know what sort of person I'm dealing with. Women who color their hair a brash color do so to stand out, and yet you strike me as an introvert."

"It's real, okay?" Under my breath, I added, "Trust me, if I could change it to something normal, I would." Dyes didn't take to angelic hair. I'd tried. Several times.

"If you could change it?" His eyebrows dipped. "Is it against your *faith* to dye your hair?"

"I'm not wasting the twenty-four hours you so generously allotted me on a discussion about my hair, okay?"

A corner of his mouth tilted up. "What shall we discuss then? The weather?"

"Ways you can become a better man."

He snorted. "I'm a lost cause, Feather. If I were you, I wouldn't bother."

"But you're *not* me." I brushed my forearms to ward off the nippiness of the April night.

"I'd much rather discuss your hair."

"And if you truly believed you were a lost cause, why give me a second chance?"

No longer smiling, he said, "I have my reasons."

My skin broke out in goose bumps. "Which are?"

"Unimportant."

I should've signed off and picked someone else. Someone who didn't look like a predator who enjoyed playing with his food.

"Are you going to lock me up and torture me?" I found myself asking.

"I promised you twenty-four hours, not an explanation for making that promise."

He started toward Amir, who stood on the threshold of the limestone mansion like a steel beam, glowering at me as though I were some rat Jarod had plucked out of the sewers and brought home to keep as his pet.

"Are you coming, Feather? You only have twenty-three hours and forty-seven minutes left to make me amend my terrible ways."

The mocking tone of his voice wasn't lost on me. He didn't believe I could change him. Truth was, I didn't believe it myself, but I desperately wanted my missing feathers, so I jolted forward, my bronze heels scraping against the cobblestones. As I passed by the fountain, my gaze wandered to the statue's ruined back.

Not an omen, Leigh.

Then why did it feel like one?

A full body shiver skittered through me as I entered the house.

"You seem captivated by my fountain," Jarod said.

I looked up into his dusky face. "Shame it's broken."

"I thought you had a fascination with broken things."

I examined his hooded eyes. The lighting in the vestibule was low, but I could tell they were a shade of brown so deep they could be confused with black. "Duty, not fascination," I answered as I sidestepped him.

Muriel wasn't there tonight, and the door that led to the incubi den was propped open, so I treaded over to it.

"Your bag, Feather," Jarod said. "I don't allow cell phones inside my home."

I tucked the supple leather against me. "I won't use it."

"Another reason to leave it behind."

I bit my lip, then shaking my head, I unhooked the bag from my shoulder and held it out. Amir seized it.

"He'll take good care of it," Jarod said.

His bodyguard didn't seem like the type to take good care of anything. He seemed like the type who crushed throats with his giant fists and skulls with his meaty head.

As I started to turn, Jarod asked, "Are you going to fix her up once you're done with me?"

"What?"

"The statue in my fountain." He unfastened the collar of his white shirt.

"Depends." I watched him undo another button, revealing a scattering of dark chest hair. "Did you keep her wings?" I raised my gaze up the length of his neck, catching the sharp bob of his Adam's apple.

"No. I turned them to dust."

"Then there isn't much I can do for her." I treaded past him, praying my fate would be kinder than his statue's. That I'd leave *La Cour des Démons* with my wings intact.

Or heavier.

Heavier would be good.

13

$\mathcal{T}$he den that had been used for the party was in fact an outsized dining room. The long, varnished table must've been pushed to the side last night, because I couldn't recall seeing it, and considering it could comfortably seat sixteen people, there was no way I could've missed it.

A faded tapestry of a hunting scene stretched the length of one wall; three sets of French doors, all giving onto the courtyard, ran the length of the other. The ceiling was the most spectacular part of the room. Cherubs—the way humans pictured them to be, winged and chubby—flew across a blue sky or peeked out from behind fluffy clouds.

"Uncle had it decorated for my mother as a wedding present. It was her favorite thing in the house. I've been meaning to have it painted over."

I whipped my gaze off the mural.

"I was thinking eggshell. Or maybe I should go with black. To match my soul."

I sensed he was trying to rile me up. If he'd wanted to erase his mother's favorite thing, he would've done it before. "Why do you want to get rid of your mother, Jarod? Was she not nice to you?"

The sharp lines of his face hardened. I wasn't sure if he was angry with me or with the woman who'd found cherubs endearing. I suddenly wished his file had told me more about him.

"Do you eat anything besides rainbows, Feather?"

His question jarred me. "Rainbows?"

The sharpness dulled from his features. Which wasn't to say he looked soft. There was nothing soft about Jarod Adler.

"Pots of gold, but only for breakfast," I ended up saying.

My answer earned me a smile I might've called devastating if I weren't still terrified about what lurked beneath it.

"I'll let Muriel know."

"Does she have a supplier?"

"And here I assumed zealots were dull."

"You have a surprisingly large number of preconceived notions about zealots. I'm assuming I'm not the first zealot you've encountered."

His gaze dug into mine.

Before I could ask him about the others, the doors of the dining room opened.

"*Pardonne-moi,* Jarod. I didn't know you were entertaining."

"You're mistaken, Mimi. *I'm* the one being entertained."

Mimi? Did Jarod have a nickname for every woman in his life? Not that I was a woman in his life—even though, technically, I *was* a woman and would be in his life for the next twenty-three and some hours.

Muriel raised an easy smile. In spite of her heavy makeup, she was a beautiful woman. "Would you like some dinner?"

"I'd love some dinner."

Her smile grew. "Will your guest be joining you?"

"She will," Jarod answered for me.

"Thank you," I said before she left.

"Of course." She shut the door.

"She cares a lot for you," I said.

Jarod shrugged out of his jacket and tossed it on the back of one the upholstered dining chairs before dropping into the seat at the head of the table. "She's paid to care."

I startled. "That's not why she cares."

He scooted back and crossed one foot over his knee, his pant leg riding up, revealing a red sock that matched the pocket square I'd spied adorning his jacket. "She wouldn't stay if I cut her off."

"I don't believe that."

"Of course, you don't. In your world, everyone's good and kind."

My throat went dry. "In *my* world?"

"You obviously live in a bubble, Leigh. It takes someone supremely guileless to stroll into my lair expecting kindness."

I wasn't sure whether to be relieved or offended.

He stretched his neck from side to side, and it cracked. "So, now, tell me why you need to win this bet. What is it you stand to lose?"

"Something I want."

"Which is?"

"Unimportant," I said, tossing the word he'd used earlier back at him.

"I have no doubt it's unimportant, doubtlessly superficial, but color me interested. What is it you want so badly you're willing to spend a day with someone as terrible as me?"

"Why do you do what you do?"

"Excuse me?"

"Why do you kill or torture, or whatever else you do in your organization?"

I was expecting him to lob another question at me, but he leaned back and draped his arm over the carved wooden frame of his seat that looked more throne than house chair. "Because I enjoy punishing people."

A frisson went through me. "Why?"

"Why do you feel the need to fix people, Feather?" Jarod was a professional deflector. Every time I got too close to something, he either mocked me or changed the topic.

"To give them a chance at a better life."

"Well, I enjoy punishing people because it gives the ones they've wronged a chance at a better life."

"How do you choose who gets punished?"

"Usually by large donations, but the first of every month, I allow the destitute to come and plead their case. I'm like a real-live Robin Hood."

I took the seat to Jarod's left. "Robin Hood was a robber and murderer who considered himself above the law and gained notoriety by being a petty criminal. You shouldn't pick him as a role model."

That wiped the easygoing expression right off Jarod's face. "You're not a feather; you're a quill," he grumbled.

Before I could tell him I wasn't trying to make him mad, the tall double doors swept open, and Muriel trotted in along with two men wearing starched gray uniforms. While one placed embroidered placemats and fabric napkins folded like fans before us, the other set down dinner plates topped with roast chicken, thinly sliced carrots, and a dollop of what smelled like mashed potatoes.

Muriel proffered a gravy dish.

I seized the silver ladle to drizzle sauce over my fragrant meal. "Smells delicious."

"It's Jarod's favorite," she answered.

That made me level a narrowed look on Jarod who was busy watching his wineglass being filled.

Muriel wasn't staying for his money. At least, not *only* for his money. Did he truly not see this? Did he really believe everyone had an agenda?

Before I could refuse wine, my glass was filled. As the waiter twisted the bottle with a flick of his wrist, his gaze drifted over me.

"Eyes up, Sylvain," Jarod barked.

The boy snapped his gaze to the tapestry, cheeks flaming.

"Get out," Jarod said.

He backed up, almost tripping over the burgundy and forest-green patterned rug, and then scurried away.

Jarod clutched his fork. "Fire him, Mimi."

My lips parted. Was he serious?

Once Muriel and the second waiter had retreated and sealed me in with Mister Moody, I asked, "Because he looked at my hair? *You* looked at my hair, Jarod. *Everyone* looks at my hair. It's really not worth firing someone over."

He stabbed his chicken and pushed a bite into his mouth. After swallowing, he said, "Don't tell me how to run my household, Feather."

I sat up a little straighter. "You *touched* my hair; he didn't. He didn't even comment on it."

Jarod finally raised eyes so black they looked made of onyx.

"He wasn't looking at your hair," he said before taking another bite. "He was staring at your tits. Then again, they're spilling out of your clothes, so maybe you wanted him to stare."

Like the waiter's, my cheeks blazed. My cleavage was on display but not purposely. I didn't say anything and neither did Jarod. We ate in a silence so tense I could feel it on my skin, sticky like molasses.

Once he'd scraped his plate clean, he seized his wineglass. "You should try the wine." His voice wasn't loud, yet after the quiet, it felt like he was speaking through a megaphone. "It's a 1978 Chateau Lafitte."

I lined up my fork and knife on the side of my plate and drank some water. "I told you yesterday, I don't drink."

"This isn't a drink, Feather. It's history in a bottle. Liquid gold. Ambrosia of the gods."

"I can't."

"Try it."

"Jarod, I can't."

"Try it, or I'll spend the next hours in my room while you squander them sitting down here alone."

"You don't understand."

"Explain it to me, then!"

"My *faith* forbids alcohol."

"Your faith is senseless. One sip won't kill you."

I bit my lip, not because I was hesitating but because I was growing angry with him for being so pigheaded and was worried about saying something that might cost me a feather.

"I won't tell," he said.

I gritted my teeth. "I. Can't."

He pushed away from the table and rose.

When he started for the door, I said, "You're not being fair!"

"Stop expecting me to be fair. I'm not a *fair* man. What I am, though, is a man of my word. I *will* leave if you don't at least sample my wine. I'm not asking you to get wasted. I'm asking—"

Tears pricking my lids, I snatched my glass and gulped down its dark content. I tried hard not to taste it, not to enjoy the velvety texture coating my palate, not to savor the sweet and earthen flavors draping over my tongue.

I tried hard to hate it but couldn't. So, I decided to hate the man who made me break the rules. "You're a cruel man, Jarod Adler."

He returned to his seat. "Wasn't it delicious?"

"I hated it."

The jabbing pain I'd expected for drinking wine hit me now. I clenched my molars and slammed my glass down. The stem shattered from the base, nicking my palm, but the flesh wound was nothing compared to the agony of having lost another feather.

Tears dripped off my chin as the silvery piece of down fluttered to the rug. "Coming back here was a mistake."

I needed to leave before I was plucked like the bird I'd just eaten. My throat closed in time with my eyes, and tears streamed down my cheeks, fusing with the spilled wine that wet my shimmying thighs.

1 4

abric was wrapped around my sliced hand. I opened
my burning eyes to find Jarod crouched beside me,
tending to me.

Even though I trembled with anger, it struck me that it wasn't
the taste of the forbidden that had cost me a feather but the lie
that ensued. At least, this was my assumption. Sick of assuming, I
took Jarod's still full glass and drained it.

And then I waited.

And waited.

Nothing happened.

Nothing. Happened.

That just soured my mood further, because I couldn't blame
Jarod for the damage to my wings. It was all on me.

"You didn't hate it, did you, Feather?" His light tone incensed
me.

"Don't ever threaten me again," I whispered indignantly. "If I
say no, it means *no*."

His breath caught on an inhale. *"Pardon."*

The knot in my throat loosened. Out of all the answers I'd
expected from him, *sorry* was not it.

The doors of the dining room flew open, and then quick
commands were exchanged. A moment later, Jarod tightened the
napkin around my hand and delicately rested it atop my lap

before moving aside so the waiter could sweep away the broken glass and mop up the table.

As I watched the stain spread like fresh blood on the white dishcloth, I heard Jarod ask, "*Mimi, tu peux aller lui chercher quelque chose à se mettre? Et un pansement.*" *Can you get her something to wear? And a Band-Aid.*

"*Non,*" I said. "To the dress."

Both Jarod and Muriel looked at me.

"It's black." Even if wine had soaked into the fabric, it wouldn't show.

"It's also wet," Jarod said.

"It'll dry." I wasn't putting on one of the dresses from his closet of oddities. Even though mine wasn't the most comfortable, it was mine. It hadn't touched some other woman's skin; it hadn't absorbed some other woman's perfume. "I'm sorry I broke your glass," I said mechanically. "Let me know how much I owe you."

The heavy fluted crystal would probably cost me my entire allowance. Everything in Jarod's house struck me as expensive.

"I have enough wineglasses to last me six lifetimes."

Not that he would get a single more if he didn't amend his ways. I made a deal with myself: if I lost one more feather, I'd leave.

No more lying for me.

"Would you like dessert, Leigh?" Muriel asked. "I made chocolate mousse for the staff this afternoon."

Even though my stomach felt like a giant knot, I murmured, "Sure."

She came back a few minutes later carrying a single crystal bowl filled with mousse so dark it resembled Jarod's eyes. After she placed it in front of me on a fresh table setting, she demanded to see the cut. I hesitated to show her, sensing my skin was healing. What if the flesh had already hemmed shut? How would I explain where the blood had come from? I thumbed the slender wound, wincing as I coaxed the skin apart, then raised my hand.

Delicately, she unwrapped the napkin and sprayed my palm with antiseptic, blowing to lessen the sting before affixing a Band-Aid. No one had tended to me since I'd developed wing bones, and her careful ministrations stole some of the despair of having lost another feather.

"Thank you," I whispered.

She smiled as she gathered up the soiled napkin. "Let me know what you think of the mousse."

When she was gone, I asked Jarod, "You don't want any?"

"I don't like dessert."

I frowned. "How come?"

He shrugged, lifting his freshly filled wineglass to his mouth. "Just never did." He closed his lips around the rim and tipped the glass. I watched him swallow, watched his spiky Adam's apple jump in his elegant throat.

Before he could catch me staring, I turned to the mousse, which was so airy it weighed nothing. I slipped the bite into my mouth and all but moaned when the lush chocolate hit my tongue. I'd often wondered why chocolate wasn't a sin. Not that I was complaining. If it had been, I would've had to live without it, and what a drab life that would've been. I took another spoonful and buried it inside my mouth, sealing my lips, so no embarrassing sound escaped this time.

After swallowing, I licked my spoon clean. "You're missing out. This is divine."

He swirled his wine, then lifted it, but before taking a sip, he said, "More for you." The timbre of his voice had turned huskier, as though the alcohol had chafed his vocal cords. "I'm trying to decide how old you are."

"How old do you think I am?"

"How about you just tell me?"

"Twenty. I'll be twenty-one soon."

"Where were you born?"

"I was born . . ." I was about to say in Elysium but couldn't speak about my first home to mortals. "I grew up in New York but was born somewhere I have no memory of." Not a lie, since I'd been carried into a guild the second my umbilical cord was severed.

"Do you have siblings?"

"Two sisters. One who's fifteen and another who's my age."

A small groove appeared between his eyebrows. "So, a twin?"

I patted the mousse with the back of my spoon, evening out the top. "Sort of. We're not blood sisters." When he frowned, I added, "We grew up together. In an all-girls boarding school."

"Because your parents are missionaries?"

"What?"

"Tristan told me they were preachers."

"Oh. Uh. Not preachers. More like guards. I don't have much contact with them." My parents were both Abaddon Erelim—sentinels of the celestial underworld.

He set down his wineglass, and a drop sloshed out. "Who do they guard that they had to toss you into a boarding school?"

Jarod's inquisitiveness made avoiding lying difficult. It reminded me of the *neither-yes-nor-no* game I used to play with Celeste when I helped out in the guild's nursery, the one that, without fail, she would beat me at.

I went with: "My parents guard a prison." Which was sort of true since they patrolled Abaddon.

He let out a low grunt that, coupled with his disapproving stare, made my spine stiffen.

"You don't get to judge them, Jarod."

"Perhaps, but you do. And you don't seem to be bothered by having been abandoned."

"Because I don't see it as abandonment."

"What do you see it as?"

Instead of locking horns, I turned the tables on him. "So, you grew up with your uncle? Was he a nice man?"

"Uncle was the founder of *La Cour des Démons*, so no, he wasn't a nice man."

"Was he nice to you, at least?"

"He was good to me. He gave my parents a roof when they had none, adopted me after Mom passed away, and then left me all of this." He gestured to the house.

"How did he die?"

Jarod hooked his foot on his knee and jostled it. "Didn't you look my family up? It was all over the tabloids."

I should've, but in my haste to arrive here then forfeit this mission, I hadn't.

"He was in a car accident." He stared at the sleepy courtyard and the lit fountain beyond his window. "Which was no accident."

His confession didn't shock me. Mob bosses had many

enemies and didn't meet kind ends. Jarod would incur the same fate if he didn't change professions.

"Aren't you scared of getting killed?"

He shot me a withering smile. "I'd rather die from a bullet than from boredom."

"Normal jobs aren't all boring. Especially if you find something you're passionate about."

"Let's talk about you again."

"I don't like talking about myself."

He linked his fingers behind his head and leaned back. "What are your favorite sexual kinks?"

My cheeks felt like they'd been torched.

"You don't need to blush, Feather. I'm the last person who'd judge you."

"That's not why." I dropped my gaze to my mousse. "I just don't want to discuss sex with you."

"Why not?"

"Because I don't know you."

"Is that the reason?"

"It's one of them."

"What's the other?"

Ugh. Tristan said he was a pit bull but so was Jarod. "Because the discussion won't bring me any closer to my goal."

"I thought your goal was getting me to perform one kind act."

"It is."

"How about I perform it in the bedroom?" He picked up the long-stemmed glass of water beside his wine and drank long and deep.

I gaped at him, and then, once I recovered from his lewd suggestion, I said, "First off, that wouldn't count. And secondly"—*I'd lose all of my feathers because sex out of wedlock is a sin*—"I'm saving myself for marriage."

He sputtered, choking on his water. I didn't think anything could stun Jarod Adler, but preserving my virtue apparently could. I supposed the women who ran in his circle weren't the sort to care about virtue and vows.

He wiped his mouth on his sleeve, then ran a slow finger around the rim of his glass, making the glass sing. "How interesting." His dry tone belied he didn't find it interesting in the least. Inane, outmoded, heinous, but most definitely not interesting. "My offer stands for the duration of our tryst—in case you feel like reconsidering."

"I just told you, I'm not having sex before marriage."

"The best part of sex isn't penetration, Feather."

Heat shot through my veins, blotching the rest of my skin.

He grinned at my discomfort.

I shook my head. "Stop trying to get under my skin."

"Oh, I'm not trying to get under your skin. Just under that dress."

I wondered why he was so intent on disconcerting me, and then it hit me. "You get a kick out of intimidating people, don't you? It makes you feel powerful."

He didn't speak. Didn't move. Even his chest seemed to have grown stiller. He hadn't expected me to figure him out.

"I'm not scared of you, Jarod Adler." Not anymore. I didn't delude myself into thinking that his bite wouldn't sting as much as his bark, but I couldn't be killed, and as long as I didn't lie or swear, I wouldn't lose another feather.

He uncrossed his long legs and got to his feet. "Well, you should be."

When his back was turned, I reached for the feather that had deserted my wings earlier.

"Hi, I'm Leigh."

Trevor swung his gangly legs over the dizzying precipice below us.

"Your parents are really worried about you."

He eyed me before snorting and returning his gaze to the blue-gray river rushing underneath the metal railing we were perched on.

"They have a lot of people out looking for you."

He kept his gaze on the Hudson. If he'd truly wanted to jump, he would have already. The fact that he'd been sitting up here since nightfall and it was almost dawn told me he didn't want to end his life.

What he wanted—I'd learned it from his holographic file before heading downtown—was to end the sorrow eating at him since his kid brother ventured into a swimming pool while Trevor played video games in the living room.

"How did you find me?" he finally asked.

I squinted at the hint of lavender flaring on the horizon. I couldn't tell him I'd been given his precise coordinates but I couldn't lie either. "Ending your life . . . it won't bring Sam back."

"How do you know about Sam?"

"I read about him."

The accident of the little boy found floating in a swimming pool had shaken the entire city, raising controversies about parents entrusting younger children to their older siblings.

Trevor's red-rimmed gaze dropped to the river below us.

"Your parents love you."

I touched his arm, and he flinched.

"No, they don't. I killed my brother."

"You didn't kill him."

"I did!"

I recoiled from the harshness of his tone.

"I was supposed to watch him, and instead I was—I was playing Fortnite." His voice broke, in volume and in strength. And then his shoulders hunched, and he started to shake. "I can't go back."

"Accidents happen."

"He died because of me."

"Do you believe in life after death, Trevor?"

The shadow of facial hair lined his trembling upper lip. He was only a year younger than I was, but grief had lent his boyish face a grave edge.

"Because I do," I said. "And I believe your brother was collected by angels and brought to Heaven."

He watched me without saying a word.

"I believe he's looking down at you and wishing you wouldn't feel so much grief and guilt."

Trevor leveled his glum gaze on the horizon.

"I believe he'd want you to get away from here and find your parents."

"I told you . . . they hate me."

"They don't hate you, Trevor."

"Stop saying that. You don't know them! And you know nothing about me!"

I knew everything about him and about them. I knew he was worth six feathers, which was more than most twelve-year-olds. I knew jealousy had earned him his first sinner point—he'd peed in his cousin's field hockey trophy. He'd netted the other five points for having left the patio *door unlatched and wearing headphones to play his video game, thus missing the loud splash.*

He grabbed my shoulders and shook me.

Wait . . . no. That wasn't possible. The only time he'd touched me that day was to take my extended hand, finally allowing me to help him back up onto the iron railing.

He'd never shaken me.

"Feather?"

I blinked up into a set of eyes shadowed by so many lashes it was impossible to tell what they hid.

"Are you okay? You were swaying." Jarod stopped shaking me, but his palms remained on my shoulders as though he was worried that if he removed them I'd keel over.

How long had I been unresponsive? "Sorry."

He rose from his crouch and reached over me, and then he was crouching again, pushing a glass of water into my hands. "When I was a kid, I'd faint at the sight of blood."

I took a sip, my head still swimming from the memory of my first encounter with Trevor. "Not anymore?"

"I wouldn't be very good at my job if I fainted now, would I?"

My throat went dry at the reminder that I was in a Triple's home.

Sharp. I needed to stay sharp.

I emptied my water glass to clear my mind of my previous mission so I could focus on my present one.

15

*M*uriel and one of Jarod's armed guards stood in the marble foyer, hands clasped in front of them.

"Can we clear away dinner, Jarod?" Muriel asked.

He nodded to her before heading up the stairs.

Was I supposed to follow him? Did he have another reception area upstairs? I didn't move, waiting for his instructions.

"Feather, are you coming?"

Thumbing the adhesive strip of my bandage, I clipped across the marble toward the curving staircase, feeling every set of eyes grind into me. His staff probably assumed I'd come to bed the boss. Even though I longed to set them all straight, what they thought he and I would do tonight didn't matter.

As I started to ascend the carpeted steps, Muriel called out Jarod's name.

He gestured for me to keep going. "I'll be up in a minute." He returned to the older woman and spoke in hushed tones with her.

I peeked over my shoulder but didn't dally, suspecting it would be construed as eavesdropping. On the landing, a collection of seascapes in sumptuous carved frames dotted the cherry-paneled walls, thick dabs of lavender, gray, and gold giving life to tormented oceans tossing ships with bloated white sails. I wanted to touch the paint, but what if it set off an alarm? Besides, it was probably not a good idea to touch art. I leaned forward and squinted to make out the signature at the bottom—*Aivazovsky*. I sensed I'd read the name somewhere before. Perhaps, in a museum?

When I straightened, my back bumped into a body.

Reflexively, I tucked my wing-free shoulder blades in. Without turning, I said, "Do you have to stand so close?"

"I didn't think proximity bothered you considering how you hung on to Tristan last night."

I spun around. Even in my three-inch heels, Jarod towered over me. "I let him lead me around because he was familiar with your house and I wasn't."

He let out a short snort that suggested skepticism.

I balled my fingers, ungluing one of the sticky flaps of the Band-Aid before pushing it back in place and crossing my arms to create a barrier between our too-close bodies. "Why are you so intent on making me feel trapped? Do you think it'll make me run?"

His gaze eddied like the squall in the seascape. "Possibly. Or possibly I enjoy watching you squirm."

"Tough luck. I don't squirm." I squared my shoulders. "So, what's on this floor?"

"My bedroom."

"The entire floor?"

"No. There are two other bedrooms, but they're far less interesting than mine."

"What am I doing up here?"

"I need a shower and a change of clothes, and you need to find a way to make me kind. Since I don't intend on going back downstairs until morning—Mimi just reminded me tomorrow is the first, and you now know what happens on the first—I thought we could continue our extraordinarily enlightening conversation in my bedroom."

I raised my chin a notch. "You're not planning on trying anything on me?"

The smile toppled from his face, and his eyes grew harder. "During my free time, I track down rapists and child molesters and get rid of them. Even the ones locked safely away in jails. So, please never insinuate something of the sort again." He turned sharply, his polished Oxford shoes squealing on the hardwood, and pushed through a set of doors.

My arms collapsed against my sides as I trailed after him. "You can't go around killing people."

"I don't expect you to understand. Your kind has a skewed view of justice."

"My kind?" My spine tingled as though my wings were about to pop out.

He slung his jacket over the back of an antique desk chair, then started on his cufflinks. "Fanatical devotees of higher beings." He tossed them on an orange tray.

When he untucked his shirt, I jolted my gaze to the art over his canopy bed. The pastel-hued depictions of rosy-cheeked women with golden ringlets contrasted sharply with the dark wood paneling and the bedsheets that shone like liquid steel in the subdued lighting coming off his bookcase.

I needed to get off the subject of religion that hit too close to home. "You really love art, don't you?"

"Uncle did."

"But you don't?"

He shrugged. "I haven't gotten rid of them."

I looked back at him, forcing my gaze not to dip to the dark hair blanketing his pecs. "Why can't you ever give me a straight answer?"

He shot me a withering smile. "Consider yourself lucky you're getting answers from me in the first place. I don't make it a habit to divulge anything about myself. Not to friends. Not to strangers."

"Why are you undressing in front of me?"

"Where would you like me to undress, Feather? This is my bedroom."

When his fingers dropped to his belt buckle, I whirled around. "I'll wait for you on the landing. Come get me when you're showered and changed."

"Weren't you enjoying the show? I haven't taken off my clothes in front of a woman in a long time." I had a hard time believing that. "Perhaps I'm not doing it well?"

Thankfully, I had my back to him, so he couldn't see how flustered I'd become. I pulled his door shut and then walked to the other side of the landing, my heels clicking in time with my ratcheting breaths.

I'd been wrong to let down my guard around Jarod. I wasn't sure what game he was playing, but I didn't like it. I peered over the blackened-iron railing, longing to race down the stairs and through the courtyard.

Would his bodyguards let me leave?

I wrapped my trembling fingers around the banister.

Asherceleste.

I squeezed my fingers, my palms molding around the cool metal, the injured one smarting.

I couldn't leave without trying to help Jarod.

You can't die, Leigh, I reminded myself for the umpteenth time.

Sure, he could torture me, bruise my skin, or put a bullet through my flesh, but my angelic blood would heal me. As long as I had wings, I was immortal.

I closed my eyes and forced my breathing to slow, forced my heart to quiet. I was going to be okay.

"Did you change your mind about spending the night with me?" Jarod's voice had my palms skidding off the banister.

He was leaning against his door frame, arms crossed over a black silk bathrobe that stopped right above his knees. He'd either taken the quickest shower, or I'd just spent an inordinate amount of time contemplating my calamitous fate.

"I thought you weren't scared of me." His lips were quirked in a deprecating smile.

Was it that obvious? "You confuse me."

"And here I thought I was an open book."

If he was an open book, then I was the queen of Elysium, and there was no royalty in my world. "Did you ever have another ambition than taking over after your uncle?"

His dark brows slanted. For a long minute, he said nothing, then, "No." The stretch of silence told me he *had* wanted something else.

"What would you have rather done?"

"I just told you. *Nothing.*"

"You hesitated." I walked back toward him. "And now you're getting mad."

A grunt scraped up his throat. "This isn't me getting mad,

Feather. You haven't seen me mad. You don't want to see me mad."

His silken robe fell open, revealing that hard, hairy torso of his. I hadn't seen Asher's chest but I'd seen his arms—golden and hairless—and imagined his chest would be bare and sculpted. Why was I envisioning Asher's pecs? I wanted to marry him for his status, not his body, even though his—as opposed to Jarod's—was undoubtedly beautiful.

"See something you like?" Jarod's voice sounded an octave deeper.

Everything about this sinner was so very dark, as though he'd been steeped in tar at birth and that tar had colored his hair, eyes, and soul. If he'd had wings, they, too, would've surely been pitch-black.

"Interesting," he said.

"What is?"

"Your silence."

"Why is my silence interesting?"

"Because I asked you a question, which you seem unable to answer."

"I'm not *unable* to answer. I simply choose not to."

He cocked his head to the side. "And why is that? My body clearly appeals to you. You can't keep your eyes off of it."

A blush stung my cheeks. "I've just never seen anyone as hairy as you before."

His eyes sparked with amusement. "As hairy? You do realize I'm a man, right? Most men have hair on their body. Some even have hair on their backs, which, thankfully, isn't my case."

A sultry, smoky fragrance lifted from his skin, reminding me of the incense one of my sinners burned while she conducted seances, pretending to speak to the dead to rob her gullible customers of their hard-earned salaries.

I swallowed. "Can we go back to discussing something you could do to help me win my bet?"

He pressed off the door frame and gestured to his bedroom that seemed darker than when I'd stepped out. "After you, Feather."

As I squeezed past him, his chest hair whispered against my shoulder, raising goose bumps. I rubbed my exposed skin, trying to friction away my body's reaction to his before he could jump to the conclusion it had been brought on by attraction.

Because I wasn't attracted to him.

Not in the least.

I was attracted to people pure of soul and heart—not people who were cloaked in darkness inside and out.

16

$\mathcal{I}$ took a seat on the edge of the cowhide recliner propped next to his bookshelves. Like in his study, only old, leather-bound books with gold embossing on the spines graced his shelves.

"Did you turn up the heat?"

Jarod smirked. "That's your body's reaction to mine, Feather."

He strode over to a silver tray topped with an etched crystal decanter filled with clear liquid, a stainless-steel ice bucket, and two empty tumblers. As he served himself a glass, I folded my legs, but that almost tipped the chair forward, so I uncrossed my legs and planted my feet firmly on the floor.

He smiled. "You should lay down. We're going to be here a while."

"Don't worry about me."

He dropped two ice cubes into his glass, then splashed whatever was in the decanter over them. "It was my mother's favorite chair. She would spend her afternoons reading in it."

For some reason, his anecdote made me slide backward and settle into the rigid shape that was surprisingly ergonomic.

He took a sip of his drink, the ice clinking against the glass. "She died in it."

My body stiffened, and I bolted up, no longer feeling comfortable. I stared at the cowhide, expecting to see a blood splotch on it, but the coarse hairs were white and brown—not red.

"It wasn't the chair that killed her." He took another swig of his drink.

"I-I imagine it wasn't."

He stared beyond me at the desk on the opposite side of the room, and a lock of hair fell into his eyes.

"How *did* she die?"

Silence ebbed between us before he said, "Stabbed herself."

I gasped.

The souls of people who committed suicide were neither brought to Elysium nor to Abaddon. They were deemed too weak to be recycled, because angels considered life a gift not to be tossed away and wasted. Another law I wanted to change. I believed that every soul—that wasn't irrevocably stained—deserved to be escorted through the Pearly Gates and at the very least judged by the Seven before being deemed unsalvageable and discarded into the ether.

"Why did she kill herself?"

"Because she loved my father too much and me too little." Even though his voice was quiet, it cut like broken glass.

"Oh, Jarod . . ." If he'd been anyone else, I would've hugged him, but Jarod didn't strike me as someone who'd enjoy a hug, much less welcome one.

"Don't pity me," he muttered. "She was catatonic and miserable after my father passed away. Her death was better for everyone."

"You don't actually believe that."

"Would you care if your mother died?"

"I don't know my mother." Plus, she couldn't die. Unless she gave up her wings, but only angels who favored Earth ever considered giving up their wings. Considering she didn't even travel to the guilds, I doubted she loved Earth all that much.

"Look at that. The sinner and the saint have something in common."

That drove all thoughts of my mother out of my mind.

"Both of us motherless," he added.

"I said I didn't know mine, not that she was dead."

"Don't want to have anything in common with a sinner, do you?"

"I'd be happy to have something in common with you, Jarod." A familiar pain stabbed my spine, and my thumb, which had been toying with the Band-Aid, flicked it right off my palm.

Not another feather.

Please, not another one.

My eyes filled with heat as downy barbs skimmed my ankle before settling beside the fallen bandage.

This man would be the death of my wings if I didn't leave now.

I raised my wet gaze back to his. "Jarod, I should—" I stopped short when I caught him staring at the space next to my bronze shoe. "What are you looking at?"

He walked over and crouched. The air in my lungs turned solid.

Impossible . . .

He didn't have wings.

He couldn't possibly see—

He picked up the Band-Aid and balled it up before flicking it toward his bookshelf. "Want a fresh one?"

He unglued my wounded hand from my hip and checked my scar. "Look at that . . . all healed."

"It wasn't deep," I said.

He let go, and I pulled my hand back to my side.

I itched to retrieve my feather but couldn't risk being zapped into another memory. *Later.* I'd grab it later. It wasn't as though it would disappear until it was touched. Which had me wondering about the feather I'd lost in the hall last night. Had a human unintentionally touched it? They couldn't see it, but if their hand glanced over it, the memory would sink into their minds. Some humans brushed it off as a dizzy spell, some as a déjà-vu, some as a divine vision.

Yesterday's feather had probably been sucked up into a vacuum.

As my gaze arced off the floor, it tripped over Jarod's body and the robe that gaped wide. Oxygen jammed in my throat, and I forgot all about my lost feather.

I traced the whorls of pastel paint on the canvases above his bed with my eyes. "Could you put on some underwear, please?"

I caught the flash of teeth in my peripheral vision. Of course, my discomfiture amused him.

"I assure you, it doesn't bite," he said.

"Forget it." I headed toward the door. I'd made a promise to myself to leave if I lost another feather and was going to uphold that promise.

"Where are you going?"

"Home. I'm going home. This was a bad idea."

"You'll lose your bet."

I laid my palm on the metal handle. "At this point, I have more to lose by trying to win this bet than by forfeiting."

"Will you stay if I get dressed?"

My pressure faltered, and the handle sprang up without unbolting the door. "Don't you want me gone? You called me bland and spineless. Not to mention a stalker."

"The word I used was soft, not bland."

"Was it supposed to be a compliment? Because it certainly didn't sound like one."

"I don't give compliments because sugarcoating life doesn't teach resilience."

"It might not teach resilience, but it shows compassion."

"I'm not a compassionate person, Feather. Not sure what led you to believe I was . . ."

I turned toward him. "Even though it isn't your job, you punish child molesters and rapists."

"Like I said, I punish them because your kind doesn't. Your kind's too busy trying to locate a glimmer of hope in their putrid souls."

I sucked in a breath at his admonishment. "You're right, Jarod. *My kind* scratches at the ugliness to find a spark of beauty. *My kind* tries to save sinners instead of ending their miserable lives."

We glowered at each other from across the room—well, I glowered; he just looked at me in that steady, inscrutable way of his. I reminded myself that Triples didn't get their score by being docile and moral; they got it by being cruel and selfish.

He started toward the opposite end of his bedroom. "I told my guards not to let anyone in or out until morning."

A gasp rocketed through me. "You're going to keep me here against my will?"

His long fingers curled around the sleek wooden edge of a door frame. "I didn't force you to come back, Feather." He slipped out of sight, but his voice drifted to me. "You're welcome to hang out in the dining room until daybreak. Everywhere else is under alarm, so unless you want my guards rushing at you with raised guns, I suggest you stick to the dining room."

My jaw dropped on another gasp. "Keeping me against my will is wrong."

Jarod padded back out barefoot, wearing a black T-shirt and tapered black sweatpants. He hadn't seemed the type to own sweatpants, nor had he seemed the type to lock up women. No, that wasn't true. He did seem like the type who'd do something as callous.

He dragged his hand through his hair that curled harder as it dried. "You seem to think I have a moral compass." He opened a set of French windows, the metal bar clanking as it retracted from the ceiling and floor, allowing the glass-paned doors to swing out.

My fingers became fists which I longed to pummel into Jarod's arm. He was bringing out the absolute worst in me. Thankfully, rage didn't cost feathers, but hitting him would. When he didn't reappear, I went to find him.

I burst onto a narrow stone balcony lacquered in moonlight. It took my eyes a moment to adjust to the obscurity and another to spot Jarod reclined on a lounger.

"Let me leave, and you will *never* hear from me again." Frenzied heartbeats swarmed my body. "I promise."

He twisted his head to look at me. "By all means, Feather, go downstairs."

"I don't mean your bedroom; I mean your house."

He checked his wristwatch. "Five hours from now, they'll disarm the place to let the supplicants in. You'll be able to leave then."

"Why?"

"Why what?"

"Why don't you disarm your house now?"

"Because Amir and Mimi are the only ones with the code to

my alarm system, and they went to sleep to recuperate after yesterday's festivities."

It felt like a lie. How could he not know the alarm code to his own house? I eyed the courtyard below and noticed movement in the shadows—a guard. I walked over to the stone balustrade and measured the drop.

"The last person who *hopped* from my balcony broke his spine."

I froze.

"Don't worry. He didn't suffer long. My guard put a bullet through his skull."

My mouth parted.

Jarod turned his eyes to the sky that stretched over us. Not a single star pinpricked the chilly darkness. Like in New York, stars lost out to smog and ever-burning city lights. "And before you start doling out sermons, know that he was a hitman paid to assassinate me."

"Would your guards put a bullet in my skull if I tried to escape?"

Jarod linked his fingers over his abdomen. "If I ordered them to, yes."

"Would you order them to?"

"Do you want to kill me, Feather?"

I shook my head.

"Then you have nothing to worry about. Now, why don't you take a seat on that other lounge chair and tell me all the things I should change about myself."

"I'm fine standing." My tone was short.

He flicked his gaze to my footwear. "In those heels?"

I leaned my hip against the rough stone handrail. "Tell me about how tomorrow works. What sort of help do people come to you for?"

"It varies, but it usually involves some form of physical retribution or monetary donation."

"People come to you for handouts?"

"You seem surprised."

Begging in a subway station was one thing, but sticking a cupped palm out to the Mafia lord was quite another. Not to mention Jarod's money was probably tainted by blood. "What do you ask for in return?"

"Nothing."

If that were true, it would mean he was generous, and generosity wiped sinner points off scorecards. Ever since he'd been recorded in the Ranking System, his score had never wavered.

It hit me then why this must be—the money wasn't his to give. Dirty money expunged any good act done with it. "And the physical retribution? What does that entail?"

"It varies from beating up spouses to frightening bosses."

"Do you do the beating up or the frightening?"

"What sort of savior would I be if I didn't do any rescuing?"

There he went with his Robin Hood complex again. "Do you do background checks to verify claims before you go in guns blazing?"

"I know you think me amoral, but I didn't think you thought me stupid."

I sighed. "I don't think you're stupid, Jarod. Conniving, calculating, controlling, but not stupid."

"Thank you."

I shifted, because the stone was digging into my joint. "Those weren't compliments."

"My uncle was all of those things, and more."

"I take it you idolized him?"

Jarod moved his linked hands to the back of his head. "He came from nothing. Dropped out of school at thirteen, then worked at a stud farm outside of Paris for six years. He started by shoveling horse shit before working his way up to training them. One of the horses he coached ended up breaking every racing record two years in a row, making his stables millions. The owner gave my uncle five thousand euros to thank him. Five thousand euros—" Jarod snorted.

"He could've been given nothing."

"Ah . . . forever the voice of reason."

"I wasn't implying he didn't deserve more."

"No, you were implying he should've been grateful for his winnings."

I shrugged one shoulder. "So, how did he go from horse trainer to"—I nodded toward the courtyard—"this?"

"Why don't you sit down? You're giving me a crick in my neck."

"I'm sure your neck is fine," I said.

"You're ruthless."

I rolled my eyes. "Then what happened?"

"Then he graciously thanked his boss and gave back the bonus."

"He gave it back?"

"Every penny, and then he asked his boss to gift him the scrawny foal of mediocre lineage which Uncle knew was supposed to be sold to a nearby stud farm for a pittance. He'd observed the foal and had discerned something in the horse's muscle structure which both his boss and the breeder had missed."

Mosquitos buzzed around the single sconce peeking out from the thick ivy climbing up the limestone, their drone interrupted by the occasional squeal of tires on the road outside Jarod's mansion.

"To my grandparents' horror, he brought the colt home. They lived in the suburbs and only had a backyard." Amusement flickered over his face. "They told him he couldn't keep that creature in their home. My grandmother had a friend in a nearby village who had a big property. She enquired if she'd be willing to take in the horse. Her friend agreed but made Uncle promise to care for it. When his savings ran low, he asked the woman if she had any work for him. She found him tasks to do around the house—she had a very old house, and everything inside needed fixing. He ended up spending most of his days there. And then, the summer after the old lady's granddaughter visited, his nights, too."

"Why is that?"

"He fell in love."

I tried to reconcile the image of the ruthless Demon Court founder I'd conjured in my head with the picture Jarod was painting of a hardworking, love-smitten, honest man.

"They trained the horse together, and once the horse turned two, my aunt, who was a slip of a woman, became the jockey. Ever heard of *Le Démon*?"

I raised my brows. "Was that what he named the horse?"

"Apparently the yearling had a fiery personality." His lips stretched tight over his teeth. "After it won the *Prix de l'Arc de Triomphe*, thus becoming the greatest horse to have tread French racetracks, Uncle got a great kick out of reading the headlines: *Le Démon champion.*"

"I imagine he made a lot of money with that horse." I'd been so absorbed by his tale I hadn't realized I'd inched closer to the free lounge chair.

"*A lot* is an understatement. That horse enabled him to buy this place"—he tipped his head to the side—"and a stud farm in Chantilly."

I finally sat down, sensing the story couldn't have a pleasant ending since the Adlers weren't known for their horse-breeding skills.

"About a year later, while Uncle was away negotiating breeding rights, someone broke into their stables and put a bullet through *Le Démon*'s skull and then another through my aunt's chest when she tried to save her horse."

I jolted.

"Uncle spent weeks tracking down the assassin. Turns out it was his former boss. The asshole felt like Uncle had gypped him and said my aunt was shot because she got in the way. That it was an accident.

"Uncle went to the police with the evidence he'd amassed, but they tossed out his case as insubstantial. The thing is, it wasn't. He'd even recorded the confession, but the chief of police told him he'd obtained it illegally, and so it was inadmissible in court.

"That's when he took matters into his own hands. Visited his former boss and shot him—first to wound and then to kill. He was caught and tossed in jail. The government tried to seize his assets, but he'd put everything in my father's name . . . my father who was still a minor back then. To make a long story short, he spent the next few years collecting valuable contacts and learning *skills*. He was out on good behavior a decade after he was put behind bars."

"Good behavior?"

Jarod shot me that murky grin of his.

I observed the pale walls of the house dotted by glass so shiny

I imagined it was cleaned daily. "So, prison made him create this place?"

"No, Feather, injustice made him create this place. Prison simply gave him the tools to build it."

I nibbled on my lip.

"Are you thinking horrid things about me and my uncle?"

"Actually, I'm thinking what a good storyteller you are, Jarod. You've made me feel something other than fear and aversion for your family."

His eyes gleamed. "Careful, Feather."

I folded my legs. "About what?"

"You might actually start to like me."

I squeezed my knees tight. "Just because you tell a good story doesn't make you likable. Now, if you let me lea—"

"Go." He jutted his chin toward his bedroom. "There's no alarm."

"You lied?"

"I lied."

"Why?"

"Because that's what I do. I lie. I blackmail. I extort. And sometimes, I kill. I'm a bad, *bad* man, Feather."

"Why did you want me to think I was your prisoner?"

His gaze ran over the orange hair I was twisting into a long rope. "Because it amused me."

I released my hair and lowered my hands to the thick cushion. "It amused you?" I croaked, genuinely hurt that he'd gotten a kick out of my turmoil. As my hair unraveled against my shoulder blades, I pushed myself up, the cruelty of his parting words making my movements all jerky.

He watched me, and the weight of his stare made my eyes heat with aggravation.

"Have a good life, Jarod Adler."

He didn't speak, not even to say goodbye. Not even to say good riddance.

I paused on the threshold between his balcony and bedroom. "Was any of the story you just told me true?"

"Perhaps." He returned his gaze to the sky. "Perhaps not."

Ugh. The man was infuriating. Why couldn't he ever give me a straight answer? As I turned to go, he said, "See you later, Feather."

I looked over my shoulder at his prostrate, relaxed form. "No, you won't."

Although he didn't gaze away from the deep indigo firmament, I noticed the corners of his mouth lifting.

The gall of him. Thinking I would come back.

What was it with him and Tristan convinced they were so irresistible?

After tonight, nothing and no one—neither altruism nor Celeste—could drag me back to this place.

$\mathcal{T}$he first thing I did after I retrieved my bag from the vestibule and exited Jarod's home was type *Le Démon racehorse* into my phone's browser. As the results of my search loaded, a car honked.

I jumped, almost dropping my phone.

The white-haired driver from yesterday circled the sedan and drew open the back door. "Monsieur Adler insists I drop you off at your place."

I swallowed. I didn't doubt Jarod had asked his driver to drop me off. What I doubted was the destination. I bet Jarod had instructed the man to drive me out of the city . . . out of the country even.

"Please thank Monsieur Adler for his *generosity*, but I'd rather walk."

"Mademoiselle, it's the middle of the night."

I found his comment borderline humorous. Warning me about the dangers that might lurk in the darkened streets. Wasn't he aware of whom he worked for?

I wheeled around and clip-clopped down the shadowy arcade, checking over my shoulder when I heard the car door shut. Red taillights flared, but the car didn't move. I bet the driver was relaying my refusal for a ride to Jarod. I quickened my strides and crossed the road. When I looked back, the sedan had vanished.

Once the Place des Vosges was behind me, I returned my attention to my phone's screen and clicked on the first article: *Isaac Adler and his prized stallion.*

I scrolled down until I landed on a picture of a young man— not much older than Jarod—with a head full of out-of-control brown curls and shiny blue eyes. So this was the infamous uncle?

I studied his features for similarities to Jarod's. Their cupid's bow mouths were the same, as well as the faint squint with which Isaac looked out at the world. But where the squint lent Isaac an impression of youth and carefreeness, it gave Jarod an impression of snark and disdain.

I read the article, then researched the murder, and read as much as I could stomach. Had the man who'd murdered Isaac's wife and horse ended up in Abaddon, or had his cruelty earned him a triple score? The Ranking Room didn't offer information on past sinners, but perhaps, one of the guild workers would know what had happened to him.

For all his talk about being a liar, Jarod had spoken the truth, and that comforted me.

As I was about to tuck away my phone and concentrate on not getting lost, it started to ring. I picked up immediately, because the only people who had my number were members of the guild and a few of the sinners I'd helped back in the States.

"You turned down my driver." Jarod's voice almost stopped my heart.

"How—how did you get my number?"

"I guessed it."

"No you didn't."

"Fine. I didn't." Something rustled on his end. "Amir retrieved it for me earlier."

So that's what they did to personal effects left in their custody: they rifled through them. Had they also planted a tracker in my bag?

Didn't matter. I'd be in a Channel on my way to New York in no time.

"Why are you calling me, Jarod?"

"To check that you haven't been attacked at knifepoint. It's the newest thing in this city. Crazies stabbing you for no reason."

I checked the street, my pulse quickening. Getting stabbed

wouldn't be pleasant. Until I completed my wings, I'd bleed like a human but heal quicker. I stopped at a deserted crosswalk, watching the glowing red hand of the pedestrian traffic light instead of scanning my surroundings like a skittish girl.

"You really expect me to believe you care about my safety? You'd probably reward the person who did the stabbing."

For a moment, there was no sound on his end. "If by reward, you mean quarter him, then yes, that's exactly what I'd do."

The red hand turned into a white stick figure, and yet I couldn't get myself to cross the street. "Why?"

"Why what, Feather?"

"Why do you care what happens to me?"

"Because my city isn't safe. Because you're a woman walking alone at night. Because you left my place angry, and for some inexplicable reason, your anger makes me feel guilt. I don't feel guilt over anything."

I pursed my lips, finally setting off across the zebra stripes even though the white stick figure was blinking. It wasn't as though there were *any* cars. No, actually, that wasn't true. There was one car. I squinted to see the driver behind the tinted windshield.

"You're having me followed?" I sputtered.

"I'm having you guarded. For your safety."

"You're unbelievable . . ."

"I'm told that often but usually after I've bedded a woman. Not before." His voice had taken on a husky quality, which combined with his words, made my steps falter.

"You're never going to *bed* me," I said.

"You know what I like more than justice? Challenges. I love challenges. So I accept your challenge."

Although the river was still a block away, the sound of it *whooshed* against my eardrums. "That wasn't me challenging you. That was me telling you I wasn't interested."

"I know what you said, but I also know what your body said. And you were most definitely interested."

I growled a little. "You think the entire world revolves around you, don't you? Well, let me clear something up for you . . . I'm not interested in getting naked with you. All I was interested in was making you a better man so that I could have a chance at being with the man I *actually* want." My breathing had turned labored as though I'd shrieked. I hoped I hadn't.

Several windows were open in the buildings surrounding me, and the last thing I wanted was to rouse people in the middle of the night.

"How would making *me* a better man up your chances at being with the one you want?" There was no longer anything husky or taunting in his tone.

I sighed. I didn't want to discuss Asher with Jarod. Besides, it wasn't as though I could explain our point system. "Look, you and I aren't friends. And like I said earlier, we won't be seeing each other again, so—"

"How does making me kinder benefit your love life?"

"I'm going to hang up now."

"I allowed you into my home. I shared my family's history. The least you can do is explain your intentions."

"Don't try to guilt-trip me."

"I don't appreciate being used, Feather."

I shut my eyes briefly and squeezed the bridge of my nose. "I was upfront about this being a bet."

"I didn't realize it was to get another man. I thought it was just a silly wager with a friend. Now, I feel like a fool. I don't like to feel like a fool."

"You're not a fool, okay? And I didn't mention the object of my bet, because it had nothing to do with you."

I waited for him to say something snarky or threatening, but what came through the receiver was neither snarky nor threatening. "You're a romantic, Feather."

I glanced down at the water wrapping around the bridge's foundations, at the gray foam and white whirlpools. "You got that from what? Me telling you I was saving myself for marriage?"

"No, I got that from your choice of reading material."

My arm tightened against my bag, which made my book dig into my waist. Had Amir given Jarod a detailed report of its contents or had Jarod gleaned the storyline from his brief glimpse of the cover?

"Your appreciation for food," he continued. "Your conviction that kindness lurks in everyone."

"Because it does."

"No, it doesn't." I was about to argue when he added, "Romantics marry for love. If you need to win a bet to get this guy, then you're not in love with him."

"Of course I'm not in love with him. I've only met him once. People don't fall in love the first time they meet."

There was a long pause on his end, as though he were mulling over the fact that a romantic didn't believe in love at first sight. "I guess I'm wondering why you're so dead set on marrying this person then."

"I have my reasons." Reasons I didn't care to share with him.

"You were willing to spend time with the most reviled man in Paris to win over this person. That tells me you *really* want to be with him."

I sighed. "And what? You care about what I want now?"

"How much *do* you want this man?"

I sighed. "I've never wanted anything more."

"Then why are you giving up?"

I stood up a little straighter. "I'm not giving up. I'm changing my method of obtaining it."

"Come tomorrow morning."

I pushed away from the bridge railing. "Jarod—"

"Listen to the supplicants. Find one who strikes your fancy, and I'll help them."

I sensed there were strings attached to his offer, and I was afraid of those strings snagging around my feathers and yanking more out. "Is this a trap?"

"Was tonight a trap?"

I was still unsure of what tonight had been. Besides a very strange evening.

"See you in a couple of hours, Feather."

"No, you won't."

"Sure, I will."

"No, you won't. And tell your driver to stop following me."

Jarod didn't answer.

"Jarod?"

When I lowered the phone from my ear, it displayed my home screen. *He'd hung up* . . . Of course, he'd hung up. I didn't understand much about Jarod, but I did gather he didn't like to be told what to do.

And then, when I was tailed by his chauffeur all the way back to the guild, I gathered one more thing about the Triple: he didn't take orders from anyone.

18

I didn't think I'd run into anyone on my way to the Ranking Room to sign off from my mission, but people were up. Well, two girls. They were checking holo-images of sinners, comparing notes. When I stepped inside the guild, both looked up from their feeds.

They trailed me with their eyes as I took a seat at the high table and pressed my hand against the glass panel.

"Are you the American who took on Jarod Adler?" The girl's blonde hair was cut pixie short which displayed ears festooned with diamond studs.

The other Fletching turned wide blue eyes on me. "Are you crazy?"

"I must be to have thought he could be redeemed." I folded the fabric of my dress until it pleated like an accordion. It was stiffer where the wine had spilled.

"*Chérie,* if only you'd asked us. I think twelve of us from this guild tried to help the guy. He's irredeemable, not to mention a complete ass."

"When Laura"—the blue-eyed girl tipped her head toward her friend—"showed up on his doorstep, he told his bodyguard to dispose of the garbage."

"Didn't even spare me a passing glance," Laura confirmed. "But Leo, from Guild 8—it's the all-male guild in Paris—he had an even worse time. Jarod made that bulldog of his—what's his name again?"

"Ethan?" the other answered.

"You mean Tristan?" I supplied.

"Yes. Tristan." She shuddered. "That guy whipped Leo's back until it bled."

I released my dress, which remained creased. The faint whiff of mulled blackberries and dank cork combined with the image of a flagellated back made bile lurch up my throat.

"To think Tristan's sinner score is only seventy-eight. The guy's a demon with a capital D."

Laura toyed with one of her earrings. "Yeah, he's totally worse than Jarod. Sometimes, I don't get how the Ishim score sinners."

Neither Tristan nor Jarod had seemed like monsters to me—devious and domineering, sure, but not evil executioners. At least, not Tristan. And Jarod . . . well, Jarod had issues and possessed the potential to be cruel, but he also possessed the potential for compassion.

The thought took me by such surprise that I blinked at his 3-D image flickering from my holo-ranker. I stared into those pitch-black eyes of his, watched his thick lashes sweep over them. If I truly believed this, then why was I signing off from him?

"You're from the New York guild?" The girl's blue eyes blazed against her dark brown skin.

"I am."

"Do you know a Fletching named Eve?"

"She's my closest friend."

"Huh." Laura crossed one leg over the other.

My skin prickled with wariness at her tone. "Why, *huh*?"

"Didn't she tell you to stay away from the Triple?"

This time, it wasn't wariness that made my skin crawl. "She warned me he ran the Court of Demons and that was the reason for his high score."

The dark-skinned girl pushed her kinky curls behind her ears, but they sprang right back out. "I know we're not supposed to influence each other, but if you and I were best friends, and I'd already attempted to reform someone like Jarod Adler, I'd find a way to keep you from signing up."

"She . . . she took him on?"

Laura shot me a wary look. "She didn't tell you?"

I swallowed, my heart banging harder than when Jarod declared me prisoner in his house.

"I shouldn't have said anything. Please don't tell the Ophanim," Laura's friend said. "I just assumed you knew."

"I won't tell anyone." My voice sounded flat.

I tucked my chin into my neck and stared at my scarred palm, tracing the pale line with my eyes, watching it shimmer and blur as tears rose. If I didn't get my weeping under control, I could take the place of the broken angel statue in Jarod's fountain. I'd fill that basin up before day's end.

"Maybe you should get some better friends," she added.

"Marie!" Laura hissed.

"What? It's not a sin to give advice."

"Your friend probably had a reason for not telling you about her time in Paris with Jarod." Laura was trying to make me feel better about Eve's betrayal, but her comment had the opposite effect.

Eve had urged me to select Jarod, because she knew he was an impossible sinner and wanted me to fail. It wasn't jealousy that had made her lose a feather, but deceit.

How could you do this to me, Eve?

I got up brusquely and speed-walked to my borrowed bedroom, the guild's quartz halls closing in around me. The elysian sky beyond the glass-domed ceiling usually comforted me, but not tonight. Tonight, everything inside of me hurt. I kicked off my shoes after entering my temporary bedroom, forgetting Celeste was inside.

Celeste who'd warned me Eve wasn't genuine.

I'd fought so hard to defend her. Disappointment made a sob lurch up my throat. I flung myself onto my bed. A minute later, the mattress dipped, and a soft hand touched my spine.

"Hey . . . what's up?" Celeste sounded groggy.

"I'm sorry for waking you," I croaked.

"Forget about waking me. What happened, Leigh? Did he hurt you?"

I shook my head. "Not he. *She.*"

"*She?*"

"Eve," I murmured.

"Eve?"

My shoulders shook on another sob.

"Is she here?" This time, there was nothing groggy about Celeste's voice. It was all steel edges and alarm.

I sat up and wiped my cheeks on my forearm. "How are you so wise and I'm so stupid?"

"You're not stupid, and I'm definitely *not* wise. I mean, have you seen my wings? I have that whole plucked bird look going for me . . . But more importantly, what did Eve do now?"

"She told me to pick Jarod."

Celeste slanted her eyebrows.

"She told me to pick him because she knew I would fail," I added in a splintered voice.

"I still don't understand."

"She tried to reform him, Celeste." I crimped my pillow with my fingers. "Eve knew it would be an impossible mission. That's why she told me to take him on."

Celeste's eyebrows jumped.

"I lost three feathers, and I haven't even signed off from him." My wings would eventually heal, but my heart . . . I wasn't sure it could ever heal from her duplicity.

Celeste didn't say anything, but I could tell thoughts were swirling behind those keen eyes of hers.

I relaxed my fingers on the pillow and hung my head, my orange hair curtaining off my face. "I should've listened to you."

"Leigh?"

"Yeah?"

"I'm not going to let you fail."

I jerked my head up and fixed her with my swollen eyes.

"First things first, you're going to make me a promise. You're not going to sign off just yet, deal?"

I swallowed. "But, Celeste—"

"*Deal?*" she repeated, tone inflexible.

I loosed another ragged breath. "Jarod brings out the worst in me. I lost two more feathers for lying!"

"About what this time?"

I grimaced. "About wine tasting awful."

"You tasted wine?"

"He made me "

She scrunched her nose. "He *made* you?"

"He told me that he'd leave and never allow me near him again if I didn't sample the bottle he served with dinner."

"Hold up . . . you had dinner with him?"

I walked Celeste through my strange evening, not leaving out a single detail. I told her about Jarod's exhibitionist tendencies—or whatever trying to make me uncomfortable in his bedroom had been—his odd flirtatiousness and even odder phone call and invitation after I'd left. And then I explained how I'd found out about Eve's betrayal.

"Everyone on the holo-rankers can be reformed. They wouldn't be on there if that weren't the case." Celeste took both my hands in hers. "Leigh, you're the most determined and patient angel in the human world."

I rolled my eyes.

"Don't roll your eyes at me. I'm being totes serious right now. You're the best of our kind."

"I'm really not."

"You're the only Fletching in the history of Fletchings who acquired over nine hundred feathers without ever losing one. And you probably wouldn't have lost any feathers if you hadn't decided to take on a Triple."

"I bet there are others."

"No. There aren't. I actually looked it up because I was curious. Now, go to sleep, and tomorrow, we'll pay your sinner a little visit."

"Celeste, I don't think . . . I don't want you to come with me."

"Why not?"

"Because it's the Mafia, honey."

"*Aw.* Are you worried about me?"

I flicked her wrist. "Yes, I'm worried about you."

She shot me a smile that touched her eyes. "Nothing to worry about. I'm the most resilient—and according to your bestie—the most loathsome Fletching flitting around."

Annoyance hardened my bones. "Eve called you loathsome?"

Celeste's smile grew, dimpling her cheeks. "I called her *way* worse. Cost me a feather. Well worth it, though."

I shook my head. "Celeste, Celeste, Celeste. What am I going to do with you?"

"You're going to get your butt to Elysium, marry Asher, and then start changing those stupid laws of ours."

For the first time that night, I smiled and swore I'd try my best.

She stuck out her pinky and wiggled it. "Pinky promise."

"Because my word isn't good enough for you?"

"Your word's okay. Your pinky's better."

I didn't see how my pinky could best my word, but I indulged her and hooked it around hers. And then I gathered her against me and gave her a long hug.

Into her snarled hair, I said, "I don't think I can ever forgive Eve for what she did to me." I breathed in the clean, warm smell of Celeste's skin, like freshly laundered sheets that had just come out of the dryer. "It's just you now. Just you."

Her wiry arms squeezed me surprisingly hard. "You and me against the human world."

I sighed into her hair. "And the angelic one."

19

I slept as though someone had clocked me upside the head, a deep, dreamless sleep that eased the throbbing in my temples but did little to soothe the throbbing in my chest.

Sleep had offered me reprieve, but the instant my lids had opened, Eve's betrayal had washed through me like an arctic waterfall, leaving me chilled to my wing bone marrow. I curled my fingers around my warm pillow, pondering whether to contact her through the guild's holo-com system.

Confronting her while emotional was probably not a good idea. Besides, I didn't feel like seeing her face on our holographic phone. *If* she even picked up my call. She was probably too busy collecting one of her fourteen remaining feathers.

I suddenly remembered her reluctance to take on a sinner in Paris. She must've known I would figure out what she'd done.

A small hurt sound formed at the back of my throat. I tried to stifle it, but it climbed out of me and got lost in the *whoosh* of the bedroom door carving the air.

"I was just coming to wake you." Celeste carried a large mug over to me. "I made you a vanilla latte."

"Thank you." I sat up and took the mug. "I don't think—I don't think I want to—"

"Nuh-uh." She flung the comforter off my legs. "You're going, and I'm going with you."

"Celeste—"

"If you don't go, Eve wins."

"Maybe I don't want to win anymore."

"And I don't want *her* to win, so get up. Drink your syrupy coffee, then get dressed. We leave in fifteen."

I gave Celeste my hardest stare—or tried to. Glaring at her proved quite difficult, considering how she rolled her eyes at my attempt to look angry.

"Besides, you made a pinky promise. Those are airtight."

THE ARCADE WAS dark with bodies when we arrived on the Place des Vosges at noon, the line of supplicants wrapping around the block. I wondered how long Jarod had been doing this. Unless his uncle had started the monthly tradition?

"Le culot de ces deux-là." The gall of those two. A bony hand clasped my forearm and twisted me around. *"Hé-oh. Derrière."* Get back in line.

I shrugged the woman's hand off. "We're not here to—"

Before I could finish my sentence and explain we hadn't come for an audience with Jarod, Celeste snarled, "Don't touch my friend."

"I've been waiting for over two hours!" the woman, who'd gripped my arm, squawked.

I pulled Celeste back. "We're not here for the same reasons you are."

The woman knotted her arms in front of her. "Why are you here then?"

The person behind her, an elderly woman with a cloud of gray hair, wound a protective arm around a young boy.

The looks lobbed our way ran the gamut from annoyed to concerned to downright aggressive. *"Elles sont peut-être des putes,"* I heard someone whisper. *They're probably whores.*

"La petite est un peu jeune pour se prostituer, non?" another answered. *The small one is a little young to prostitute herself, isn't she?*

Celeste's fingers jammed into fists. "We're not—"

"Celeste . . . it doesn't matter." I grabbed her fist, pried her fingers loose, and dragged her toward the blood-red doors guarded by Amir and another brawny guard dressed in an impeccable suit.

"*Bonjour*," I ventured.

Without a word, Amir jutted his head toward his fellow guard, who inserted a key in the metal plaque.

When the woman at the front of the line started forward, elbowing me, Amir shot out his thick arm to bar her way. "Not you."

I slid past the woman, then past the two guards, towing Celeste behind me.

"Just you, Mademoiselle Leigh," Amir said, propping the door open.

I was startled he knew my name, but he *had* rifled through my bag. "Celeste's my sister."

"Jarod mentioned you'd come. He didn't say anything about a *sister*." The way he spoke the word told me he didn't put much stock in the fact that we were related.

"Please, Amir," I said. "She's just here to keep me company."

He took Celeste in. "My orders—"

"Can you at least ask him?"

Footsteps resounded, and then familiar blue eyes sparked in the obscurity of the covered porch. "I thought I heard your voice."

My heart swayed with relief at the sight of Tristan and then with anguish. As I absorbed his easygoing smile, I decided the two girls I'd met in the Ranking Room had gotten erroneous information. He couldn't have flogged an innocent Fletching.

I smiled. "Hi, Tristan." When I caught his gaze wandering over my shoulder toward Celeste, I said, "This is my sister, Celeste."

Tristan inspected my friend. "Sister?"

Celeste narrowed her eyes, measuring Tristan right back. I was glad I hadn't told her about his reputation, because she was far less trusting and forgiving than I was, and if she suspected Tristan of violence, she'd haul me away from the Court of Demons, Triple or no Triple.

"Yes, *sister*," she said with a little growl. "You don't see the resemblance?"

Tristan chuckled. "Now that you've opened your mouth, I do. Come on in, ladies."

Amir's lips shifted as though he were about to protest, but in the end, he simply squeezed them tight and went back to skimming the street and the endless line of people desirous to meet with his boss.

*C*eleste's neck rocked from side to side and back to front as we walked through the courtyard where ivy and roses the color of fresh snow scaled the trellises drilled into the limestone walls. Jarod's home seemed somehow less forbidding drenched in sunlight, more pretty castle than haunted fortress.

Unlike *La Cour des Démons*, the stone angel appeared just as bleak in the light of day. Had Celeste noticed the chipped stone? From how fast her gaze whizzed off the statue and onto the grid of diamond-cut windows, I guessed the sliced wings had eluded her assessment.

Instead of going through the usual entrance, we entered through the set of French windows that gave onto the checkered marble foyer. The sight of the sweeping stairs made goose bumps burst over my skin. I rubbed my bare arms but stopped when Tristan's eyes leveled on them before trailing to my nipples.

"Are you cold, Leigh? Would you like my jacket?"

"No," I said quickly before adding an even brisker, "thank you, Tristan."

His comment—or was it his stare?—drew Celeste nearer to me.

"*Bonjour*, Leigh."

I spun around at the raspy yet feminine voice.

Reddened lips curving, Muriel stepped out from Jarod's study, carrying a silver tray topped with a porcelain tea set. Her hair was swept back in another elaborate hairdo that glinted auburn in the sunlight bouncing off the crown moldings.

Celeste glanced up at me to ascertain if Muriel was friend or foe. When I smiled back at Muriel, Celeste's taut shoulders relaxed.

A string of expletives had all of us turning toward Jarod's study. The door swung open, almost unhooking from its shiny brass hinges. A thick man with sweat coating his flushed brow growled a particularly unsavory word as he yanked on the leash of a chihuahua whose tiny claws clicked nervously on the marble.

I pivoted toward Jarod, who was seated in one of his plush green armchairs, an arrogant smile tugging at his lips. I must've paled under the weight of his scrutiny, because Celeste stepped even closer, her shoulder brushing my arm.

Tristan gestured to the open door. "You ladies go on ahead. I'll go collect the next candidate."

As he plodded away, whistling, I swallowed, my throat alarmingly dry. I shot down my saliva a few more times but found no relief. It would probably only come once I left *La Cour des Démons* and its daunting owner.

I nudged Celeste into the high-ceilinged study. The patterned drapes on the two sets of French windows had been drawn open today, allowing light to bounce in. Where the room held fewer shadows, Jarod's face did not. Even the ray of sun slashing across his dark irises and razor-sharp jawbone did little to brighten his features.

"How was your night, Feather?"

Again, I swallowed. Again, it did nothing to moisten my throat. "It was okay. And yours?"

"Lonely."

"Feather?" Celeste piped in. "You call her Feather?"

He turned those unnerving eyes of his on Celeste. "She didn't tell you about my little nickname?"

A supple groove appeared between her eyebrows. "Why do you call her Feather?"

"Because I'm soft and spineless, apparently." I was glad to hear my voice grow a little sturdier.

Jarod's smile broadened.

"Unicorn noodle," Celeste muttered under her breath.

"Celeste!" I gasped, scouring the air around her skinny black jeans to make sure no purple feather drifted down.

"Pardon my French."

Jarod chuckled. "I'd never heard that one." He crossed his ankle over his opposite knee. When his steel-gray trouser leg rode up, I caught a hint of ochre-yellow.

Jarod seemed to have a thing for colorful socks, the same way I had a thing for bright accessories. And here I'd thought it impossible to have anything in common with this man.

"Will your friend be observing the interviews?"

"Would you mind if she did?"

His eyebrows shifted, vanishing behind a wayward chocolate-brown lock. Was he surprised I'd asked for his permission? His composure returned swiftly, and he shrugged. "Just don't hover."

I nodded and started toward the back of the room when Jarod called out my name—well, the name he'd given me. "Feather, sit next to me."

I startled.

Celeste pushed onto her tiptoes to align her mouth with my ear. "I'll go stand by the window. This way, I'll have your back. *Literally.*" Soon, her lithe form melted into the shadowed recess between the mahogany bookcase and a small varnished game table topped with a chessboard.

As I folded myself into the seat nearest Jarod, he said, "Here are my rules. Don't interfere with the interviews. Just listen. You get one joker. In other words, one person will benefit from my help thanks to you. Choose wisely."

At the loud knock, Jarod perched his chin on a closed fist. "Come in."

His transformation from lively to blasé was startling. I blinked, wondering if I was imagining the hardening jaw or dimming gaze, but the mask he'd worn the night we met—and I wasn't referring to the masquerade one—was firmly back on.

I turned toward the study's entrance.

The woman who'd elbowed me when I'd gone ahead of her in line strutted inside, glittery sneakers casting tinsels over the mahogany paneling. "I'm sorry. I thought you were done. Would you like me to wait outside?" Her tone was so syrupy I wrinkled my nose.

Jarod disregarded her question. "What brings you here, Mademoiselle . . ."

She frowned at me but must've understood I wasn't a supplicant. "Guanod," she finally answered. "Can I sit?"

She started to lower herself into a chair when Jarod said, "No."

She popped back up. After recovering from the shock of Jarod's ban, she jutted her pointy chin toward me. "She's sitting."

"*She's* not here for my help."

"What is she here for then?"

Jarod flicked his gaze toward Tristan, who pushed away from the wall, his crisp blue dress shirt glinting silver as he threaded himself around the furniture.

"Mademoiselle Guanod, I'll ask you one last time before my employee escorts you back out . . . how may I be of service to you today?"

Her eyes twitched, as though annoyed she was being treated so unsympathetically.

"I'm making her uncomfortable, Jarod." I was already scooting to the edge of my seat, ready to join Celeste in the back of the room, when his voice rang out sharply.

"Leigh, sit."

I wasn't sure what shocked me more—the use of my real name or the inflexibility with which he gave me the order.

I balanced on the edge of the seat cushion a couple of seconds before scooting back, afraid he'd cancel my joker if I didn't abide by his rules. His eyes didn't stray once toward me. They stayed glued to the woman whose forehead was scrunched in confusion.

"Next!" Jarod said.

"What?" When she saw Tristan closing in on her, she barked, "I didn't even—"

"Do you know how much my time is worth, Mademoiselle Guanod?"

"But I've been waiting—"

"Come back next month," Jarod said.

Tristan took ahold of her elbow, but she whipped it out of his grasp. "My ex-husband is refusing to pay the alimony he owes me!"

Jarod inspected his cuticles, perfectly and utterly uninterested.

"He put all our money into offshore accounts before filing for bankruptcy so he wouldn't have to share with me. All I want is for you to talk some sense into him."

Jarod didn't say anything, didn't even glance at her.

Tristan, on the other hand, said, "Men can be such bastards. Now, please, follow me."

When he placed his hand on her, she batted it away. "Don't touch me." Tears sprang to her eyes, glistening like the hefty diamonds fastened to her earlobes. "Can you please just talk to him, Monsieur Adler? Threaten him a little?"

"What do you think, Feather?"

I jerked my attention toward Jarod. "Um." Between being put on the spot and the way his inky eyes lingered on mine, the air became pinned to my lungs.

"Should I help her?"

The woman's soul didn't strike me as pure. Hurting, perhaps, but not in dire need of help. "Do you still have a roof over your head, Mademoiselle Guanod?"

"What does that have to do with anything?"

"My advisor asked you a question." Jarod drilled the woman with a glare. "Have the decency to answer."

Her teeth clenched. "Yes. I have a home."

"And do you feel safe in your home?"

Her green eyes, a shade darker than mine, rippled with hesitation. "No."

"She's lying, Leigh." Celeste's voice was low.

The woman jolted. "Who the hell's that? Another one of your *counselors*?"

"Would you like to cash in your joker, Feather?"

Wringing my fingers in my lap, I shook my head. Although I didn't doubt this woman feared for the quality of her life, she didn't fear for her life, and I wanted Jarod to help someone who did.

"Very well." Jarod flicked his fingers.

The woman growled as she trounced across the jewel-patterned rug ahead of a cheery Tristan. As she wrenched the door open, she fired out, "Since when do you employ whores to counsel you, Monsieur Adler?"

I blinked, and then a blush mottled my skin. I tugged on the spaghetti straps of my clingy gray dress, trying to heave the fabric higher. I thought it was conservative, but if I came across as—

"Tristan." Jarod didn't utter anything more than his second's name, and yet I sensed a loaded command attached to it.

Especially when Tristan nodded.

Once the door shut, I spun on the seat cushion. Before I could open my mouth, Jarod said, "No one gets away with insulting one of my guests."

"Except you." Celeste's voice made the tendons in my neck strain against my still flushed skin.

A nerve ticked at his temple. "Except me."

"She was just mad, Jarod. People say mean things when they're mad."

"Is your sister always this charitable, Celeste?"

"Always. It's her only flaw."

I was too anxious about the woman's fate to roll my eyes at their side conversation. "Please, Jarod. Don't do anything to her."

He cocked his head and fixed me with eyes that sparked with mischief. Except he wasn't a child, so his idea of mischief wouldn't be sticking itching powder in her bed. "*I* won't do anything to her."

My heart banged. "And Tristan?"

"I'm not his keeper."

"You might not be his keeper, but you're his boss." Fingers still toying with my dress straps, I worried my bottom lip.

Jarod's expression flattened. "You shouldn't let people get away with insulting you."

I should've worn a loose T-shirt. Or a turtleneck. Or—

"And stop doing that."

My hands froze on my dress's straps.

"You don't look like a whore." Jarod glared at the oil portrait of the bay horse on the wall between the French windows. "I've been around enough of them to know."

My exhale rushed out of me. For some reason, even though I wanted to thank him for his reassurance, the last part of his proclamation bothered me. "Why do you hang around that type of woman, Jarod?"

"Because I could never subject an innocent girl to the sort of life I live . . . to the sort of people who keep me company."

I was about to point out that changing his way of life would allow him to open his heart to the type of woman who'd desire nothing from him besides his love but was interrupted by a sharp knock.

A gangly man with undereye circles so purple they resembled bruises walked in behind one of Jarod's guards. Upon not seeing Tristan, I fretted for the woman with the diamond studs.

"Your name?" Jarod's question redirected my attention to the hunched newcomer.

"Sasha."

"What can I do for you, Sasha?"

The man didn't look at me or question my presence. Then again, he barely looked away from the carpet beneath his scuffed sneakers. "I run a small restaurant with my wife, and these men . . . they"—he rubbed at the collar of a plain black T-shirt—"they come in every night and demand a consequent portion of our earnings. They say it's to pay for their services. They claim they're neighborhood vigils." Sasha's voice was so soft it barely carried over to me. "I'm not sure if they're in your employ"—he flicked his eyes up to Jarod, then back down to the carpet—"but my wife doesn't feel safe around them, so we were hoping you could maybe tell them that we don't require their services." The man swallowed, his Adam's apple bobbing in his long, scrawny throat.

Jarod brushed the scruff darkening his jaw. "In which neighborhood is your restaurant?"

"The Twentieth. Just off Belleville. On Rue Levert."

Jarod kept rubbing his stubble. "Feather, what do you think?"

"Yes," I said without hesitation. But perhaps, I should've hesitated . . . I should've waited to see if he would've helped Sasha without me cashing in my joker.

I took in Jarod's profile, the strong, even lines of his face, his lips that parted to say, "Today's your lucky day, Sasha."

For the first time since he'd stepped into the room, Sasha straightened his head and stared at Jarod with such shock I didn't care if I'd used up my joker for nothing. The medley of gratitude, hope, and joy that washed over the man made everything which had come to pass in the last few days suddenly worth it.

"I-I don't know how to thank you." Gratitude glimmered in his eyes. "Both of you." He looked at me, then back at Jarod.

Jarod lowered his hand from his face and looked toward me. "Around what time do these men drop by?"

"Ten. Every night at ten."

"Give my guard the address of your restaurant before leaving. My advisor and I will stop by around nine thirty so we're there to greet these *vigils*." The way Jarod pronounced the word made me realize these men mustn't be in his employ, which reassured me more than anything.

Sasha performed spasmodic bows before spinning around and grappling for the door handle. He pumped it jerkily, then stepped out, but stuck his head back in to proclaim his gratitude a second time.

As soon he was gone, Jarod muttered, "You're not about to cry, are you now, Feather?"

A tear had curved down my cheek. I palmed it away. "Thank you."

"For what?"

"For volunteering to fix his problem yourself . . . And in person."

His eyebrows arched. "You make it sound like it's the first time in my life I've done something nice."

"Isn't it?"

His palm connected with the arm of his chair—noiseless, yet I felt the impact. "My reputation is truly abysmal."

I blinked, stunned he was trying to make himself pass as a benevolent person. Sure, he conducted these monthly open houses, but if he gave away favors for nothing in return, then his score would've dropped. The fact that it hadn't wavered since he'd been ranked a Triple told me he must either demand compensation in return for his generosity or send emissaries to help.

Unless he did handle these situations himself, but in that case, it would mean he committed such heinous crimes the rest of the month that they steamrolled all the good he did.

I glanced over my shoulder at Celeste. My friend was outspoken and rarely kept quiet, so the fact that she hadn't made a peep confounded me a little.

"Will you hold Sasha to an IOU?" Celeste finally asked, her mind operating on the same wavelength as mine.

He frowned. "An *IOU*?"

"Will you call in a favor at a later date?"

"I never expect anything in return from these people."

"Because they have nothing to offer?"

"Because that isn't the reason I help them."

"Why *do* you help them?" Celeste continued. "To better your conscience?"

He narrowed his eyes. "I help them because I can."

I stroked the armrest, leaving dark tracks in the velvet before brushing the fibers back. "Jarod?"

"Yes?"

"Would you have helped him if I hadn't cashed in my joker?"

His eyes flashed. "You'll never know."

And yet, I knew. Or at least, I sensed I knew. "Can I stay and listen to more, or do you want me to leave?"

"I don't think having you stay would be very wise. You'd have me save everyone and their mothers."

I shot him a rueful smile. "I'd certainly try."

"A shame you're all out of jokers."

Would he have given me another if I'd asked? I'd settled for one because that was all *I* needed, but Jarod would need to help more than one person to bring his score down. And no, it wasn't one life for one point—some acts could win him dozens of points, just as some acts could lose him a handful.

The Ranking System was like a scale that weighed kindness and maliciousness, then established a sum. Even though its inner workings remained a mystery to everyone besides the archangels and the Ishim, who were in charge of it, the way we'd been taught about it was that it was comparable to weight loss. At the start of a diet, the pounds slipped off fast, but then the numbers on the scale dropped slower as the body habituated itself to the new regimen.

"I'll pick you up at nine sharp tonight." Jarod's voice broke me out of my musings. "Don't keep me waiting."

"I know. I know." As I rose, I skated my palms over my thighs to smooth out my dress. "Your time's worth a fortune."

Jarod shot me another one of his disarming looks before turning his attention to Celeste. "Will you also be joining us later?"

"If Leigh wants me there."

"I don't." As much as I appreciated her support this morning, I didn't know what to expect from the last part of my mission. If it happened to be dangerous, and Celeste got hurt in the crossfire, I would never forgive myself.

"Well then, *au revoir*, Celeste."

"To our paths never crossing again, Monsieur Adler," she said sweetly.

"Celeste!" I chided her.

Jarod observed her with a quiet smile. "I like your friend, Leigh, and I don't like many people. She's honest. Most people aren't."

I wondered if he liked *me* but then stopped wondering this, because one, it was strange, and two, I didn't need Jarod to like me. I just needed him to like doing good deeds so he would keep doing them once I ascended.

As I curled my fingers over the door handle, Jarod's voice cut through the study. "Is it with you that she made the bet?"

Celeste glanced over her shoulder at him. "Excuse me?"

"Her bet. To marry some formidable male specimen." His tone smacked of so much sarcasm my shoulder blades tightened.

Keeping my gaze on the cool bronze handle, I waited for Celeste to answer, praying she wouldn't tell Jarod there was no bet, since our kind didn't make wagers.

"Wasn't with me," she said at last.

"Have you met the man Feather wants to marry?"

I looked back at Jarod, found his gaze sliding up the peach waves of my hair before settling on my chin.

"I did," Celeste said.

"And do you approve?"

"They're perfect for each other."

A blush crept into my cheeks. I forced the handle down before I blazed any redder. "I'll see you tonight, Jarod." In my haste, I bumped into Tristan.

"Leaving so soon, Leigh?"

"Yes." The word came out slightly strangled.

"So, this is *adieu*?" Tristan's eyes shone like pieces of cloudless sky.

"Not quite yet." I glanced back at Jarod who was staring intently at his right-hand man as though trying to glean from his mind what had happened to the torn-jean lady. "I'm coming along tonight."

"Are you?" He looked at Jarod. "How . . . exciting." He didn't sound very excited that I was coming; he sounded miffed. I supposed they were rarely shadowed by outsiders.

"Will you be coming along too?" I asked, as slow footsteps sounded on the marble.

The elderly woman with a dollop of gray hair hobbled into the foyer, leaning heavily on her grandson.

"*Allez-y, madame.*" Tristan gestured to the study.

Celeste slinked behind me as I stepped aside to let them pass.

Tristan closed the door behind them.

The wood was so thick it ate up the voices inside, yet I heard Jarod's deep timbre seep through. "What happened to the other woman, Tristan? The one you escorted out of here."

"I put her in a cab."

Celeste cranked her head to the side. "You didn't hurt her, then?"

Tristan snorted. "No, I didn't hurt her." Since he didn't flinch, I assumed he was speaking the truth. Unless he was an exceptional liar.

I breathed a little easier. Even though I should've left then, let them *work*, I couldn't help myself from straining toward the study to hear what was being said. "How many people do you usually help out on days like these?"

"I'm not at liberty to disclose that sort of information."

"*Do* you help people, or is this some pretty front to hide what you actually do?" Celeste asked.

When Tristan's eyes snapped to hers, my heart leaped right into my throat. Undermining the Mafia was probably not recommended.

I stepped in front of her to shield her from Tristan's serrated gaze. "What she meant to say—"

"Is exactly what I said. I'm sorry, but I have a hard time believing you guys are do-gooders." I knew she meant because of their sinner scores. Well, Jarod's score. Unless she'd looked up Tristan on the holo-ranker.

A soft, unsteady voice whispered through the wood. Although I couldn't catch all that was being said, I heard the word—*prison*.

I itched to press my ear against the wood, but Jarod's demand that we leave twisted through me. It wouldn't be right to eavesdrop. Still, I tried to collect a little more of the conversation while Tristan and Celeste stayed locked in a staring contest. The air crackled between them.

I laced my fingers around her wrist to break her concentration. "Does Jarod usually go help people out in person?"

Tristan unfastened his gaze from Celeste's. "Depends on the help we sign up to provide."

"So, what we'll be doing tonight . . . it's not out of character?"

The door behind me groaned. Hand curled around the boy's neck, the older woman tottered out, her gait seemingly wobblier than when she'd entered, but that could've been due to the tears flowing into her wrinkles.

Were they tears of relief or disappointment? As they shuffled past us, I hunted the boy's face, hoping he'd be easier to read than his grandmother. Although his long blond bangs obscured his downcast eyes, they didn't hide his matching wet cheeks.

Whatever they'd come for, they hadn't gotten.

Soles squeaked on the marble, and then Tristan blurred past me, going to the woman and boy, and preceded them across the sunlit courtyard.

"You can't help everyone in this life, Feather." Jarod's deep voice rumbled toward me like a swell of thunder.

Did he mean him or me? I supposed it didn't matter who this

you was. He was right, it was impossible to help everyone, but he had the power to help so many. Had the woman and child not been worthy of kindness?

A new theory blotted out all the others: his score had never wavered, because dangling hope that wasn't obtainable was the epitome of cruelty and negated any good act he might perform.

Wordlessly, I stepped out of his line of sight and then out of his realm.

I hadn't packed many clothes, and although laundry was an easy task in the guild thanks to our angel-fire hampers, I found myself spending my allowance on a dress in a cute French boutique that afternoon.

It wasn't the sort of thing I would've normally picked—emerald-and-gold leopard print over two layers of gauzy black chiffon —but today was not a normal day. Today was my last day on Earth, and I wanted to wear a beautiful human creation. Besides, it seemed to be the sort of dress Parisian women sported, and since Jarod and Tristan were always so impeccably dressed, I didn't want to stick out like a sore thumb.

As I clopped down the pedestrian street in black stilettos, the airy layers of chiffon swirled around my calves. What if Jarod and Tristan showed up in black cargo pants and black tees?

Too late to change outfits now. Soon, Jarod would arrive, and like he'd reminded me, he didn't like to be kept waiting.

When I reached the main boulevard, the chauffeured vehicle, which had trailed me home, already hugged the curb, hazard lights carving the dark street.

My stomach rumbled, reminding me I'd skipped dinner. Then again, I'd devoured a giant pink macaron stuffed with sweetened whipped cream and raspberry *confiture* after my shopping expedition. My taste buds still tingled with its delectable flavor. Since food could be conjured into existence in Elysium, I'd wish for that pink morsel of paradise often.

Elysium . . . I was so close I could almost taste the brine and sunshine ricocheting off the quartz walls of the capital wreathed by the smoking Nirvana Sea; I could almost hear the celestial tongue, which would become more familiar to me than any human language.

The white-haired driver stepped out of the car and drew open the door to the back seat. I stole one last lungful of oxygen before folding myself into the black sedan. The first thing I noticed was that Jarod was wearing a black suit, which meant I wasn't over-dressed. The second thing I noticed was that his eyes were stained by shadows and fatigue.

Had he given an audience to all the hopefuls lined up outside his home?

I touched his knuckles. "Are you okay?"

His dark gaze lowered to my bold fingers. I pulled them back and curled them into my lap.

He sighed. "It was a long day."

"It's almost over," I reminded him with a smile.

He lifted his gaze from the spot of skin I'd touched and set it on me, or rather on my neck and then lower. His expression darkened as it skated back up my body. "We're not going to the theater, Feather," he all but growled. "We're going to the Twentieth, one of the sketchiest neighborhoods in this Goddamn city. What the fuck got into you to wear . . . *that*?"

"You and Tristan are both wearing suits."

"I'll give her my jacket," Tristan offered, his fingers already dropping to the button.

Jarod shot him a glare before shrugging out of his own jacket and lobbing it at me. "She'll wear mine."

Once I'd recovered from the shock of the woolen slap, I speared my arms through the sleeves, the platinum silk lining warm against my bare skin. "Did you find anyone worthy of saving after I left?"

He stared out his window at the ebb and flow of cars around us. After almost a full minute, he turned back toward me, and then almost a full minute after that, he said, "Perhaps."

My lungs filled with Jarod's mineral, sweet scent. "Why do

you always have to be so enigmatic? After tonight, we won't see each other anymore."

My argument backfired. "Why would I share details of my life with someone I won't see again?"

"Forget it," I grumbled.

We rode in silence after that. Well, not in complete silence. Tristan, at least, chatted with me, asked me where I was going next. I told him *back to New York*—not a lie. Then he enquired as to my plans once I got home, and I glanced at Jarod, wondering if he'd informed his friend about my *bet*.

"I'm not sure yet," I said.

Jarod, who'd seemed lost in thought, deadpanned, "She's going to settle down as one does at . . . how old are you again, Feather?"

"Twenty." I ran my fingers through my hair, which lay in gentle waves against his jacket. The color might've been jarring, but at least, my angel-blood made my locks naturally glossy and soft.

Tristan twisted around. "You're getting married?"

"I'm thinking about it." But it was Asher, not me, who needed to be thinking about it. The choice wasn't mine.

"Who's the lucky man?" Tristan asked.

The gold accents woven throughout the leopard print glinted as I rolled the fabric between my fingers.

"Yes, Feather, who's the lucky man?" Jarod repeated tauntingly.

I nibbled on my bottom lip, not feeling like discussing Asher any further, because it wasn't making me happy. "You don't know him."

My gruff tone made Jarod smirk. "Perhaps we do know him. We know a lot of people, don't we, Tristan?"

Tristan's teeth gleamed in the dim interior.

"Not *him*," I said.

"What's his name?" Jarod needled me.

"I don't want to tell you."

"Why not?"

I decided to use his exact words. "Why would I share details of my life with someone I won't see again?"

Jarod's eyes seemed to spark in the obscurity. *"Touché."* After a beat of silence, he asked, "What would happen if I didn't help Sasha tonight?"

His question, coupled with his heady cologne, had my lungs struggling for air. "You promised him. And me."

"But what happens if I tell Francis to turn around and drop us off at *L'Ami Louis* instead?"

I didn't know who this Louis was; all I knew was that his place wasn't our destination. My knuckles whitened on the fabric. "You're having second thoughts?"

"I'm hungry, and considering the sound coming from your stomach, so are you. *L'Ami Louis* has the best *foie gras* in all of Paris. Do you like *foie gras*, Feather?"

I gaped at him. "You're thinking of going back on your promise because you're hungry?"

"Don't look so outraged."

"I'm not outraged; I'm shocked that you'd let your stomach take precedence over your soul."

"There you go about my soul again. My soul is unsalvageable however many good deeds I do."

"That's not true, Jarod!"

A dark lock fell into his eyes. He pushed it back, but it tumbled over his forehead again. "Feather, you don't know me. You don't know what I've done. *All* I've done."

"I'm sure it's all very terrible, but everyone can change. You just need to want to change."

"Maybe I don't want to change. Francis—"

Sensing he was about to tell his driver to double back, I said, "Jarod, please." I wasn't past getting on my knees to beg. Hopefully, it wouldn't come to that. "Sasha is counting on us. On *you*. Please let's go to him."

He regarded me a long time, as though weighing the pros and cons of keeping his promise to the restaurant owner.

"After we get rid of his unwanted solicitors, we can go to dinner. I mean you and Tristan. You don't have to take me to dinner." Sweet Elysium, could I sound any lamer?

Again, Jarod evaluated my plea quietly. I'd rarely met anyone as comfortable with silence as Jarod Adler.

"Monsieur Adler?" Francis asked.

Gaze not wavering off mine, Jarod flicked his fingers toward the windshield. "Proceed to Rue Levert." Once his driver gunned the car back into the right direction, the mob boss crossed his ankle over his opposite knee. "I'm holding you to dinner, Feather."

"Thank you," I whispered.

We rode the rest of the way in silence—Tristan typing on his phone, the driver concentrating on avoiding motorized scooters, and Jarod staring out his window.

Soon, we were traveling down a street lined with pale rectangular buildings devoid of ornate carvings and a crowd that didn't glitter like the one swarming Saint-Germain. The car slid to a stop in front of a restaurant with a red awning inscribed with loopy white letters forming the word *Layla*.

Our arrival attracted more than a little attention. I was suddenly glad for Jarod's jacket. As the driver opened my door, Tristan pulled something out of his jacket pocket—a little black gun. He checked the barrel, then slid it into the waistband of his pants.

Guns caused so much damage. I was about to ask Tristan if it was truly necessary when Jarod said, "Try not to shoot yourself this time."

Tristan snorted. "*T'es drôle.*" *You're funny.*

Jarod grinned, which knocked some of the earlier worry off his face. When he saw that I was still planted on the back seat, he mused, "Having second thoughts about tagging along, Feather?"

I pulled the jacket even tighter and hopped out. Tristan joined me first, then Jarod circled the rear of his car and walked straight into Layla's, and we followed.

A woman toting a slab of slate covered in chalked scribbles gasped, her fuchsia-tinted lips forming a perfect "O" on her otherwise colorless face.

"Sasha!" she called out, her voice a tad strangled.

Sasha looked up from a bottle of wine he was uncorking beside a table of four.

She wrenched her head toward us.

I smiled at her, which just seemed to deepen the fine lines puckering her brow.

Sasha poured the wine at record speed into his diners' glasses, then set the bottle on their table before hurrying to greet us. "*Bonsoir*, Monsieur Adler."

"Have they arrived?" Jarod asked, pleasant as usual.

Sasha's eyes darted nervously around him. "Not yet. Please, sit. Layla *chérie, la bouteille.*" *Layla darling, the bottle.*

As he led us to a table propped against the roughcast wall, his wife all but tossed the piece of slate on a chair before bustling toward the L-shaped wooden bar in the back and through a swinging door. Jarod selected the seat facing the street and leaned against the coarse wall, examining the small space and the two dozen or so people crowding it. The conversations hadn't picked up again, everyone still much too busy gaping. I loosened my grip on the jacket, the attention fanning heat through me.

Tristan pulled out the chair opposite Jarod's for me, then sat beside me just as Layla bustled over holding a dusty bottle of red wine with a tattered label. Jarod gave the bottle a cursory glance while Tristan read the label slowly.

"*Château Montrose '01.* You spoil us," he said, flashing Layla his customary flirtatious grin.

Her cheeks pinked as she uncorked the bottle in one quick pull and tipped it toward my glass. I was about to refuse but remembered alcohol hadn't cost me any feathers. Besides, declining their gift might offend them, so I let Layla pour.

Once she returned to the table she'd been taking the order from when we'd arrived, Tristan raised his wine. "*À la tienne*, Leigh."

"To all of our health," I countered, lifting my glass and clinking it against his. I waited for Jarod to pick up his glass, but he was still assiduously observing the room, from its timbered ceiling to its clusters of bare bulbs that puddled light on each square table.

"Leigh," Tristan said, pointing to his eyes, then to mine. "I'd rather dodge seven years of bad sex."

"Excuse me?"

"It's customary to look into someone's eyes when you cheer. To prevent bad luck in the bedroom. Or wherever else you enjoy getting naked." He added that last part with a lascivious wink that I'd come to understand was part of his arsenal when interacting with members of the opposite sex, so I neither took his words nor his wink personally.

Keeping my eyes on Tristan's, I took a sip of wine, the sweet alcohol burning a path down my throat. I expected to feel the pinch that preceded a falling feather, thinking that yesterday had been a fluke, but no feather fell.

Relief made me take another sturdier swallow. This time, there was no burn, just a lush aftertaste that reminded me of the cherries growing in the guild's orchard, which we would harvest before our wing bones appeared and our preoccupations changed. I took another sip of the unctuous nectar and licked my lips.

"Has anyone ever told you that your mouth is a work of art, Feather?" Tristan took a slow swallow of his own drink.

I startled at his use of Jarod's nickname. Somehow, it sounded wrong coming from him. Apparently, I wasn't the only one who had that thought.

"Don't fucking call her that," Jarod snapped.

Tristan's smug countenance teetered at Jarod's admonishment. "Won't happen again, boss." He tipped his glass and drained it, then scraped his hands over the silvering hair at his temples, and got up. "I'll go sit at the bar. Don't want any blind spots."

As he trudged away, I said, "Possessive of your nicknames, huh?"

Jarod side-eyed me, fingers stroking the stubby stem of his wineglass. His nails were all neatly trimmed and buffed, almost shinier than my own, which I'd painted a shimmery nude.

Between the radiator warming the right side of my body and the alcohol roiling through my veins, the heat became unbearable, and I shrugged out of the jacket. "Do you know what the men look—"

"Put the jacket back on." Jarod's words were low and clipped.

Since his gaze was cemented to the group of five guys at the neighboring table, how had he even noticed me taking it off?

"*Je me la ferais bien, celle-là.*" I'd do her.

I blinked at the man who'd spoken, more boy than man with his face full of pimples and sparse facial hair.

Jarod popped his cufflinks out of his cuffs and rolled up his shirtsleeves. "Feather, put the damn jacket back on," he ground out again.

As I flung it around my shoulders, the man-boy leaned back in his chair and smirked at Jarod. *Creep.* Jarod's chair legs scuffed the wooden floors. Before he could get up, I clamped my fingers around his forearm.

"Remember why we're here," I murmured, trying to soothe his temper. *To improve your soul, not to soil it.* "Don't throw it away over some stupid remark. In the grand scheme of things, it doesn't matter."

Jarod's nostrils flared. "It matters to me."

For a Triple, he was awfully righteous. "Please," I said again, and that last whispered plea dismantled his thirst to teach the creep a lesson.

23

Sensing trouble, or perhaps, privy to what the pimply-faced boy had said, Sasha rushed toward us, sweat glistening on his brow. "I'm so sorry, Monsieur Adler."

He pivoted toward the table of five guys and requested they leave. Even though his voice was quiet, the tension inside was unmistakable. When one of the guys grumbled and told him he'd never come back and like hell if they'd pay for their meal, the knobs of Sasha's spine strained against his gray cotton shirt.

Chair legs scraped, and then the pimply man-boy swiped the half-full wine bottle from the table before spitting at Sasha's feet. The viscous glob landed right by the owner's worn sneakers. I pressed my lips together. I'd miss certain humans; others, not so much.

I felt something shift underneath my fingertips—the tendons in Jarod's forearm. I'd forgotten I was still holding on to him. I snatched my fingers away just as the door swung shut behind the ill-mannered group.

"Keep the jacket on this time," he said.

I yanked the jacket so tight it all but choked me.

The room grew uncomfortably quiet, and the silence grew until it became an almost solid mass. Tristan was poised on the edge of a stool at the bar as though ready to leap off. It was only when Jarod relaxed that Tristan did too.

Sasha's hands trembled as he piled the plates of the five men who'd left, and the tremors seemed to grow worse under his customers' scrutiny.

I started to get up to help him when Jarod said, "Don't."

I frowned, uncomprehending as to why I couldn't help lighten Sasha's load. I was about to protest and remind him that my calling was to help people, when he shot me a look so stern it pinned my thighs to the wooden seat.

"All of your meals are on us tonight!" Jarod's voice sliced through the small room, amplified by the roughcast walls and low timber ceiling. "So, order that second bottle of wine or sample the entire menu for all I care."

The clink of silverware meddled with low gasps. Two glasses rattled on the platter Layla was setting down on the bar, and the dregs of wine inside one of the glasses splashed Tristan's jacket sleeve. He muttered under his breath, and Layla turned crimson. She rushed behind the bar and returned with a wet towel. Whispering apologies that carried over the growing hubbub, she started to pat his jacket when Tristan grabbed the towel from her, removed his jacket, and finished the job.

"Monsieur Adler, that's too generous," Sasha croaked, clutching the stack of plates against him. "You don't have to do that." Shiny brown sauce dripped off the doddering stack and down his bony wrist.

"Come to think of it, all your meals in this establishment will be comped for the next month if you bring Sasha and Layla business," Jarod added.

Sasha gaped at Jarod, clinging on to the plates so hard I worried they might shatter. "*M-Merci.*"

Jarod shrugged. "Don't thank me yet."

Sasha nodded before scampering off.

"That was really kind of you, Jarod," I said, attempting to decipher this puzzle of a man.

"Startling, I'm sure." He finally took a sip of wine.

Although diners had gone back to cutting through browned lambchops or scooping up creamy, scalloped potatoes, all of them darted curious glances our way. I was about to ask him if most people in Paris knew him when Layla bustled over to ask if she could bring us anything else. Although the smell of food had my stomach rumbling, I sensed now wasn't the time to indulge.

"Just some bread, please," Jarod said.

"Right away." She rushed back to the bar, then returned carrying a wire basket filled with slices of springy baguette. After depositing it on our table, she went back to taking food orders.

I heard one woman ask for all their appetizers and main courses. Either she and her husband were famished or they were going to milk Jarod's offer. Probably the latter.

I smiled. "Planning on distributing antacids?"

"Gluttony is a deadly sin, so their souls should suffer accordingly, don't you think?"

His comment, combined with its mocking delivery, temporarily impeded my brain's ability to shape an answer.

"Besides"—his fingers stroked up his glass—"it'll give you a jolly band of new sinners to assist. Surely, not as entertaining as yours truly but easier considering how well-versed you are in gluttony."

How well-versed I am in gluttony? My palm dropped to my soft stomach. "Just because I enjoy eating doesn't mean I have a disorder," I said, wishing I was comfortable enough in my skin that jabs at my physique didn't sting.

Jarod's fingers plummeted from his glass, the side of his hand hitting the scratched wooden tabletop. "What?"

I scrutinized one of the many grooves in the wood. "Forget it."

"Don't tell me to forget it. Why did you just take my remark so personally?"

I filched a piece of bread from the basket and peeled the doughy center from the thin, hard crust. "Was the *you* supposed to be a universal you?" I stuffed the bread inside my mouth. *Take that, Jarod Adler. I don't care what you think of my body and my love for food.*

But I *did* care. Too much. The same way I cared when Eve urged me to cut carbs.

"That wasn't—Feather, I didn't—"

"I said forget it."

The glass door of the restaurant jangled, and three men strolled in, grins as wide as their shoulders. All of them sported hair on their faces but none on their scalps. A chill swept up my spine, and I didn't think it had anything to do with the cool air that had drifted in when they'd entered.

One of them winked at Layla, who went as rigid as the slate menu she was holding. He snickered as he followed the other two mounds of muscle toward the bar where all three dropped heavily on barstools two seats down from Tristan.

Tristan glanced up from the jacket he was still cleaning. The guy who'd winked at Layla spun on his stool, a diamond stud sparkling in his right earlobe. Once he faced out, he placed his elbows on the bar behind him as though he owned the place. The door behind the bar flapped open, and Sasha, arms laden with plates, froze before looking toward Jarod.

Jarod, who'd grown as still as the wingless angel in his courtyard.

Earring-guy's gaze skidded over to him. When Jarod stood, the thug elbowed his friend, whose jaw twitched. I felt useless sitting so far away but was afraid to get in the way if I went to them. Besides, my mission was to guide, not to perform the acts in the sinner's stead.

As I observed the men's body language, I ran my thumb along the lapel of Jarod's jacket, coaxing his scent out of the silken wool. Instead of calming me, it had my heart racing harder.

The man beside Earring-guy shifted on his stool, and then his hand slipped under his T-shirt as though he were scratching his stomach.

When I caught the gleam of silver, I gasped Jarod's name and shot up, the jacket springing off my shoulders and hitting the back of the chair before pooling on the floor. Thankfully, Tristan had seen the weapon too. He leaped in front of Jarod, gun brandished. Over the din of chair feet, strident shouts rang out, rivaling the thunder in my veins.

Tristan cocked the hammer, and the man jerked his hands in the air. The knife clattered to the floor. Tristan kicked it backward, and it bumped against Jarod's shiny Oxfords.

He stepped on top of the blade and said, "*You,* call Mehdi and put him on speakerphone."

While Earring-guy's fingers tapped his phone screen, the guy beside him narrowed his eyes, first on Tristan, then on Jarod.

I didn't like the way he was watching Jarod and stepped closer to my sinner. I wasn't supposed to interfere, but I also wasn't going to sit back and watch men rip each other apart. Especially when I was immortal, and Jarod wasn't.

The man's gaze sparked with amusement at the sight of me. "Cute bodyguard," he said, which earned him Tristan's elbow in the temple and which earned *me* a hard scowl from Jarod.

A few years ago, I'd stepped in front of a yellow cab and gotten flung several feet in the air to protect a child whose mother had pushed out the stroller without checking for oncoming traffic.

Even though Jarod might've believed me useless, I knew I wasn't.

A barked "What?" rose from the cell phone Earring-guy was holding up, stealing Jarod's attention away from me.

The Demon Court lord cracked his knuckles. "Been a while, Mehdi."

Silence answered him.

"You never drop by to visit anymore," Jarod continued.

"Jarod?" Mehdi's voice hitched.

"I was afraid you'd forgotten about me." The ghost of a smile floated over Jarod's lips. "You're overdue for a visit."

The guy Tristan had hit rubbed his temple, green eyes slitted like a snake's.

Mehdi cleared his throat. "I've been busy."

Jarod ran his gaze over the three men before him. "I can see that."

"I was planning on ringing you this week, actually."

"Were you now? How delightful. I'll tell Tristan to look out for your call. Oh, and congratulations, I heard you landed a very profitable wedding for your eldest daughter. Should I send my gift to her honeymoon suite in the Seychelles or to her apartment on Avenue Matignon?"

"How—" Mehdi sputtered but stopped himself from voicing the rest of his question. He was probably wondering how Jarod knew where his daughter was honeymooning.

"Were you planning on informing me about your little side business?" Jarod asked.

The guy next to Green-eyes shifted on his stool, casting glances around him. I became acutely aware of how quiet the restaurant had become. I looked over my shoulder to find Sasha and his wife huddled in a corner, the only remaining people besides us. I hoped that Jarod's offer to comp meals would make the customers forget the heated altercation and return, if not tonight, then soon.

"I was—it's not—" Mehdi was unable to string full sentences together.

"*La Cour des Démons* doesn't condone racketeering, but you know that, don't you?" Jarod continued, sounding as censorious as Ophan Mira when she would catch me reading one of my human novels. "I expect you'll return the funds you've confiscated from all the establishments you've been hitting up for the past year."

There was a loud bang on the other side of the phone as though Mehdi had punched something. Green-eyes's attention flicked to one of his buddies before skipping back to Jarod.

"Earlier today, your son graciously provided Tristan with a detailed list of the restaurants and cafés you've sent your little *emissaries* to raid. Tristan will be contacting them one by one to confirm they've recovered their funds before our meeting." A string of muffled swear words made Jarod smirk. "I can't wait to see you too, old friend."

At the same time as the phone screen went dark, the green-eyed guy bounded off his seat, snatched my wrist, and rammed me against his front. His beefy arm wrapped around my throat, squeezing the air out. I clawed at his skin, wheezing. He backed away, dragging me with him, then seized a bottle from a table and swung it against the back of a chair. Red wine splashed over the floor and sprayed my bare ankles, dribbling inside my shoes.

The guy pushed the razor-sharp edges of the bottle against my collarbone. "You shoot us, I slice her neck." Rancid-smelling spittle smacked my cheek.

Jarod's eyes became as black as the barrel of the gun Tristan was pointing at the two others. "I wasn't planning on shooting any of you, but now . . ."

The man choked me harder, and the room went grainy.

"Don't," I murmured. To my attacker and to Jarod. I didn't want to be the cause for bloodshed. Bloodshed would erase all the good Jarod had done tonight. Even if it wasn't his finger on the trigger, if he ordered the hit—

"*Putain, lâches la meuf, Mo!*" Earring-guy shouted. To beg his friend to release me meant he sensed this wouldn't end well for the three of them.

When stars danced at the edge of my vision, I summoned my wings. They wouldn't help me fly out of the man's grasp, but my wing bones would press him back like an invisible hand, hopefully lending me enough room to wriggle out. As they burst from my shoulder blades and my feathers snapped out, air trickled back down my throat, sharpening my vision.

"What the—" The man sputtered as I twisted around and shoved my palms into his torso. I wasn't supposed to use violence, unless under duress.

I decided I was under duress.

He stumbled, and then his backside hit the ground. A gun went off. I spun around to find one of the men trying to pry the gun from Tristan's hands while Earring-guy was yelling at him to stop.

Something sharp carved through my calf, tearing a scream from me. I toppled forward, falling right into Jarod's rigid arms. For several breaths, he didn't move, but then, he twirled me around and kicked Mo's wrist right as he swung his makeshift weapon again. The bottle rocketed out of his grip and landed on the floor with an earsplitting crash.

Another gunshot went off.

This time the bullet sank into flesh. Earring-guy seized up as his friend's brain matter exploded all over him. And then he paled and stumbled away, heaving. Tristan got to his feet, wiped the blood on his forehead with the sleeve of the jacket he'd cleaned so assiduously, then aimed the gun at the guy who'd attacked me. The bullet zipped through the air and ricocheted off a plate.

"Jarod!" I screeched when I saw Mo grab a steak knife.

I lunged to put myself between them. Jarod wrapped an arm around my middle and whisked me up and around. As my heels met the ground, a growl lurched out of Jarod's throat and lashed my feathers.

I tried to look over my shoulder, but my wings were in the way. I magicked them out of existence and twirled in Jarod's arms.

Another shot pealed through the restaurant. Mo dipped his

chin and looked at the dribbling hole in his chest. His eyes rolled back, and he flopped against a table before crashing to the ground.

My ears rang, and my throat constricted at the stench of hot blood and acrid vomit. Jarod's complexion had paled considerably, and his eyes had this glassy sheen to them that made me skate my palms over his jaw, down his warm neck, and over his back. His shirt had been slashed. When my fingers came away sticky and red, I realized Mo had hacked my sinner's back.

"He cut you!" I yelped.

"I know, Feather. I was there."

I blinked at his dry humor. It wasn't funny. None of this was funny.

"I'm fine," Jarod added.

He didn't look fine. He looked white as the fish congealed on one of the plates next to us.

"Let me see," I said.

"I said I was fine."

"Jarod—"

He clasped my wrists. "I said I was fine. It's just a superficial scratch."

"Scratches don't bleed that much," I said but then caught Tristan raising the gun on Earring-guy, who was on all fours, emptying the contents of his stomach. "Tristan, no!"

His finger squeezed the trigger, and the man fell face-first into his own vomit.

Tears ran down my cheeks at the massacre.

My fault.

This was all my fault.

If I hadn't pushed Jarod to take up this task.

If I hadn't let my guard down and allowed myself to be used as a pawn in this power play.

Oh, Great Elysium, what had I done?

My wings reappeared, and I curled them around me, wishing they could protect me from all this death, but all they accomplished was hiding the spectacle. I could still smell the bitter cordite; I could still hear the squeal of approaching sirens.

"We should go before the police get here," Tristan said, his voice so incredibly calm I wanted to smack him.

How could he be so unaffected by taking three lives? Because he was used to it?

I tucked my wings back, bile rising at the sight of the carnage. I looked at Tristan, who was pushing his gun into his waistband, then at Jarod who was staring at my shoulders.

I blanched.

Could he . . . could he see my wings?

My heartbeat strengthened, vibrating against my palate, making the inside of my mouth taste like a penny.

"*Mon Dieu. Mon Dieu,*" Sasha's voice rose from behind me.

That's what had caught Jarod's attention.

Not my wings.

Not. My. Wings.

Besides, if he could see them, then he could touch them, and I hadn't felt his fingers on my wings. Or had I? My chaotic pulse seemed to have numbed my body and thinned my memory.

"We wait for the police," Jarod said calmly, turning his gaze to one of the fallen bodies. "And, Tristan, call the cleanup crew."

Tristan's jaw clenched as though he wanted to protest, but he pulled out his phone and scrolled through his list of contacts.

They have a cleanup crew on call? How often did this sort of thing happen? I didn't ask, because I didn't want to know. I kept my wings tucked but present, finding comfort in their familiar weight. A few minutes later, two cops walked into the restaurant, guns raised.

"Monsieur Adler," one of them sputtered.

The female officer flanking the other cop frowned.

"Put the gun down, Christine," the first one hissed.

Even though it seemed to take everything in her to force her arms to holster the weapon, she did. "What happened in here?"

I wasn't sure if Jarod would explain. He didn't seem like the type to explain.

"They were bad men," Layla said, index finger trembling in midair as she pointed at the three bodies. "They attacked Monsieur Adler's girlfriend. It was self-defense."

My cheeks pinked. In the scope of things, being called Jarod's girlfriend should've been the least of my worries. My wings reflexively curled around me as though they could somehow shield me from everyone's scrutiny, because *everyone* was looking at me now. Actually, that wasn't true. Jarod was staring at the broken bottle that lay on the ground, its serrated edges darkened by blood. His and mine.

Another wave of uniformed men and women came in—police and EMTs.

"I'll take care of everything, Monsieur Adler," the male cop was telling Jarod, who gave him a slow nod.

I shouldn't have found Jarod's ties to the police surprising, yet the scope of his influence didn't cease to astonish me.

"The cleaning crew's on their way," Tristan said. "Should I call Francis?"

Jarod nodded again, his eyes now riveted to the crimson splotches tarnishing the shine of my patent stilettos.

"Leigh, are you riding back with us?" Tristan asked.

Jarod's gaze banged against me. "Did you expect her to fly out of here?"

I blanched.

Tristan frowned, looking between Jarod and me. "Um, *non*."

It wasn't my imagination. Jarod sounded annoyed. Was it with *me*?

I took a step toward him. "I'm sorry, Jarod. About tonight. This isn't what—"

He snorted. "You're just sorry my trigger-happy associate made you lose your bet."

I startled, stopping a few feet from his rigid form. "No." I shook my head. "I'm sorry I interfered."

"You think things would've gone down differently?" Jarod asked.

"Leigh, Leigh, Leigh." Tristan grinned. "Welcome to *La Cour des Démons* where justice is restored one bullet at a time."

My stomach clenched.

"Call Francis," Jarod said. "And give Sasha some money to cover the meals and the damage."

Tristan nodded, seeking out the man we'd come to help but had failed. As he gave his statement to the female cop, I stared at Jarod, desperate to understand the source of his anger.

"Thank you for keeping your promise. And for not shooting anyone yourself," I said gently.

Even though it was selfish of me, I wondered if the Ishim

would consider his intervention tonight an act of valor. He had neither given the order to kill nor held the gun that stole three lives.

And he'd protected me.

How I wished I understood their system better.

Just as I had that thought, three winged men marched into the restaurant, wringing a gasp from my lungs.

Angels had come.

And not just Malakim.

*a*sher strode over to us, flanked by two gold-robed Malakim. Where Asher's wings were deployed, the turquoise and copper glittering in the dim lighting, the other two angels had their wings tucked into their backs, only the gilt tips of their feathers peeking out. Unlike the Malakim, Asher wore jeans and a white T-shirt that made his torso appear broader than when I'd seen him in his leathers.

"Get the souls out of here," he murmured, nodding toward the bar.

Cloaked in angel-dust, the Malakim wound around the police, then squeezed in next to the riddled corpses before kneeling and placing their palms on the dead men's chests. Like honeyed threads, the souls stuck to the pads of the Malakim's fingers. They coaxed the glowing threads until they detached themselves from the immobile bodies, and then both angels closed their fists and rose.

It wasn't the first time I'd watched the Malakim extract souls, and yet my amazement never tarried. My heart gave a hopeful thud that, one day, I'd be able to perform this type of magic. Granted, the angels didn't deem this magic, but to me, the process felt magical.

The realization that only two Malakim had come made my gaze return to Asher.

Asher who was talking in low tones with Jarod.

I forgot all about the unharvested soul as I noted the familiarity of their interaction. This wasn't their first meeting.

Asher's alarming reaction the night I'd given him my sinner's name washed over me. He *knew* Jarod. Personally. Although this shouldn't have shocked me—the Seraphim were reputedly omniscient—the awareness grated against my wing bones.

What had Asher told me again?

Don't spend too much time trying to reform a Triple. His words trickled through me clear as the night he'd spoken them.

Tristan sidled up next to me. "I don't know about you, but I'd really like to break out of this joint."

I crossed my arms. "Do those two know each other?"

"The guy's some distant cousin. Every time he stops by, he warns Jarod to behave better."

Distant cousin? That was the cover Asher used? I supposed no one would be the wiser. It wasn't as though Jarod would force the Seraphim to spit into a test tube to have his DNA mapped out.

As though he heard us discussing him, Asher's turquoise eyes beamed into mine.

"Tristan, let's go." Rigidly, Jarod began to stalk away.

"Wait," I called out.

Jarod halted, his bloodied shirt sticking to his back, and glanced over his shoulder at me. "For what?"

For me, I thought but then looked at Asher. Had Asher been sent to escort me back to the guild? Since when did Seraphim collect Fletchings from their missions? Was I in trouble?

"My cousin will see you home," Jarod said. "Apparently, you two have met."

Tristan cocked an eyebrow.

"Small world," I mumbled, fingers clamping around my forearms, crimping my pebbled skin.

Jarod scrubbed one hand through his gelled locks, flipping back a curl obstructing his obsidian eyes. "Take care, Leigh."

The use of my angel-given name iced me almost as much as his tone.

It sounded like goodbye.

As he finally walked away, Tristan tailing him, I told myself that I'd see him again. Sinners didn't sign off; only Fletchings had that power.

As long as I didn't sign off, Jarod Adler would remain my sinner.

25

"You're pretending to be his cousin, Seraph?" I snapped as we made our way out of the restaurant after I'd collected Jarod's fallen jacket. I hadn't meant for my words to come out reproachful, but I felt blindsided. This wasn't fair of me, though. Asher had tried to tell me, not in so many words, to stay away from Jarod.

Asher slid me a look, his eyes impossibly colorful in spite of the darkness of Rue Levert. "I've come to know him well."

"But cousin?" Lies didn't cost feathers once wings were filled out, but still, it was in poor form to lie. Especially when you were at the top of the hierarchy and expected to set an example.

Asher loosed a deep sigh. "I apologize, Leigh, but you're familiar with celestial policy. We're not allowed to discuss sinners with Fletchings."

I bit my lip and nodded, tightening my grip on Jarod's jacket. "Am I in trouble? Is that why you showed up tonight?"

"The Ishim told me they were collecting souls in Paris squandered by a man named Tristan."

I searched our darkened surroundings for Ishim or Malakim but found no other angel. No other human either, for that matter.

"I assumed Jarod would be here," Asher continued, "and since you took him on, I expected you would be, too."

"Which doesn't answer my question, Seraph . . ." I returned the full force of my stare on him. "Am I in trouble?"

Asher ran a big hand through his shoulder-length golden locks. "Yes."

My mouth went very dry. "How much trouble?"

"We're not supposed to influence Fletchings, but, Leigh"—he stopped walking, and my heart climbed into my throat—"you need to sign off."

"Why?"

"Do not ask for I cannot tell you."

"Please."

Asher scrutinized the graffitied storefront of a hookah shop where fluted glass pipes were coated in a layer of dust so thick it was impossible to guess their colors. "Do you want to ascend?"

"Of course I want to ascend."

He shifted his gaze back to mine. "Then sign off."

"Seraph—"

"I beg you, Leigh, no more questions. This conversation will undoubtedly already get me in trouble." He scanned the sky as though angels were hovering above us.

I silently assembled all the scraps of our conversation, trying to puzzle out the reason I should sign off from Jarod. "I can't die," I reminded him.

"If you don't complete your wings in time, you could," he answered softly.

"But I still have fourteen months."

His Adam's apple jostled, which made me realize how it had sounded—like I no longer felt an urgency to ascend. "Perhaps, but this mission has already cost you feathers."

Shame made me tuck in my wings. I didn't think three feathers were that noticeable, but he was an archangel . . . all-seeing. "I'll earn them back. Jarod's willing—"

"Not if you don't select another sinner!"

A protective instinct surged within me, which was nothing new. I'd always been protective of my sinners.

I squeezed Jarod's jacket against my hardened stomach. "He didn't shoot anyone tonight. He didn't even *punch* anyone. And he protected me. Surely, that will take a digit off his score."

"His score cannot change."

"But he's in the system."

"And he shouldn't be," he shot out, fast and low, gaze skimming the sky and street again.

Besides the occasional vehicle rumbling past us, we were alone.

"I don't understand, Seraph. Are some crimes so unforgivable?"

What could Jarod Adler have done that merited a permanent score of a hundred? I ran through my years of celestial lessons, sensing the answer to that question suspended just out of reach.

And then it hit me, robbing me of breath and heartbeats. "He killed an angel," I said on a gasp.

But *how*? Only angel-fire could kill us once our wing bones appeared. And before that, we weren't allowed out of guilds. Unless a celestial child had escaped into the human world—I couldn't imagine Jarod killing a child but then remembered he'd earned his score when he was eight. *An accident?*

"It wasn't an accident," Asher said softly.

I hadn't realized I'd voiced my thoughts. "So he did kill an angel?"

Asher was back to being silent and unhelpful.

"How is that even possible, Seraph?" I whispered, my voice as thick as the coating of dust on the hookahs. "We're immortal."

"Not all of us."

Not all of us? I almost choked on my next breath. "He killed a Nephilim?"

The fact that the blood on his hands wasn't that of a child shouldn't have alleviated my dread, but it did. Nephilim were the black sheep of the angelic race—mortal, wingless, soulless.

When they ran out of time to seal their feathers to their wing bones, they were pitied. When they voluntarily forfeited their wings, they were considered heathens, worse than Triples.

Asher neither confirmed nor denied my suspicion, but I could tell I'd assembled the pieces he'd given me correctly.

"He was eight. Children make mistakes."

"It's late, Leigh. Let me fly you home."

I'd only been flown over the human world once before when

I'd gotten lost in a sketchy part of Queens. I'd called Eve who'd passed on the message to Ophan Greer. It wasn't completely uncommon for Fletchings to become disoriented, but it was humiliating. I'd cried so many tears that the city had blurred past me, a mess of leaden concrete and riotous lights.

Asher spread out his wings, and their breadth and beauty pinned my lips shut, but then I remembered he'd brought them out as a means to an end: getting rid of me and my pesky questions.

I backed up, Jarod's jacket folded over my rigid arms, lending my skin some warmth.

"You have nothing to fear. I will not drop you."

"I'm not scared of falling, Seraph."

"Then why are you backing away from me?"

The smell of Jarod drifted from his jacket and replaced the scent of spice and wind gusting off Asher's skin. "He was a kid," I repeated. "Surely, his soul shouldn't be bound to extinction."

Asher narrowed his eyes. "He was a child who knew what he was doing. Now, please—"

"How could he know? Humans can't see what we are."

Asher pressed his lips so tight they lost their fullness. He looked severe then, and it reminded me that I was in the presence of one of the Seven and probably not behaving accordingly, yet no feather had detached itself from my wings.

Suddenly, Jarod's nickname popped to the forefront of my mind, and my lids snapped high. "He does know what we are!"

Asher's lips thinned some more.

Humans couldn't see us; only angels could.

"He's a Nephilim," I sputtered. "That's how he can see us!"

Like a slow-moving movie, I recalled the way he'd tracked the feather I'd lost in his bedroom. And at Layla's . . . my wings had snared his attention not Sasha's sobs.

"I never said that," Asher growled, snapping his wings and rocketing into the starless sky, leaving me alone on that strip of pavement with no phone, no money, nothing but a man's jacket and my own two feet to carry me home.

Had he left because he'd lost patience or because he'd feared revealing classified secrets?

Stunned and disoriented, I waited for him to take pity on me and return. When he didn't, I started walking, attempting to remember how we'd gotten to Rue Levert.

Jarod had warned me this part of Paris was of ill repute, so I was extra conscientious of my surroundings, crossing streets when passersby addressed me too rowdily or lewdly. By the sixth vulgar remark, I put on Jarod's jacket. And then it hit me to check his pockets. There was no phone, but there was a wad of cash so thick I felt like everyone could see the bulge of it once I'd stuffed it back inside.

At a taxi stand, I got into a cab.

"Where to, mademoiselle?" the man asked.

I hesitated. In the end, I said, "Place des Vosges."

I needed to return the jacket to its owner, and I wanted answers. And since Asher couldn't give them to me, I'd seek them out from the source.

The source who'd killed an angel-blood.

My conscience waged a war with itself as the taxi cut through the city streets. Jarod was dangerous, but I was immortal, so no true harm could come to me. Besides, he'd had his share of opportunities to hurt me. Sure, he'd taken great pleasure in making me uncomfortable, but tonight, he'd been almost . . . *sweet*.

Besides the gluttony comment.

The taxi jolted to a stop at a red light. As I stared at diners sitting in a restaurant that spilled onto the sidewalk, a thought twisted inside my mind. I'd once helped a teenage girl quiet her urge to fill her stomach with pounds of food she'd heave up minutes later. Could one of the feathers I'd lost in Jarod's home have belonged to this girl with destructive cravings?

If Jarod managed to see the memories contained in feather shafts, then he had angel-blood. But angels didn't have scores. Not even Nephilim.

Especially Nephilim since they lacked souls. Yet he was in the system, so he *had* a soul.

I growled in frustration because something didn't add up.

The cabbie glanced into his rearview mirror. "Everything all right, mademoiselle?"

No. *Nothing* was all right. Everything was all wrong. Instead of lying, I said, "Long night."

Thankfully, he didn't prod. "Is there a particular address you'd like me to drop you off at?"

When the manicured, block-long grassy square came into view, I said, "Right by the arcade, thank you."

He pulled up on the corner of Jarod's street. Eighteen euros glowed on the meter. Tenting the jacket around me, I pulled out the wad of cash and looked through it for a twenty, but the smallest bill I found was yellow and bore two zeroes.

When I handed it over, the man shook his head. "I don't have change for two hundred."

"I don't have anything smaller."

"I take credit cards."

"I'm sorry, but I don't have one."

It wasn't my money to hand out, but I couldn't not pay. "Please just take it. And do something good with the extra money." I'd explain my predicament to the Ophanim. Hopefully, they'd understand and give me an advance on my allowance so I could reimburse Jarod.

The man eyed the yellow bill suspiciously. When he still didn't take it, I laid it on his armrest and scooted out. And then on feet that felt wedged too snugly inside my patent stilettos, I trudged underneath the arcade toward the crimson doors.

I wiped my clammy palms on my dress, then pressed the buzzer, and waited. I wasn't sure if I'd be allowed in, but the familiar click granted me entry. I traversed the cobbled courtyard, eyes cast on the starbursts of lights tangled in the ivy and white blooms.

A low creak sounded as Jarod's bulked-up bodyguard Amir opened the door I'd been escorted through the first night.

"Is Jarod home, Amir?"

"He just arrived." Amir didn't search me, simply led me through the quiet dining room with its cherub-adorned ceiling. Between the fountain and fresco, it felt like Jarod's house was thumbing its nose at me.

He had a connection to our world, but what was it?

At the bottom of the stairs, Amir said, "I'll be in the vestibule once you're ready to leave."

I nodded, then started my journey up the stairs, the evening running on a loop inside my mind. What would I find upstairs?

The truth? More enigmas? As I reached the landing, I slipped Jarod's jacket off and draped it over my forearm. It felt wrong to have sheathed myself with something that didn't belong to me.

Steeling my spine, I let out a breath, took in another, and then I lifted my hand and knocked.

26

"*C*ome in, Leigh."

How—how had he known it was me? Was my knock distinctive? And *Leigh* . . . not Feather?

I opened the heavy wooden door a sliver, then wider. The room was so dark I didn't spot Jarod lounging on the cowhide recliner immediately. Ever since he'd related the story of his mother, I felt like the scent of rust and salt lingered in the air.

I closed the door behind me, staring at his profile edged in pale light. "You forgot your jacket." I extended it toward him, but the gesture was senseless considering the distance that separated us.

He didn't reach out for it, and I didn't come closer.

"Just toss it on the bed," he said warily.

I stepped toward the canopy bed and laid it neatly on the tucked steel-gray comforter. "I borrowed one of your bills to pay for my cab," I said before turning around. "I'll give it back to you later."

"If you borrowed one of my bills, then you must've noticed I had many and therefore have no need for repayment." His gaze was on the golden letter opener he was slowly rotating between his index fingers.

Each time the blade caught the glow of the sconce outside his window, a vane of light swept over his stubbled jaw, his patrician nose, and the curl of his sooty lashes before vanishing in the unruly waves of his dark hair.

"I can't accept your charity, Jarod."

"It's not charity if it's a gift."

"I'm not allowed to take money. Not yours. Not anyone's." When he didn't respond, didn't even spare me a glance, I segued toward the matter that had brought me back here. "I didn't know you had a cousin."

The letter opener stilled.

"Is he from your mother's side or your father's?"

He kept his gaze on the object balanced between his hands.

"Jarod?"

"Has anyone ever told you that you ask a lot of questions?"

"Has anyone ever told you that answering with a question is called deflecting?" I crossed my arms. "Tell me how you and Asher are related, and I'll leave."

"You use the threat of leaving a lot. You shouldn't threaten someone with something you are incapable of doing."

My arms fell out of their knot. "I *am* capable of leaving."

"Then walk out my door and never come back." His lips barely parted, yet I heard each word loud and clear. Too loud, and too clear.

"Jarod, please, I only want to help—"

"So you can marry fucking Prince Charming?"

I recoiled. My first instinct was always to recoil when someone lashed out at me. My second instinct, though, was to fight back. I fisted my fingers until my nails bit into my palms. "What do you care who I marry?"

It was on the tip of my tongue to add that I didn't want to get married anymore, because one, the husband I'd wanted had shown me a face I hadn't particularly liked tonight, and because two, there was no way in Abaddon I'd collect my missing feathers before the month was out.

"You're right," Jarod finally said. "I don't care who you marry."

My breaths were coming in spurts as though I'd run from Layla's all the way to *La Cour des Démons*.

"Why don't you tell me how *you* know him, *Leigh*?"

The sound of my mutilated name falling from his lips was a punch to the gut. "I asked first."

"We aren't ten. You're in *my* home. *My* bedroom." Each sentence was a new jab, but the finishing blow came when he said, "And I've been indulging your petty whims since you've inserted yourself into my life, so I'll ask again, how do *you* know *him*?"

My temples throbbed. I was tired. Tired and hurt he'd felt the need to raise his voice and be so insulting. I wasn't his enemy. "Asher's the man I wanted to marry." As silence stretched between us, I worked hard on soothing the ache in my chest caused by my shattered hopes and squandered feelings.

"Why am I not surprised?" The sneer in his voice made my heart ratchet anew.

"*Wanted*," I repeated, stressing the past tense. "He left me behind on the sidewalk, because I asked too many questions." I snorted even though it wasn't funny. "I guess I infuriate all the men in your family. Next thing you know, Tristan will complain about my inane curiosity and have me tossed out of here."

Even though I couldn't see Jarod's pupils from where I stood, they seemed to bleed into his irises and then into the whites around them. It was an impression—no one's eyes could go dark from lid to lid, yet that was the way Jarod's eyes looked in that moment. "He left you stranded on a sidewalk?"

"Don't act like you care."

He lowered the letter opener, curling the fingers of one hand over the blade. I expected to see blood trickle down his wrist and into his rolled shirtsleeve, but the blade must not have been very sharp.

"Besides, you abandoned me first, so you have no right to judge him." My voice wasn't loud, yet the hurt inside of it seemed to ring across the large room.

Elysium only knew why Jarod's desertion stung. He'd entrusted me to Asher. He hadn't left me alone in unfamiliar territory.

He sat up and swung his long legs over the edge of the seat, planting his feet wide and pressing up. "I apologize for leaving you."

"I didn't say it to receive an apology."

"You should've called me. I would've come to pick you up."

The crazy thing was that I believed him. "I left my phone at—" I'd been about to say *the guild* but switched it to, "home." I reached up and pushed a lock of hair behind my ear with unsteady fingers.

Jarod followed my hand's trembling arc back to my hip. I balled my fingers to stifle the tremor before more pity could crowd his expression.

"Asher's a cousin on my mother's side," he said.

My lids fluttered from the shock of his voluntary admission. Here I'd thought I would never get an answer from him. Or that if I did, it would take more coaxing.

"I met him the day my mother . . ." He swallowed, his Adam's apple jostling heavily in his throat. "The day my mother died."

I recalled something Tristan had said: that Jarod had lost both his parents by the time he was eight and that he'd destroyed the wings of the stone angel after his mother passed. And then I measured it against what I knew: that he'd been ranked a Triple that year.

My nerves began to jangle so fiercely I suspected Jarod could hear them. "How did she die again?"

He opened his fingers to display the golden letter opener. "Stabbed herself with this." A slender, bloodied wound marred his palm—the blade wasn't as blunt as I'd estimated.

Knives couldn't stop angel hearts, at least, not winged one's. Which meant Jarod's mother was a Nephilim, but Nephilim couldn't have children, so Jarod must have been adopted. Which meant I was wrong about him being able to see what we were.

But that suddenly wasn't important anymore. "Did she plant it inside her chest . . . herself?"

He lobbed the letter opener at his bookcase where it clanged against a spherical glass bookend. "No. *I* put it there."

I gaped in horror at Jarod. "Why?"

"You should run away now, Feather." He turned his face away. "And this time, *stay* away."

Even though I tried to stay away from the cracked sinners, I'd been around enough of them to learn that a truly dangerous person didn't avert their eyes when they delivered a threat, much too desirous to savor the fear they instilled.

"You killed your mother, Jarod?" I repeated softly.

He raised his chin, leveling his bottomless eyes on me. "Why does this surprise you? My soul's putrid."

"I don't believe that."

"You should come to terms with the fact that some people have no good in them and that I'm one of those people."

"Did she hurt you?"

"Hurt me?" He gave a dark laugh. "I told you already. She wasn't interested in me, Feather."

The return of my nickname on his lips solidified my resolve to dig for the soul that lay beneath the granite shell he'd built around himself.

"Why are you still here? *Leave!*" he barked.

"Stop trying to scare me."

He took a step toward me, his expression turning almost feral.

I stood my ground. "I need to understand one last thing."

Even though Nephilim couldn't have children, the fact that he'd destroyed an angel's wings made me wonder if his adoptive mother had told him stories about us, or if, for some reason that defied all logic, he could see what we were.

I let my wings ripple into existence, then snapped them out as far as they could extend.

His gaze jumped to the spires of his canopy bed.

"You see them, don't you?"

"Them?" he asked, using that bored tone of his.

"Look at me, Jarod."

Slowly, as though it physically pained him, he dragged his attention back to me.

My heart held very still. "You know what I am, don't you?"

"A pain in my ass," he muttered.

"Besides that," I deadpanned.

A nerve twitched next to his eye. Sensing he'd be harder to break than elysian quartz—not that I'd ever tried, but I'd heard only angel-fire could cut through it—I stepped closer. Human hands fell through our wings like powdered sugar through air, but angel-bloods could feel our feathers.

I took the fingers he'd balled and pried them open. Surprisingly, he let me straighten them. Without breaking eye contact, I lifted his hand toward my shoulder, then beyond it.

For a heartbeat, I worried I was wrong, that his fingers would slip right through my feathers. But as our hands neared my wings, his exhales pulsed harder against my brow. Right before I could set his hand on the peak of my wings, he put up some resistance, but it was too late. I hoisted my wing until its tip brushed his palm.

He shuddered so hard it shook his entire body. Shook mine, too.

His touch sent a slow shiver through each shaft, making the vanes tremble. I reasoned that the sensation had everything to do with the discovery that my sinner was an angel and nothing to do with the feel of his skin against my feathers.

His eyes sparked, then sparkled like the Eiffel Tower at night.

I swallowed, trying to quell the tremors sinking into my wing bones. "You're one of us," I whispered, my voice hoarse with emotion.

But *how?* Had his mother, a Nephilim, conceived him, or had he somehow run away from a guild before his wing bones could materialize?

Gently, I released his wrist, allowing him, now that I had my answer, to snatch his hand back.

Although his eyes kept shimmering, he parked his fingers back next to his side. "I am *nothing* like you," he growled, spittle smacking my forehead. "Unlike your kind, I don't seek to do good for personal gain, to better my soul, or grow those appendages you believe make you so glorious and superior." He stepped back, then stalked past me, grabbing his jacket from his bed.

"Jarod!" I swung around, my feathers swaying from my brusque spin. "What are you doing?"

"What you're incapable of: *leaving.*"

Before my next breath, he'd flung his bedroom door wide and trampled down the stairs, his furious footsteps echoing against the runner and then against marble. As another door clanged shut, rattling the very walls of the house, I drew my wings around me. My feathers quaked as his words reeled through me, scoring me deeper and deeper.

It's not personal. Not personal. Then why did it feel like he hated *me?*

A tear curved down my cheek, and I raised my hand to scrub it away but froze at the sight of my skin.

I'd attributed the shine in Jarod's eyes to emotional turmoil, but it wasn't the sight of my wings that had made them glitter. It was the sight of my skin.

Its reflection.

I'd just smoldered Jarod Adler.

Oh, Great Elysium, what was wrong with me? My body must've been wired defectively, because why else would it want to seduce someone who detested all I was and all I stood for, someone who'd murdered their own mother?

I watched my flesh glitter, then snapped out of my daze and sought out the switch to turn off the absurd glow. Since I'd never smoldered, I realized I had no idea how it worked. All I knew was that I should be able to control it.

My heart was beating too fast, which must've caused my flesh to light up. I flared my nostrils, inhaling long and deep, then exhaled until my lungs cramped. The scent of Jarod almost choked me, but I persevered, sensing I needed to relax in order to stop shining. I repeated this breathing sequence until the vibrations in my chest decreased and dowsed my radiance.

27

On the upside, the shock of smoldering Jarod tempered the shock of learning he'd murdered his own mother.

As I tucked my wings back, I caught the gleam of the letter opener that had ended a Nephilim's life. I watched it suspiciously, as though it might levitate and stab me.

What had prompted an eight-year-old to kill his mother? I'd heard Nephilim often lost touch with reality, the pain followed by the absence of their burned wings progressively consuming their minds. Had she become so crazed that Jarod took it upon himself to end her suffering?

As I moved across his bedroom, the glossy wood creaking under my weight, I let my gaze stray off the letter opener and onto a decorative purple-stingray box that held up a row of leather books, then higher toward the crown moldings of the pale ceiling. This would be my last sight of *La Cour des Démons*, because I couldn't come back. Not after all Jarod had said, and certainly not after my skin's humiliating display of affection.

Besides, I had nothing to gain by staying.

My footing faltered. *Ugh.* Jarod had called my kind selfish, and I'd just proved him right.

But our kind *wasn't* selfish. My blood heated with indignation that he'd planted this seed inside my mind and that it had dared take root.

Building our wings didn't only benefit us; it benefited humans. If we didn't earn our feathers, then we couldn't ascend to Elysium. Our race would become mortal and perish, and in turn humankind, because no virtuous souls would be harvested and re-implanted into wombs to counterbalance the incessant influx of depraved ones. Not to mention that humans who spent their lives bettering the world would no longer be rewarded, and those who spent their time spoiling it would no longer be punished.

Without us, the apocalypse humans had feared for millennia would come to pass and ravage the world angels kept in equilibrium.

So, no, Jarod Adler, we aren't selfish. We are necessary.

Why couldn't I have come up with all of this in his presence? Why did my mind work with a broadcast delay?

Jarod Adler obviously didn't understand our system. How could he, though? He hadn't grown up in a guild. Perhaps, his scorn for angels stemmed from that. Perhaps, that was why he'd murdered his own mother. Because she'd robbed him of the opportunity to live among us.

As my theory solidified, I stepped onto the landing and bumped into a soft body.

"Muriel!" I gasped, reaching out to steady her.

"Leigh? Is everything all right? I heard doors slam." She rubbed her eyes, smudging her residual mascara.

"Everything's . . ." I'd been about to say fine, but that would've been a lie. I sighed. "Jarod and I got into a fight, and he left."

She frowned, her navy eyes running over my face as though to decipher the reason for our fight. Then she sighed. "And I suppose you did not resolve it since my boy's weapon of choice is always flight."

Her boy. Had *she* had sexual relations with an angel? "Is he . . . *yours*?"

Her forehead grooved. "I raised him from the time he slipped out of his mother, screeching at the top of his little lungs, so yes, in a way . . . in many ways, I consider him mine."

"You were there at his birth?"

"Mikaela decided to have it at home, and I assisted the midwife."

How was this possible? How could a fallen angel create life in her womb? Was it a fluke, or was what I'd been told about Nephilim untrue?

It must've been a fluke, because Ophanim didn't lie.

Mikaela. I rolled her name around on my tongue. "Was she a good mother?"

Muriel's pupils eddied. "There's a bite to the air tonight." She tightened the belt on her blackberry-colored cashmere bathrobe. "How about we continue this discussion over a tisane?"

I desperately wanted to say yes, but remembering the late hour and my manners, I said, "You'd surely rather return to bed."

"And I will. After our tisane." She smiled. "Come."

I trailed her back down to the marble foyer and through a door carved into the wall beside the base of the stairs. A narrow passageway opened onto a pantry organized around an oval table cinched by six metal chairs and a wall of glass cupboards filled with fine china.

Muriel pulled a kettle off its base and filled it in the copper sink.

"Can I help?" I asked.

"Just take a seat, *chérie.*"

I pulled out one of the chairs, its legs grinding against the yellow tiles beneath it. As the water heated, Muriel extricated a polka-dot porcelain teapot from a cupboard, then bent over a drawer filled with colorful canisters. She selected a yellow tin box festooned with lavender lines.

"Do you like chamomile?"

"I like everything."

Smiling, she popped the top off the box, poured dried buds into a strainer, then grabbed two teacups with the same polka-dot pattern as the pot, and set everything on the table. As the tea steeped, she went back for a large round tin. She removed the lid, and a buttery aroma wafted straight into my stomach.

"Chocolate *sablés,*" she said. "I made them this morning."

I dipped my hand inside the tin and fished out a cookie. When I bit into it, I swore I could hear the arias twittered by our rainbow-winged sparrows. I committed its taste to memory to conjure it up in Elysium. Perhaps, my diet would consist of only chocolate shortbread and macarons.

I must've moaned, because Muriel smiled as she poured the tea.

"I cannot think of any word to describe how incredible these are." The hard, crumbly treat melted on my tongue.

"They're my grandmother's recipe. I could teach you how to make them?"

"I would *love* that," I said before remembering I'd be gone by tomorrow. I curled my fingers over the warm porcelain. "I mean maybe. I'm not sure I'll be allowed back inside this house anymore."

Muriel lifted her cup and blew on the billowing steam. If she was curious as to why I'd be barred from the Court of Demons, she didn't ask.

"So . . ." I said. "Mikaela?"

"Ah, Mikaela. She was a"—her cheek dimpled as though she were biting the inside of it—"complicated woman. One day, she'd be giddy with happiness, the next, she'd hide out in her bedroom. Jarod's uncle referred to her as bipolar, but I believe her mood swings were rooted in something deeper . . . something from her childhood. She rarely spoke about it, but right after Jarod's father passed, she contracted this fever that lasted days. As I sponged her forehead and administered medication, she would moan that they'd taken her wings and hadn't that been enough? Why had they taken the man she loved?

"She rambled on about a place called Elysium and then about another called Abaddon." She took a sip of her tea. "It's one of the names for Hell," Muriel explained, thankfully mistaking my shock for confusion. "It was at this point that I realized she must've incurred a strict religious upbringing. Perhaps, in a convent? I tried to find out, but she would drift in and out of consciousness, and after her feverish episode, she was never quite the same.

"Jarod was four then. Even though his uncle and I tried to shield him, he became a quiet child, kept to himself. Some days, I'd find him curled against his mother; others, I'd find him sitting on the floor of his closet, hugging his knees against him." She took another sip, then set her cup down. "Monsieur Isaac—his uncle," she added in case I didn't know the man's name. "He told me to move into Jarod's apartments since Mikaela had become quite incapable of caring for her son. They lived in the right wing of the house." She lifted her eyes to the ceiling, probably to indicate where the right wing was.

"It's not the wing he lives in now?"

"No. He took over Monsieur Isaac's apartments."

Apartments? Is that how they called bedrooms here in Paris?

"Night after night, Jarod and I would fall asleep in separate beds, but morning after morning I'd wake up to his tiny body snuggled against mine."

My chest tightened as I imagined Jarod as a child, clinging on to what little warmth and stability he could find.

"Monsieur Isaac walked in once and flew into a rage about how I'd defiled the propriety of his family. He ordered me to return to my service apartment. Jarod cried for twenty-four hours straight. He cried until Monsieur Isaac came to my room to fetch me and ordered me back into Jarod's." A smile stretched over her lips, as though she still savored winning that battle.

"His mother was still alive then?"

"She was, but once her husband passed away, she became a ghost in this house, existing but not truly there."

Had her husband passed to our world or had he been a Triple like Jarod? And what of Isaac?

I poured myself some more tea. "I heard Jarod was the one to find her the day she . . . the day she died." I drank even though the buds had steeped so long the ochre liquid had turned bitter.

Muriel's eyes gleamed, but I couldn't tell if it was with sadness or anger. "We'd just returned from the park where he'd made a friend, Tristan—Jarod didn't spend much time around children, so this was momentous for him." Her lips softened before pursing, creating rays of tiny wrinkles around them. "He ran up the stairs to tell his mother, and I chased after him, because he hadn't removed his shoes, which were full of sand." Tapping the tabletop with her fingertips a few times, she heaved a deep sigh. "Mikaela was . . . she was"—Muriel inhaled slowly —"bleeding. *Profusely.* I ran down to call for help. When Amir, Monsieur Isaac, and I made it back upstairs, Jarod's hands were"—she shuddered—"they were covered in blood." She closed her eyes, her wrinkles deepening. "And Mikaela had stopped breathing."

My saliva turned thick as plaster in my throat. "He told me he killed her."

Muriel's lids flipped open. "He did no such thing!"

I jerked at her tone.

"I'm sorry, Leigh. I'm sorry. I didn't mean to take it out on you, but I hate that he still believes he's to blame. I hate that he still thinks removing the knife was the reason she bled out." She huffed, fiddling with the collar of her robe. "Leaving it in wouldn't have kept her heart beating."

Even though I'd sensed he wasn't to blame for his mother's death, hearing Muriel confirm it loosened the tension coiled around me.

"After that, Jarod was never the same. Not that anyone expected him to come out unscathed. Who would? He'd never been a sound sleeper, but his night terrors grew so terrible he never slept through a single night. Still doesn't. Monsieur Isaac told me I shouldn't worry. That *our* boy—and yes, I say *our*, because Jarod had become very much ours by then—"

"Sounds like he was always yours."

Her taut lips relaxed a fraction. "Monsieur Isaac and I were the ones to raise him. Even when his parents were alive, they weren't very involved. When he wailed at night, I would rock him, and when that didn't settle him, I'd take him out in his pram and roll him back and forth across the cobblestones until the dips and bumps eased him to sleep." Her eyes glistened at the memory. "Monsieur Isaac, he took care of Jarod's education. Taught him to read, write, count, reflect. Monsieur Isaac wasn't known for his patience, and yet with Jarod"—her smile added some brightness to her haggard face—"he had an endless supply. He would've moved mountains for that boy."

"Jarod respected him very much."

"He did. He respected him. Loved him. Trusted him. And Jarod doesn't trust many people, Leigh."

"I suppose I wouldn't either if I'd lived through what he did."

"Especially women," she added, holding my gaze.

"Except you."

"Except me."

She kept watching me, and the intensity of her gaze made me dip my gaze to the yellow surface of the tea.

"Do you know that he's *never* dined in a tête-à-tête with a woman?"

I studied the pattern of blue dots on my cup until they began to superimpose. "Probably because he doesn't like food."

She leaned forward in her chair. "No, he just doesn't like the company of most women."

"He doesn't much like *my* company, Muriel."

"I don't believe that." She placed her dry palm over my hand. "He's never let a woman venture upstairs either."

I studied her knuckles that were as fine as her fingers. I didn't want to sully the image Muriel had of Jarod, so I didn't share the reason he'd had for herding me into his bedroom. I didn't tell her that it had been to make me squirm.

"He hates my beliefs. Hates what I am," I said instead. Which didn't surprise me now that she'd told me about the only other celestial example he'd had.

She released my hand, dragging hers back across the table. "What you are?"

Heat snaked into my neck and cheeks. Why couldn't I have picked other words? Or spoken none at all for that matter? "I have a strong faith, and he hates it."

"Jarod abhors religion—*every* religion."

"And I understand, but not all pious people are the same." I supposed my wings hadn't been a very convincing factor in this argument. I bet he hated all winged creatures, be they butterflies or angels. I drained my cup, then pushed away from the table and stood. "Thank you, Muriel. For the talk, the tea, the cookies, the kindness." I tried to fit a smile onto my lips, but it wouldn't hold. "He's lucky to have someone like you in his life. You're a saintly woman."

She tipped her head up and watched me. Even though Jarod wasn't biologically hers, there was something in the way they observed a person that was very much alike—a quiet, profound surveillance, as though they were looking at the soul instead of the envelope encasing it.

"To love isn't saintly . . ." she said at last. "To love is natural. Have you ever loved someone?"

Eve surged inside my mind. She'd known Jarod was an impossible case, which was why she'd suggested him. Had she known why? Had her archangel mother imparted classified information to make sure her daughter didn't waste her time?

My lips must've puckered because Muriel said, "No one?"

I thrust Eve into a dusky recess. "The girl you met yesterday. Celeste. She's like a sister to me."

"What about parents?"

"I don't know them."

Her eyebrows shot up. "A parental figure, then?"

"I had many teachers. Most were nice."

She watched me in that silent way of hers again. "It's late. You should sleep here tonight."

I could just imagine Jarod's expression if he returned and found me in his home. He'd probably say, *See, you're incapable of leaving.* It probably shouldn't have made me smirk, but for some reason, that reason surely being extreme exhaustion and moderate immaturity, it did.

"Celeste will worry if I don't come home," I ended up saying.

Since I was twenty, the Ophanim no longer cared about my whereabouts.

I'd never realized how alone I was, and that realization erased my smirk. I'd always believed belonging to a community was enough, but a community wasn't the same as a family.

Muriel, whom I hadn't even noticed getting up, wrapped me in a hug. "You're a sweet girl."

Sighing, I nestled my chin in the crook of her shoulder and let the sweet-butter scent clinging to her cashmere robe ease the residual tightness in my chest. What would it have been like to sneak into someone's bed after a nightmare instead of having to self-soothe by counting the stars in the elysian firmament?

"Come by tomorrow afternoon. I'll teach you how to make *sablés.*"

"I'd really love to, but I can't," I said, extricating myself from her arms.

"Then, the day after."

"Muriel, I . . . I can't come back. Jarod wouldn't want me to."

She frowned.

Before she could ask me for an explanation or challenge my assertion, I strode out of the little pantry through the cool marble foyer and burst into the courtyard with its ruined angel. I finally understood why the little boy had maimed her. How I wished I could show him we weren't all like Mikaela, but he would never be receptive.

Besides, I needed to move on before I ran out of time to complete my wings. I had no desire to become a Nephilim.

I bit my lip and was still denting the fleshy tissue when I exited onto the street and someone called out, "Mademoiselle!"

28

*J*arod's white-haired driver held the door of the sedan open for me. "Monsieur Adler asked me to see you home."

My heart, which had become lodged in my throat when Francis had called out to me, began its slow pilgrimage back into my rib cage.

Was Jarod afraid I wouldn't leave if someone didn't physically extract me from his territory? That was probably it. What else could it be? Concern for my safety? I snorted. Jarod Adler was most certainly no longer concerned for my safety.

Even though owing Jarod any more than I already did was unappealing, walking home in the dead of the night in a pair of stilettos was even more so.

"*Merci,*" I said, sliding into the back seat.

The door made a quiet suctioning noise as it sealed me into a space that smelled of crisp leather but also of Jarod. I rested my cheek against the headrest and watched the moonlit street, wondering where he'd gone off to in the middle of the night. Was it to visit a woman and lose himself in the pleasures of the flesh? I suddenly damned my passion for romance novels for instilling images I would never have thought of had I read celestial texts instead. I shut my eyes, but that spurred my imaginings, so I pried my lids up and focused on the city that glistened like labradorite.

As we neared the guild, I caught a poster advertising bank loans with two-hundred-euro bills printed all over it, and my mind zipped right back to the sinner I was trying to forget. We weren't allowed to take anything from humans they didn't willingly give us, and even though he'd insisted I keep his money, he'd said it after the deed, failing to unbind me from my celestial obligation. I couldn't afford to lose another feather.

Could I give the cash to his driver? Would he pay Jarod back?

I felt a niggle in my shoulder blade as though a shaft were loosening already. Sighing, I decided to visit him tomorrow. I needed sleep to recover from all that had happened and a shower to wash off the grime and blood.

After thanking Francis for the lift, I walked to the guild, arms wrapped around myself for warmth.

The guild was calm at this hour. Only the sparrows roosting in pairs on the Atrium fountains disrupted the silence with their honeyed cooing. One of them launched into song upon spotting me, and then the others followed suit. The melody grew, dispelling some of the chilliness in my bones.

Had these celestial creatures not been so skittish, I would've held out a finger for them to perch on, but they weren't fond of human contact.

A little like Jarod.

I sighed, listening to them a while longer before making my way toward the fire-lit quartz hallway, wishing the stone had the power to melt the lingering ice in my veins. As I passed by the last fountain, I thought of the one in *La Cour des Démons*, and instead of making me sad, it incensed me.

It was unfair that Jarod had been saddled with a skewed knowledge of us.

It was unfair that his number could never drop, because the Ishim thought he'd killed a Nephilim.

I spun on my heels and changed directions. In the Channel, I yelled, "I request an audience with Seraph Asher."

And then I waited, clutching my elbows.

I had no idea how long it would take my message to reach Elysium. I stared into the beam of pure light until my eyes stung. I supposed the archangel wasn't at my beck and call, but he'd have to show, right? Or would he send an emissary to tell me he was otherwise engaged? I began to pace, wishing I could scale the wall of the Channel and access Elysium.

I'd never questioned our rules, but at that moment, I began to find fault in them. Why were we separated from our parents? Why were we kept in guilds in the human dimension? Why did we have to relinquish our wings if we wanted to live among humans? On Earth, we aged, perhaps slower, but still our faces wrinkled and our flesh sagged.

I understood that laws were indispensable to the smooth functioning of a society, but how many of ours still made sense? Hadn't we—our people and our world—evolved?

"Leigh?"

My name made me snap around. Asher stood in his leathers, turquoise wings retracting.

"I thought Nephilim couldn't have children," I said on a single breath.

The tendons in his biceps pinched. "You thought correctly."

"Yet Jarod Adler's mother was a Nephilim. Which means he's a hybrid. Which explains why he can see us."

Asher remained silent.

"How is that possible, Seraph?"

His jaw clenched, and I worried he'd be as elusive as earlier. But I was wrong to worry. His expression softened. "We believe Mikaela was with child before she was stripped of her wings, and by some miracle, the embryo held on."

"Has this ever happened before?"

He speared his hand through his long hair, which slid like molten gold around his fingers. "I am not at liberty to share this with you."

I nibbled on my lip. "There's one thing I don't understand."

A corner of Asher's mouth lifted. "Only one?"

"You're right. There is more than one thing, but let's start with the most pressing one. The Ishim thought he was human. They didn't know he was a hybrid, correct?"

Asher slanted his thick blond eyebrows. "Correct."

"Why is he still in the system now that his lineage is known?"

"We're all in the *system*, Leigh. How do you think the Ishim control your feathers? They're not constantly watching you; they're watching your souls. All of our souls."

My brows arched up very high. "We're in the guild's sinner system?"

"A derivative of it that's only accessible to the Ishim and to the Council of Seven, but yes, your soul is being weighed on the celestial scales at all time."

Why were we never taught this? "Then, I suppose my question is, why is Jarod still in the *mortal* system?"

"Because he never lived in a guild, so he never developed wing bones."

"If he was brought into a guild now, could he develop them?"

"They won't form after puberty."

"Why was he never brought into a guild?" I twirled a lock of hair around my finger, then watched the copper coil loosen and bounce back against my patterned dress.

Asher scrubbed a hand down his face. "Because he killed a Nephilim."

"No, he didn't."

"He murdered his mother, Leigh. A Nephilim. Even if Jarod was in *our* system, he'd have been considered a Fallen, so he would've incurred the same fate."

"Except he *didn't* murder his mother."

"What are you talking about?"

"I'm talking about the fact that the Ishim who ranked him made a mistake. Jarod Adler did *not* kill his mother."

His eyebrows slanted deeper. "Just because he fed you a different tale—"

My temper sparked. "*He* didn't feed me any tales."

Asher's pupils dilated against their brilliant backdrops.

"Jarod's convinced taking the knife out of his mother's chest made her bleed out, but it was the *planting it inside* that killed her, and she did that all on her own." The same storm captured in those canvases back at Jarod's house raged behind my breastbone. "Are the Ishim truly so dense that they can't tell the difference between murder and succor?"

My breath hitched as though someone had jabbed the letter opener into my wing bones. I shut my eyes, nostrils flaring. I wasn't surprised that criticizing the Ishim had cost me a feather.

I'd been livid before, but now I reached a whole new level of anger.

I flung my lids wide, cranked my neck back, and yelled into the dark elysian sky. "Punish me all you want for decrying your fallible system, but don't punish a man—an angel-blood—for *your* mistake!"

"Leigh!" Asher thundered.

I gestured to the skylight. "They made a mistake, Seraph."

"You weren't there that day," he said coolly.

"Just because I wasn't there—"

"Well, I was." His voice had dropped. "I'm the one who found him with the weapon in his hand."

I touched my throat, mouth gaping. That's how Jarod knew him so well.

"Before becoming an archangel, I was an Ishim. I'm the one who gave him his score, and I marked him *after* he confessed."

"He was eight, Seraph! He was probably in such shock that he had no clue what he was confessing to."

Asher tossed his hands in the air, turquoise feathers bristling at his back. "He's the nephew of Isaac Adler. Isaac Adler was a Triple and died a Triple. Not to mention the boy's mother was a Nephilim."

"So that makes him automatically evil?" I shot back. "Since when are we judged by our kin?"

A body materialized in the Channel. And then another. And another. All wore sleeveless belted gray tunics over gray suede leggings, all had metallic wingtips. I'd met Ishim a few times over the years. They'd visit the guilds to explain their jobs. I remembered being dazzled, but that was back when I'd thought their system faultless.

One of the Ishim, a woman with wild blonde corkscrews and a pointed chin, came to stand beside Asher. "Seraph?"

"I have the situation under control, Ish Eliza. I do not require assistance."

Eliza turned, fanning out her lilac wings as though to shield the archangel from my sight. "Seraph Claire sent us."

I snorted, which captured the attention of all four angels. Not that Asher had looked away from me. Angel-fire hadn't shot out of his palms, but I doubted that was for lack of want.

He was probably worried of the repercussions of barbecuing a Fletching.

Eliza's gold-tipped feathers swayed as she whirled back around. "Careful, Fletching. You've lost many feathers recently."

"Are you reminding me or threatening me?"

Her dark eyes narrowed. "We don't threaten."

As she glanced up at Asher and added something in the celestial tongue, probably so I wouldn't understand, the Channel filled with sparkling motes of lavender smoke, and then spiky heels clacked against the quartz as the waifish body of a woman with a river of black hair and eyes the color of summer grass materialized. I'd met this woman only once, at her daughter's wing bone ceremony, but Seraph Claire was quite unforgettable.

"The Ophanim of Guild 24 seem to be lacking at their task of instilling manners in our Fletchings," she said, her feet coming within inches of my blood-speckled heels.

I'd always found Eve's mother intimidating, but tonight, not much intimidated me. "I'm sorry my behavior offends you, but the Ophanim aren't to blame."

She folded her fine-boned arms in front of the gauzy white chiffon dress she wore cinched by a leather corset covered in the same translucent jewels that festooned her ears and neck.

"The sinner your *daughter* suggested I help out has been unjustly ranked. Not only have I come to discover that he's been placed in the wrong Ranking System, but I have also come to discover that his rank is frozen at a hundred because of a misunderstanding on the Ishim's part."

"It was no misunderstanding!" Asher boomed, and I swear the stone surrounding us trembled.

I blinked but then shook my head. "Ask Jarod again, Seraph. Ask his nanny who was there. Or his guard Amir."

"I'm not going to run around collecting biased testimonials." A pulse point throbbed in his corded neck.

I gasped. "Biased testimonials?"

"Both of you, quiet!" Eve's mother snapped. "You are a Seraphim, Asher. Behave like one. And you"—she poked a manicured finger in my direction—"are a Fletching. Remember your place."

I ground my teeth so hard I was probably chipping the

enamel. How I ever considered being able to marry a complete stranger for status was beyond me. Jarod was right. I was a romantic, and there was no way in Abaddon or Elysium I would marry for any other reason than love.

I shifted my attention to Eve's mother. "I'm not trying to get anyone in trouble, Seraph Claire. I'm trying to get *one* person out of trouble, and that person is Jarod Adler."

"For someone not trying to get others in trouble, you're quick to name names," she said. "The first thing out of your mouth when I showed up was that my daughter made you take on this mission."

"You're right. That was low of me. How I got here doesn't matter." Not anymore. Not in the scope of things. "What matters is what I do now that I *am* here."

"The best thing you can do, for your sake and for all of ours, is apologize to my fellow Seraphim for the slanderous way you've handled yourself."

I pressed my lips together, reeling. "I didn't know that speaking the truth required an apology."

"Don't be a smart aleck, Leigh. Apologize to Seraph Asher before he asks the Ishim to remove yet *another* one of your feathers." Her gaze dipped to the platinum feather at my feet.

I straightened as though someone had skewered my spine with a metal rod. Even though I didn't feel like apologizing, I realized it wouldn't help my fight for Jarod's soul, so I swallowed my pride and spit out, "I apologize for raising my voice, Seraph Asher."

But I don't apologize for letting it be heard.

Asher stared at me over the lilac fence of Eliza's wings. I sensed he, too, was seeing a stranger. We weren't the same people who'd ridden through the Channel days ago.

Jarod Adler had changed me. He'd removed the rose-colored glasses through which I saw our world and the people ruling it. Humans weren't perfect, but we weren't either.

"I accept your apology, Fletching," he said.

Fletching? Relegating me to my status added another wall between us.

Seraph Claire turned sideways so that I was left staring at her aquiline profile. "Now that this situation is resolved—"

"Will you at least take my findings under consideration?" I asked.

She twisted her head toward me, her black hair swishing over her platinum-tipped fuchsia feathers.

"He's the leader of the mob in this city," Asher said. "Even if he didn't murder his mother, his soul is far from pure."

"Far from pure shouldn't lock up his score." I gazed at both archangels and then at the three angels in charge of ranking souls. "I'm not looking to cause an uproar in Elysium, but I am looking for justice, and the just thing to do, since his soul can't be removed from the sinner system, would be to free him of his status."

Claire tipped her head to the side. "Does your plea to lower the sinner's score have anything to do with my fellow archangel's impending nuptials?"

As color crept into Asher's neck, I gaped, stunned she'd think I would be so self-serving.

"My husband picked a Triple to win my hand, so it's an honest question that deserves a yes-or-no answer, Fletching."

Heat coursed through my veins as though I were made of angel-fire instead of blood. "My dream has always been to become a Malakim, to interact with souls, harvest them, and see to their safe return into the human world, but for a moment, becoming a Seraphim spouse held more appeal, so, yes, I picked a Triple, because I wanted to complete my wings in time to be considered by Seraph Asher. But this mission reminded me that helping sinners has never been a means to an end. I adore the adventure, the experience, the contact. I love to see the change happen over the course of weeks. Months. Nothing satisfies me more than watching someone hold out a hand they would never have offered before I entered their life." I inhaled slowly, deeply. "So, to answer your question, I have no ulterior motive in asking you to unbind Jarod Adler's soul."

Eve's mother watched me and then she watched the air around my hips on the lookout for a falling feather. When none tumbled, her gaze arced back up. "Your honesty and empathy are commendable, but use those qualities to help other sinners. Jarod Adler's score will not change." She turned toward Asher and tilted her head to the side. "Right, Seraph?"

He leveled his turquoise eyes on me. "Right." That simple word felt like the most eloquent slap.

I backed away. "By damning him, you're damning me."

"What are you talking about, Leigh?" He was back to using my first name?

"I tie my fate to his." I halted my retreat. "I won't sign off until his status is reevaluated."

Claire spread her wings as though to appear fiercer. "Are you blackmailing us?"

"My life matters as much as his, Seraph, and if to the Seven, that's not at all, then so be it." I pivoted before the reddening tips of my ears and the heat creeping into my jaw could reveal the desperation and fear strumming through my veins. For all my selflessness, I was scared.

My chest felt too tight, my invisible wings too heavy, my gaze unfocused. I stopped running at some point and leaned against the wall of a deserted hallway, flattening my palms against the warm stone. I'd taken my immortality as a given, but there were no givens in this world.

I'd been born an angel, but perhaps, I'd die a human.

Just like Jarod.

*a*fter the maelstrom quieted inside my head and chest, I retreated into my bedroom. Celeste was sound asleep, air whistling through her heart-shaped lips.

Would she be proud of me or horrified by what I'd just done? Eve would've been horrified. Instead of annoying me, thinking of her saddened me. To say I was grateful she'd made me sign on to Jarod Adler would be a stretch, but I no longer loathed her for it.

I kicked off my shoes and carried them into the bathroom, sliding the door shut behind me so as not to wake Celeste. After rinsing the blood off them, I stripped and stepped into the shower, lathering my hair, body, and wings. The suds rolled over my impermeable but not invulnerable feathers. To think my entire life had been a race to earn them. What would I do now that I no longer had any finishing line to run toward? Would the Ophanim kick me out of the guild? Would I be forced to return to New York? Would I even be *allowed* to return?

If angels refused me shelter, where would I live? My breath caught. No shelter meant no allowance, no protection. No allowance meant no food. They wouldn't kick me out, would they? It would be too cruel a punishment. Unless they'd use my predicament to strongarm me into signing off from Jarod Adler. Great Elysium, I hoped their thinking didn't align with mine.

Contemplating all the luxury I might need to give up, I turned off the tap, then dried my exhausted body with a towel that felt woven from celestial clouds.

After getting dressed in leggings and a boxy T-shirt, I packed a bag with the bare necessities and placed it on my nightstand. If they came for me in the middle of the night, I would at least be a little ready.

What I still needed was money, more than my remaining handful of twenties. I didn't dare pad back out of the bedroom and wake an Ophanim, because what if they'd been filled in and given instructions to show me out?

I lay down on top of my covers and stared at the door, imagining it opening and shutting more than once, but the only thing that shut were my eyes.

MY MATTRESS DIPPED, and my lids flew open. I scrambled into a sitting position, gathered my knees against my chest, and seized my bag.

Celeste blinked her large eyes at me and touched one of my knees. "Sorry. Didn't mean to scare you awake."

My heart walloped my ribs so hard I panted like I'd run a mile.

"What's wrong?"

Sensing I was in no danger, I relaxed my fingers around the strap of my bag before pulling them back toward me. "Did you just wake up?"

"No. I've been awake for three hours." She cranked her head toward the nightstand. "I brought you some coffee."

My eyes opened wider. "You've been out of the room?"

"Um. Yeah. I was starving. On my way back, I stopped by the Ranking Room. I was hoping, well hoping and fearing—honestly, I don't know how I'm going to survive without you—that your sinner's score had changed."

I sat up a little straighter. "And?"

Her lips twisted. "It didn't."

Not surprising. What was surprising, though, was that the guild wasn't abuzz with my misconduct. Were the archangels and

Ishim keeping it under wraps since it stemmed from their mistake?

"What happened last night, Leigh?"

I sighed, then covered her hand with my own. "So much, Celeste. So much happened last night."

As I recounted the awful night, her expression puckered and scrunched.

"Are you disappointed in me?" I asked when she still hadn't spoken a word and I'd finished speaking all of mine.

Her lashes hit her brow bone. "Disappointed? Are you kidding?"

"I challenged our system and criticized an archangel." I didn't regret what I'd done but regretted the hostility that had limned the discussion.

Celeste's gaze slickened. "You're asking the girl who grew up challenging the system if she thinks you did something wrong? Leigh, I'm—I'm so proud of you."

I squeezed her hand, which had turned rigid against my knee. "Then why do you look like you're about to burst into tears?"

"Because . . ." She tugged her lip into her mouth. "Because your big, stupid heart might just cost you your immortality." She sniffed, and tears coursed over her freckles. As she stole her hand from under mine, she said, "And I don't want to lose you." She scrubbed her face, but instead of whisking away the wetness, she spread it. "And if they kick you out, then I'll leave, too."

I pushed some hair off her shiny cheeks. "No, you won't. You're going to complete your wings. Especially if I can't. Someone has to go up there and call them out on their erroneous management."

Surprisingly, my attack on the celestial system didn't cost me a feather. Maybe, the Ishim were taking pity on me, or maybe, they'd moved my soul to the department of unsalvageable items.

I kneeled and hugged Celeste, resting my chin on the top of her head. "Thank you."

"For what?"

"For not calling me crazy."

She let out a pulse of air. "You *are* crazy. But so am I. Welcome to the dark side, Leigh. I have to warn you it can get sort of lonely."

I smiled and smoothed out her soft hair. "Not anymore. We're together now, so not anymore."

She pressed harder into me the same way I imagined Jarod had curled into Muriel. We didn't need many people in our lives; we needed one, and I had my one. A scrawny fifteen-year-old with a heart of steel.

Was his charm a disguise he donned to enhance his appeal?

"Are you interested in him, Ophan?"

"Me?" She let out a chirp of laughter that made a sparrow pause mid-note. "Don't get me wrong. If I were attracted to men, possibly. Not only is the Seraph not my type, but also, he lives in Elysium, and I love it here." She smiled at me. "Once you ascend, you'll see that the human world is more . . . full. Diverse. Fun." She shifted her eyes toward the octagon of brilliant blue sky over the Atrium and dropped her voice, "Everyone's so solemn up there."

"Ophan Pauline!"

A matronly angel with topaz feathers and graying hair appeared in the doorway of the office.

Pauline's blue eyes sprang wide. "Uh-oh," she said on an exhale, but soon, her easy smile returned. "I'll be right with you, Eleanor. Just filling a Fletching's pocket."

"And mind," the older angel grumbled.

"Bye now, Leigh," Pauline singsonged. "Have a beautiful day!"

I wasn't sure how beautiful it would be. After all, I was about to visit someone who despised me more than the Seven. The irony of my situation wasn't lost on me.

Hooking my bag to my shoulder, I set off by foot toward *La Cour des Démons*, indebted to Celeste for forcing me into espadrilles with wedge heels instead of the strappy sandals with toothpick heels I'd wanted to wear. As I wandered through the winding streets, my long black skirt swished around my ankles. I looked like I was going to a funeral—my own. At least, my orange hair added some color to my otherwise all-black outfit. Never imagined I would've found something pleasant to say about my hair. Then again, I never imagined I would argue with an archangel about the celestial system.

I walked through a bustling, open-air marketplace lined with buckets of rainbow-hued flowers and crates of juicy produce. I exchanged a ten-euro bill for two baskets of plump raspberries. After placing one delicately inside my roomy handbag, I ate the contents of the other on the way to Jarod's home, and it restored some sweetness to my presently bleak life.

When I arrived in front of the blood-red doors, I hesitated to slip the bill under them and retrace my steps, but the niggling feeling in my shoulder blades spurred me to ring. As I waited, the memory of smoldering Jarod walloped me upside the head. *Ugh.* I'd conveniently forgotten about it.

The lock clicked, and I pressed my palm against the lacquered wood. The cast-iron lamp flared to life, vanquishing the darkness gathered beneath the covered porch. How I wished it could vanquish the darkness crowding my mind, too.

I licked my teeth. When I felt a little seed in the seam of my front ones, I licked them again, the superficial undertaking momentarily sloughing off some of my stress. To think I'd grinned at a gaggle of kids chasing each other around a gated playground. Most of them hadn't paid attention to me, but a little girl with crooked pigtails had stared steadily at me.

It had felt as though her soul were judging mine, which was impossible, because when souls were re-implanted into wombs, the memories of their past lives and of their time in Elysium or Abaddon were erased.

As I crossed the courtyard, a new thought barreled into the others. What if the fault in the celestial scales extended to the rest of our *system*? My fist, which I'd raised to knock, froze in midair. What if the claims some humans made about remembering past lives weren't fabricated? What if a few memories slipped through the cracks?

Even though my knuckles hadn't made contact with the door, Amir drew it open.

"Muriel told me you'd be stopping by." His nose seemed even more crooked in broad daylight.

Muriel? Right . . . The baking lesson. Hadn't I told her I wouldn't be able to take her up on it? Some parts of the night had stayed crisp, and others had started to blur. Unfortunately, it was the parts I wished to forget that I couldn't.

"She's in the pantry," Amir said when I still hadn't moved or spoken. "Told me to send you right through when you arrived."

"Is Jarod—is he here?"

Amir leveled his dark eyes on my bag. "Monsieur Adler has asked that no one disturb him until this evening." I started to slide my bag down my arm to hand it over when he said, "You may keep your bag."

Huh. I bent my arm, and the bag settled in the crook of my elbow. "Well then, I guess I'll go find Muriel."

I walked past him, then crossed the dining room, keeping my eyes on the tapestry depicting a violent hunt complete with snarling hounds and deer with mangled necks and bloodied fur. It beat looking at the mural of innocent, blushing cherubs.

I gritted my teeth, trying to squelch my growing rancor. I didn't want to become an embittered person like Jarod. That would just make me unhappy. Besides, not all angels were bad. Just some. Just like humans.

The checkered marble foyer was empty except for the bodyguard standing vigil next to the dining room.

I glanced up the stairs, wondering if Jarod was in his bedroom or in his study. "Muriel's expecting me," I ended up saying even though the guard hadn't asked.

He gave me a perfunctory nod, his gaze barely scraping over me as though he'd been warned not to make eye contact after what had happened to the waiter. Why had Jarod even cared about who'd looked at me? He'd already known what I was back then.

He'd already hated me.

When the man made no move to block my path, I walked toward the pantry and pulled the concealed door open. My mouth watered at the smell of caramelizing onions and woodsy thyme. Jarod was lucky to have someone in his life who could create such delicious aromas.

I set my bag down on the pantry table, removed the paper-wrapped offering stained with juice from the bruised fruit, and carried them through another small passageway that gave onto a kitchen that couldn't be called anything but grandiose.

The floor was covered in weathered mosaics depicting a fleur-de-lis—the symbol of French monarchy. Did the house date back to that time in history, or had Isaac Adler purchased the tiny tiles and installed them in his kitchen? A strip of glass along the top of the far wall let in a bar of sunlight that reflected on the garland of copper pans dangling over an island which resembled an outsized butcher's block.

"*Ma chérie*, you arrived just in time." Muriel appeared from another little passageway.

I couldn't help but smile at her endearment. I extended the little basket. "I bought you some raspberries."

"*T'es un ange.*"

My muscles seized up. As she circled the island and eased the packet I was crinkling out of my hands, I gaped at her. Had she meant *you're an angel* literally or figuratively?

She selected a plump berry and popped it into her mouth, which she'd reddened with lipstick. "*Hmm . . . une vraie merveille.*" *Hmm . . . delicious.* She smiled, and it settled my nerves. If she knew what I was, she wouldn't smile at me. "*Merci.*"

I shrugged. "It's nothing, Muriel."

"No one has ever bought me raspberries, so it is something to me."

My wary heart slowed, and I returned her smile.

"Are you ready to learn how to make *sablés*?"

It hit me that there was nowhere else I'd rather have been than in this serene kitchen in the company of this patient and warm woman. After all, I no longer had a sinner to reform; I no longer had missions to undertake or wings to complete.

I had absolutely *nothing* to do.

Instead of feeling bereft, I felt unfettered.

I was removing the first batch of cookies from the oven when the kitchen's doorway filled with the shape of a body. I almost dropped the tray. By some miracle, I managed to slide it onto the butcher block island, my hands shaking inside the oven mitts.

"Finally taking me up on cooking classes, Jarod?" Muriel said, slicing a roll of chilled, salted chocolate dough into perfect disks.

Gaze affixed to me, he said, "Not a chance of that ever happening, Mimi." A smirk played on his lips, and I knew exactly what he was thinking . . . that I was a piece of gum he'd stepped on, sticking tiresomely to his person.

"Thank God I found myself a good disciple then," Muriel said, sliding me a wink.

"Still can't get Amir in here?"

"The problem with that man isn't getting him in here; it's getting him out of here. He inhales all of my cooking."

"He's part giant," Jarod said, sticking his hands into the pockets of his suit trousers, which he wore with a tucked white button-down opened at the collar, but no jacket.

Muriel laughed. "He is, isn't he?"

Their good-natured banter felt like being chained under Damocles's sword, conscious it was about to skewer me yet unable to move out of the way.

"What brings you to my kitchen, Leigh?" He caressed the syllable of my name instead of deforming it, surely trying to lure me into a false sense of security or to maintain a pleasant appearance in front of Muriel.

"Baking cookies," I said, nerves brimming.

His smirk turned into a smile full of perfect teeth that seemed almost phosphorescent set against his dark afternoon shadow. "You don't say. And who are you baking cookies for?"

"Not for you," I said before realizing how rude that sounded, so I amended my words with, "Because you don't like desserts."

His eyes sparked.

"Oh, *flûte*. I forgot to do something." Muriel wiped her hands on a striped kitchen towel. "I'll be right back." She walked down the passageway she'd appeared from earlier, then turned and vanished up what I imagined were stairs, since I could hear her thick heels clacking against cement.

I willed her to come back, but she didn't. When I turned back, Jarod was circling the island. I tried to reassure myself that since his hands were still in his pockets, he wasn't planning on strangling me. When he bent at the waist, I backed up.

He inhaled the steam rising from the deflating cookies. "I told you I was a lost cause. Yet you're back."

"I just came to return your money."

His gaze slid to the cookies. "And you stumbled into an apron on your way to me?"

My lips parted, unsure how to interpret his question. It sounded like he was teasing me . . .

He was so close I could no longer smell the sweet aroma lifting from the tray. All I could smell was him. His stare turned so intense I checked my arms poking from the oven mitts to make sure I hadn't lit up like a string of fairy lights. My skin was blotchy and smeared with flour, but thankfully not shimmering.

When I looked up, my chin bumped into Jarod's fingers. I was so startled by his touch that I forgot to breathe.

"You had some flour on your chin," he said, lowering his hand, rubbing his thumb against his index finger to get rid of the powder, which had transferred from my skin to his.

I touched my chin, which felt as hot as the baking tray, unsure what to make of his kindly gesture until I recalled his total and utter disgust.

"Let me—I'll just go grab . . ." I backed away from him, leaving my sentence aborted. I hurried to the pantry, dug out the yellow bill, then returned to Jarod, and brandished the money. "Here."

He recoiled as though I were offering him a live snake. "I told you I didn't want it back."

"And I told you I couldn't keep it."

His mouth thinned. When he didn't take the money, I laid it on the island beside the tray. There. It was done. I wouldn't lose another feather, which was ironic considering I stood to lose my entire wings.

I glanced around me, then down at the cookies, realizing all that was left for me to do now was leave. "How's your back?"

"My back?"

"You were bleeding last night."

"*Right.* My back's fine. Are you done baking?"

My throat constricted. Swallowing, I nodded and slid the oven mitts off. I laid them beside the blackened tray and glanced toward the passageway that had swallowed Muriel.

"Can you tell her I said"—I cleared my throat, fixing my gaze to his Adam's apple—"thank you?"

"Your voice seems to be working fine."

I blinked up at him.

"You should tell her yourself."

"Oh. Um. Okay."

I started to turn when he asked, "How well do you play chess?"

"Chess?"

"You know . . . the board game where you have to defeat the king?"

"I know what chess is, Jarod, but I thought you wanted me gone."

He wedged his hands back into his trouser pockets. "I do. Eventually."

Why did he want to play chess with me? Surely, his motives were twisted. And then it hit me. "It's not going to cost me any feathers."

"What?"

"If you're trying to mutilate my *appendages*—"

He sputtered, and then he laughed, and it wasn't dark and slimy but melodic and deep. I had to remind myself that he was laughing *at* me.

"Ruining my wings isn't a game," I said, pinching my shoulders together as though to safeguard my invisible wings from Jarod, even though I'd ruined them far more than he ever could.

And for *him* of all people.

He sobered up immediately, and then one of his eyes twitched. "I . . . I . . ." He rubbed the back of his neck. "I . . ." Jarod at a loss for words? *That was a first.* "I didn't suggest playing as a way to hurt you. But if you don't want to—if you'd rather leave . . ."

The look he wore was so at odds with his usual, intractable confidence that my protective stance slackened. "I thought you couldn't stand the sight of me."

His hand was still on his neck, but he was no longer scouring his skin. "Last night, I felt cornered. I don't like to feel cornered."

"I didn't mean to corner you, Jarod. Or to scare you."

His lips quirked into a lopsided smile. "*Scare* me? Don't give yourself too much credit."

"Why did you leave, then?" I twisted my long hair and let it unravel over my shoulder, its brassy shine a close match to the copper jam basin, which hung over the kitchen island.

"Because I needed to think, and for some reason"—he reached over and slid the lock I'd been toying with between his fingers —"I can't do that around you."

What was it with him and my hair? "Is it my hair color that distracts you?"

"*Hmm.* I can't decide if it's orange or pink."

"It's sort of both," I said, watching the heavy fringe of lashes shadowing his eyes.

"Rose gold." As he ran the strand through his fingers, his knuckles grazed the skin of my collarbone and then the side of my breast.

I stepped back, and my hair fanned out from his fingers and settled over my heaving chest. "Why do you enjoy making me uncomfortable?"

"That wasn't my intent."

I pushed my hair over my shoulder and crossed my arms. "What *was* your intent?"

"I'm not quite sure anymore." His gaze stroked up my throat. "Can I ask you something?"

"You can ask. I might not answer."

His lips quirked at my response. "Why did your skin emit light last night?"

I moistened my dry lips. Out of all the questions, he had to ask that one.

One of his eyebrows lifted. "So?"

"I'm choosing not to answer." I squeezed my fingers around my biceps and took another step back, as though if I stepped far enough away, the question would sink into the void between us and vanish.

He smirked. "Is it very terrible?"

"No, it's not terrible."

"Then, why can't you tell me?"

"Because I'm not allowed to disclose information about us to humans," I whispered.

He tilted his head to the side, and a curl of dark hair fell into his probing eyes. "Except I'm not entirely . . . *human*."

"Please drop it."

"Your silence, coupled with the high color in your cheeks, speaks volumes." He stalked toward me, and I steeled my spine to avoid bolting. "I think I have it all figured out."

"It happens when we're tired." The lie rushed out to cover the truth.

I gritted my teeth, anticipating the cost of saving face. Even though I didn't gasp when the Ishim robbed me of another feather, sweat beaded on my brow. Jarod's smirk turned into a frown when he caught the glint of the feather drifting toward the mosaic. The loss should've saddened me, but I was way too busy seething to care.

"What . . . no gloating?" I snapped.

He stared at the fragment of my being rocking beside my espadrilles. "I'm sorry, Feather."

I doubted he was. When the downy barbs began to blur, I lifted my gaze toward the window, hoping the bar of sunlight would burn away the annoyance pooling behind my lids.

"Are you going to pick it up?" His voice was soft, probably a distortion caused by the rushing in my ears.

"No." I was afraid of reliving a significant episode in view of my precarious state.

"Does it hurt when it detaches itself?"

Sensing I'd gotten myself under enough control, I shifted my eyes back toward him. "Yes."

He raked his fingers through his hair, pushing his wayward locks back.

"Before meeting you," I said, my voice feeling as raw as my wing, "I'd never lost one."

He winced, as though it was *his* body that had endured the assault. "I told you that you should leave, Feather."

Leaving wouldn't change anything, not now that our lives and fates were plaited together. Still, I said, "I should."

Jarod backed up, giving me space to maneuver around him. When I glanced toward the doorway, he said, "But I'd rather you didn't."

My heart missed a beat.

"Playing chess against myself is quite dull." He smiled, but it didn't reach his eyes.

I let out a soft snort.

"I might even let you win," he said. "To make up for being such a . . . what was it your friend called me?"

"Unicorn noodle."

"Yes. That." The smile on his lips reached a little higher.

I sighed. "Fine. But I'm just accepting in order to teach you some modesty."

"Modesty, huh?" Jarod's eyes sparked with amusement.

"You probably don't even know what the word means."

His lips parted around a chuckle that turned into something deeper, louder, more magnificent, that vibrated against the copper pans and the mosaic tiles and made my fallen feather seesaw.

Like the first time we'd met at his masked party, he crooked his finger under my chin and cranked my head up. "Stop looking at it."

He was no longer laughing, and I realized I missed the sound more than I missed my feather. "Make it disappear, then."

He held my gaze. "Are you sure?"

I slid my chin off its perch and nodded. I was hoping that seeing what I'd done to earn the wings he'd been so intent on destroying would give him pause.

When he crouched and delicately wrapped his fingers around my feather, I braced myself for disgust or perverse glee. He neither wrinkled his nose nor smirked.

After a stretch of silence that felt as interminable as Ophan Greer's etiquette classes, he opened his eyes and tipped his head toward me. I gripped my elbows harder, the pointy bones digging into my palms.

Shadows steeped his eyes as he stood. "I wish you'd never come to Paris."

Pain streaked through my chest.

"You are too sweet for my world, Feather." He rolled the fingers which had clutched my feather into a hard fist. "For your own world, too."

"I found what I was looking for!" Muriel's shrill voice made me leap backward, even though it sounded like it was coming from far away, as if to warn us she was heading back down.

My cheeks flushed as I realized that was probably her intent. Oh, *Great Elysium* . . .

Jarod must've come to the same conclusion, because the gloom barreled right off his face, replaced by a look of pure hilarity.

"At least, she didn't ask if we were decent," he murmured, which vivified my blush, which, in turn, increased Jarod's smile. "Don't look so horrified."

I side-eyed him. "Don't look so amused."

He grinned as he wandered toward the pantry. "If you decide to stick around a while longer, I'll be in my study setting up the chessboard."

"*R*eady to give up yet?" I asked smugly, admiring the army of smooth ivory pieces lined up on my side of the board.

I'd taken Jarod up on his offer to play chess, in part because I was a masochist and in part because Muriel had insisted I stay until all the cookies baked, and apparently, one batch had to be refrigerated for two hours before they cooked.

"Do I strike you as someone who gives up?" Jarod had raked his fingers through his hair so many times while playing that his wavy locks were distractingly mussed.

"Being bested twice wasn't enough?" I goaded him.

"Careful. Smugness surely costs feathers."

Even though I hadn't felt any pain, I glanced over my shoulder. "Apparently not."

"You know what?" He pushed away from the game table.

I stroked the smooth crown of his queen, which I'd just lifted from the board. "You forfeit?"

As he stood, he shot me a bold smile that made my finger slip right off the piece. "Never. However, we're taking a break from playing."

"In other words, you forfeit."

His eyes flashed behind his chaotic locks. "In other words, I'm taking you to dinner." He extended his hand.

"Dinner?" I wrenched my shoulders back and shot my gaze toward the windows that glowed sapphire. Where had the afternoon gone?

"You know, that part of the day when we eat and drink?" he said, lowering his hand back to his side.

I watched his fingers settle against his pant leg, staggered he'd even extended them. Then again, since I'd walked into the study, Jarod had been surprisingly . . . *nice* to me, as though he were afraid I might shatter or spook if he spoke too roughly.

"Never heard of it," I said, pressing myself up. "But I'm intrigued. Will you tell me more?"

The tension in his body eased. "Some people deem it the best part of their entire day."

"You don't say?" I said, keeping up the innocent pretense.

It struck me I hadn't lost any feathers for lying. The same thought must've gone through Jarod's mind because he gazed at the floor.

"Apparently, the Ishim have a sense of humor," I said. "Who would've thought?"

"The Ishim?"

My mouth went dry before I remembered that Jarod, for all his hatred of our kind, shared our blood, so I wasn't breaking any rules by telling him about angels. "Your cousin didn't tell you about Ishim?"

"My *cousin* has always been quite . . . disobliging."

I didn't want to think about Asher, because thinking about the archangel reminded me of my glum fate. "That's the least of his faults."

Jarod rested his hand on the door handle but didn't flex his fingers around it. "Least of his faults? Here I thought soul mates were faultless."

"Probably in the eyes of *their* soul mates." I stared at the chest hair spilling out of Jarod's open collar. The man was part bear, the complete antithesis of slick, golden-skinned Asher. Even though it was ridiculous, I suddenly appreciated the sinner more for it.

"Do you like *foie gras*?"

My gaze scaled up the graceful column of his throat before perching on his midnight-bright eyes. "I don't know. I've never tried it."

"Let's go find out, then." He tipped his head toward the door he must've opened while I'd compared his torso to Asher's.

"Who won?" Muriel asked, coming down the wide sweeping stairs, an empty bottle of spirits in one hand. I assumed she'd refreshed the tray of *digestifs* in Jarod's room, because she didn't strike me as someone who'd down a bottle of alcohol, then parade it around.

She'd changed into a black kimono-like outfit, that accentuated her trim waist, and applied her usual thick coat of kohl and vermillion lipstick.

Jarod unrolled the sleeves of his shirt. "Would I ever allow a woman to lose? You taught me better than that, Mimi."

She beamed, whereas I pivoted to gawk at him, a few of his most questionable moves cropping into my mind.

"You let me win?" For some reason, a torrent of disappointment washed through me and blistered my tone. I didn't even care about winning, so my reaction was all kinds of absurd.

Jarod's fingers slid off the button which he was trying to stab through his shirt's cuff. "I was just trying to save face in front of Mimi and Luc."

I assumed Luc was the guard standing sentry beside the dining room.

"Can't have my household finding out about my subpar chess skills," he continued. "They'll lose all respect for me."

I rolled my eyes. "Now, you're just being dramatic."

An easy smile tipped his mouth, and it substituted the weird upheaval in my chest for another that had nothing to do with feeling duped.

"Dinner's ready when you are," Muriel said, stealing my attention off Jarod.

"Merci, Mimi, but we're going to dine out tonight."

Remembering the roasted lamb shank she'd basted while I'd shaped crumbly dough, I said, "But Muriel prepared an entire meal."

"Which Amir will only be too happy to eat," she said.

I searched her face for disappointment but found none. She seemed genuinely happy Jarod and I were going out, which made all sorts of questions pop into my mind.

"Can you call Sybille and tell her we're on our way?" Jarod

asked Muriel before addressing me, "Did you have a coat, Feather?"

I shook my head. Before he could suggest I borrow one from his weird cloakroom, afraid I'd end up with a scrap of leather encrusted with silver spikes and the perfume of another woman, I said, "But I don't need one."

"It's warm tonight," Muriel said. "You two should be fine."

Jarod eyed the courtyard, seemingly unconvinced, but he didn't put up a fight. What he did do was climb up to his bedroom while Muriel phoned Sybille.

I smoothed out my long black skirt, glad I'd picked it instead of the navy eyelet dress Celeste had suggested. Although both outfits were understated, the eyelet dress looked better suited for a picnic.

When Jarod trundled back down, hair slicked back with gel and suit jacket on, my lungs tightened. How I hadn't guessed his heritage was beyond me. The man was far too handsome to be a mere mortal. He even smelled too good for a human.

He adjusted his pocket square—orange tonight. "Ready?"

Feeling exceedingly unsophisticated, I crimped the fabric of my skirt. Perhaps, I should've borrowed a dress from the foyer closet. The emerald one came to mind, but I'd felt like a sausage encased in satin. Probably looked like one, too.

"Feather?"

This is dinner, Leigh. Not a date. I shoved my insecurities away. "I just need to get my bag."

"What for?" Jarod asked.

I arched an eyebrow. "My wallet. And so I can get home tonight."

Jarod stood by the door his guard had opened. "Get it after dinner."

"My wallet won't serve much of a purpose *after* dinner."

"Your wallet won't serve much of a purpose *during* dinner either. Unless you want to offend me."

"But—"

"I'll keep an eye on your bag," Muriel said. "Don't worry."

I wasn't worried about it getting stolen. "You'll still be up when we get back?"

204 | OLIVIA WILDENSTEIN

"You know me. I'm not much of a sleeper." She tipped her head toward Jarod. "Better hurry before they close the kitchen."

Close the kitchen? How late was it? Without a phone or a watch, I realized I had no clue.

Relenting, I followed Jarod out of the house.

As the Demon Court's porte-cochère clanged shut behind us, Jarod said, "Don't know what spell you put on Muriel, but she usually doesn't like anyone. Especially women."

I eyed Luc, who walked behind us, along with a second suit-clad bodyguard.

Even though they kept their distance, I lowered my voice to say, "You do know we don't have any magic, right? Well, at least, not when we're Fletchings. It's only when our wings are complete that we get our dust and fire."

"I was teasing you about the spell part."

I'd imagined as much.

"So, fire, huh? What can you do with it?"

"Pretty much everything you can do with human fire." I studied the seams in the pavement, thinking, *That's what they used to burn your mother's wings off.*

"And dust?"

"We can cloak things with it. Make them invisible."

He nodded. "How practical."

A heaviness settled in the pit of my stomach as I realized I might never receive these gifts. Before my negativity could tinge my mood, I changed the subject. "I've been meaning to ask, does Tristan know about us?"

"Yes and no. I told him about your kind when we were younger, when your peers began showing up to reform me, but he thought I was employing the term loosely. Besides, like most humans, he's wired to only believe what he can see and he can't see you. He just considers the lot of you zealots."

"I heard he whipped someone who showed up to help you. Is it true?"

My curiosity caused shadows to gather in Jarod's eyes. "If he did, it wasn't on my orders."

A weight lifted off my chest.

We crossed the road and cut across the leafy, manicured square, little clouds of dirt puffing around our feet.

"So, where is it you're taking me?"

Giving the row of geometrically clipped linden trees his undivided attention, he said, "A restaurant called L'Ambroisie. It was my uncle's *cantine*. He ate there every lunch, even on Sundays and Mondays when it was closed to the public."

"I like the name."

"Knowing you, you'll like more than the name."

"*Knowing me*?"

"Knowing your appreciation for food." He side-eyed me. "And just so we're clear, last night at Layla's, I wasn't implying you had a problem with it."

"I know."

"You do?"

"I figured you learned about Delia from one of the feathers I lost in your house."

I had a passing thought for the girl, hoping she hadn't relapsed into her bulimia. I hadn't visited her in a few months because she'd moved to Florida, and we weren't supposed to travel for any other reason than our current missions.

I should've carved out some time to go see her like I'd promised. I supposed I could head there next.

Next . . .

I felt like I was standing on either side of a fault line and the ground was shifting. Until Asher gave his verdict, I would straddle both worlds, uncertain as to where I would land—in Elysium, on Earth, or in the chasm between.

"Where's Tristan?" I asked, to stopper my drab thoughts.

"Either in someone's bed, or on a flight back from Marseille."

I twisted a lock of hair around my finger, imagining Tristan's trip had something to do with Jarod's line of work.

"Why are you still here, Feather?"

His question made me come to a standstill. "I thought you wanted me to come to the restaurant."

"I'm not talking about the restaurant."

Tiny rocks had slid inside my open shoes, and I wriggled my toes to push them out. "I don't give up on people, Jarod."

He'd stopped walking too. "Feather, I'm a lost cause. When will you believe it?" Dust veiled the shine of his dress shoes. "You have to let my case go." He sighed, and it smoothed the hard

206 | OLIVIA WILDENSTEIN

contours of his face. Even his bladed cheekbones seemed softer. "Let *me* go."

I glowered a little. I wasn't mad at him. I was mad *for* him. "What part of not giving up don't you understand?"

His pupils swelled and shrank. "You're just going to get hurt."

"What do you care if I get hurt?"

He held my gaze for a blisteringly long minute. "I need to get my revenge in chess and won't take any pleasure in winning, or playing for that matter, if you're a whimpering mess."

My lips bent, then straightened, then bent again. "A whimpering mess," I muttered, shaking my head. "I don't whimper."

"You cry a lot."

"I'm sensitive."

Had he stepped closer? Perhaps, it was an impression brought on by his arresting presence. Like a magnetic force, Jarod Adler absorbed everything around him, from buildings to trees to the very air. He wasn't just a sinner or a hybrid, he was a vortex, who'd sucked me straight into his world.

"Is the restaurant close?" My voice was disturbingly breathy.

He seemed to have leaned forward a little, because the heat of his body lapped against mine, and since he wasn't made of fire, his area of radiation wasn't disproportionate like my brethren's.

"It's across the street," he finally said, pivoting.

My nose and forehead felt suddenly cold, which was weird. Not to mention perturbing. Maybe, Jarod was right. Maybe, I had to let him go—not his case, but his company—because staying might lead Asher to believe I was fighting to save Jarod's soul for the wrong reasons.

Jarod placed his hand on the small of my back and spurred me back into movement, first across the pedestrian walkway and then down the sidewalk. I glanced up into his face that was focused on the cars slowing to a stop at the edge of the thick white zebra stripes.

I knew he didn't hate me, but that didn't mean he liked me. Perhaps, he just felt indebted that I'd invested so much time and lost so many feathers. That was probably all it was.

He looked down at me once we reached the opposite side of the road. "What thoughts are slinking through that mind of yours?"

"I was wondering why you were being so nice to me."

"How else am I going to get you into my bed?"

My lips parted.

He tossed me a lopsided smile. "I'm just kidding, Feather."

I smacked his chest, but regretted it when I remembered Luc and the other guard were watching us. Hopefully, they wouldn't pull out their guns and aim them at me for assaulting their boss. When neither reached for a weapon, I relaxed.

Jarod was still rubbing the skin I'd hit. "Angels are such violent beings."

I rolled my eyes.

"Truthfully, though?" His expression cooled. "I tried being mean to you, and you stayed." The tips of his fingers slinked to the indent of my waist, gripping instead of just guiding. "I'm hoping kindness might scare you away."

"*He* came by to see me this morning," Jarod said, swirling the diminutive glass of amber wine a man in dark tails had just poured him from a bottle labeled *Château d'Yquem.*

Jarod dipped his lips inside, then nodded his approval.

The sommelier filled my glass before topping off Jarod's and leaving with the bottle nestled against his chest as though it were a newborn infant.

"Who did?" I picked up my glass and sniffed the liquid curiously. Delicious notes of spun sugar and candied apricots eddied off the golden surface. I took a small sip and all but purred when the nectar hit my tongue.

Maybe, I did purr, because an even heftier smugness draped over Jarod's already complacent self. "Good?"

"Ambrosial." I took another sip, then licked my lips.

Jarod's gaze lingered on my mouth before moving to the golden-framed fabric panel depicting a head of cabbage and various other pastel vegetables behind me.

I set my glass back down beside a plate so ornate it belonged on a wall instead of on a dinner table. "You were saying someone came by to see you."

"Right." He cleared his throat and returned his attention to me. "My dear cousin stopped by."

My eyebrows jolted. So that was why Asher had returned to Paris . . .

I sat up straighter. "What did he want?"

"He wanted to know what lies I'd been feeding you."

My pulse detonated, speeding my blood flow to the point where my limbs felt vaporous. "And what did you tell him?"

"The same thing I told him when he arrived on the scene seventeen years ago." Jarod reclined in his chair, nursing the wineglass that looked like it belonged to a doll's tea set in his hands. "That she's dead because of me."

My spine locked up. "But that's a lie. Muriel told me what happened."

"You never considered Muriel fabricated a story to protect me?"

Had Muriel fibbed to cast Jarod in a better light? Had I just raised Heaven and Hell over a lie?

I caught the flutter of a nerve beside his temple. Even though he had no wings to shed feathers from, the mixture of pain and anger lacquering his irises told me Muriel's account was truthful. Not only that, but if she had lied, she wouldn't have placed him on the scene of the crime. She would've cast him as far away from it as humanly possible and would certainly not have mentioned he'd touched the murder weapon.

"A woman who cares so deeply about someone else would've invented a much better lie. One where the little boy she loved wasn't in the house and wasn't clutching the blood-soaked letter opener."

He pressed his lips together.

"And before you try to convince me otherwise," I said, my voice barely over a whisper even though his bodyguards had stayed in the street and there was only one other table occupied at this late hour, "sliding a blade *out* of someone's heart isn't what put the hole there in the first place."

"The best lies contain some truths."

"I'm certain you're well-versed in lying, Jarod Adler, but I'm also certain your eight-year-old self did not murder anyone."

A tendon flexed in his neck. "I wanted her dead. I wished it so often. I even told her."

"Your loathing wasn't what killed her."

A waiter arrived with a platter, which he placed on a little stand. He removed my pretty plate and replaced it with another equally sumptuous one at the center of which stood a work of organic art—a toasted brioche cleaved in half and topped with a thick slice of pink *foie gras,* upon which had been pinwheeled a fig and spice paste. The delightful sight and smell buffeted some of my anger and indignation.

Once the waiter left, having deposited a delicate poached egg with chanterelles in front of Jarod, I said, "You have to tell Asher the truth."

"I have." His lips barely stirred around his words.

"You told him you didn't plant that letter opener in her chest?"

Jarod smacked the tabletop, and it made the cutlery jump and the wine shiver. "Doesn't fucking matter who planted it in her fucking heart."

"It does matter," I hissed, sensing the eyes of the sommelier and the couple seated by the window. "You're a *Triple,* Jarod. A Triple doesn't get a chance at another life. If your number doesn't go down, this one'll be it for you. When you die, it's game over."

Every line on his face tensed, which led me to deduce he'd never been told any of this. But then he leaned further forward and spat out, "One's plenty. I don't need a second life."

"Needing is beside the point. Your soul shouldn't be annihilated because of some technical error."

"Will you let it go?"

"It's not fair, Jarod."

"Life isn't fair," he growled. "When will you get that through that coddled brain of yours?"

A strong desire to bolt wound up my muscles, but I stayed seated, because me leaving was what Jarod wanted, what he expected. My fingers curled around the arms of the chair. I wasn't strong yet felt like I could tear the wood clean off. Maybe, I should. At least then, I'd have something to throw at the pigheaded sinner.

"Get out!" I thought he was snarling at me, but he was turned toward the sommelier and the couple.

"Who do you think—" the man started.

"Sybille!" Jarod shouted, and the perfectly coiffed matron who'd greeted and seated us clip-clopped inside the room.

"Please escort monsieur and madame out. And put their meal on my tab."

"Of course, Monsieur Adler." She squared her shoulders, then calmly explained how terribly sorry she was to abort their meal in such an abrupt matter.

Chair legs scraped the parquet, and then muttering how he'd never been thrown out of a restaurant before, the man yanked on his date's hand and pulled her up and out before she managed to hook her quilted bag's chain strap onto her shoulder.

Even though I felt bad about their dismissal, I was also grateful to no longer have an audience.

I turned my glare back down to my plate, the pinkish liver, yellow bread, and muddy paste smearing together.

"Leigh?"

"What?" The word snapped out of me like Cupid's arrow— not that Cupid existed. Angels only dealt in souls, not in hearts.

"Let me worry about my soul, okay? Let it be my burden, not yours."

I lifted my wet eyes to him. Great Elysium, how this man could infuriate me! "It's too late for that."

His face had been scrubbed clean of anger. In its stead was confusion. "What do you mean, it's too late?"

I closed my eyes and palmed my cheeks. When I opened them again, he was right there, his chair tucked in next to mine.

He captured one of my wrists and towed it off my face. "What do you mean it's too late?" he asked again.

"Do you know how celestial missions work?"

He twisted his lips. "You earn feathers for helping people."

I nodded. "But we only earn them for the people we sign up to help on the Ranking System. Sinners are ranked by degrees of sinning, the worst rank being one hundred." I locked my eyes on his, and slowly, like a ripple smoothing, he came back into focus. "A Triple."

"What I am," he said slowly.

"Exactly. If I'd managed to get your rank down, I would've earned your number in feathers, and since I was only missing eighty-one before taking you on, I would've ascended. But your score is locked, because the Ishim—the rankers—are certain you killed a Nephilim—a fallen angel—and even though, in my world, Nephilim are detested, especially those who choose to give up their wings . . . like your mother." I paused, allowing him a moment to digest all I was sharing. "Spilling angel-blood is the gravest and most unforgivable sin."

A flurry of emotions took flight over Jarod's face. "Whether I killed her or not, Feather, my soul is far from shiny."

"I can work with far from shiny."

He lowered his eyes to the starched white tablecloth. "It'll be a waste of your time."

I cupped his prickly jaw to bring his gaze back up to mine. "No deserving soul is a waste of my time."

He laid his hand over mine, and the heat of his palm penetrated into my knuckles and warmed my chilled skin.

"Don't tell me to let you go, Jarod. Because I can't. I won't."

He glided my hand off his jaw but didn't release it. "You said it was too late. What did you mean?"

"I can only earn feathers for the mission I'm signed on to. If I don't sign off from you, I don't complete my wings. If I don't complete my wings, I can't ascend." I left out the part about them falling off my back in fourteen months' time. I'd laid enough on his plate for one night.

His grip became bruisingly tight on my fingers before slackening and vanishing altogether. He moved his hand to his armrest. "Why?" His voice simmered with rage again. "Why would you sacrifice your wings for a stranger?"

"Because my people—*our* people—robbed you of your right to access Elysium. I will not let them rob you of your soul."

"Feather . . ." he whispered, but his voice carried no more heat.

Before he could plead for me to let him go again, I said, "I want no part in a bigoted world."

"This one's not much better."

"At least humans don't pretend they're something they're not."

His lips bent a fraction. "Some do."

I tossed my hands in the air, then banded my arms in front of my chest. "Fine. You win. This world isn't better than ours. Is that what you want to hear?"

"Hey . . ." Jarod clasped the back of my neck, which I tried to keep twisted away from him but failed to. "I'm sorry for being such a venal, ungrateful ass."

I side-eyed him.

"Thank you for fighting for my soul."

I still didn't say anything.

"But I don't want your soul to get damaged in the celestial crossfire." His thumb set on my neck.

"Don't worry about my soul, Jarod," I said in a toneless voice.

"I'll make you a deal."

I felt my eyebrows lower.

"I'll stop worrying about your soul when you stop worrying about mine."

I was surprised my hammering pulse hadn't knocked his thumb off my skin. "I'll stop worrying about it when you admit to Asher you didn't plant that letter opener in your mother's chest."

"I already did."

I broke free of his hold. "What?"

"I told him I only removed it."

"You couldn't have led with that?"

"I could've, but then, I would've missed out on all the fun and surprises of our sparkling dinner conversation."

I gaped at him, then snapped my jaw closed. "I would've told you all of it if you'd asked."

"I know." He plowed his hand through his hair.

"You're so infuriating."

"Hey, I didn't sign up to me." He smirked. "You did that all on your own. Should've spent more time scrolling through available sinners and vetting the contenders."

Telling him my best friend had forced my hand was on the tip of my tongue, but it felt venomous. Hadn't I been spiteful enough for one evening? Besides, I wasn't focusing on the most important aspect, which was that Asher had heard the truth from Jarod's lips. Maybe the archangel was adjusting my sinner's score as we spoke. Or, at least, unlocking it.

Soon, Jarod's soul would lighten, and his rank would drop. Perhaps, one day, he'd even dip beneath the bar of fifty and avoid Abaddon altogether.

My chest flared with hope and with something else . . . nostalgia. If Asher was correcting Jarod's score, the countdown to my ascension would begin. I would be locked out of this world for a century until the archangels bestowed the key to the Channels upon me.

My gaze strayed over the beveled mirrors hung in thin gold frames, the crystals dripping like fat raindrops from the lavish chandelier, the crushed velvets, and sculpted granite mantles before returning to the sharp ridges of Jarod's face.

How I would miss this world and these imperfect humans.

"You haven't tasted the *foie gras* yet," Jarod said, scooting his chair back across the table from me. "I'm dying to see what you think of it."

I concentrated on the here and now. "*See?*"

He picked up his diminutive glass of wine, swirled it, then tipped it inside his mouth. "Your skin is very expressive, Feather."

On cue, my cheeks warmed, so I angled my face toward my plate and focused on my food. "And your skin is very hairy," I muttered under my breath.

He rended the quiet room with a bark of laughter.

*W*hen we got back to his home after our delicious meal, my body couldn't decide whether it was sinking or floating. I'd had too much to eat and drink, but I'd also tossed an anvil off my shoulders.

"Do all angels enjoy food as much as you do?" Jarod's gaze lingered on his statue, on her chopped wings.

"No. We're urged to live a life of moderation. Haven't you noticed how thin all the others are?"

Jarod shifted his attention from the stone to my flesh. "What exactly do you think you are?"

"Certainly not thin." I suddenly regretted overindulging tonight—not that it had cost me any feathers. The thought that it might had crossed my mind and stuck like a fly to a cobweb. Hadn't kept me from eating the three desserts Jarod had ordered, though.

"And thank God for that."

"God doesn't exist," I deadpanned.

He snorted, but a smile tugged at his lips.

I sighed, touching my full belly. "Next time, don't order the entire menu."

"Next time, huh?"

"Not that there needs to be a next time," I mumbled, surely

turning the color of the candied beets, which had been served atop a small mound of tangy goat cheese.

"Would you like there to be one?"

I side-eyed him, and then I side-eyed Luc, steeped in the shadows of the porch. He didn't seem to be paying attention, but how could he not? Nothing else was happening around him.

I tossed the ball back in Jarod's court. "Would *you* like there to be a next time? And don't play the *I asked first* card."

His smirk reached all the way into his eyes that seemed as luminous as the glass chandelier Muriel had left on in the checkered marble foyer. "Surprisingly, I'd love to share another meal with you, Feather."

"*Surprisingly*," I muttered.

"You did hear all I said after that word?"

Considering my heart had grown wings of its own, *yes*, I'd heard all of the words that had followed. Would there even be a next time, though? I wished I could magick my wings into existence to test their weight, but Jarod hated them as much as he loathed desserts.

"I did," I said, starting up again, but Jarod barred the entrance to his house by extending his arm.

"You have to answer my question to gain entry into my domain," he said.

"I just did."

"I meant the question I asked before that one."

"*Surprisingly*, I'd love to share another meal with you, too." *Lunch.* Whatever happened, I would still be around for lunch.

His smile didn't grow, but it firmed up like the caramel cage around the *praliné* ice cream I'd devoured while he'd watched on, nursing a second brandy. "Zero points for creativity, but one for enthusiasm."

"What?"

"You rank us; only fair I rank you."

I shook my head but smiled.

"Don't worry, your superior looks earn you lots of points."

I wasn't sure whether to blush or balk, so I did both, which made Jarod chuckle. He retracted his arm, then held the door open for me.

It took my legs a moment to work after that offbeat compliment. *Superior.* Did that mean he considered me beautiful or a notch under? What was a notch under anyway? Cute? Puppies and children were cute. Was that how Jarod saw me? Like a child? More importantly, though, why did I care how he saw me? He was my sinner, not my love interest.

Sighing, I stepped past him and into the house that was so quiet I felt the need to whisper, "I'll just get my bag—"

"How about one more drink?"

I twirled around as Jarod clicked the door closed behind him, no bodyguard in tow. "I don't need one more drink."

He circled me. "Since when do we need the things we want?"

"I don't *want* one either, Jarod."

My answer blotted his pleasant mood.

"But I'd enjoy spending more time in your company."

By increments, the darkness cleared from his face. "You could've led with that," he finally said, which elicited a cheek-splitting grin on my part.

"Zero points for creativity, Monsieur Adler," I teased him. "You just recycled words I used earlier."

My mind blanked when he linked his fingers with mine and pulled me into his study. After he sealed us inside, he flicked on the sconces and the light fixture over the oil portrait of the horse, then released my hand, crossed the wide room, and heaved the curtains closed.

I watched him move around the room with a manner so elegant and dark it was bewitching. As he poured himself a tumbler of something, my gaze slid down the length and breadth of him. He was a man sculpted from obsidian and starlight, not flesh and sins. If anyone was the sinner in this room, it was me.

The girl who couldn't stop watching.

The girl who couldn't stop wondering if his breath would taste like fire and spice, or mineral and sweet like his fragrance.

"Tired, Feather?"

"What?" My voice sounded like it was coming from miles away.

"You're sparkling."

The rushing stilled in my ears.

Oh . . . sweet cherubs . . . no.

I feigned a yawn, which made his mouth tick up as he stalked back toward me.

"Do you need to be plugged in?"

"Very funny."

He waggled his eyebrows. "You could always take a nap in my bed."

Even though there was no mirror, I suspected that even my eyeballs had started glittering. Did that happen?

When he got close enough that I could smell the smokiness lifting off his drink and the sweetness lifting off his neck, I eyed the drapes, keen to cocoon myself in them until my skin returned to normal. But then, what?

Perhaps leaving this world wasn't such a bad thing.

"Now that we're friends, why don't you tell me the truth about why your skin lights up?"

I swallowed and backed up a step. "I'd really rather not."

He took a step forward. I backed up again. We performed this little dance until my tailbone met solid wood, and I was trapped.

"Would you rather I guess?"

"Nope."

"I have a very pertinent deduction."

"Keep it to yourself."

His eyes glittered fiercely, but how much of that was my skin and how much of that was his perverse glee to embarrass me?

"I believe you glitter when you're turned on."

"Nope." *Please, please, Ishim, don't steal a feather from my wings.*

Jarod lowered his gaze to the floor. No feather had fallen, and this obviously baffled him, because the little customary dip materialized between his eyebrows.

Had he said smoldered, and I'd refuted his claim, would I be down another feather?

His eyebrows drew so close together they almost touched.

He was disappointed. Was it because he hadn't guessed right or because he'd wanted to be right?

Desirous to put a smile back on that stupidly gorgeous face of his, even at my expense, I explained, "It's called smoldering. Only women of our kind do it. Males extend their wings, which is called winging."

He waited in silence for me to elucidate further.

I licked my lips before I confessed, "It happens when we want to attract someone."

"*Y*ou want to attract me, Feather?" His voice sounded like crushed velvet, and it did all sorts of improper things to my body.

I rolled my eyes, trying to play the smoldering off as an unfortunate mishap. "I don't do it on purpose."

He frowned.

"I don't tell my body to shine to get you to look at me. It just happens." *Twice. It's happened twice. Once was a mishap, but twice?*

"So, your subconscious wants to attract me?"

"Exactly." On the plus side, sparkling like a disco ball hid my mortifying blush.

He tipped his head to the side. "So *subconsciously* you really want me."

"Exactly," I said again but then realized how that sounded and squeaked like the time I'd walked through a dark alley in New York and came upon a rodent the size of a minx. "No. I mean, yes." *Ugh.*

His forehead smoothed, and his cocky grin returned.

I shifted my gaze to the horse painting. "Can you stop looking at me like that?"

"Like what?"

"Like I've just faceplanted into a lamppost."

"If that's your interpretation of my stare, then I really have to work on it."

I could tell his smile had increased from the lilt in his voice.

"Feather?"

I tugged my lip into my mouth and gnawed on it.

"Look at me."

"I'd rather not," I mumbled over a mouthful of flesh.

"Please?"

Still not freeing my lip, I pressed the back of my skull into the wood, wishing its grainy surface could dip and swallow me whole.

He raised his thumb and freed my lip from my teeth. "If I had wings," he said huskily, "they'd be stretched from one wall of this office to the other."

My heart froze, then turned liquid, melting into every extremity in my body.

He stroked the edge of my lip, then leaned over, and pressed his mouth to mine, and I swear I no longer smoldered, I burned, a hot, hungry flame that he'd stoked with all his dark smiles and sultry words.

I was so stunned that I didn't kiss him back, the same way I didn't close my eyes. Wasn't I supposed to close my eyes? What did the heroines in my books do? They wrapped their hands around the necks of the person kissing them. I could start there.

As my hands rose, they bumped the drink he was still clutching, sloshing the contents on his pants.

Oh . . . crap.

Jarod jerked away.

"I'm s-s-sorry," I stammered. "I was trying t-to—"

"Cool me off?" His curved lips glistened.

"No. I was—*ugh*—" I suddenly wished I could be struck down with angel-fire. "Trying to do something with my hands."

His smile turned so wicked I regretted explaining my clumsiness. "And what were you trying to do with your hands?" His brazen timbre covered my smoldering skin in goose bumps.

I shut my eyes, wishing that because I couldn't see him, he couldn't see me, but I'd learned during a long-ago game of hide-and-seek with Eve that disappearing didn't work like that.

The heat from his body vanished, and then something clinked

—glass against wood? I didn't peek to find out, still dying of mortification. Suddenly, the air's temperature swelled again, and fingers laced around my wrists, towing them gently upward, setting them around his neck.

I still didn't look, and the anticipation of his next move had my heartbeat radiating, making every inch of me vibrate with its wild tempo. His fingers stroked up the silk of my camisole, tracing the indents of my waist, the outer swells of my breasts, the bare skin right below my armpits, the crests of my shoulders, the dips around my neck.

Where one hand sank over my shoulder and traced a line down my spine, the other combed through my hair until it cupped the back of my head. I held my breath as sensations undulated through me, each one more debilitating and delectable than the last.

I gripped Jarod's neck, and the sinews tautened like stretched twine. I dipped the fingers of one hand below his shirt collar and speared the fingers of the other through his stiffened locks.

His spicy breath warmed my forehead, then the tip of my nose, and finally my parted lips. "Ready to try this again?" he murmured.

Keeping my lids clasped shut, I nodded.

His nose brushed mine before pressing into my cheek, and then his lips closed over mine, stealing my breath and making it his.

This kiss was surely going to cost me a feather. Perhaps, all of them. And yet, when he opened his mouth and dipped his tongue against mine, I welcomed him in, mirroring his pressure and stroke.

Our mouths moved silently over one another, our tongues exploring and connecting and licking. Celestial arias mingled with the rush of our heartbeats, gorging my ears with rapturous music.

His stubble roughed up my chin, leaving a titillating burn in its wake. I tightened my hold on his neck to bring him closer even though his nose already dug into my cheek and my hardened nipples gouged his chest. As though we were of one mind, his hand crimped the fabric at my waist and the skin beneath it, blighting every atom of air between us.

Our bodies fit as though created for one another, my soft

curves filling all of his hard dents. As I explored his mouth, a new hunger streaked through my body, made my heart contract and thighs tremble. His kisses became more demanding, and I gave him everything I had to offer, which was probably not very much to a man like him, a man so used to getting *all* he wanted.

My lower belly ached from the hard press of his zipper, but there was no pain in that ache. The brandy, which had soaked into the fine wool of his suit, transferred to my skirt, hot and wet and smelling of spice and desire. His scent tormented me almost as much as his taste.

Panting hard, he broke the kiss and leaned his forehead against mine, a gelled tendril of hair tickling my temple. His palm released the back of my head and pressed into the wall behind me, heaving his body off mine. The distance was unbidden, and I tried to coax him closer, but it was like trying to shift a marble statue.

"Unless you want me to rob you of the rest of your innocence," he murmured huskily, "you have to give me a minute." He pushed a tangled orange lock behind my ear.

I slid my hand out of his hair and around his corded neck, feeling his pulse drilling his throat. Worried that he might snap out of whatever spell had made him kiss me, I kept both my hands on his body.

He might've let me go, but I wasn't ready to let *him* go.

My heart shook as a terrible thought coiled through my mind. If Asher amended Jarod's score, I would have no choice but to let him go. As the selfish thought took root and twined around my lungs like a vine, heat smacked my lids.

"I don't want this to be our last kiss," I croaked, my voice sounding like it was crumbling.

Jarod swiped my bottom lashes with his thumbs, whisking away the moisture pooling there. "I'm not done with you."

When I lowered my lashes to hide my stinging eyes, he wound my hair around his fist and levered my face up.

His gaze roved over mine, searching for the source of my insecurities. "Will your people try to keep us apart? Is that what's frightening you, Feather? Because I won't let them come between us. I won't let anyone or anything come between us."

A sob splintered out of me. "If Asher changes your score"—

my voice broke—"I ascend. In the next twenty-four hours, I could be gone."

His eyes flicked faster over mine. "But then, you can come back down to me."

I swallowed, but it did nothing to quell the lump bloating my throat. "Not in your lifetime, Jarod," I murmured.

"What do you mean?"

"New angels must spend a century in Elysium before they can return, so that all the humans they've come in contact with are gone."

He didn't say anything for so long that the vine around my lungs grew thorns.

Suddenly, he released my hair and began to pace the length of his office. "Call him! Tell him I lied."

I gasped. "No, Jarod! For all my selfishness, I want your soul to survive."

He wrenched his hand through his hair, shoving the dark waves out of his eyes. "I should have a say in that!"

"Jarod—"

He halted and whipped his attention off the rug and onto me. "Can you feel your feathers growing?"

"No. They're too light, but you can see . . ." I let my voice trail off before I could utter a suggestion that would surely incense Jarod even further.

"Your wings. Bring them out."

"Jarod . . ."

He arrowed straight for me. "Do it, Feather. Now."

I hesitated, remembering the pain they'd caused him.

He gripped my chin. "Please."

He thought I hadn't made them materialize because he hadn't said please? *Oh, Great Elysium, this man.*

Heart smarting, I pulled my wings out of hiding and prayed, for the first time in my life, that new feathers hadn't formed on my wing bones.

I didn't glance over my shoulder, didn't extend my wings to test their weight. Since I usually earned so few feathers at a time, I'd never noticed a change, but a hundred feathers . . . I'd surely feel a difference.

Jarod's Adam's apple bobbed as his gaze skirted over the edges of my silver feathers. His hand fell away from my face in slow motion, leaving traces of heat behind. "Where would they . . ." He swallowed. "Where would the new ones appear?"

"On the edges," I whispered.

Nerves quivered under his skin, and his overly bright eyes spoke of dread. "How can you tell if they're new?"

"They're smaller . . . softer." I thought of all the feathers I'd earned over the years, of how I'd relished stroking the untainted down. A shudder passed through me at the memory, and it made the silken barbs sway, tickling my bare shoulders and the backs of my arms.

"I can't see, Feather," he said, which made hope spring through me. But then, I understood he couldn't see because my wings were tucked in too tight. "Stretch them out."

My wing bones felt made of rusty steel instead of celestial magic. As I extended the web of sinew and cartilage, a bead of cold sweat formed on the nape of my neck.

Jarod paled.

The bead rolled down my spine, tunneling between my contracted shoulder blades. "Are they—do you see something?" I finally twisted my neck as far as it would turn. When that didn't help, I curled my wings until their outer edges touched in front of me.

Jarod stepped back, and I wasn't sure if he'd added the space because he was horrified or needed some distance to examine them. I traced the outermost fringe, Jarod's keen eyes shadowing my fingertips' path. I didn't think my heart had thumped once since I'd made my wings appear. When I'd probed every rachis and vane, I shook my head.

His eyebrows lurched up. "No?"

I kept shaking my head. All at once, blood gorged my veins, air expanded my lungs, and my heart revved up. The lump in my throat took more time to recede, but once it did, I managed to croak, "No."

Color slowly leached back into Jarod's face. "No?" he repeated, as though he hadn't heard me.

Before I realized what I was doing, I took his hand and ran it over the rim of my right wing. "You see? No fluffy ones."

He sucked in a breath, which he held until I towed his fingers away from my feathers and released his wrist.

"I'm sorry."

"For what, Feather?"

"For having made you . . . *touch* them. I know how much you loathe them."

A beat passed. "I do loathe them, but for an entirely different reason tonight." He reached up and glided his palm over the silver vanes. When his hand curved and stroked the underside, a full body shudder went through me. "Tonight, I hate them because they could take you away from me."

I gasped at his confession.

"Tonight, I hate them because they're the fucking most beautiful things I've ever laid eyes on, and yet I have this violent urge to cleave them from your body." He glided his hand back up with a gentleness that didn't match the tone of his voice or the fire in his eyes. When he stroked his way back down, and my teeth knocked together from the pleasure that shot through the barbed shafts, he snatched his hand back.

"Am I hurting you?" Genuine worry crimped his features.

"No, Jarod. You're not hurting me."

"Then why—why did your body shake?"

I smiled at how innocent he suddenly looked, like a boy who'd never touched someone else's flesh. How I wished that were the case. Just the way he kissed told me I wasn't the first woman he'd used his lips on. Before the thought could fill me with jealousy, I pushed it away.

Far. Away.

"How about you take a wild guess?" I said. "You're good at guessing."

His pupils eclipsed his irises, and then both his hands flexed open and settled with no restraint on the underside of my wings.

I gasped from the almost brutal impact and shivered so hard Jarod banded one arm around my waist and dropped the other away from my body. "No pain. I promise."

He searched my eyes.

I let my head loll against his neck and asked something of him that would surely cost me a feather. "Again. Do it again."

I heard him swallow. Without removing his arm from my waist, he lifted his other hand and drew it achingly slowly over the downy curve. My spine spasmed as a bolt of pleasure electrified the web of cartilage holding my feathers together. I understood then why it was forbidden to touch another angel's wings without their consent.

I nestled my head into the crook of Jarod's neck as he tracked his fingers slowly up and then back down. My knees softened until all that was holding me up was his rigid arm. I moaned against his neck, inhaling his scent.

"Feather?"

"Hmm . . ."

"Faster? Slower?"

"I don't know. I've never . . . no one's ever . . . touched my wings." A soft whimper escaped my lips. I tried to muffle it against his skin, but considering how he seemed to grow a whole foot taller, I imagined he'd caught the sound.

He trailed his palm leisurely, and even though it was the sweetest form of torture, I growled, "Faster."

A slow chuckle rumbled through his chest. For a long second, I didn't think he'd listen to me, but his strokes sped up and pressure built inside my body and sizzled against my skin, and my heart . . . my heart distended, as though trying to break free from my rib cage to penetrate Jarod's.

I panted against his neck, then alternately nipped the taut flesh and moaned against it, rendering his breathing as patchy as my own.

The world suddenly stilled, then exploded. The floor, the ceiling, and the walls of Jarod's house fell away. Only glittery starlight and my dark sinner remained.

Jarod's fingers came to rest on my hip, supporting me as the sparkle faded and the study's walls closed back around us. Then he pressed his lips to my temple, stamping their shape into my skin.

A long, *long* time later, he murmured, "Lie to me, Feather."

"Wh-what?" I stuttered back to reality.

"Lie to me."

I pulled away from him.

"How many feathers did I make you lose? Three, four?"

My eyes widened.

"How many do you still need to earn?"

The fog of my orgasm—or was there another name for what I'd just experienced?—cleared. "Eighty-six. I think."

"Lie to me twenty times," he said, cradling my face between his palms. "I know it'll hurt, but speak them so that if Asher lowers my score tonight, or tomorrow, or next week, it doesn't rip you from my arms." He touched his mouth to my parted lips. "Please . . ."

My chest cracked right open. "I hated the feel of your hands on my wings."

My wing bones tensed, and then a feather drifted down like a clump of dawn-lit snow.

"Again," Jarod said. "Please, baby, again."

I told him how I'd hated kissing him.

I told him how I thought he was as ugly on the outside as he was on the inside.

I told him so many lies that when I was done, a sparkling silver heap littered his rug, and my cheeks were wet from my pain and his kisses.

37

*P*ounding on the door made us spring apart.

After I'd spoken twenty lies, perhaps more, enough to satisfy Jarod that I wouldn't be stolen from his world, he'd led me to one of the armchairs. I'd magicked my aching wings away as he'd slid me onto his lap and embraced me with arms that felt like steel bands.

"Jarod!" Tristan's voice made me blink my gummy lids open.

Jarod stroked my cheek with his long fingers.

"I know you're in there," Tristan said.

"He's going to tear down my door if I don't let him in," he muttered. "But if you don't want to see him—"

I sniffed, and his eyebrows knitted together.

"I'm okay. Let him in. I should get back to the guild anyway."

"*Jamais de la vie.*" *No way.* "You're not going back there, Feather. Not tonight."

"Ja-arod," Tristan singsonged. "Come on, man. Let me in."

"Stay. Please," he said, his tone urgent.

"I'm not going to vanish through a Channel. You made sure of that." I tried to smile, but the aftermath of shredding my wings was still rippling through me.

"Fuck that. I want you here. With me. I *need* you here."

Warmth spread through me. "Okay, okay. I won't go home." I smoothed the furrows from his brow with my fingertips.

230 | OLIVIA WILDENSTEIN

"I'm coming in," Tristan warned. "Hope she's decent . . . Or that you're willing to share."

Jarod muttered, "*L'enculé*," before giving me one last fleeting kiss.

The door soared wide.

I sensed Tristan's eyes on me.

"Well, well," he said in a voice that was so chirpy it sounded like he'd awakened from the longest and greatest nap of his life. "If it isn't the stray I found on your doorstep."

Jarod's body firmed up so fast it felt like I was sitting on concrete. "Don't you ever fucking talk about Leigh like that!"

I straightened my hunched spine and peeked over my shoulder.

Tristan raised both his palms. "*Pardon*, Jarod. It was meant as a joke."

"Ask for her forgiveness, not mine," Jarod growled.

"I'm sorry, Leigh," he said, his gaze roaming over my mottled face. "Everything okay?"

I nodded. Everything was okay *now*.

Another figure appeared behind Tristan—Muriel. "Jarod?" Even though she didn't attach any other words to his name, I sensed she was asking him if he was all right.

"Mimi, can you take Leigh upstairs?" I must've gone a shade paler, because he added, "She'll stay the night in my old bedroom."

Muriel retied the belt on her cashmere robe. "*Viens, ma chérie.*" *Come, my darling.*

Was I really staying the night in Jarod's house? I'd never slept anywhere but in guilds . . . Then again, I'd never done a lot of the things I'd done tonight.

As I reached Muriel's side, Jarod said, "I'll be up as soon as I can." His expression was so full of worry that I wanted to run straight back into his arms and tell him I was truly all right, that I'd never been this all right. Instead, I held his gaze and smiled.

He didn't smile back, but his breathing seemed to even out.

As Muriel closed the door, I heard Tristan say, "Had to yank a few fingernails out . . ."

That sentence was like a cold shower, waking me up to the fact that the man I'd just ruined my wings for did terrible things or ordered others to do them on his behalf. He might share my kin's blood, but Jarod Adler was no angel.

I touched my lips as nausea rose, making my stomach contract.

What had I done?

What was I still doing?

I needed to go home. I opened my mouth to tell Muriel I'd changed my mind, when she said, "I think Tristan enjoys what he does a little too much." Darkness smudged the thin skin underneath her eyes.

I stopped at the bottom of the stairs. "And Jarod? Does he enjoy it too?"

"Jarod inherited his uncle's sense of duty and morality."

"So, he doesn't . . . *hurt* people?"

"We don't discuss his job, Leigh. The same way I never discussed it with Isaac. But I trust that if he *hurts* people he does it for a reason."

Money was the first one that came to mind. Revenge was another. Control. Many more words flowed freely through my mind, none easing my qualms.

"Come now," Muriel said.

Suddenly, the staircase looked as though it led to a dungeon instead of apartments crafted in rich satins and glossed wood.

"I-I . . ." Nerves skittering like claws against my skin, I glanced toward the pantry where I'd left my bag, then toward the study where the men spoke in such low tones it was impossible to hear what they were discussing.

I want you here. With me. I need you here. Jarod's plea and imploring gaze reeled through me.

I'd promised to stay, and I was a woman of my word. Jarod had such little faith in angels—for good reason—that if I left, what would remain of his faith?

The rules of my mission might have changed, but not its reason. I'd signed up to sprinkle light into his darkness. My methods were unorthodox, but if they led Jarod to become a better man, then it would be worth it.

Sighing, I decided to follow Muriel up those stairs and see where they led.

38

I trailed Muriel through the set of tall doors opposite Jarod's bedroom. As she flicked on some lights, I understood why she'd referred to the bedrooms as apartments. We'd entered a large hallway decorated with framed charcoal drawings of women with cubic faces and asymmetric breasts in various stages of undress. When I read the scribbled signature at the edge of the thick vellum, I realized I was staring at works of art that were worth an insane amount of money.

Muriel walked past them as though they'd become one with the cherry-wood paneling behind. She'd probably seen them so often they no longer impressed her. At the end of the hallway, she opened one of two doors.

"This was the room Jarod grew up in."

I was expecting a little boy's bedroom made up in a palette of blues and whites, complete with ships in bottles, dangling paper planes, and baskets brimming with toys. The only thing I'd gotten right was the blue, but it was far from the shade of the noon sky I'd envisioned. This was the color when twilight and dusk collided, a blue that was almost black.

I took in the king-sized bed boxed into a dark wooden alcove with built-in shelves that didn't seem suited for a child. "Was it redecorated?"

Muriel stared around the room as though to check everything

was still in its place. "No."

I peered out the window that gave onto a tall gray wall crusted in pigeon droppings and exhaust gas. The view was a far cry from the sumptuous courtyard with its stone fountain and tangled ivy.

Muriel turned on the light in an adjoining bathroom made of white and gray stone tiles. Polished silver fixtures reflected my pale face, haggard green eyes, and snarled brassy hair. While I smoothed my hair back, Muriel opened the cupboard beneath the sink and removed a stack of folded towels, which she deposited on the side of a claw-footed tub.

"Why don't you take a hot bath? I'll bring up your bag."

"I can go get it, Muriel."

"Nonsense. Stay here." She patted my hands, which I was wringing together.

Was she afraid I might bolt if I went back down the stairs? The thought did cross my mind.

Before leaving, she turned on the bath faucet, and the gushing noise replaced the quiet stillness. "Do you need clothes?"

"I actually packed some." I blushed as I realized how that sounded. When she arched an eyebrow, I added, "I did something that made my family mad, so I wasn't sure I would be welcomed home."

She scowled. "No mistakes are ever grave enough to turn away family."

I shrugged, and the movement reawakened a battery of little aches. Where the twinge of one lost feather faded relatively swiftly, the pain of losing so many loitered. "I might've been over-dramatizing. Maybe they wouldn't have locked me out."

"Well, *our* doors are always open to you, *ma chérie*."

Her unmerited benevolence combined with the steam rising from the bath made the air suddenly too thick to breathe.

"You don't even know me, Muriel. Maybe I'm a horrible person."

The corners of her navy eyes crinkled along with those of her mouth. "You make my boy laugh. I haven't heard him laugh in years. So even if you were horrible—which you're not—I'd coerce you to stick around, just to hear that sound again." She squeezed my shoulder as she walked past me. "I'll be right back."

I was still standing in the exact same spot when she returned, watching the round mirror over the sink cloud and blur my reflection until I looked more wraith than angel, which seemed appropriate considering how unangelic I felt.

I SOAKED in the bath until my muscles softened, my skin pruned, and the water turned tepid, then I towel-dried slowly, squeezing the foamy water from the ends of my hair.

I was just slipping on a fresh pair of underwear and an oversized Eagles T-shirt one of my sinners had gifted me years ago when a knock resounded.

My stomach tensed. "Come in."

As Jarod appeared in the doorway, I tugged on the hem of my T-shirt wishing there was more fabric to tug. So much of my legs was on display. What if the sight of my soft thighs made him gallantly retreat to his own bedroom?

I searched his face for repulsion but found mostly fatigue. He slid his hands inside his pants pockets and leaned against the wooden frame, taking me in first before gazing around his bedroom as though he hadn't visited it in years.

He'd shed his jacket and rolled up his shirtsleeves, displaying lean, tanned forearms dusted by the same dark hair that peeked out from his open collar. I wasn't sure if being attracted to hairy men was a thing, but possibly it was my thing, because the sight of all that virility was tightening various muscles in my body.

"See something you like?"

I gulped, then crossed my arms, trying to strangle the thrashing inside my chest before it made the rest of my body vibrate. "I remember you asking me this when we met."

One side of his mouth ticked up as he pushed away from the frame, kicked the door closed, and ambled toward me. "And I remember you avoiding replying."

I stood my ground as he reached me. Without heels, the top of my head barely cleared his chin.

He looked down at me. "Were you afraid that declaring your overpowering lust would cost you a feather?"

"Overpowering lust . . ." I rolled my eyes. "I'll admit, I was intrigued."

"Intrigued, huh?" Smiling, he pulled one hand out of his pocket.

Anticipation that he was about to touch some part of my body skittered in my blood. He didn't, though. He rubbed his jaw, and the chafing sound made goose bumps spread over my skin.

"Well, I was intrigued by you the moment I saw you hanging on to Tristan's arm in your little mask."

My skin palpitated from his nearness. "The only thing that intrigued you back then was finding a way to destroy me."

He stopped rubbing his jaw. "I wanted to destroy your dress. And Tristan's arm," he added as an afterthought.

His hand finally bridged the distance between our bodies, coming to wrap around the back of my head. I wondered if he was going to kiss me, but instead he just stared, and his dark eyes seemed to darken some more.

"I'm sorry for what Tristan said downstairs."

"It's okay," I said, gripping onto his shirt in an attempt to keep myself upright, even though I had no doubt his hands were doing a better job of ensuring my verticality than my own. "You called me a stalker, remember?"

He dropped his forehead to mine. "I'm so glad you stalked me, Feather."

"You didn't look glad."

"Showing emotion gives people leverage over you."

"Your uncle taught you that?"

He nodded.

"Wish someone had taught me that."

The look of seriousness that invaded his face made me worry I'd said the wrong thing. "The world was an immensely drab place to live in before you burst through my doors, so full of light and color."

"Color, huh? Are you talking about my hair? I've always hated how colorful it was," I added mournfully.

"I'd say your hair's the sexiest part about you, but I'd be doing the rest of your stunning body a great deal of injustice."

The heat in my cheeks made its way toward the juncture of my thighs. "No one's ever called me sexy before."

"Only because they're better-mannered than I am." He tugged on my hair, tipping my head back at an almost painful angle.

"And just so we're clear, no one besides me gets to call you that from now on."

The heat of him, the growl of him, the feel of him threatened to make my heart jump right through my parted lips. I licked them, and his eyes flared. "You're smoldering, Feather."

"Seems to happen a lot in your presence." I moistened my lips again. "Are you going to just look at me or do something about it?"

His lips curved into a smile so satisfied it rubbed my nerves raw. "What is it you want me to *do*, Feather?"

"You could kiss me for starters," I suggested, my voice barely audible.

His dark eyes absorbed the glowing mess I'd become. "Where?"

I sucked in a breath.

Jarod pressed his mouth to my collarbone. "Here?" he whispered huskily, and I shivered. "Or . . ." He tugged on the collar of my T-shirt, and his mouth bore down on my shoulder. "Here? Or . . ." When he dragged his tongue in a straight line up the slope of my neck and tugged my earlobe inside his mouth, I worried for my ribs' safety. He pulled away to inspect the effect of his kisses.

"Anywhere, Jarod. Just—don't stop," I begged.

"Careful what you wish for, Feather. I'm an extremely creative person." He let go of my hair, and his hands tracked down the pebbled skin of my arms.

Not that my mind was at its most lucid, but what the heck did creativity have to do with—*oh!*

Jarod dropped down to his knees, his palms skating down the sides of my legs. When his hands swirled around my calves, and he kissed the inside of one knee, then the other, I all but choked on a gasp. Or was it a moan? The next kiss fell just below the hemline of my T-shirt.

I scrambled to grab some part of him, managing a handful of hair. "Wait! Stop—" My heartbeats tasted like metal. "I—" If Jarod took this any farther, my wings were going to go up in smoke.

Ophan Greer had taught us it was improper to have relations of a romantic nature outside of wedlock, yet my earlier orgasm hadn't cost me anything. Was it because Jarod wasn't completely human? Or because wings weren't *sexual* organs?

Jarod rose, then cradled my face. "I'm sorry."

A mad chuckle leaped out of me and made his brow crease. I sobered up, not wanting him to think I was laughing at his apology. "Oh, Jarod. Please don't be sorry."

He frowned.

"I'm just scared the Ishim are going to cremate what's left of my feathers." I shrugged, and my back stung again. Latching on to the hem of my T-shirt, I explained, "I grew up being told that sex out of wedlock was a carnal sin that would send me straight to Abaddon."

His eyebrows knitted, but at least, his nostrils stopped flaring in anguish. "So, without completed wings, you could be taken to Abaddon but not to Elysium?"

The dissonance of his conclusion struck me. "You're right . . . it makes little sense." Why hadn't I considered asking Ophan Greer this?

"You didn't lose any feathers for what I did to you earlier."

"I know."

"Have you ever wondered if the rules you were given were simply a way to keep you in line?"

"Not before I met you."

His pulse leaked through his thumbs and drummed against my cheekbones.

"I don't want to rush you into something you're not ready for, Feather, especially if giving you pleasure causes you pain, but I also don't want you to push me away because you're scared of your people. Because if that's the case—"

"You'll make me lie until I have no more feathers to lose?" I joked, but it wasn't really a joke.

Jarod's gaze sharpened. "What would happen if you did lose all your feathers? Would it get rid of your wings?"

The pressure of his palms and stare suddenly felt overwhelming, so I extricated my face from his grip, took a step back, and stared at the gray carpeting beneath our feet, tracing the edge of a discolored spot with my toe. I'd been willing to give up my wings to save Jarod's soul, and then I'd ruined them to make sure I wasn't ripped from Earth during the night, so my reaction to his question was incongruous.

"I shouldn't have said that." He sank down on the edge of the bed, the mattress springs groaning underneath his weight. "I just *loathe* your system and wish—I wish I could protect you from *it*. From *them*."

But he couldn't protect me, because if he stood between them and me, he'd get hurt . . . perhaps, irreparably so. "I shouldn't be here, Jarod," I said, staring at the dark locks of hair that were sticking out at odd angles around his head. "I shouldn't have stayed."

He whipped his head up so fast his neck cracked.

"I don't want them to hurt you, Jarod."

His head jerked back some more in surprise. "Me?" His tone was almost maniacal. When he started laughing, I realized he wasn't taking my concern seriously.

"I'm not trying to be cute," I said, frustrated.

His eyes still danced, but he sobered up, and then he pulled on my hand and towed me toward him until I had the choice between toppling ungracefully beside him or falling into his lap. Toppling would have been the safer option, but I'd forfeited safety the day I'd pushed my palm into my holo-ranker's glass screen and my name had appeared over Jarod Adler's three-dimensional picture.

He roped my waist to keep me in place, and then, in the most serious voice I'd ever heard him use, he said, "The only way they could hurt me would be by taking you away."

I traced the ridge of his brow, thinking about a long-ago conversation I'd had with Eve. I'd asked her if she believed in soul mates. Instead of asking me where I'd come up with that harebrained idea—I was certain she assumed I'd read it in one of my human books—she'd answered, *Yes.*

I'd been so surprised that I'd gaped at her for two solid minutes.

And it's terrible when it happens, because it means the Malakim did a subpar job of wiping away the souls' memories and giving them the blank slate they need to start their new lives. Usually those souls—the ones who remember—spend so much time hunting down souls from past lives that they don't work on improving themselves. They just squander their time on Earth.

After that, I'd balked at her, but for a completely different reason.

Maybe you shouldn't be a Malakim, Leigh.

Wh-what? I'd stuttered.

You're so governed by your love of love that sometimes I think it might not be the best calling for you.

I'd gotten very defensive, then. *Just because I'm a romantic doesn't mean I'd disregard celestial ordinations.*

She'd come to sit on my bed and had hooked a hand around my shoulder. *Leigh, I didn't say this to upset you. I just don't want you relegated to working as an Ophanim because you didn't have the heart to scrub souls of their previous lifetimes.*

"What are you thinking about?" Jarod asked, stealing me out of the memory.

"A conversation I had with a friend a long time ago."

"Are you sure it was with a friend? You look about ready to punch someone."

His comment gave me pause, because I realized that sending me to Paris wasn't Eve's first unsympathetic act toward me. For years, she'd made me doubt myself. Why had I been so intent on not seeing her for what she really was, which was *not a friend*?

"She's the reason I'm here." I traced the stitching in the hem of my T-shirt. "She suggested I take you on, because she must've known your score was locked and I wouldn't be able to earn my feathers in time for—" I stopped talking, not thinking it wise to remind Jarod of my prior desire to marry the archangel.

"In time for what?" When I didn't respond, he imprisoned my restless fingers. "In time for what, Leigh?"

"Remember that bet I told you about?" I stared at the span of the hand cocooning mine.

"The one to marry another man? The one you had forty days to win?" He made a sound at the back of his throat. "How could I forget?"

"I didn't understand it then—because I didn't think anyone in the system could be irredeemable—but she sent me to you to remove me from the competition." I peeked at him through a lock of hair that had tumbled into my eyes.

He tucked the strand back. "I've never felt such conflicting emotions toward a person—part of me wants to break her neck and another part wants to prostrate myself at her feet."

I couldn't decide if I was horrified or moved by his declaration. Both. I was both.

"How did this girl know so much about me?"

I bit my lip. "Apparently, she tried to reform you."

He bobbed his head a few times. "What color feathers does she have?"

"Why?"

"Many angels have shown up on my doorstep. I find remembering the color of their wings, when they display them, easier than their faces or names."

"Yellow with gold tips," I said.

When the corner of his mouth curled up, I took it he remembered her.

Even though I wasn't sure I wanted to get an answer, the masochist in me asked, "Did you take her to your bedroom and give her a strip show too?" I was deeply disturbed by how jealous I sounded.

He ran his thumb over the edge of my jaw, no longer smiling. "You're the first person—besides Muriel and Tristan—who's seen the inside of my bedroom."

I was sure he was just saying that to quell my jealousy. Then again, he didn't need to be in his own bed to have sex. And why was I thinking about Jarod having sex? *Ugh.*

He returned the hand he'd set over mine to my waist and dragged me closer. "To tell you the truth, I was just as shocked as you were to have let you inside."

"You didn't look shocked."

"Probably because most of the blood in my body had gone south, incapacitating my brain and facial expressions." He shifted and something dug into my thigh. Something too hard to be a wallet and too thick to be a cell phone. "Same way I'm so turned on right now I'm afraid I'm going to end up bruising your thigh." He dropped his voice. "Or my dick."

My mind blanked, and my pulse scattered throughout my body like embers from a fire. I didn't move and neither did he, as though handing me the reins to whatever it was we'd started mere hours ago.

I turned toward him before gliding off his lap to straddle him instead. "I think it would be wise that I didn't completely damn my soul tonight. But perhaps, we could test the boundaries?" My sore back was apparently not sore enough to keep me from rebelling.

His hands rose to my ass but didn't apply any pressure. Which I doubted was for lack of want. The strain in his posture told me he was waging a war with himself not to drag me any closer. "What do you have in mind, Feather?"

What I *didn't* have in mind would've been an easier question. I really had read way too many romances. Or perhaps, I'd just been bridled for far too long.

I rocked my hips, and the bulge in Jarod's pants rubbed against my underwear.

The sensation that shot through my core made both our breaths catch. It also made Jarod clench his jaw and his fingers.

"Our clothes stay on," I whispered into his ear at the same time I shifted my hips.

He made an unintelligible sound that was part groan, part growl.

The third time I did it, he ensnared my mouth and lashed my tongue, doing to my mouth what I wouldn't allow him to do to my body. As I rocked back and forth, his zipper began to chafe the sensitive skin beneath my black lace underwear. One of his hands left my ass to cradle the back of my head while his other dragged me nearer.

When heat started to build between my thighs, my spine tightened as though preparing for feathers to loosen and rain down around us.

Jarod ripped his mouth off mine, his breaths coming out in hot, hard pants. "Your wings? How are your wings?"

The fact that he cared shot emotion through my chest. "They're fine."

I tried to grind into him, but he held me away, his gaze skirting the carpet and bed. When he was satisfied the Ishim weren't admonishing me, his hold relaxed, and I moved over him. He shuddered and closed his eyes, his lashes fanning his cheeks. I kissed one lid, then the other.

"Fuck, Feather." He sounded angry, feral almost, as though the pressure of his zipper was hurting him.

"Want me to stop?"

His eyes flew open, and he barked a laugh that was not a laugh at all considering how tense his lips were. "What I want is for you to come before I cream my pants."

I blushed. "Oh."

He shook his head, seemingly surprised the girl who'd come up with the idea of dry-humping could go red in the face. Or maybe, I was tossing my insecurities out on him, and he wasn't surprised in the least.

As his hips danced against mine, his mouth slid down the length of my throat, nipping and suckling every piece of exposed skin. Heady sensations whirled deep inside my belly, racing like thunder on scorching summer nights, popping like lightning, threatening to drown our world.

Thighs trembling, I closed my eyes and rocked, and the power of that single, slow stroke rent me in half, smiting Jarod's name out of my lungs, liquefying my bones, singeing my flesh. A choked curse spewed from Jarod and echoed against the walls that had seen him grow from an innocent child into a man who was a lot of things, but not innocent.

But who truly was? Not Eve who'd spent her life pushing me down. Not Asher who'd ranked a man unjustly. Not Celeste with her sharp tongue and sharper wit. Not Tristan who'd removed fingernails from a man. And not me.

Not anymore.

As Jarod's wet heat absorbed into my underwear's lace, filling the air with a sultry, musky scent, I realized I hadn't lost a feather. For all their rules and dictates, pleasure wasn't heresy to my kind. I wasn't sure whether to feel outraged that I'd been spoon-fed lies or grateful that it wasn't a sin.

"You might destroy my soul after all," Jarod said slowly, lazily strumming the base of my spine with his fingers.

I smoothed back his wild hair. "Your soul is safe, Jarod Adler, but I won't make the same promise about your pants."

He tossed his head back, and the dark, radiant waves of his laughter lapped at my heart, all at once dashing it to pieces and solidifying each beat.

39

*T*he divide between wrong and right frayed further that night. After stopping by his bedroom for a shower, Jarod returned wearing his black robe over a pair of black briefs molded to his body. He locked the door, then tossed the robe onto a valet stand.

The soft glow of the bathroom light edged the solid span of his shoulders, the muscles swelling his long thighs, and the dark curls of chest hair that became a mere scattering over the ridges in his abdomen before thickening again below his navel. The man was a masterpiece of flesh and muscle, tortured and torturous.

He watched me looking at him but didn't make light of it, didn't ask if I liked what I saw. There was probably no doubt in his mind that I found him—*all* of him—to my liking.

"Would you rather I don't sleep here tonight, Feather?"

His question jolted my gaze off the sharp dents in his narrow waist. "It's your house."

He smiled. "Might be my house, but it's still your choice."

I tugged my bottom lip into my mouth. Was inviting him to lay beside me a good idea or the worst one I'd had yet?

I lifted the comforter and slid toward the middle of the huge bed. Apparently, I wasn't done making questionable decisions.

A vein throbbed in his neck and along one of his arms. I watched his skin palpitate as he approached the bed. I still couldn't believe he'd grown up sleeping in a king-sized bed, then again, he'd grown up like royalty, and princes didn't sleep in bunk beds.

When his thumbs hooked into the elastic band of his briefs, I freed my lip. "Please keep it on."

I neither trusted him nor myself. Now that I'd dipped a toe into the forbidden lake, I wanted to submerge my entire body, but my mind and heart weren't ready for more. Not so soon.

"I don't want to use you any more than I already have," I added, as his body aligned with mine.

He quirked a dark brow. "Use me?"

"I'm angry at angels tonight."

He stroked the side of my body, raising goose bumps underneath my T-shirt. "I have no objections to being used by you."

"It's not a joke."

"Am I laughing?" He wasn't even smiling. "Leigh"—his voice was low and serious—"do you regret tonight?"

"No, but what if I do tomorrow?"

He rolled onto his back. As he studied the white ceiling, his Adam's apple bobbed in his throat. "In the morning, you'll head to your guild and sign off from me."

My mouth fell open, and I rasped, "Jarod—I don't—"

"Wait. Listen." He turned his face toward mine. "I'm surrounded by people whose scores are probably high double-digits. I'll help you reform them so the feathers I stole from you grow back."

His words wrung a gasp from my parted lips. As I scooted onto one elbow, I blinked down at him. I had *no* regrets about ridding my wings of feathers. I just didn't want to regret sleeping with him to test the boundaries of our system.

"You'll complete your wings." His jaw clenched. "Maybe even in time for Asher's—"

"Jarod, stop! I don't want Asher."

"But do you want me?"

From the pain lancing inside my chest, all of my doubts about being intimate to test the limits of my world left me. His altruism made a tear slide down my cheek and fall on my tensed forearm. I tried to answer him, but instead of the word *yes*, I choked on a sob.

Jarod started to raise his hand but paused in midair. When a new tear dripped off my chin, he sighed and tunneled his arm beneath my bent one, toppling me onto him before pressing my shaking body against his.

I pressed away from him so he could see my expression. "Yes," I croaked. "I want you."

He gave me a kindly smile, the sort people put on to be polite. "You don't have to say—"

"Shut up, Jarod Adler. Shut. Up. I'm never signing off from you. And not because of your soul anymore. I'm not signing off because of your damn heart."

The planes of his face readjusted, his confidence slowly blazing back and extinguishing the uncertainty my stupid tongue had caused.

"I was talking about regretting losing my virginity when I felt so mad. I'm a romantic, remember?" I said gruffly.

His lips quirked. "My damn heart thanks you and promises to make your first time"—he rolled us over, caging my head with his forearms and my thighs with his knees—"and all the ones after, fucking romantic."

"I'm not sure those two words fit together."

He lowered himself a fraction, and his hard length stroked up the inside of my leg. "I think they fit what I have in mind to perfection, Feather."

My entire body went on high alert. "Jarod," I warned.

He kissed my nose, then pried himself off me. "It's going to be a long, *hard* night," he said, dragging out the word.

I smiled. "Your sense of humor leaves me speechless, Monsieur Adler."

Letting out a soft chuckle, he gathered me against him, locking my back against his front.

His *very* hard front.

Was he really expecting me to fall asleep like that? The heat of his skin and the bulge prodding my tailbone made me squirm. I didn't manage to put more than an inch between our bodies before his big palm erased the space.

He slid himself a little lower, settling his stiffness underneath my ass, then dropped a kiss on the top of my spine. "Better?"

I was too focused on all the points of contact on our bodies to answer.

When he pressed his mouth to the curve of my neck, my body finally softened and molded to his. "I'm not hurting your back, am I, Feather?"

How long would it take me to get used to how sweet he was underneath all that snark? "You're not."

"Good." His palm was a warm iron on my stomach, all at once keeping me close and branding me.

"Jarod, are you going to stay all night?" I prayed my voice didn't smack of desperation.

It wasn't that I was scared of staying alone in this bedroom, but I was in the home of a Mafia boss. For all his guards and security, what if bad people came in the middle of the night? The irony of my deliberations hit me. The mob wasn't made of saints and innocents.

I realized he'd never answered me. His breaths had gentled against my neck even though the hand holding me hadn't. He'd slipped into sleep so easily I had trouble believing that spending the night next to a woman was a first for him.

Frustratingly, that new deliberation kept me awake long into the night.

40

*T*hree knocks followed by Muriel's voice announcing I had a visitor had my lids flipping up. I tried to get up, but a hand tugged me back, and I only managed to sit. I stared down at the hand, then at the body attached to it, and my heart went haywire.

I'd spent the night in the Court of Demons.

I'd slept next to Jarod Adler.

He and I had . . . we'd . . .

One side of Jarod's mouth perked up as he observed my heating complexion.

He chucked me under the chin, probably to slam my lips shut before answering Muriel in a languid yet authoritative tone, "Mimi, tell Leigh's guest to make themselves comfortable in the study," which caused my mouth to gape wider.

Oh . . . sweet . . . baby . . . cherubs.

Muriel now knew Jarod had spent the night with me. She'd probably imagine all sorts of things.

I decided that I would never again leave this room. Not even for my guest. And why did I have a guest? It wasn't my home. Had Muriel mentioned a name? I wanted to ask, but by the time I located my voice, Jarod bumped the inside of my elbow, and I tumbled onto his bare chest with an *oomph*.

I hissed his name as I struggled back up, my palm pressing against the surprisingly soft dark curls on his chest.

"Yes, Feather?" His voice was deliciously deep and infuriatingly sprightly.

Once I managed to lever myself up, I said, "Muriel's going to think—she's going to think—*ugh* . . ."

The second corner of his mouth ticked up. "What is it she's going to think?" He gently combed back my mad hair. "That I spent the entire night inside of you?"

"Yes. I mean, *no*." I almost wished I could've started smoldering, because I was pretty certain my color rivaled the Demon Court's porte-cochère.

When Jarod chuckled, I rolled onto my back and smacked my forearm over my eyes to make the world disappear since I couldn't make myself vanish. The mattress dipped. I waited for Jarod to move my arm, but it wasn't my arm he touched, and it wasn't his hand that touched me. His hot mouth landed on mine, and my arm stumbled off my face, plopping onto the brassy mane fanned over the pillow.

A moan fell from my lips as his hand glided up my waist, my ribs, and . . . *oh*. I gasped as he palmed one of my breasts, crinkling the washed cotton T-shirt over it. He swallowed the sound, keeping up his steady assault and adding one to my nipple.

The hands trying to lift him off wound around his neck, tangled into his hair, and deepened the kiss. When he settled his lower body between my legs and pressed his thick bulge against my entrance, sanity finally clocked me.

I slid my mouth off his and panted his name into his mussed hair followed by: "We have to stop."

He sighed, and the sound was muffled by my skin. When he vaulted off the bed, cool air slicked over my warmed skin, pebbling it. I missed the weight and heat of him, the mineral and musky scent of him, and yet the reasonable part of my brain, which had shrunk considerably during the night, celebrated having been listened to.

Jarod smiled down at the mess of limbs and scattered heartbeats he'd made of me before extending his hand. I took it, allowing him to pull me up. I bumped into his body, unsteady like a toddler learning to walk.

Splaying his palm on my waist, he tilted his head down. "Do you want to meet Celeste on your own?"

"Celeste?" I was fully awake now. "Celeste's here?"

"That's what Mimi said."

Crap. Crap. Crap. I swirled away from Jarod and rooted around my handbag for my phone. Ten missed calls. All from Celeste. I was the worst friend. I should've called her or sent her a message that I was safe and sound. I pulled out a violet crepe slip and was about to yank off my T-shirt when I remembered Jarod was in the room.

His gaze was riveted to me. "Don't stop on my account."

Skating my fingers through my hair in an attempt to tame the thick mass, I said, "Turn around."

When he didn't, and I'd given him ample time to do so, *I* turned, pulled off my T-shirt and slipped on the dress that coasted like hot oil down my body, stopping mid-calf, then fastened the strip of brown leather I used as a belt. It was only after I was done buckling yesterday's espadrilles that I looked up at Jarod. He hadn't moved, and his eyes had gone serial-killer dark.

I walked over to him and chucked him under the chin, giving him a dose of his own medicine. "I'll see you downstairs." I kissed his scruffy jaw. "Maybe give me a little time alone with Celeste, though, okay?"

His Adam's apple worked in his throat as he offered me a heavy nod. My pleasure at leaving him in such a perplexed state —only fair—faded when I remembered our wake-up call. I hoped Muriel didn't think terrible things of me . . .

Steeling my spine, I went downstairs to find out.

"*Bonjour, ma chérie.* Your friend's in the dining room. I laid out some breakfast." Muriel sounded so cheery that I was both relieved and mystified. "Would you like scrambled eggs? I'm making some for Celeste." She smiled wide, revealing the thin gap between her front teeth that somehow added to her classical beauty.

"Um. Sure." Even though the guard who stood in the check-ered foyer didn't look my way, a blush pricked up my neck. "Thank you," I added, all but diving into the dining room.

Celeste's gaze rushed to me, but she stayed seated, rigid as a breadstick, amber eyes rimmed with circles that rivaled the tint of my dress. "Had a good night? Because mine sucked."

"I'm so sorry, honey. My phone was on silent mode." I took the seat next to hers. "But I told you I was coming here."

"You didn't tell me you'd be sleeping over! This is a freaking mobster's house," she hissed.

"I know."

"Do you?" she said so harshly I bristled.

"He's my sinner; not yours." Even if her heart was in the right place, her words were out of line.

She must've sensed she'd overstepped because her brow pleated. "I started imagining—I was so worried."

I laid my hands over the ones buried atop her narrow lap. "I know, sweetie, but I promise you don't need to be worried. Jarod didn't force me to stay, and he was a perfect gentleman."

Celeste must've trusted me, because her gaze didn't stray to the rug underneath my chair for a fallen feather.

I squeezed her clammy hands. "Thank you for checking up on me, though."

Her big eyes filled with tears, and she lunged toward me, hooking her arms around my neck. "I'm going to miss you so much."

I smiled into her hair. "Just because I stayed over one night doesn't mean I'm moving in with Jarod."

"Oh, Leigh," she sobbed.

"How about we spend the whole day together? And tonight, we can go to that Japanese ramen place in the First you wanted to try."

Sniffling, she pulled away. "You'll be gone before tonight."

"Gone?" I frowned. "Where is it I'm going?"

"Asher revised his score."

My pulse went from zero to a hundred in a second. "What?"

"Asher changed Jarod's score."

Ice. I became ice.

"You're going to ascend today. And I won't see you for—" Her lower lip overtook her upper one and wobbled. "For so many years. Maybe forever at the rate I'm building my wings."

Asher had altered Jarod's sinner score? He'd admitted his wrong and made it right?

Even though a part of me had dared hope for this, had even prepared for this, I had trouble wrapping my mind around it. "Wow. I'm—I—*wow*."

Celeste palmed her shiny freckled cheeks. "You did it, Leigh."

I stared past her at the silken sashes hooked around the heavy drapes, letting in the morning sunshine. Even though the fountain wasn't carved from polished stone, the angel seemed to shine.

"Now you just have to get him to pick you so that you can—so that you can keep changing things."

I blinked away from the statue. "I'm not going anywhere."

Celeste's dimples made an appearance. "You're not going to be able to change the century-year rule until *after* you're married."

"Celeste, I'm not getting married, and I'm not going anywhere."

"But—I—what?"

I slid my lower lip between my teeth, trying to decide how best to explain my self-inflicted predicament. "Last night, I decided I wasn't ready to leave so I . . . so I chose to *lighten* my wings."

Her dimples vanished.

"I made a lot of feathers fall. I'm not certain how many . . . just enough that if Asher changed his mind, I wouldn't be dragged away from Earth. I'm not ready to leave." Jarod's face flashed behind my lids—his crumpled hair, his heavily lashed eyes, and his chiseled body. I shivered as I recalled the gentle strokes of his hand and his not so gentle lips.

Celeste's mouth popped open.

I smiled. "So, you're not losing me today."

She neither closed her mouth nor said a thing.

"Or tomorrow."

As I watched my confession work itself through her, I wondered if Asher had changed Jarod's score because he realized he'd made a mistake or because he'd sensed my growing affection for the sinner and wanted to take me away from him. Then again, *I* hadn't sensed it, so the archangel probably hadn't either. Unless the Ishim had somehow watched me interact with Jarod and told Asher I'd smoldered the sinner. I chose to believe he'd unlocked Jarod's score out of righteousness.

I magicked my wings into existence, curious to see if their

weight had changed. Bringing them out awakened a shallow ache. I stretched them out under Celeste's watchful gaze, casting tinsels all over her dazed face and the heavily upholstered dining room. Their weight hadn't changed so much as their breadth. Even though my new feathers were mere puffs of down, they edged my wings like the softest fur, prolonging their gilded range. In a few days, they'd be fully grown.

I stroked them, pondering what memory of my time with Jarod each one contained. How did the Ishim slip memories into the shafts? Did they sift through my mind and allot memories, or did their well-oiled system attribute memories at random? I suddenly wished I'd asked more questions about the Ishim instead of focusing on the Malakim, whose ranks I'd wanted to join since I was a pintsized Fletching.

The doors of the dining room opened, and Jarod swooped in, hair combed and slicked back, body ensconced in a tapered navy suit and white dress shirt which he wore unbuttoned at the collar. My breath caught. Would it ever stop catching at the sight of him?

Celeste twisted around in her chair, then twisted back toward me as though on a spring. She still didn't say anything, but her jaw stiffened.

"Good morning, Celeste. Hope I'm not interrupting any idle chitchat," Jarod said, and I rolled my eyes. He'd perfected his dull and dominant pitch to such perfection that, had I not tasted the honey beneath all the snark, I might've taken offense.

"And here I was, almost missing you," I said, beaming at him over Celeste's shoulder.

He answered me with a smile that barely dented his smooth flesh but made his eyes glow. "To what do we owe the pleasure of your visit, Celeste?"

Celeste's brows drew together at my grin. "You did it for him? You trashed your wings for *him*?"

"I did it to stay," I said, picking my words carefully.

"To stay *with him*."

"And with you, Celeste. You know how much I like it here."

My words mustn't have reassured her, because she blanched. "You can't fall for a sinner. That's not right."

My grin flattened. I hadn't expected her to pat me on the back and hug Jarod, but I also hadn't expected her disgust. "Tell me, Celeste. Why isn't it right?"

"You're supposed to fix people, not play house with them."

Jarod slid me a look but didn't intervene.

"I don't expect you to understand." I skated my hands off hers. "But I also won't tolerate you criticizing my choices. You're my friend—my only friend—and I value your opinion . . . I value *you*, but you're not allowed to judge me."

"But he's a Triple, Leigh," she said, as though his number automatically made him despicable.

"*Was* a Triple," I fired back.

Jarod's eyebrows jolted, and then his gaze traveled to my wings, to the downy edge of them, before locking back on my face, shock warring with another emotion. I wasn't really sure what the other emotion was. Maybe it was only shock. A lot of it. Even though we'd spoken about the possibility of Asher amending his judgment, we hadn't put much stock in it.

"Asher's going to be furious," Celeste said.

"Why would he be furious? He made a mistake and corrected it," I said.

"Because he fixed it to get you up there!"

"Why am I not surprised?" Jarod's eyes darkened, their shade matching his timbre. "Your kind's incapable of performing a good deed without a vested interest."

"Our kind is your kind too," Celeste snapped.

Jarod leaned forward, placing one forearm on each side of the fine porcelain plate topped with a fan-shaped cloth napkin. "Unless I'm mistaken, I have no wings."

"You have our blood," she said.

"Blood ties us to people; sometimes to the wrong ones. My only affiliation is to the Adler name, to Tristan, and to the woman running my household."

Celeste balked, but I didn't. I couldn't even fault Jarod his disregard for angels. What had they ever done for him besides spoiling his childhood and unjustly stealing his chance at joining our ranks?

"Leigh, I love you like a sister, but staying here is selfish. You might not love Asher, but you know that marrying him—"

"Marrying him?" I sputtered. "Celeste, he might've liked me at some point, but trust me, that point's in the past."

"He winged you!"

"In. The. Past," I replied calmly but firmly.

Jarod's fingers balled into fists, which made me regret explaining angelic courtship.

Celeste shook her head. "You're deluding yourself."

"Doesn't it matter what I want?" My pitch rose. "And what I want is to stay here. I don't want to marry Asher, because I don't like Asher. Not in that way."

Her eyes filled with tears. "So what? You're giving up on this chance of a lifetime—of several lifetimes—for a couple of months with *him*?"

"Months?" Jarod's voice was like a bullet zinging through the growing tension.

I couldn't tell if he was stunned by the idea of having so little time with me or if he calculated our relationship's lifespan in days.

It didn't change that I had no desire to marry Asher.

Besides, I wasn't delaying my trip to Elysium for Jarod. I was delaying it for myself. I wasn't ready to leave. Once I was, I'd only have a handful of feathers to earn, which I could do relatively quickly.

"She has thirteen months left to ascend, after which her wings will fall off her back like chicken meat."

"Celeste!" I admonished her.

"The same way your mother lost her wings . . . unless she'd already ascended. Then the Seraphim would have burned them off her back. The pain of that is apparently so excruciating it drives people to madness."

"My mother went nuts because my father died, and he was the love of her fucking life."

"Your mother went nuts because she lost an essential part of herself, and that part wasn't your father." Celeste crossed her spindly arms. "If you don't believe me, ask Leigh. She knows this as well as I do."

His Adam's apple jostled, and I realized he'd never been told how his mother had lost her wings. Had he thought she'd just unhooked them and handed them back to the archangels like they were nothing more than Halloween props?

I pursed my lips. "What if it's a lie, Celeste? To dissuade us from staying in the mortal realm."

"Fine. Let's say it is—which I don't believe—you'll still lose your immortality. Have you thought about that?"

"I didn't say I would *never* ascend. I said I wasn't ready to leave right now." I kept my eyes on Celeste, but then, curiosity got the better of me, and I darted a glance at Jarod.

Tension raced along his shoulders and neck, sharpened every line on his face, tightened his eyes, which he lowered to the porcelain cup filled with a foamy expresso. He lifted it off its matching saucer and shot the contents back, then yanked the napkin from his plate, and shook it out before slapping it onto his lap. All of his gestures led me to think he was angry, but was it because he no longer considered me an ally in his battle against angels or because he didn't want me to desert him?

"No one's holding her back," he said, eyes locked on the croissant he'd plucked out of the bread basket. He ate it in three bites, guzzled his glass of orange juice, then pushed away from the table. "I have business to attend to."

"Jarod?"

Although it looked painful, he turned toward me. "Yes?"

"I'm not going anywhere."

I waited for the harsh veneer to crack and peel off the man who'd spent the night holding me against him as though afraid I'd use my wings to fly away.

"Don't stay on my account," he said curtly, before stalking out of the dining room.

It wasn't his veneer that cracked but my heart.

I left shortly after Jarod.

I'd drunk my coffee but hadn't managed to eat anything. In a daze, I'd walked out of *La Cour des Démons* with Celeste. We ended up at the Louvre where we took in every exhibit. Besides its triangular-shaped glass dome, nothing about the museum stuck with me, not a single canvas or sculpture. All of it had just smeared into one endless strip of marble and paint.

Even though I sensed Celeste wanted to bring up Jarod's dismissal, she didn't. At least, not until we'd left the famed museum and started meandering through the adjacent gardens.

"Leigh, are you going to sign off from him today? Now that you've accomplished your mission . . ."

I bit the inside of my cheek, my heart feeling as scrambled as the eggs Celeste had eaten for breakfast.

"You can't earn more feathers if you stay signed on," she continued. "Not even if you manage to knock another point off his score."

Two ducks pecked each other on the octagonal pond but not out of love. Out of dominance. As one of them took flight, trailing glittery drops of water, I thought of my wings, how if I hadn't ruined them, I would've also taken flight. A chill enveloped me even though it was in no way cold.

"It's not too late," Celeste said.

I clutched my elbows, slowly rubbing the goose bumps away. "Too late?"

"To earn your wings before Asher's engagement period is over."

The Tuileries Gardens turned gray and flat. "Just because Jarod doesn't care if I stay or leave doesn't change the fact that I don't want to marry Asher. If I'm going to spend an eternity with someone, I want it to be with a person who makes my heart soar."

"S-O-A-R or S-O-R-E? If it's the latter, you have two contenders all lined up."

I side-eyed her.

"Crack a smile. Even a tiny one. I don't like grumpy Leigh."

I offered her a diminutive smile that stuck for all of a second. Then Jarod's parting words came barreling right through my brain again like a subway train. I sensed he'd spoken them out of anger, but even if that was the case, they'd hurt. He was a grown man, and grown men shouldn't conceal their wounded pride behind barbs. It was petty. He was better than that.

Celeste sighed. "What happened with Jarod yesterday? How come you ended up staying the night?"

I closed my eyes. She was only fifteen, and even though she was mature, I wouldn't corrupt her young ears with all I'd done. Besides, it was private. Last night belonged to Jarod and me. "I hadn't planned on staying, but when I got there, Muriel insisted on teaching me how to make shortbread, and, well"—I shrugged—"I couldn't say no. And it was fun. And then Jarod arrived, and I gave him back his money, but then, he suggested a game of chess, and one game turned into two, and before I knew it, it was night." I raked my hand through my hair, realizing I hadn't even brushed it when I'd gone upstairs to get my bag. "He invited me out to dinner, and it was really nice." My voice faltered. It took me a couple of breaths to steady it again. "Since it was late, he offered me his guest bedroom." The sun pricked my eyes.

"Are you in love with him?"

I jerked my gaze back to her. "I've known him all of four days." An intense four days, but still . . .

"But you like him?"

"Yes."

"So, what happens now?"

"I don't know, Celeste. I don't know what to do."

She slid her hands into her skinny jeans' pockets, her oversized blue plaid shirt flapping like a piece of tarp.

"What should I do?"

"Don't ask my advice, Leigh." Her attention was on the dust billowing around her black combat boots, which she wore come rain or shine, winter and summer alike. "Because I'm biased."

I nodded, then went right back to brooding silently as I followed Celeste out of the park, across the river, and all the way back to the guild. Even though I wanted to lose myself in the maze of twisted streets for a few more hours, I entered our celestial sanctum.

The air was alive with the twittered arias of the rainbow-winged sparrows perched on the quartz fountains and the tinkle of feminine voices. Three Fletchings were moving on the other side of the Atrium, laughing about something one of them had said. How I envied their carefree manner.

Their laughter faded, replaced by a series of rapid-fire whispers, "C'est elle, non?" "Je n'arrive pas à croire qu'elle a réussi." "Incroyable." It's her? I can't believe she succeeded. Incredible.

They were talking about me.

About my startling exploit.

News traveled fast.

One of the girls—the blue-eyed, pixie-haired blonde I remembered from the Ranking Room the night after my disastrous dinner with Jarod—looked straight at me. "How did you do it?"

Respectful of the archangel who surely didn't want the news of a wrongful score traveling the halls of the guild, I said, "I didn't give up."

Celeste glanced at me, then back at the girls, who seemed to be waiting for me to add something more.

When I didn't, the blue-eyed girl said, "Your friend Eve was looking for you. I think she's in the cafeteria."

The scent of the heavy pink blooms blanketing the quartz walls became stifling.

Eve was *here*? I gaped at Celeste, wondering if she'd known, but her eyes were as wide as my own.

For several heartbeats, I barely moved. Only my fingers twitched, creasing the hammered purple silk fabric of my dress.

There were only two reasons Eve would have come—either she'd completed her wings and had traveled to Paris to say goodbye like she'd promised or she'd heard I'd earned a hundred feathers and had come to . . . *what*? Congratulate me? Check that I hadn't cheated?

Whatever her reasons for using the Channel for a visit, I realized I didn't want to see her. I was afraid of what I might say to her. Sure, her plan had backfired, and I'd won, but what was it I'd won?

Awareness that angels weren't virtuous, me included?

Doubt as to whether I wanted to spend an eternity in Elysium or a single lifetime on Earth?

Lucidity that I couldn't marry a man for status?

A broken heart, because I cared too deeply for an emotional cripple?

I started to back out of the Atrium, suffocating on the smell of petals, when my name echoed against every single slab of translucent quartz. Jaw clenched, I looked over my shoulder at the girl with the heavy black hair and sharp hazel gaze who'd been the bearing wall of my childhood. Where had she been when my house crumbled? When I was left in the rubble?

"Congratulations," she said. "I just heard the news."

I searched for a glint of genuine happiness but found only uncertainty. Which was new for Eve.

"I trusted you," I said tonelessly. "And you played me for a fool, Eve."

"The engagement was my dream, Leigh, not yours."

I bottled up my desire to shout, because we had an audience, and they weren't aware of the finer details of my mission. "And what? That was reason enough to throw away fifteen years of friendship?"

Eve's lashes flapped like the wings of the sparrow swooping around one of the statues.

"You could've talked to me," I said. "We could've discussed it. You didn't have to—to set me up to fail."

"But you didn't fail. You *never* fail."

Celeste wrapped a hand around my forearm as though to remind me I wasn't alone. "You really have no shame."

"Stay out of it, winglet," Eve barked.

"Don't speak to Celeste like that," I answered so sharply that Eve's entire body jerked.

"Piece of cherub dung," Celeste muttered under her breath, just loud enough for Eve to hear.

Scowling, Eve knotted her arms in front of her body. "Have the Ishim taken pity on you, or do you have no more feathers to lose?"

"Don't be a bitch, Eve! Celeste's never done anything to deserve—" The pinch to my wing bones reawakened their soreness.

As a feather fell from my invisible wings, the Atrium was plunged in the deepest of silences. Even the fountains seemed to have stopped gurgling and the sparrows to have stopped singing.

"How—I thought you'd earned a hundred feathers?" Eve sputtered.

I scrutinized the glittery feather. "I did."

"But then . . . *how*?"

Whispers erupted among our audience.

"Being around Jarod cost me many." I didn't add that most had been molted by choice. It was none of her business. None of anyone's business. "Aren't you happy? I won't be entering Elysium before you after all."

She wet her lips. "How many do you have left to earn?"

"Why? You have another sinner to suggest?" My sarcasm made her flinch.

"I'm sorry, okay?" she mumbled.

And it struck me then that I wasn't sorry. "*I'm* not." I stared around the courtyard, first at the Fletchings amassed in the corners of the grand Atrium, then at Celeste whose forehead was scrunched in worry, then at the bright dome of elysian sky before returning my sun-stung gaze to Eve. "This mission has taught me so much. Has brought me so much."

The awe and tenderness that had softened Jarod's face last night and again this morning filled me with a single certainty—I wouldn't leave Earth or sign off from him until he and I had a little chat.

I peeled Celeste's fingers off my arm. "I need to go."

"Leigh—" I thought Celeste was about to tell me it was a bad idea, but instead, she said, "Be safe."

I sent her a quick smile.

"And call or message me this time. Please!"

I nodded as I exited the guild, leaving behind a whole bunch of little fires I hoped the Ophanim would manage to douse before the smoke reached Elysium and brought down the wrath of the Seven.

As though I'd downed an electrical charge, all of my muscles zinged as I raced down the stairs of the subway station and through the maze of tunnels. The train doors opened just as I reached the platform.

The carriage smelled rank, but it didn't prevent me from inhaling great big gulps of air to slow my careening heart. A bead of sweat slid between my shoulder blades and made me shiver even though I was flushed from the heat of my run. As the train rattled in the city's underbelly, I thought of Eve, of what seeing her had made me feel, and realized that my anger had turned entirely to disappointment, in her and in myself.

I was done being a feckless doormat, and ironically, it was all thanks to the girl who'd treated me like one.

42

*W*hen the blood-red doors opened, my chest flamed with anticipation.

I stepped over the raised threshold, smacking right into a body.

"Whoa there." The cigarette Tristan must've just taken out of a pack toppled from his fingers and rolled against my espadrilles.

"S-sorry." I crouched to pick it up. As I handed it over, I couldn't help but search his nails for the blood from the torture session he'd boasted about last night.

"He's not here, Feather."

My nickname made my attention snap back to his face. "Where is he?"

"At the spa." Tristan tapped the cigarette against his palm.

"The spa?"

"You know, that place people go to in order to relax?"

For some reason, I couldn't picture Jarod at a spa.

"I was just heading out to see him. Want to hitch a ride?"

"He won't mind?"

Tristan lit up and sucked on his cigarette before blowing the smoke out of the corner of his mouth. "Nah." He tipped his head toward Jarod's chauffeured car, which idled behind me. After opening the door for me, he slapped it shut, then went around the car and got in. Cranking his window down, he asked, "Did I ever tell you the story of how Jarod and I became friends?"

I set my bag at my feet and crossed my legs, smoothing the material of my dress. "No, you didn't."

"I met him at the playground. I was ten and waiting on a park bench for my mother to finish blowing one of her customers in the building across the street."

My hands froze on the violet crepe, and I gasped.

"I got bored, so I went into the playground. *Maman* would always spend the money she made whoring herself on booze, so I'd learned to make my own way. Playgrounds were great hunting grounds for cash and food, what with mothers and nannies so distracted by their kids. Plus I was small for ten, so I didn't attract suspicion.

"Muriel was there. I didn't know who she was then, of course. Just saw that she wore a very shiny watch with lots of diamonds. I thought she was Jarod's mom, 'cause nannies didn't own Cartier watches. I debated whether to steal it from her. I was getting pretty good at pickpocketing at that point. I was going to go for it when I saw that the kid she was watching like a hawk wore an equally blingy timepiece. Even though I doubted such a young boy would sport something of value, I approached him to check. Lo and behold, it was an Audemars-Piguet."

I wasn't sure what that was but imagined it was expensive.

"So, I hung around and befriended him, and he seemed plenty happy for the company. Anyway, I filched the watch. He didn't notice a thing; Muriel didn't either, and she was right *there*." He sucked on his cigarette, then flicked it out of the moving car. "I should've left then. Actually, I tried, but the little twerp begged me to play one more game, and I didn't have the heart to turn him down. During that last game, the watch slipped and fell into the sand, right at Muriel's feet."

He smiled.

"You should've seen her face. She went purple and lobbed words at me I'd never even heard, and I had a very *flowery* vocabulary. Of course, it called attention to us, and soon we had an audience. Jarod's bodyguard—Amir—and a cop even joined the fray. I thought for sure my days as a street urchin were over, that I'd be sent into juvie or placed in the system."

He powered his window up.

"Jarod handed the fucking watch to me. I thought he was trying to frame me, not that I needed framing . . . I was the biggest attraction outside of the Mona Lisa that day. The cop started to move toward me when Jarod said, '*He didn't steal it; I gave it to him.*'" Tristan's smile increased. "When Muriel asked him why, he said I looked hungry." He shook his head, letting out a short snort.

"Did you take the watch?"

"Of course I took it. I *was* hungry. And I needed clothes that weren't two sizes too small and shoes in which my toes could lay flat."

"So, how did you become friends?"

"He saved my ass that day, so I came back and saved his, first from boredom, and then from one of his uncle's dealings that had gone wrong."

The sedan glided to a stop and the locks retracted.

"You can leave your bag in the car." He hopped out, then came around to my side. As he opened my door, he said, "Can I give you a word of advice?"

Scooting out, I nodded tentatively.

"Don't get attached. Leeches don't encounter a pleasant fate in *La Cour des Démons*."

Shock sank into my veins. "Are you calling me a leech?"

"Are women anything else? You suck our money, our energy, and, if we're lucky, our cocks." He slammed the door shut, and the sound made me jump.

Seventy-eight . . . His number, which had probably increased since Layla's, swam across his tanned face and glacial blue eyes. Suddenly, I could picture him injuring one of my peers.

"You had a bad example, I get that. But it doesn't give you the right to badmouth me or my gender."

"I'm just telling it like it is, Feather."

"Stop calling me that!"

"Doesn't bother you when Jarod says it."

"You're not Jarod." *You're the watch thief who got off scot-free and just called me a leech.*

He cranked up his chin. "I think I misjudged you."

My heart thumped. Was he going to apologize? Not that his

apology would erase his insult. I waited, but all he did was flash me another grin before gesturing toward a set of porte-cochère decorated with metal grommets.

I trailed him inside a courtyard that smelled of burning oil and orange blossom, toward outsized white lattice doors. Sitar music echoed off the sapphire tiles that lined every wall in the spa's entryway.

A woman dressed in a midriff-baring gauzy outfit greeted Tristan with a kiss on both cheeks. "You're a little late . . ."

Did he have an appointment too?

The woman's gaze slid over to me. Was she going to ask me if I wanted a massage? Even though I'd had some in the past, having accompanied my spa-addicted ex-best friend repeatedly back in New York, I was in absolutely no mood to relax at that moment. At least, not until I spoke with Jarod.

Bodies moved in the shadows. I knew Jarod had bodyguards, but I couldn't get used to their constant presence. Without meaning to, I backed into Tristan, who snuck out his arm and laced it around my waist.

"Don't worry about them," he said.

He was right. The person I needed to worry about was him.

As I extricated myself from his grip, I wondered if Jarod was aware of his friend's shady depths. Probably not if he kept him around . . .

I understood then, that to truly save Jarod's soul, he would need to disentangle himself from Tristan and the toxic adoration his second vowed him. Unless I could help Tristan become a better man.

The glow of colored glass lanterns tinted his silvering hair pink and green and cast squares of light into the eyes he'd trained on me. Not enough, though, to read his mind.

43

*T*he dim hallway was lined with thick candles dripping wax over the sapphire tiles and casting dancing shadows across the walls.

When we arrived in front of a door crafted from pure bronze, I finally spoke up. "You should give women another chance, Tristan. They're not all nefarious."

He grunted.

"If you open your heart—"

"Then I give someone the power to destroy it. I'm touched by your concern, but not the least bit interested." I was about to protest when he added, "Jarod and I, we like our lives just the way they are." He raised his fist and rasped on the metal, and the clangor reverberated inside my chest. "I hope you understand what I'm saying."

We were greeted by a man with the smoothest head and the densest beard.

"A latecomer," Tristan told the guard blocking the doorway.

I'd been expecting silence and more relaxing string music. Instead, the cavernous space beyond the guard resonated with tinkling laughter, gruff tones, and splashing water.

Baldy gave me a once-over before stepping to the side and revealing a sight I wished to forget immediately.

Two naked women lounged next to a luminescent rectangular

pool, their skin glistening with oil. Another one gyrated, half-submerged in the pool, over the lap of a middle-aged man. Dragging the girl's wet hair back, he canted his round head to the side to catch a clearer glimpse of me.

"You spoil me, Jarod," he said.

Jarod, whose spine—or what I could see of it rising over the mosaic basin's edge—was marred by a red scar I'd missed last night.

"Excuse me?" Jarod's low timbre made goose bumps sprout all over me.

The girl in the pool stood and inched seductively toward Jarod, water sloshing around her submerged waist.

Horror struck my veins. "I-I shouldn't be here."

"Nonsense, *Feather*." Tristan's ashen breath was low and sultry in my ear. "The prime minister's a huge fan of redheads. Your presence will give us some extra sway."

I sucked in some air that hissed through my gritted molars. "I'm not a—"

"Tristan, why is the girl still clothed?" the politician asked.

Because I hadn't come for the freaking orgy! I'd come for the man throwing it. What was it with Jarod and orgies anyway? Was this some kink of *his* or a French bartering tool?

Jarod turned around then, and although I was glad his eyes were no longer on the naked woman massaging her nipples, they were filled with so much fury that sweat dotted my brow. "What the—Tristan, get her out of here, now!"

"*Non, non.* Bring her closer," the minister said.

Wisely, Tristan didn't press me any closer. I would've broken his arm and each one of his fingers had he set a single one on me.

"Such a divine hair color. Is it real? Actually, don't tell me. I'd love to uncover this on my own," the politician added with a smile that made his already round cheeks puff up some more.

Jarod's jaw hardened. Voice clattering against the perspiring tiles, he barked, "This one hasn't been vetted for venereal diseases yet. She shouldn't even be in here."

The thick man tittered. "You know I like to live dangerously. Come closer, *ma petite.*"

"Tristan!" Jarod growled.

Tristan grabbed my arm. I tried to shake him off, perfectly

capable of getting my own self out of this damn spa, but his grip hardened, denting my flesh.

The bearded bodyguard was obviously not on Jarod's payroll, because he blocked our exit.

"With all due respect, Jarod," the minister said, "I'm perfectly capable of making informed decisions when it comes to my sexual health."

"With all due respect," Jarod gritted out, "the girl's not on the menu today."

The minister finally turned his deep-set eyes on Jarod. "If I didn't know any better, I'd venture she's not on *my* menu, but perhaps, on yours? Which is all the more intriguing. You usually have no problem sharing *les bons coups*."

I gulped, because that last expression could mean one of two things: profitable business ventures or good lays.

"If you want my help eliminating your *problem*, tell your fucking guard to step away from the fucking door."

"*Hmm*." The man stroked his weak chin. "I won't touch her, but I'd really like a better look before she leaves."

Jarod climbed out of the pool in one fell swoop, not a stitch of clothing on his body. As he pounded toward us, panic seized my chest.

"What the fuck got into you to bring her here?" he growled, several degrees past anger.

Tristan stood his ground calmly. "She wanted to talk to you. Said it was urgent."

Jarod skewered Tristan with his black gaze before setting it on me.

"Get me my clothes," he barked.

I scanned the room for them.

"Not *you*," he said, his voice low but in no way calm.

Tristan unhanded me and moved away, then tossed Jarod a small white towel to sop up the water ribboning down his arms and legs, matting the dark hairs to his taut skin.

"Leaving already, Monsieur Adler?" the minister asked.

Without turning, Jarod said, "We're done here. I'll let you discuss the finer points with Tristan."

He tossed the towel aside, then took the clothes Tristan

tendered, yanking on each item with a ferocity that belied the extent of anger brewing beneath that steady, fearsome body of his.

As he belted his pants, he shot his gaze to the bearded guard and hissed, "Out of my fucking way, or I'll have your pregnant girlfriend stop by your wife's Zumba class and introduce herself."

Anger and fear made the bodyguard's bald head sweat. Without consulting his boss, he unbolted the door.

"Go!" Jarod's order set me in motion.

I marched down the blue-tiled hallway, heart banging in time with Jarod's footfalls.

The scantily clad woman, who'd greeted us, scurried out from behind her welcome desk. "Is everything okay, Monsieur Adler?"

Even though it wasn't her fault, he glared at her, which made her shrink back. Without answering, he stepped past the lattice doors and into the courtyard, matching my rapid strides.

He didn't speak a word to me the entire way back to his house. Barely even glanced my way. Not wanting to make a scene in front of his driver, I didn't say anything, but my own anger rose steadily as the car bumped over the cobbled street of the graying city.

44

*W*hen we got back to his house, Jarod ordered me into his bedroom, and even though I wanted to tell him that intruding on his meeting hadn't been my idea, I sealed my lips and climbed his stairs.

The sound of his voice must've alerted Muriel he was home, because she popped out of the pantry. When she caught sight of me, she blinked. I cut my eyes to the bedroom door and shoved it wide.

Jarod marched in behind me, then slammed the door shut. "What the fuck, Leigh?"

"I thought you were getting a massage!" I growled right back.

"Did my line of work slip your mind?" He plowed his hands through his damp locks. "The prime minister is a wormy sleazebag. Want to know what his last assignment was? Make his mistress vanish after he strangled her to death!"

A gasp burst out of me. I didn't ask whether he'd made the corpse disappear. I doubted he'd have had a second meeting with the man if he'd failed that first job. I also didn't ask why he was still conducting business with a murderer, because his line of business *hadn't* slipped my mind.

"Those are the types of people I deal with, and you just walk in like I'm at a fucking tea party! Fuck!" Jarod's voice clanged over the panes of glass that glowed cerulean from the dwindling daylight.

"I'm sorry, but Tristan told me you were at a spa. He didn't mention anything about a business meeting."

Jarod halted his mad pacing, but his wild pulse kept gorging the artery in his neck. "It doesn't make any fucking sense. Why would he do that?" Even though I wished he'd trusted my word, he scanned the air around my hips for a tumbling feather.

My annoyance turned to disappointment. "Probably so I would catch you with another woman and leave once and for all."

Jarod's lashes hit his browbone. I locked my hands at my sides and squashed my lips together before I shared Tristan's warning, the one about leeches. I was afraid it would be the drop that made Jarod's anger boil over, but not at his friend.

At *me*.

After several long minutes, he exhaled wearily, the fight draining from him. "Why did you come back, Feather?"

His broken tone pitched away my disappointment and fear. "Did you really think I'd leave?" I hated how accustomed he was to being abandoned.

"I hoped you would. This world—*my* world—it's not for you."

"How about you let me decide where I want to go." I walked over to him. "Where I want to *be*."

His features contorted. "You didn't tell me you'd lose your wings if you didn't complete them."

I laid my hand on his bristly jaw, and he shuddered.

The scene at the spa played out again in my mind, making my wings feel of little importance. "Were you . . . were you with one of the women this afternoon?"

His eyebrows shot up, vanishing behind his tumble of unruly locks. "Of course not."

"I thought—"

"That I fornicated with women in front of clients? I get paid to fix problems, not to screw around."

"You were naked."

His lips relaxed a fraction. "The prime minister—like many people I deal with—are concerned about wires, and I'm concerned about concealed weapons. Conducting business in our birthday suits is a win-win." I must've wrinkled my nose, because he added, "Didn't like my full frontal, Feather?"

"I was a tad too stressed out by your murderous glare to concentrate on much else."

"*Murderous glare.*" He snorted. "Wasn't you I wanted to murder; it was everyone else." He leaned his forehead against mine. "I don't like that the prime minister saw you. That any of them saw you. That bodyguard of his is a real asshole."

"Thank Elysium, I'm immortal."

He straightened his neck, putting space between our heads. "I thought . . ."

"As long as I have wings, I can bleed, but I can't die, so you have nothing to worry about."

He looked at my shoulders even though my wings weren't on display. "One more reason you need to complete them."

I slid my hand down to his neck, capturing his heartbeats in my palm. "Let that be my choice, Jarod."

"Fuck, you're stubborn." He sighed.

"And it paid off." I looked into his obsidian eyes. "You're no longer a Triple."

"So, my soul isn't doomed after all . . ."

"As long as you keep on doing good deeds, but you need to get your rank under fifty."

"Why?"

I snagged my lip and slid it between my teeth. "Anything above a fifty, and you end up in Abaddon."

"Hell?"

"Yeah."

"It really exists?"

I nodded. "But there's no devil. It's run by Erelim—celestial sentinels. They also run Elysium. My parents are both Erelim in Abaddon. I think."

Something gleamed on his shelf. When I realized it was the letter opener, a chill fluttered over my skin. Was it the same one that had stopped his mother's heart? And if it was, why did he keep it?

"I'm imagining it's not all licentious raves and lava-filled Jacuzzis down there."

"No." I licked my lips. "It's like a prison . . . except the cells are magicked to make you relive your worst nightmares over and over."

"My version sounded way more fun."

"If you stop trying to push me away, I can help get your score down."

"If I keep you close, Feather"—he linked his arms behind my waist—"my score's not going to go down, because I'll be dismembering anyone who so much as looks in your direction. Not to mention all the sinful things I'll be doing to your body." The reverberation of his voice combined with his words made me shiver.

"The dismembering part is unnecessary since I'm immortal," I said a little breezily.

"I'm glad you have no objections to my second point."

I swallowed. "Might cost me feathers."

"Also, might not." His thumbs stroked the base of my spine. "We'll have to test it out."

My breath caught on its way in, which made my lungs convulse, which in turn made me wheeze and hack like the time I choked on a mangosteen pit and Eve went pro wrestler on my chest. I slid my hand off his face and thwacked my chest until my coughing quieted.

How I wished I could thwack Eve's face out of my mind the same way . . .

I'd spent years with her, so I supposed it would take years for her not to surface before everyone else.

Jarod traced the downward bow of my mouth, picking up on my suddenly somber mood. "Am I scaring you?"

I shook my head. "It's not you. I just had a visitor today, and seeing her didn't make me very happy." I tried to smile, but my lips were so tense it probably looked like I was sucking on sour candy. "Her visit even cost me a feather."

"Why?"

I didn't want to talk about Eve, but I also didn't want her hanging over Jarod and me like a dark cloud. So, I told him how she'd dropped by the guild to congratulate me on reforming him, and I told him I'd called her something not very nice because she'd insulted Celeste's wings, which led me to tell him how worried I was that Celeste was missing so many feathers.

"My little fixer." He stamped a long kiss on my forehead.

"I try, but I can't fix everything."

Against my brow, he said, "I have an idea. Celeste should sign on to me. I'll find something nice to do, so she can fluff up her little wings."

My eyes slicked with tears. I wanted to say yes and cover his face with kisses for having suggested it, but signing off from him would make my residential status even more precarious. If I couldn't find a low-ranking sinner in Paris, I'd have to leave. And if I didn't sign on to anyone else and inadvertently helped someone out, I'd win one feather for every kind act.

Jarod slid his index fingers along my lower lash line. "What is it, Feather?"

I explained the complexity of my situation.

"Then you're not signing off from me." He kissed my eyelid, then the other. "But that doesn't mean we can't help Celeste. How about she signs on to Tristan? I bet he's worth his weight in feathers."

The suggestion locked up my bones. I didn't want Celeste anywhere near Tristan. "I—um. Once she's done with her current mission, we can explore that possibility."

Jarod frowned. "I'll keep him in line, if that's what you're worried about. I'm already planning on giving him a good tongue-lashing when he gets back from the meeting."

"You realize it'll just make him hate me more, right?"

"Leigh, he doesn't hate you. He just feels threatened. A woman other than Muriel sticking around is new to him. New to me, too."

"So, you do want me to stick around?"

He bumped my nose with his. "I was trying to do the selfless thing, which is completely out of character for me, so it might've come out a tad harshly."

If I'd learned anything in the past few days, it was that Jarod Adler didn't possess a selfish bone in his entire body.

"If I was a better man, I'd call Asher and make him take you away from me. And keep you away."

"Don't you dare," I whispered harshly, winding my fingers through his damp locks and capturing his lips before he could spout any more ghastly ideas.

His warm skin smelled of eucalyptus and orange blossom, and it reminded me of where he'd been, which intensified the storm raging through me. I wanted to replace every trace of that pool and of those other bodies with my scent.

"What am I going to do with you?" His raucous voice thrummed my already fierce pulse.

"*Not* push me away."

"Fine." Foreheads still touching, he backed me up, and up, until the backs of my knees hit the edge of his canopy bed.

I sank onto the mattress.

"Lay down, Feather."

Although the good girl in me, the one who'd grown up abiding to the Ophanim's strict teachings, became a little flustered, the other girl, the one who'd devoured romance novels like sweets, complied. I scooted farther back before uncoiling my spine.

He watched me, and my already sensitive nerves jangled. In slow motion, he climbed my body, then slid the thin straps of my dress off my shoulders. He lowered his mouth to my neck and scorched kisses over my collarbone, shoving the silky fabric aside until my breasts met cool air, then put a little distance between our bodies to take in my exposed flesh.

"I would ask if all angels are as beautiful as you are, but I've seen them, and fuck if any hold a single feather to you."

I started to roll my eyes when he swirled his tongue around one of my nipples. My back arched from the jolt of pleasure, and I gasped, "Jarod."

Supporting his weight on his forearms, he dragged his mouth to my other breast and laved the pebbling peak.

Surely, a feather would fall.

Maybe, one did.

It wasn't as though I could feel anything over the intense waves of pleasure coursing through me. He tracked kisses down the seam of my ribs, growling when he encountered resistance. Rising to his knees, he attempted to take off my belt, but his hurried fingers grappled clumsily. I pushed his impatient hands away and accomplished what he couldn't. The instant the leather unraveled, Jarod hauled it off my waist. Instead of tossing it to the ground, he ran it between his fingers.

His dark eyes flashed with a look that made my skin pebble over completely. "Do you trust me, Feather?"

I nodded.

He took one of my wrists and wound the leather around it, then picked up my other wrist, and proceeded to do the same before pulling the cord taut. I watched him attach it to one of his bed posts before tying a pretty knot, the end of which he placed in my mouth.

"One tug, and it'll loosen." His husky voice made me swallow. He dragged his fingers down my body, curling them into the material pooled around my waist. He eased my violet dress down my legs, his buffed nails caressing the tops of my thighs.

Only a scrap of lace remained on my body, and from the way he was eyeing it, I suspected it wouldn't stay there long.

But I was wrong.

He didn't take it off, simply grazed his knuckles over the material. My blood jammed in my veins as he repeated the maddening stroke.

His gaze sharpened on the lace. He hooked one finger underneath the damp material and pressed it off me. For an interminable moment, he studied my bared body, and panic flared inside my chest.

But then, his fingers started moving over me, and his head lowered to the apex of my thighs, and my insecurities dissolved like grains of sugar in scalding water. The first flick of his tongue had my hips bucking and my skin lighting up.

He scooted his tall body down the bed, getting comfortable, then draped my legs over his shoulders, nudged the lace to the side, and pressed a soft kiss to my glittering core.

I spit out the leather cord so I could catch my breath. But that didn't help. As I choked on air, my spine arched again, and the leather ties bit into the flesh of my wrists.

Sweet cherubs . . . The Seven wouldn't wait for my wings to fall off; they were going to cleave them straight off my back.

Jarod's technique turned rougher. Groaning, he plundered what few shreds of innocence I was still clinging to, sawing them with each lash of his skilled tongue.

"Jarod!" I gasped, as I teetered on the edge of oblivion.

He slowed, swirling his tongue over me, and looked up, my skin's light filling his eyes. "Yeah, Feather?"

I picked my head off the bed and must've shot him one heck of a glower, because he chuckled, and the sound almost knocked me over the edge, but it didn't.

He hummed against me, and a violent desire to smack him seized me. This was torture, and he knew it. And he was enjoying it.

"You're evil," I mumbled.

"I've been telling you that all along."

I shut my eyes, the thrilling sensations cruelly crumbling away. I almost cried out of frustration but shut up when he resumed drawing lazy circles that turned smaller and tighter until they only targeted one tiny knob.

My orgasm exploded through me, wrenching my lids and lips wide open. I'm not sure if I screamed or only gasped, but if I had only gasped, it was surely the loudest gasp in the history of gasps. So loud it probably pierced the divide between the worlds and filled every Ishim's ears.

After the intense pleasure dwindled, and Jarod had rested the lace back against my no longer shiny core, reality and sanity knocked into me. "How many feathers did I lose?"

Eyebrows knitted, Jarod lifted his head and scanned the rumpled bedsheets, then levered my spine off the mattress and ran one of his hands underneath me.

The crease on his forehead smoothed, and then his glistening mouth curved with a heartstopping smile. "None."

$\mathcal{M}$y cage had stretched a little wider tonight.

That was the thought that filled my mind as Jarod loosened the ties around my wrists.

The gloating camber of his mouth and the devilish gleam in his eyes told me *his* mind was running on a much dirtier bandwidth. "Hope you enjoyed that as much as I did, because I'll be subjecting your sweet body to regular encores." He licked his mouth, and the pulsing between my legs soared.

Blood prickled my fingertips as it flooded back into my hands, and then it prickled my cheeks even though no leather cord had been wound around my throat.

Before I could speak, he leaned over and kissed me, and I froze as the taste of my pleasure hit my tongue. My surprise didn't put a damper on his mouth's grinding, and after a while, I got used to my taste and opened up for him.

I curled my arms around his back, then freed his shirt and glided my fingers beneath it, freezing when I encountered the raised outline of his scar. I popped my hands off his skin and my mouth off his lips. "Did I hurt you?"

"Hurt me?" He sounded hoarse, as though it was his vocal cords that were in pain.

"The cut on your back."

"The only thing hurting at the moment is located *much . . .*" He lowered his hovering body and pressed his hard length against the inside of my thigh. "Farther south."

Smiling sultrily, or at least, that was the look I was going for, I raised an eyebrow. "Then why are you still clothed?"

"Because if I get naked, you can forget about your first time being romantic."

All of my senses sharpened. "Maybe you can make my second time romantic."

He turned to stone. Even his chest stopped moving as though my offer had squeezed all the air out of his lungs. I wrapped my legs around his, pinning his lower body to mine.

The planes of his face tensed and twitched, and so did another part of him.

"Honey, I'm home!" The deep voice that erupted through the thick walls of Jarod's home shattered the moment.

I whipped my neck toward the bedroom door, panicked Tristan was about to barrel inside. Thankfully, the handle stayed immobile.

Expelling a rough sigh, Jarod buried his nose in the crook of my neck. "I'm very tempted to tell him to fuck off, but he and I have much to discuss." He kissed me before climbing off my body, then yanked on his bedsheets and draped them over me. As he readjusted himself, he added, "Don't think for a second I'll be forgetting about that offer." He shoved his rumpled white shirt into his pants.

I scooted onto a forearm. "I should probably go back to the guild. I need some fresh clothes."

He halted mid-tuck. "I don't want you going back there."

"It's where I live, Jarod."

"How are you supposed to keep me from murdering people if you leave?" His shirt was still half-out.

"Are you blackmailing me into staying?"

"Maybe."

"You have no shame," I murmured lightly.

"None whatsoever." He thrust the remaining piece of fitted cotton into his pants, then leaned over, pressing his fists into the mattress. "Say yes."

"What if I say no?"

"I'll tie you to my bed again."

"Not much of a threat."

He smiled wickedly.

I gnawed on my lip. "Are you certain you want me here?"

"Never been more certain of anything."

I stared around me at the vast space covered in dark wood paneling, antique books, and priceless oil paintings. When my gaze landed on the recliner, I asked, "Why did you keep the chair?" *And the letter opener?* But I didn't add that part.

All the playfulness bled out of him. "As a reminder to never give up, however fucking hard life gets."

"Jarod!" Tristan's voice seemed to have gotten closer.

Jarod pressed off the bed and strode to the door.

Before he left, I said, "I'll need to go back to the guild at some point. To get some clothes."

He looked over his shoulder. "I'll have Muriel bring you some. And tomorrow, she'll take you to Avenue Montaigne, and you can buy the whole fucking street."

I sat, tucking the sheet around my torso. "This might come as a surprise, but we're pretty tightly budgeted, so Avenue Montaigne might be a little out of my price range."

He flashed me a smile. "You're cute, Feather."

I frowned.

"Your budget's unlimited from now on."

"Jarod, I can't—"

"Consider it payment for saving my soul. Plus, you'll need some outfits for the coming week. I have to go to the opera, and I'd much rather take you than Tristan."

My mouth parted to protest again, but by the time I got my throat to work, he was gone. "That's not how it works," I mumbled.

I fell back against the fluffy comforter. My beloved romance novels were full of scenarios like this one, but they were fictional. That this sort of thing could really happen, and to me, of all people, was so preposterously farfetched that I didn't have the slightest clue how to cope with it. I could turn Jarod down by insisting it would cost me feathers, but if I lost a feather telling him this, he'd handcuff me to Muriel and make her drag me down the opulent avenue.

I pushed the shopping issue aside. I'd revisit it later when I was done examining the issue at hand—me, naked, save for a scrap of wet lace, in Jarod's bed. Had I really propositioned him before Tristan arrived? Maybe Celeste had been right to worry about me even though her worrying was misplaced. It wasn't my safety she should've been concerned about, but my sensibleness.

Sex. The act we grew up cautioned against. Here I was offering myself to a man who, although not a stranger, wasn't a boyfriend.

My body thrummed as it rekindled the softness of his tongue and the firmness of his fingers and the sweetness of his words. Running my hand idly over the silky sheets, I realized that the only regret I felt was that he'd left.

"Leigh, can I come in?" Muriel's voice had me sitting up so fast the dusky space swam and blurred.

"One sec!" I yelled, scrabbling to locate my dress. I yanked it on, then straightened the sheets at warp speed. "Come in," I blustered.

She bustled inside carrying hangers dripping with sequins, leather, satin, and lace. Their narrow shapes told me they'd all be snug, but at least, their colors were all muted. "Jarod told me to bring up some clothes. Unfortunately, we mostly have dresses. I don't think you're going to like them very much."

I thought of the outfit balled up inside my bag. It was probably too wrinkled to wear tonight. "Thank you."

She smiled. "I heard we're going shopping tomorrow."

My ears felt like they'd just come out of the oven.

"I'm hoping this means you'll be staying."

I studied the starburst pattern of sequins on one of the dresses she'd laid out on the foot of the bed. It mirrored the explosions detonating everywhere inside my body. "Uh . . ." Anxiety apparently made me devolve into a primitive, non-verbose version of my species.

Her eyes crinkled with the same smile bending her rouged lips. "I need to get back to the kitchen. I'm making soufflés tonight. I even prepared a special sweet one for you. I hope you'll like it."

Talk of food loosened my tongue. "Considering I've loved everything you've made up till now, I'm certain it'll be delicious."

"Good. I'll let you get ready. If you need anything else, just call me from the bedroom phone." She showed me what button to press to reach her in the pantry before leaving me alone with an array of dresses that would make eating way less enjoyable.

As I walked toward the bathroom, the sound of yelling made me freeze. The thickness of the floors and the plushness of the oriental rug distorted the words but not the tone with which they were delivered. Jarod wasn't having a pleasant conversation with Tristan. Part of me felt guilty, because I was certain the thunder in Jarod's voice was my fault. Another part hoped this would influence Tristan's behavior for the better. In truth, if anyone could reform Tristan, it was Jarod—the only person the former respected and admired.

Not wanting to meddle any more than I already had, I stepped into the temple of black marble that was almost as vast as his bedroom and turned on the water in a shower that contained more jets than a propeller plane and could easily fit everyone on Jarod's payroll.

46

After wiggling into a dress that made my hourglass figure look *very* hourglassy, I slid my feet into a pair of black patent stilettos. I tried not to wonder if the dress and shoes had already been worn. I also tried not to fret too much about going without underwear—the two I'd brought were presently drying on the heated towel rack after I'd had the presence of mind to wash them.

Steadying my nerves, I opened the door and walked down the stairs. As I passed Amir stationed beside the study, my cheeks heated. Had he heard me earlier? The walls were thick, but were they thick enough?

When he glanced my way, the barest flicker of something animating his impassive features, I magicked my wings into existence and cocooned my heating skin. It was silly and useless considering it only hid *him* from me.

"Um." I shifted on the checkered marble, and my silver feathers caressed the skin below the cap sleeves of my black Band-Aid of a dress. "Should I wait for Jarod inside the . . . " Before I could finish my sentence, the door of the study opened, and Jarod's body filled the frame.

"Thought I heard you." His own jaw was flushed, but that probably had to do with his impassioned conversation.

From the look on Tristan's face, I suspected it had just ended.

My nemesis observed me a moment over Jarod's shoulder before lifting his cell phone to his ear and turning away, so I was left staring at the back of his silver suit that matched the hair at his temples.

My feathers were still wrapped around me, but they'd loosened and allowed Jarod glimpses of what I wore.

His eyes turned as black as the stretchy fabric binding my curves. He took a step toward me, pressing away my wings, his fingers skimming the newest growths in the process and sending frissons straight into my wing bones.

Gripping my hips, he uttered a single word, "Wow," and that word flicked the switch on my skin, turning me into a strobe light. My smoldering ticked one side of his mouth up. Against the shell of my ear, he murmured, "Shall we skip dinner?"

My heart must've started smoldering too, because my insides felt like a brazier. "Muriel made soufflés," I whispered hoarsely, thinking it would pain her if they collapsed because Jarod and I were busy feasting on each other.

"And they're ready, Jarod," Muriel said.

I whirled around, smacking Jarod with my wings. He pressed them away, smile intact. I hoped his gestures didn't look too strange.

"Good. I'm ravenous," he said, the heat of his body licking up my spine.

When he ran a lazy knuckle on the underside of one of my wings, I magicked them out of existence. He let out a little grunt of disappointment before murmuring, "I want them out later."

I bit down so hard on the inside of my cheek that I punctured the skin and the tinny taste of blood hit my tongue.

Muriel eyed the server who'd stepped out of the pantry behind her. "Will Tristan be joining you two?"

"He will, Mimi. As soon as he finishes his call." Denting the supple flesh at my waist, Jarod nudged me into the dining room.

The server hurried to add a third place setting as Jarod pulled out my chair before taking up his seat at the head of the table. Muriel brought over a bottle of chilled white wine with a label that had seen better days. I imagined it was another deliriously rare vintage.

Jarod picked up his glass and took a sip. When he nodded to Muriel, she filled my glass.

I was drinking wine. Letting a mob boss do things to my body that would make the residents of Abaddon pray for my wicked soul. And wearing a very unangelic dress commando.

When both Muriel and the waiter left the dining room, I said, "Maybe I shouldn't help get your rank under fifty. I'm pretty sure if I ever ascend, I'll be going straight to Abaddon."

Jarod tossed his head back and laughed, which in turn made me grin.

Now I was cracking jokes about Hell? What was the world coming to?

Still chuckling, he leaned toward me and raised his glass. "To Abaddon and the magnificent angel who'll be sharing my cell."

Shaking my head, I clinked my glass gently to his, then drank, the crisp buttery flavor thrilling my taste buds. I must've hummed, because Jarod's mouth twisted into a brazen smirk.

The dining room doors swept open then. I squared my shoulders as Tristan took the seat opposite me. The room became so silent I could hear the brush of his chair's feet against the deep-hued rug.

Jarod leaned back, spinning his wineglass between his long fingers. "Tristan? I think you have something to tell Leigh."

Tristan eyed the wine shimmering in my glass. "Leigh, I apologize for having subjected you to Jarod's meeting. I have little faith in people and projected my qualms on you. My actions and words were indecent and undeserved."

I gave a quick nod, but that was mostly for Jarod's sake, because Tristan's apology was far too polished to settle me.

As he scooped out the bottle of wine Muriel had placed in a silver ice bucket at the center of the table, he said, "I thought drinking was against your faith."

"It . . . is."

"Devout people make my skin crawl. They're so convinced that prayers and higher beings can solve all of their problems it turns them into indolent, entitled societal burdens who talk out of their asses more often than their mouths." He took a swig of his wine and licked his lips. "Looting Uncle Isaac's cellar, I see."

"He's no longer here to drink, but we are."

"To the simple pleasures in life." Tristan raised his glass. "Wine, women, and punishing swine."

The waiter arrived then, holding a tray laden with crimped white ceramic dishes overflowing with golden domes that wobbled as he walked. He presented me with the tray first, and I picked up one of the plated soufflés.

"Don't touch the ramequin, mademoiselle. They're very hot," he warned.

I waited until everyone was served to break the puffed cupola with my spoon. The egg concoction deflated like an unplugged bouncy castle, discharging a ribbon of tangy steam that made my stomach grumble. I ate in silence, listening to Jarod and Tristan discuss an upcoming trip.

They left out the finer details, and the larger ones too, for that matter. All I gleaned was that they would depart for Nice in the morning on a private jet and be back in time for dinner. As my spoon scraped the bottom of my dish, I pondered how Jarod's score could decrease if he kept conducting business with shady people, because sadly, I doubted all the Court of Demons did was *punish swine*.

The waiter returned to clear our soufflés, presenting us with new ones, pink this time. "Tomato reduction," he explained.

Would there be more savory ones after this? Perhaps, I shouldn't clean off each dish, but the eggy treats were so incredibly light . . .

Dipping my spoon in, I asked, "Jarod, why don't you hold your day of succor once a week instead of once a month?"

Tristan gored his soufflé. "That would turn *La Cour des Démons* into the Wailing Wall."

I disregarded his comment, waiting for Jarod's response.

He studied his pink dome. "I don't have time to organize it every week, Feather," he said, making my hope deflate like Tristan's soufflé. "But we could hold it twice a month." He lifted his eyes to mine.

If Tristan hadn't been in the room, I would've gotten up and kissed Jarod for his concession. Instead, I held on to his gaze and expressed my gratitude with a smile.

"Tristan, find a date in my calendar for the next one and spread the word."

Jarod's order turned Tristan's cool expression crisper. "I'll get to it after dinner."

If we'd been kids, and the table hadn't been banquet-sized, he probably would've kicked my shins under the table. Since we were all adults, we contented ourselves with ocular jousting and tight retorts.

"Thank you," I told Jarod.

He placed the back of his hand on the table, offering me his palm. Without hesitation, I fed my fingers through his. Perhaps, I should've hesitated. By holding hands in front of Tristan, we were revealing a new alliance that didn't include him.

Although his face remained smooth, there was a new gleam in Tristan's eyes that hadn't been there the night he'd introduced me to his boss.

*E*ven though the food had been delicious, I'd had trouble appreciating the meal fully because of the tension that stretched like a rope between Tristan and me. How could I make him see I wasn't trying to steal his place but make my own beside Jarod? A heart-to-heart without Jarod was in order. When they returned from their trip . . . or the following day.

"You've been unusually quiet tonight," Jarod said, leading me up the stairs to his bedroom after Tristan had taken his leave.

"Just thinking."

"About what?"

"I'm thinking Tristan's afraid I'll dethrone him."

"Dethrone him?" Jarod's eyebrows jolted. "No. He's afraid you'll hurt me. And I can't blame him, because I'm afraid you'll hurt me."

"Hurt you?" I twirled toward him when we reached the landing. "I'd never."

He tendered me a smile that didn't reach his eyes. He *really* believed I would hurt him . . .

"Jarod, I promise—"

He kissed me to quiet me.

Had my sinner been burned so often by empty promises he no longer believed in them? I decided then and there that I would have to prove my loyalty and affection with actions instead of words.

I clasped his neck as he backed me into his bedroom and kicked the door closed, his hands traveling over the black spandex compressing my form. Instrumental music played softly, and I assumed it was in my head since there'd been no music when I'd left earlier. This should've preoccupied me, but Jarod's kisses were so intoxicating I wasn't surprised they filled my ears with beautiful harmonies. When our lips unsealed and the music kept playing, I realized it wasn't in my head.

Slowly, I spun.

The darkness glittered, candles burning on every surface, casting miniature pools of light on the scattering of crimson rose petals sprinkled over Jarod's rug and bed.

His arms came around my waist and pulled my back into his front. "Is this romantic enough for you?"

My throat tightened with emotion. "Who—how—"

"Didn't notice Muriel was missing throughout most of the meal?"

My embarrassment was on par with my enchantment as I took in her handiwork. I orbited back in the cage of his arms and covered his jaw in kisses, my heart puffing like a soufflé. He chuckled at my enthusiasm but then stopped chuckling when his face came away wet with my tears.

This man. "Will you ever cease to amaze me, Jarod Adler?"

He kissed my lids with such tenderness that my pulse turned molten and my skin began to gleam. "I'll never cease to amaze you if you never cease to glitter for me."

I nodded again, my hair rushing around my face.

"Fuck, if you're not the most magnificent being I've ever laid eyes on."

"I'm just a woman. With wings."

He cradled my face. "*My* woman with wings. *My* angel. *Ma plume.*" His feather.

He crushed his mouth to mine, and then his hands slid down my neck, shoulders, and arms, coming to rest on my hips. Slowly, he started to tug on the fabric of my dress, sliding it up my thighs. When his fingers grazed my bare skin, he broke the kiss. "You weren't wearing underwear?"

"I ran out of clean ones," I said, watching his pupils dilate.

"Fuck . . . me. I would've cut dinner short if I'd known. Fuck . . ." His gravelly whisper increased the glow of my skin. "Arms up, baby."

I raised my arms, and he slid the dress up my body and over my head. I almost moaned with relief as my skin broke free from the unpleasant contraption. "Whoever sewed this dress should be forced to wear it," I muttered.

Jarod laughed softly. "I'll be sure to pass this on to"—he read the label—"Hervé Léger, at the same time I tell him how much I enjoyed how it embraced your extraordinary assets."

I reconsidered my aversion to the dress . . . Concessions could be made, I thought, as I began to slide my shoes off.

"Keep them on, Feather." His timbre seemed to have dropped a full octave. "And bring out your wings."

I made them appear, and then I stretched them out as though I were winging Jarod. My skin had stopped smoldering, but my silver wings took over, shimmering in the candlelight. Jarod's eyes ran over my flesh and feathers with unprecedented hunger.

"Your turn," I said, tipping my chin toward his shirt and dress pants.

He didn't move for so long I worried my words hadn't reached him. But then, he unbuckled his belt, tossed it to the floor, and unbuttoned his shirt. He sank onto the cowhide lounger I abhorred and unlaced his shoes. He let them clatter against the floorboards, then dragged off a pair of royal blue socks. Shrugging out of his shirt, he stood up, unhooked his pants, and flung them off. His black briefs vanished next.

Unlike at the spa, I let my gaze travel over every dip and sinew, every sharp edge and honed muscle, every curl of dark hair that adorned his body. I took a step closer and ran my hand over his chest, through the soft hair that vibrated with his heartbeats, across his small, hardened nipples, then followed the trail down the seam of his ribs across his belly button that juddered when my fingertip dipped inside.

Years of warnings stilled my hand. I pushed out the Ophanim's voices, pushed out the rest of the world, as I lowered my hand to the part of him that stretched hard and proud toward me.

Jarod sucked in a sharp breath when my fingers closed over him, and then he shuddered as I dragged my fingers gently along his silky length until I reached the tip that glistened with a shiny bead of lust.

When I swirled it with my thumb, he groaned, "Feather."

I glided my hand back toward the root of his shaft, and his muscles bunched and spasmed. On my way back toward the tip, Jarod snatched my hand off him and scooped me up. My hands came around his neck as he crossed the room toward his bed.

He tossed me atop the mattress, bruising the dusting of petals, and looked me over with the ferocity of an untamed beast who'd cornered his kill. Even though the velvet edges of the petals pricked my backside, I could feel little else than my sinner's eyes. The sultry fragrance of roses churned around us, blending with the fig and musk scent coming off Jarod. Never—not even during the best meals—had my senses all been awakened at the same time.

After he climbed over me, I locked the heels he'd asked me to keep on around the backs of his legs. His wet tip glided over my soft stomach, then a little higher before slipping back down and settling heavily between my thighs.

As Jarod kissed his way up my neck, the pulse that ignited in my core rivaled the throbbing in my chest. He moved his body against mine again but didn't breach my walls. Instead, he rose to his knees and tugged on my hand as he dropped against the mattress and rolled me onto him.

Jamming a pillow behind his head, he seized my waist and forced the body I kept hovered over his down until we were aligned. "Spread your wings for me, Feather."

I stretched my wings, purring when his fingers grazed their undersides, and my body dropped another inch, sheathing just the tip of him between my folds.

"You set the pace, baby. You're in control." His obsidian gaze didn't stray off my heavy-lidded eyes.

Pressing my palms into his chest, I lowered myself another inch, gasping. He stroked my wings faster, and the pain was superseded by a growing, billowing heat. I closed my eyes and took more of him in, feeling as though he would soon reach the end of me. My wing bones tensed as the pleasure building within them began to sizzle and crackle like the candle wicks burning all around us.

Inhaling a lungful of rose and fire, I lowered myself without stopping, hissing as he stretched and reshaped me. "Jarod," I gasped.

"Look at me, Feather."

I pried my weighted lids up.

His jaw and brow were taut, as though he were also in pain, as though he was experiencing what my breasts and ass had been subjected to throughout dinner.

As he ran his palm over the bottom edge of my wings, I asked, "Does it hurt?"

He laughed, and it softened all the hard lines of his face. It also made the part of him buried inside my body vibrate, sending renewed shards of pleasure and pain coursing through my core.

Sobering up, he said, "You're in pain, though."

Before he could suggest we stop, I lifted my body a few inches and slid him back inside. The vein in his neck jumped, and his fingers tightened on my feathers as though he were about to pull them out.

I did it again.

And again.

And his hands matched my rhythm, replacing every speckle of pain with sparks of pleasure. My skin began to warm, my spine to tingle, and my pliant walls to quiver, molding around his girth and length.

The slow build detonated, flooding every corner of my being with the sweetest darkness. My limbs turned to jam, my muscles blissfully liquefying around bones that felt as springy as marshmallows.

Jarod took over then and pumped into my limp body until a new heat bulleted into me, seeping and merging with my own, spreading everywhere. I knew it was physically impossible, but it felt like it shot straight into my heart.

Between pants and groans of pleasure, he pulled me down against him, kissing my mouth. His body spasmed anew, and he poured more of himself inside of me.

Playing with a lock of gelled hair that had abandoned ship, I soaked up his heat and smell, his taste and touch.

I would sell my soul for this man.

Maybe, I already had.

48

I awakened the same way I'd fallen asleep—my ear drinking in Jarod's heartbeats and his fingers caressing my shoulder.

As I stirred, he dropped a kiss to the top of my head. I craned my neck and took in his jumble of dark locks that fell into his relaxed brown gaze.

"Morning, beautiful," he murmured in a deep rumble that sent tiny bolts of pleasure straight into my toes. He shifted, tossing a handful of petals to the floor. "How many roses did Mimi skin?"

His wording made me grimace.

"I hope you'll forgive me if, from now on, the only roses you get come in vases." He kissed the tip of my nose, then extricated a petal from my hair, and flicked it away.

I smiled, then straightened my neck, running my fingers through the dark curls rising and falling with his breaths. "Thank you for last night."

He gripped my wrist. "You did not just thank me for being a greedy asshole. I promised to let you set the pace but broke that promise almost as quickly as I came." His exhales warmed my nose and lips. "How do you feel?"

Deliriously happy. Physically drained. Instead I said, "Stunned that the Ishim didn't demand I hand over my wing bones."

His lips curved slowly as he uncuffed me. "They're either

turning a blind eye or sex isn't the heinous crime they made it out to be."

"What if it's because you're part angel?"

"Then I owe my mother's departed soul a fuckload of apologies."

I flicked his biceps. "You have such a dirty mouth. I don't think I've ever heard anyone curse as much as you do."

He grinned. "And to think I'm filtering the filth that comes out so as not to shock your pure ears."

"Not so pure anymore," I mumbled as he rolled on top of me and captured my lips in a searing kiss that made me think dirty was an inadequate adjective to describe his mouth, but suddenly, another thought tumbled over that last one, and my drooping eyelids flipped wide. "We forgot to use a condom!"

He trailed his mouth across my jaw. "I've had a vasectomy, so you don't have to worry about getting pregnant. And as far as diseases, I've never slept with a woman without a condom before."

I blanched. "A vasectomy?"

He pressed up on his forearms. "It's when—"

"I know what it is." He was twenty-five, too young to make such a rash and significant decision. "Can it be reversed?"

"Possibly, but I have no desire to be a father."

"You're so young."

He rolled off me and sighed. "I'm sorry if this is a deal breaker for you, Feather, but having kids, considering what I do, would be selfish and cruel."

I wanted to shout at him to change what he did. Instead, I laid my cheek on the creased pillow and said, "It's not a deal breaker, but one day, I might want to have children."

Before, I would've imagined this wouldn't have been an option, not if I chose to give up my wings, but his mother, a Nephilim, had had a baby, so maybe it wasn't completely impossible.

"By that point, you'll have grown tired of my Machiavellian ways or ascended and found yourself an angel worthy of filling your womb."

My throat squeezed, and my eyes stung. "How can you say

that? How can you even think it?" I turned onto my other side so he wouldn't see the tears drip off my nose.

"Hey." He dragged his fingers gently up and down my arm. When I pulled it away, bending it and burrowing it farther under the pillow, he scooted against me, curling his sleep-warmed body against my huddled form.

"Stop imagining me gone," I said.

His palm settled on my stomach, and he pulled me closer.

"Tristan and Muriel never left you."

"They should've."

"But they didn't."

"Feather, I don't want you to leave, but I don't know how to keep you close."

I turned around. "Just find a place for me in your heart. Even if it's a cramped and dusky corner."

His dark-brown irises eddied around his shrunken pupils. I worried I'd asked for too much, but he dipped his mouth to mine and whispered, "You already own more of it than I've ever given anyone."

49

"That looks nice," Tristan said, leaning against the mirror outside my changing room, chewing on a toothpick, probably to temper his urge for a smoke.

I studied my reflection or what I could see of it with him standing in the way. When Jarod had enthusiastically announced Tristan would accompany Muriel and me, I'd swallowed back my desire to protest.

"*Absolument pas.*" *Absolutely not.* Muriel shook her head at the simple black sheath that didn't do much for my curves besides swallow them whole. "Garbage bags are shapelier."

The saleslady's complexion pinked as though she felt personally responsible for the hapless cut of the garment. I went back into the changing room and traded the black sheath for a fitted emerald dress with a puffy tulle skirt that hit an inch above my ankles. After contorting my arms to zip up the corset top, I readjusted my breasts, hoping the neckline didn't make me look vulgar, and stepped out, readying myself for the firing squad.

Muriel clapped, which made the saleslady next to her loose a relieved breath.

Tristan, on the other hand, wrinkled his nose. "Jarod won't like that."

Muriel scoffed. "My boy, go." She flicked her hand toward the back of the store. "You're being incredibly unhelpful."

He heaved himself away from the mirrored wall and strolled down the long aisle of clothes fit for ballrooms and coronations.

"It's stunning. We'll take it," Muriel said to the saleswoman.

"Are you sure?" I was trying to see what Tristan disliked about it. "It doesn't make me look like an overgrown ballerina?"

Muriel rolled her heavily kohled eyes. "It does not." As I retreated into the changing room, she trailed me inside and helped me with the zipper. "I don't know what Tristan's problem is today, but if he doesn't snap out of it, I'm going to have words with Jarod."

"Don't."

Muriel's hands stilled at the bottom of the zipper. "I don't like the way he's acting."

I turned, holding the dress up with my hands. "He just needs time to adapt."

Her navy eyes drilled into mine. "Fine, I won't say anything to Jarod, but I won't promise not to have a conversation with Tristan."

It was as good a compromise as I would get.

"Try these three last ones on, and then we'll head to Valentino."

I nodded, and she let herself out. I peeled the dress off and laid it on the leather upholstered bench next to my purple dress Muriel had laundered and ironed for me even though I hadn't asked.

I wiggled into a tight black chiffon number with long see-through sleeves and tiny hook closures that fastened up the front. Before even stepping out, I knew Jarod would like it. A glimpse at the price tag made me grimace. I was tempted to pretend it didn't fit, but knowing Muriel's hawkish perspicacity, she would see right through my lie.

My lie, which would surely cost me a feather.

Tristan joined us at the register and paid in cash, handing over so many pink and purple bills guilt bubbled inside me anew. The two bodyguards Jarod had appointed to me for the day scooped up the shiny black shopping bags even though it seemed counter-intuitive considering they'd been sent to protect me, not to carry around bags. But I'd learned after the first boutique that it was useless to insist on carrying my own purchases.

The store guard unlocked the doors, which he'd sealed shut during our shopping—every establishment had done the same. Even though it was to offer me privacy, it never ceased to make me feel uncomfortable when salesclerks escorted straggling customers out of the boutique so I could roam around undisturbed.

As Jarod's bodyguards loaded the trunk of the black sedan in which they'd followed us, Muriel and Tristan walked me to the next store.

"I think I bought enough," I said.

While I'd tried on clothes, Muriel had picked shoes and costume jewelry to match each outfit.

Tristan snorted. "Jarod told me you'd say that. He also told me to spend *all* the cash he gave me, and you've barely put a dent into it."

My eyelashes hit my browbone. I hadn't tallied up every price tag, but I was pretty certain we'd spent close to thirty grand, which was insane.

Completely insane.

"Fine, but this is the last store, okay?" I mumbled.

Tristan opened the glass doors, then grabbed a saleslady and ordered her to clear the boutique. I feigned great interest in the pyramid-studded bag collection as disgruntled customers were funneled onto the street.

Muriel plucked a small red shoulder bag from the shelf. "We'll take one in each size. Which colors would you like, *ma chérie*?"

"You choose."

She picked out the colors and requested shoes to match. "Now, onto clothes."

As we started down one aisle, another saleslady made her way to us, tucking a black shirt into a black pencil skirt as though she'd just gotten into work. "This is such an honor," she gushed, pushing a strand of brown hair behind her ear. A diamond solitaire, bigger than my thumbnail, glimmered on her ring finger. When I didn't say anything, she added, "To serve *l'amie* of Jarod Adler."

Muriel pushed a hanger with a sky-blue twinset into the girl's arms.

A small *"Oomph"* flew through her parted lips as she clutched the outfit. "I'll get a dressing room going." She swiveled on boots that must've come from the store considering how fancy they were, embellished with the same pyramid-like rivets as the bags.

As Muriel pulled out almost every hanger on the first rack, I gazed out the store windows. One of the bodyguards had stayed outside and was corralling passersby. I was almost surprised no paparazzi had arrived or angry archangels for that matter.

I'd take paparazzi over Asher any day, though.

If Asher caught me shopping at the mob's expense, he'd probably physically remove me from Paris. As I looked away from the store front, I saw Tristan standing close to the dressing room the salesgirl was getting ready for me. Still sucking on his toothpick, he now toyed with the button on his jacket. The man either had a serious nicotine addiction or was bored out of his mind. Maybe a combination of both.

As the girl walked past him, she glanced his way. Tristan, though, pretended like she didn't even exist. Was it because of the engagement ring gracing her finger? He hadn't struck me as a man of many—or *any*—scruples. Perhaps, her willowy frame and thick brown hair just didn't do it for him.

"Leigh?" Muriel touched my arm. "What do you think of this skirt?" She extended a long, flowy number the same peacock-blue as the brunette's eyes.

"It's very pretty."

"Why don't you start trying things on? I'll keep looking for you." Muriel passed the hanger over to the saleslady, who stared me up and down as though sizing me up.

And not in the way of a seamstress, but in the way of someone evaluating her competition.

Was she envious that I was *l'amie* of Jarod Adler? The fact that she even knew I was his girlfriend was surprising. The only time Jarod and I had been together outside the walls of his home was at Layla's. Had we been photographed there?

I obediently trailed her into the changing room that shut with a heavy length of cloud-gray velvet. Once she'd exited, I undid the leather belt, the roots of my hair warming at the memory of the other use Jarod had found for it yesterday. I laid it down on the bench sculpted from the same smoky wood as the walls of the cabin, then yanked off my dress, and let it pool next to the belt. I tried on the eggshell camisole overstitched with strips of matching lace, pairing it with the blue skirt, then strode out to get Muriel's opinion.

As soon as she saw me, she bustled over, arms laden with yards of gauzy fabric. "*Magnifique.*"

"If I may, I know I'm new here—*first day*," the brunette announced, flashing a smile to her colleague, who was toting an armful of bags out of the back room, "but I think the skirt needs to be hemmed."

I stared down, not really understanding why since it didn't touch the floor.

"Let me pin it up, and then both of you can decide." She probably said this in the hopes to allay the deep furrows collected on Muriel's brow. "I left my pins inside." The salesgirl gestured toward the changing room, her movement slightly twitchy. Was she nervous because this was her first day?

I trailed her in, frowning when she pulled the curtain closed. How short was she going to pin the dress that she needed to screen us off?

She crouched, then before I could even blink, she sprang to her feet, squashed her palm against my mouth, and pressed a sharp blade to my neck.

"You whore, this is for my father." She slit my throat.

Blood spurted over her pretty face, coated her enormous diamond ring. I tried to speak, to yelp, but all that came out of my mouth was a wet gurgle.

She banded her arm around my waist and eased me quietly to the floor. The world began to tarnish around the edges like the labels on Jarod's wine bottles, and rushing filled my ears.

The girl cleaned herself with one of the dresses. Did she expect to walk out of the cabin and survive the wrath of my bodyguards? Of Tristan?

Even though my brain felt as though it were bobbing inside my skull, I managed to keep my eyes open. Only a smear of blood remained on the shell of her ear, which would be swallowed up by her hair if she untucked it.

What would be her next move? Attacking my guards or—

Muriel! What if she went after her?

I tried to scream again, but the gushing wound snatched Muriel's name from my gaping lips.

"Everything all right in there?" Tristan asked, and I begged him to be his usual intrusive self and part the curtains.

I wouldn't die, but they might.

Gritting my teeth, I crawled toward the drape, but the woman smashed her boot into my cheek, sending me toppling over. Unfortunately, the carpet absorbed the sound of my impact.

"Just fine. Almost done," the woman said, a hitch in her tone.

Please, please pick up on it, Tristan.

She dropped the knife coated in my blood back inside her boot, and I almost sighed with relief, because that meant she wasn't planning on attacking anyone else.

Tossing the soiled dress she'd used as a towel on top of me, the woman, who'd just earned herself an astronomical sinner score, squeezed past the curtains, pulling them tight behind her. "She'll be out in a minute." Her voice was muffled by the thick fabric. "I'm going to find her a pair of heels to showcase the skirt. I'll be right back."

My silk top became saturated with blood and stuck to my slow-pumping chest. If I hadn't had wings, a Malakim would've already arrived to harvest my soul.

"Can I come in, *ma chérie*?" Muriel asked.

Never in my life had I experienced such pain. How could humans do this to each other? Be so vicious?

Dying was a necessary part of a soul's cycle, but this type of death was inhumane. No wonder the Malakim erased a soul's memory. Trauma like the one I was experiencing would scar someone for several lifetimes.

"Leigh?" Muriel called out.

At some point, impatience would win her over, and she'd discover my gory body. I tried to use the fabric the saleslady had tossed on me to clean off the blood, but my hands shook too hard, and my fingers wouldn't even close. Muriel would be terrified, and there was nothing I could do about it.

The curtain finally swished open.

A scream rent the air, and then footfalls pounded the store's granite floor, thudding right into my skull. Muriel's face blurred in front of me and then sharpened before blurring again. Blots of silver and blue hung behind her. When my eyesight cleared again, I noticed the blots were Tristan. His skin, usually tanned and bright, was ghost-like.

"Don't just stand there!" Muriel screamed. "Call for help and find the girl!"

Tristan backed away, pale eyes wide with fear.

Before he could even turn around, a series of pops went off. Gunshots?

My head swam as Muriel's clammy palm cupped my cheek. "Stay with me, Leigh."

I really wanted to sleep.

Just for a little while.

Just until my skin mended and my windpipe sealed shut.

"Call Jarod!" was the last thing I heard her yell before the world unraveled, turning blissfully blank.

50

I awoke cocooned by something that felt fashioned from silken steel.

As the world came into focus, I realized the silk was Jarod's bedsheets and the steel was his body. I shifted, and his pulse sprang to life beneath my head.

"Leigh?" He'd never pronounced my name so sweetly.

"You're here," I whispered, my throat still aching. It would probably ache for days considering how deep the crazy brunette had cut.

I lifted my fingertips to my neck, discovering an enormous bandage.

"Don't touch it. I don't want the stitches to open."

"Stitches?" I'd never had stitches before. Never needed them. Still didn't, but I supposed Jarod had forgotten about my healing prowess. Unless Muriel had taken the executive decision to have my skin hemmed.

Ugh. Why did that verb have to be the one to pop into my mind?

He eased his arm out from underneath me, treating me as though I were as delicate as the petals we'd bruised during our lovemaking. "Yes. Stitches." His dark gaze traveled over the bandage as though he wanted to peel it off and rip it to shreds. It was probably the woman who'd done this to me he wanted to shred.

"You know, I didn't really need them." I kept my voice low, even though I doubted I could speak much louder.

He shook his head, jaw darkened with such thick stubble it seemed days had gone by since my shopping incident. Had days gone by? I looked toward one of the windows, trying to glimpse if it was night or morning . . . not that it would tell me how long I'd been unconscious.

"Two . . . fucking . . . days," he growled, as though he'd read my mind. "You've been out for two fucking days. I banged down your guild's door to get one of your kind to fucking tell me if this was normal!"

My breath jammed in my sore throat. It hurt, but I bit back the shallow gasp before it could surface and add to Jarod's worries. "They must've been surprised . . . when they opened up and found you."

"You could say that."

"Did you see inside?"

He snorted. "They like marble and fountains."

I smiled. "Quartz. Mined in Elysium." Had he mentioned being able to see them?

"They called Asher for me. He came over, and after checking on your neck, declared you'd be okay."

I winced, just imagining Asher's horrified expression upon finding me in Jarod's bed—I imagined this was where I'd been since the attempt on my life. How shallow that my whereabouts bothered me more than my condition. Then again, I was immortal, so my condition wasn't cause for alarm.

The vein at Jarod's temple twitched. "Feather, I was out of my fucking mind."

"I told you"—I ran my finger over his cupid's bow mouth—"I can't die."

He grunted, as though he didn't believe me. He had all the proof he needed, though. Yes, my throat stung more than my wings the night I'd told two dozen lies, but I was alive.

"The woman . . . did they—"

"Her skull has a great big hole inside. And you'll be happy to know—or maybe, it's just me who's pleased about this—but I was informed her soul wasn't harvested."

I wasn't surprised she'd died a Triple. "I'm only happy she's gone so that she can't harm you and Muriel."

Jarod blinked before shaking his head. "Always worrying about everyone else."

"Jarod, she mentioned she was avenging her father."

His gaze set on one of the wooden posts of his bed, tracking its elaborately carved shape to its pointed spire.

"You don't need to tell me who she was . . . I just wanted to share what she'd said."

Sighing, he returned his attention to me, the purple circles rimming his eyes resembling bruises. "She was the daughter of the man who ran the little racketeering operation we uncovered. When I shut it down, he lost a lot of money. He also lost my protection and got demoted."

"So, he sent his daughter to get back at you?"

"Apparently, he wasn't aware of her plans."

Hmm . . . I wasn't sure I believed that. "She said she'd just started working at the store. Was it a coincidence?"

"No. Someone informed her you'd be shopping on Avenue Montaigne." He gritted his jaw. "She probably picked a shop at random and crossed her fingers you'd pay it a visit."

"Who informed her?"

"Tristan found a listening device in the dining room."

Had we discussed it over dinner? I couldn't remember.

The vein throbbed harder in his temple. "Probably planted during one of those fucking parties I have to throw each month to secure blackmail material on my clients."

It was silly, but the reason for his parties comforted me.

"When I catch the little shit—because I will catch him . . . or her—I'll cut off their fucking head and plant it in on the metal gate of the park."

My stomach roiled, and bile swarmed my raw throat.

My rising nausea must've sapped the color from my cheeks, because he said, "Sorry, Feather. You didn't need to know this."

I cupped his rigid jaw. "I'm just glad she targeted me and not you."

His eyes turned as black as the rumpled dress shirt he wore, and his nostrils flared out, which told me he wasn't glad in the least.

"Will her father seek revenge?"

"His soul might . . . if it was pried out of his dead body."

"You killed him?"

"Did you expect me to let him live?"

"He's not the one who hurt me, Jarod."

"I'd been meaning to do it eventually. It just advanced the date of his funeral."

A terrible thought coalesced in my mind. "Your rank, Jarod."

He shrugged. "Probably back to being a Triple."

My lashes fluttered over my eyes a few times in horror. "We need—I need—I don't want—"

"Shh," he whispered before dipping down and sealing my lips shut with his own.

I was torn between pushing him away so I could reason with him and pulling him closer so I could get my fill of him. The latter won. I gripped his creased shirt and wrenched him as close as one body can get to another.

I wasn't sure how long we stayed tangled up, but I was sure it wasn't long enough. We only broke apart because a knock sounded. Muriel came in, wrinkles seemingly more pronounced. She chided Jarod for "roughing me up" before proceeding to check on my wound. When her breathing whistled out a little steadier, I assumed she was pleased by how miraculously fast I was healing. She still cautioned Jarod to be gentler.

Jarod and I both smiled at that.

She ran me a bath, telling Jarod to go eat the dinner she'd left out for him before it went cold. He started to protest he wasn't hungry, but she shut the door of the bathroom in his stunned face.

He must've gone down for food because he wasn't in the room when I emerged, bandage-free and in a pair of black pajamas that felt like silk. Had she bought them for me during the shopping trip?

I shuddered at the memory of that morning, and the brush Muriel was running through my damp hair slid out. As she started up again, her strokes slow and gentle, I wondered if my mother would've taken as meticulous care of me as Muriel did.

"What did you make Jarod for dinner?" I asked, not because I was especially hungry—*surprising, I know*—but because I wanted to wipe the frown that had crimped Muriel's brow since she'd marched into the bedroom.

"Green beans and roast chicken."

"His favorite," I mused, remembering her saying this the first night I'd dined with him.

"I made you some soup. Several kinds—there's beef broth, carrot, sweet pea. I didn't know which you'd like. I just assumed you'd be drinking your meals." She lowered the brush, done untangling my long locks. "Which one would you like?"

"Sweet pea. I love peas."

Her wrinkles smoothed out. "I'll be right back."

"Or I can go down—"

"You"—she pointed the hairbrush at me—"stay put."

"Okay."

"Do you want me to turn on the TV before I go downstairs?"

"TV?"

She walked toward the wall across the bed and opened the doors of what I'd assumed had just been a fancy armoire containing more books. She turned on the flat screen and left me to watch a news program broadcasting firefighters plunging into the Seine on a rescue operation.

The body retrieved was shown for only a second, but that was all it took for me to understand there would be no rescuing this person whose skin was so bloated and blue I wasn't sure I'd be able to eat anything.

"First time I toss a body in the Seine," came a voice that made me spin away from the television. Tristan stood in the doorway wearing a proud smile and a buttoned iron-gray vest over a shirt the same shade as his eyes. "Quite convenient."

I swallowed.

He nodded to the looping coverage. "It's Mehdi, the father of the girl who attacked you. In case you were wondering." He jammed his hands into his pockets as he walked closer. "No one in that family will be bothering you anymore."

"Why? Did you kill them all?"

"No. But death is sometimes not the worst fate." He studied the discolored line of skin spanning my throat. "You gave us all a fright. I'm surprised you survived. It looked . . . deep."

I studied his expression, wondering if he regretted that I'd survived. It would've been a convenient way to get rid of me. "I must have a guardian angel."

His nonchalant mask was firmly in place, making it impossible to guess what was going through his mind.

"I hope no one finds out you put that body in the river," I added.

"The police chief knows, but he's a regular at our monthly demon bash, so he won't be pressing charges." A smug grin cracked the polished veneer of his mask. "Jarod seems to be under the impression we'll stop hosting them. I hope you're not putting any ideas inside his head, because those revels are very important to what we do." The antipathy that rolled off him was so strong it was almost solid.

I wedged my lips together. I didn't want to answer, but I also didn't want him disliking me further. "I didn't give Jarod any advice concerning your parties."

"They're his, too."

I absorbed his loaded comment, analyzed it.

As he turned to leave, I said, "I'm not trying to take Jarod away from you."

The silk fabric of his vest strained as the muscles in his back bunched. He tossed me a look over his shoulder. "I'm not worried about that."

The smile he shot me before he left unsettled my stomach more than the image of the drowned man on TV.

Had Tristan meant that he wasn't resentful about the attention Jarod paid me or that he didn't think I was capable of taking Jarod away from him?

51

*T*he next few days blurred together. The only highlight was when Celeste visited. Even though she wasn't her usual *happy-go-lucky-with-a-side-of-self-deprecation* self, she'd come and stayed an entire afternoon with me. Not to mention, she'd sat through two meals with Jarod during which she was only passably aggressive. An improvement.

"I think she's starting to like me," Jarod said the following night, as I slid my feet into a pair of crystallized black heels Muriel insisted suited the green tutu-like dress I'd purchased before—

I shuddered.

Before the episode I was still desperately trying to magick out of my mind. "Who?"

He sat on the bed to fasten his black diamond cufflinks. "Celeste."

I grinned. I couldn't help it. "What exactly led you to think she was warming up to you?"

"She only called me a unicorn noodle once."

My smile increased.

Done with his cuffs, he adjusted the placket on his tuxedo shirt, then patted his lap. "Come here."

I traipsed over and perched on his thighs.

"Have I mentioned how stunning you look tonight?"

I ran my fingers over the poufy tulle. "You really think so?"

"I really think so."

"Tristan said you'd hate this dress."

"Tristan can be a dick sometimes."

I straightened his bow tie even though it was already straight. "You look incredibly handsome yourself, but then again, you always look handsome." He'd slicked so much gel on his hair it seemed almost black.

"I have something for you." He slid his hand into the breast pocket of his jacket and extricated a small velvet box.

"You've already given me so much, Jarod."

When I didn't reach for his gift, he flipped my hand over and placed the box inside my palm. "I bought it to match your eyes, not your dress, even though it'll go superbly with both."

I popped open the lid, my mouth going round before shutting to steady the rising tremors. A pair of yellow filigreed gold and emerald earrings sparkled against the black cushion. Pearls no bigger than needle heads and raindrop-sized diamonds were sprinkled throughout the setting.

"I've never owned anything so beautiful," I whispered, voice thick with emotion.

He tucked a lock of hair behind my ear, then removed one of the jewels from the box and speared it through my lobe. "They were apparently the property of the Romanov family. At least, that's what the man at Sotheby's told me when I asked him for the rarest and most beautiful piece of jewelry they had up for auction." He lifted the second earring out of the box, then gently turned my head to gain access to my other ear. "The czar had them fashioned the day he met the woman who was to become his future wife. Word has it, he even designed them and hand-picked the stones. If I had any talent, I would've done the same. Since making pretty things isn't my forte—"

I pressed my still trembling lips against his before he could demean himself any further. I was certain he was just as capable as the czar of Russia of designing something of beauty. "I love them, Jarod." I curled my hand around his neck, my thumb strumming his nape. "I love you." The words came out before I could speculate if they might scare him off. Bullets through hearts, he was used to, but declarations of love?

He stared at the faint scar on my neck. "You really shouldn't, Feather."

My heart dropped right into my glittery shoes. I hated the guilt he carried for my attack. I hated there was nothing I could say or do to dispel it.

"We should go. I have a few people to see before the show begins."

Nodding, I stood and accepted his proffered hand.

In the foyer, Muriel was waiting for us. "*Vous êtes si beaux.*"

He raised our clasped hands and twirled me. The unexpected movement made my heart bounce a little higher. "You mean *Leigh* is so beautiful."

Muriel picked a piece of lint off his black satin lapel. "You too, *mon amour.*"

He kissed the top of her head, then backed up, pulling me along. "Don't wait up, Mimi."

She grunted. "I'll sleep when I'm dead."

My heart drifted right back down. *Dead.* I'd never feared that word before, because death wasn't the end. Except for Triples. I suddenly wanted to find out Muriel's rank. I doubted it contained more than a single digit, but what if . . . what if her contact and enduring camaraderie with a mob family had tainted her score?

THE OPERA HOUSE was another architectural gem in a city that already enclosed so many—a temple of gold leaf, oil paint, and ochre-veined marble.

Jarod kept me tucked into his side as I craned my neck to take in the splendor of the vaulted ceilings.

My lips must've parted in awe because Jarod said, "How about I have this place closed down tomorrow so you can have a private tour?"

I returned my gaze to his. "You don't need to do that."

He kissed my still-parted mouth. "Consider it done. I'll arrange for a few other sites too."

"Will you come with me?" I asked hopefully.

"I can't. But how about you take Celeste? I'm certain she'll love it. Or if she doesn't, it'll give her fodder for new diatribes."

He added a crooked smile that made me shake my head. "I'll send Amir with you this time."

My heart stuttered. Did Jarod think someone else would try to attack me? I was about to remind him I was immortal, that I'd rather Amir stick to him, when Tristan trotted over to us, arm in arm with a woman who must've been a runway model considering how tall, lithe, and exquisite she was. Everything about her was sculpted to perfection from her high cheekbones to her pert nose to the sloping shape of her eyes and the dainty collarbone on display in her strapless black gown.

I burrowed closer to Jarod, feeling like a giant burr. I hadn't felt so blimpish and lackluster since that last night I'd spent in New York, standing beside flawless, gorgeous Eve.

"Jarod," the woman said, a thick accent—Eastern European possibly—coating his name, "it has been too long."

"Good evening, Petra."

She leaned over to kiss his cheeks. Even though her lips didn't make contact with his skin, hovering in that polite way of the French, my fingers twined like vines around Jarod's jacket.

"Nice dress, Leigh," Tristan said with a smirk that brought out thorns in me. Who would've thought soft, supple Leigh could get so prickly?

"I almost regret letting her out of the house looking like this," Jarod said.

Tristan's smirk increased. "I can believe it."

Jarod's right-hand man probably thought me an eyesore amid all the majesty of the Palais Garnier. What bothered me most, though, was that, as I took in the room, I joined him in thinking this.

"Amir," Jarod called out over his shoulder.

His bodyguard broke rank with the other three trailing us.

"Please escort Leigh to the *loge*."

The man nodded his meaty head.

To me, Jarod said, "I'll be up in a few minutes."

I released my death grip on his jacket, and it felt like releasing the tallest branch of a tree and freefalling backward. My wings poured out of my back as though they could somehow break my fall, but all they did was uselessly adorn my back.

Jarod cupped my chin. I thought he was going to kiss me, and

I desperately wanted him to, if just to show Petra and the rest of the women ogling him that he was taken, that even if he didn't love me, he liked me better than them. Instead, his chin bumped my emerald earring.

"You are blinding me to the surrounding world, Feather. How am I expected to look anywhere else or *see* anything else when you are near?"

I wanted his compliment to reach deep and lift my sunken heart, but part of me thought he'd spoken it only to alleviate my manifest sullenness.

He canted my face. "Smile for me."

Sighing, I raised a diminutive smile.

He leaned over and kissed my taut lips before pulling away and striding through the crowd that parted around him and Tristan as though they were kings.

The night I'd met Asher, I remembered thinking he was attractive, powerful, and kind, but the archangel paled in comparison to my sinner.

Neither human nor angel could eclipse this man whose magnificent darkness devoured even the brightest of lights.

52

a s Amir escorted me into an opulent red box situated directly across the stage, curious glances were tossed my way, ramping up my tenacious insecurities.

"Tristan mentioned Jarod was acting out of character, but kissing in public"—Petra glided toward the gold handrail of the *loge* next to which I was poised, scanning the crowd below—"that is certainly a first." She leaned her dainty forearms on the scarlet velvet upholstery that matched the chairs with their deep button tufting and golden frames.

I didn't think she was telling me this to stroke my ego, but I lapped it right up. "I take it you know him well?"

"Intimately, but not well."

I knew I wasn't Jarod's first, or second, or third, but hearing it from someone who'd come before me stung my already vulnerable heart.

Petra turned away from the sight below to examine me. "I do not think it is possible to know Jarod Adler well."

How wrong she was.

How *deeply* I relished how wrong she was.

I kept my gaze on the operagoers milling around below, flattening their ample dresses to thread themselves down the narrow rows of seats or embracing friends as though they were long-lost relatives before disparaging their outfit or Botoxed features the instant their backs were turned.

On my way up the stairs to our private box, I'd been privy to such hushed backstabbing. I'd even heard one woman comment how someone else was wearing the same dress I was, but in black, which was so much more distinguished than lurid green. My confidence level had taken another hit, but I'd raised my chin a little higher and spread my wings a little wider.

For a slender moment, I'd wished humans could see them, or at the very least, feel them. Bodies passing through them as though my feathers were no more substantial than vapor hadn't been half as satisfying as smacking them would've been.

Such an unangelic thought.

"It is Lee, right?" Petra asked. "Your name."

"Leigh," I responded, adding a long *yuh* sound to differentiate it from the word that meant ugly in French.

"Which agency do you work for, Leigh?"

I glanced at her. "Excuse me?"

"I imagine you are a model."

"A model?" I actually smiled at that. "No. I'm not a model."

"A call girl, then? Or an actress?"

I shook my head no.

She checked my left hand, and even though I wore no ring, asked, "A client's wife?"

"No," I gasped.

"Then how did you meet Jarod?"

The memory of how I'd entered *La Cour des Démons* flitted through my mind. It felt like an entire year had come and gone. "I sought him out to offer him a chance at a better life."

"Better?" She made a little sound, which I wasn't sure how to interpret until she shook her head. "Jarod leads the best of lives. He is the wealthiest and most powerful, unattached man in this city—probably in the whole country. Not to mention exceedingly handsome."

"Those aren't reasons for happiness."

"You have obviously never known hunger or poverty."

"You're right. I haven't."

The strain that flexed her dainty shoulders led me to believe she had known both.

The air changed suddenly, both in texture and scent. Without having to glance over my shoulder, I sensed Jarod had arrived. Nonetheless, I glanced to fill myself with the sight of him. Gait so proud, he advanced toward me. Petra also watched him, along with everyone in the surrounding private boxes, but I was his single focus, and that did things to me that were downright alarming.

It made me feel special. And beautiful.

It set me on fire.

My body began to pulsate with light, and his eyes glittered. How much of that light was a reflection of my own and how much of it was a reflection of the one in his heart? He backed me into the guardrail, his hands drifting to my waist, probably to keep me from tipping over the red velvet balustrade.

"Sorry I left you alone so long," he whispered before pressing his mouth to mine, and although our lips didn't open and our tongues didn't twine, it felt like one of the most intimate kisses he and I had ever shared, like his mouth was memorizing the shape of mine.

The lights dimmed then, and we took our seats. As the heavy curtains parted, his hand slid off my waist but not off my smoldering body. His long fingers played my feathers with the dexterity of the harpist in the orchestra pit, strumming and flicking each one until a melodic hum made its way through my lips.

Although he kept his eyes on the show, the smile growing on his face as my breathing turned nippier and my skin shinier betrayed where his attention truly lay. I probably should've chided him for what he was doing, but I sealed my lips and eyes and waded through the minefield of impropriety. When his fingers sent me soaring, my lips parted with a gasp that was swallowed first, by the audience's loud clapping, and then, by Jarod's lips.

After pleasure came pain, though. As though someone had punched my back with steel knuckles, I hissed, and my eyes flipped open, locking on Jarod's. He lurched back, already scanning the shadowy expanse beneath my chair. When he located the feather I imagined the Ishim had purloined for our licentious undertaking, his expression darkened like my no longer glittery skin, and his hand fell away from my body.

I apprehended his fingers. "It doesn't matter."

He side-eyed me, and I sensed that, to him, it mattered.

A duet began on the stage.

He removed his hand from mine and crossed his arms, bunching the fabric of his sleeves.

Instead of trying to pry his arms apart, which I sensed he wouldn't appreciate, I let him stew in his guilt. But I did lean over to say, "I don't want them; I want you."

"Don't say that," he snapped, his harsh tone garnering Petra's and Tristan's attention.

I shifted closer to him again. "You don't understand what they represent."

"Your safety," he hissed. "That's what they fucking represent." His gaze was still riveted to the stage and stayed that way throughout the entire first act.

Only once did they stray, and it was to glare at the hand caressing his lap.

Which wasn't mine.

Blood thrashed in my ears as I watched Petra stroke up his thigh again. How dare—

Before I could finish that thought, he plucked her hand off his lap and tossed it with a violence that made her slap her own body. "You fucking touch me again, and I will cut off your hand." And then he shot up and walked out.

Tristan followed him, but Petra didn't even flinch. It was only once the lights came on for the intermission that she, too, rose and left without an apology or passing glance.

I didn't move. In part because I was pinned to my seat by all that had unfolded in the span of an operatic act, and in part because if Jarod returned, I wanted to be here.

Minutes ticked by, and none of them returned. Only Amir had stayed, but I imagined it was more out of duty than pity.

When he turned to look at the hallway behind the box, I picked up my fallen feather. I didn't particularly want to relive an episode from my past, but I forced myself to. Jarod's outburst might've been borne from guilt, but it had served to remind me how deeply I was rejecting my kind.

The walls of a drab, gray high school appeared around me, and then the muscled body of the star running back popped into my line of sight—*Sean*. I'd posed as a transfer student, who'd helped tutor him in order to curb his habit of cheating on exams. I'd spent several weeks convincing him that he was smart and as capable of success in the classroom as he was on the field.

At the memory of his face lighting up after scoring his first B- without copying the answers off his friend, a lump clogged my throat, and the tears that had welled up finally spilled. I missed the girl I used to be and grieved for the one I'd dreamed of becoming.

I grieved for her, because I'd felt too much during this last mission, learned too much, to ever become her. I dragged both my hands over my wet cheeks, not caring if I ruined what little makeup I'd applied.

The air around me shifted, and I knew Jarod had returned.

Which didn't mean he wouldn't eventually abandon me for good.

His steely gaze scoured the floor beneath my chair, probably seeking out the fallen feather. When he didn't find it, his gaze climbed up to mine.

"You didn't leave." Every syllable splintered.

"You didn't either." Unlike mine, his tone was stiff.

When the golden-red drapes lifted, I murmured, "I'll never be the one to leave, Jarod."

He turned to stone.

The lights dimmed, and he still didn't sit.

I crimped the green tulle, trying to prepare myself for a decision I'd be powerless to overturn, trying to remember that if he left it wasn't because he didn't care but because he cared too much.

When I could no longer stand the sight of his stillness, I shut my eyes. The least I could do was not watch it happen.

A warm hand spanned my cold fingers. My lashes pulled up slowly, afraid my skin was conjuring a touch that wasn't there. But long fingers dusted with dark hair overlapped my knuckles.

Jarod forced my hand off the tulle and speared his fingers through mine, pressing our palms together until I could feel his brisk heartbeat through the pad of his thumb. I glanced at him, but his eyes were affixed to the stage and the progressing scene. He didn't say a word to me throughout the entire second act.

But I didn't need words.

Not when I had his hand.

53

 etra had never returned after that first intermission, yet her hand stroking up Jarod's lap had haunted my sleep and awakened me more than once throughout the night. Each time, I'd tracked the wisps of light trickling from his balcony and through the drawn curtains as they danced across the ceiling like ghosts until they lulled me back to unconsciousness.

Unlike me, Jarod had slept soundly, but I suspected it was thanks to all we'd done once we'd gotten home from the opera. Three times, he'd made love to me. The first was sweet, an apology for how he'd acted. The second brisk, an assurance of my desirability. The third, slow and unfinished—he never climaxed even though he made sure I did—a promise that there would be no end to us just as there had been none for him.

When morning seeped around the edges of his curtains, I stopped trying to fight wakefulness and reveled in the unspoiled peacefulness of dawn, turning onto my side to study Jarod's profile, the dense swoop of lashes brushing his bladed cheekbones, the burnt-coffee locks falling arbitrarily over his forehead, the cracked seam of his full lips parted in tranquility.

I wanted to wake up to this sight every day of my immortal life, but that was an impossible dream.

How. Unfair.

A thought skated into my mind, blasting away my little

misery-party. If he could see inside the guild, then he could enter it. It was far from ideal, but *if* I ascended, maybe I could convince the archangels to bend their hundred-year rule of no traveling out of Elysium. Within the confines of the guilds, I would raise no mortal eyebrows. Excitement began to plug all the little fissures loitering in my heart.

"Jarod," I murmured.

He stirred, but his eyes didn't open.

"Jarod?" I tried again.

"Mmm." His lashes still didn't rise, but his arm reached over and curled around my waist.

"Did you *enter* the guild?"

This time, his lids lifted, and he stared.

"I just had this idea. It'd solve our dilemma, but it's not ideal. I was hoping that if you could *see* inside the guild, then you could maybe step inside, too."

His mouth thinned. "I couldn't get over the threshold."

My fragile dream popped like a champagne bubble, and my heart crackled all over again.

"I'm pleased to hear you're considering completing your wings, though," he murmured.

"I'm not considering *or* completing them if it means they'll take me away from you." My words clattered, heavy like stones.

"Feather . . ."

"Don't."

He sighed.

"We're never having this conversation again, all right?" I croaked.

It took a long time for his mouth to form an answer, but in the end, I got the one I wanted: "Okay."

He pulled me close, and then closer—first, his tongue slid inside of me, and then, his rigid length. Raising my leg to rest over his thigh, he drove in deeper, establishing a measured rhythm that amplified the thumping inside my chest.

Heat built and curled like glittery smoke throughout my body. I looked at him, and he looked right back, and this contact became more intimate than any other place connecting in our bodies. The black of his pupils and the brown of his irises seemed to merge and swirl as he impelled himself deeper, drew back, and thrust again. The chasm of pleasure grew near, and I crushed the rumpled sheets with my fingers, twisting the silk to hold on until he was ready to fall inside with me.

"Feather," he rasped.

My fingers sprang open, and I dove.

And he dove in after me.

WE DIDN'T CLIMB out of our silken nest for almost an hour, and I would've stayed all day had Jarod not reminded me of his meetings and my private tour of Versailles.

"I wish you could come with me," I said, donning a pair of fluid black pants that skimmed the glossy floorboards of his walk-in closet in spite of my four-inch heels. The effect made my legs look almost as long as Petra's.

How I wished I could forget about her . . .

After fastening my emerald earrings, I smoothed out the simple white T-shirt I'd tucked into the pants. I so rarely wore pants, convinced skirts were best for my shape, but these were making me rethink my wardrobe preferences.

Jarod walked up from behind and laced his arms around my torso. Even though my heels were high, he still loomed over me. As he took in our reflections in the full-length mirror propped against the wall of his enormous closet, he said, "I can't let you leave the house looking like this." When I frowned, he added, "French men are not to be trusted."

I shook my head, and the spotlight showering us made my hair shine like a sunset—orange and pink and gold. "I look like I'm going to work."

"Actually, you look like you're going back inside my bed."

Before I could roll my eyes, he flung me over his shoulder.

Laughing, I smacked his back. "Put me down, you sex fiend."

He did put me down. On his bed. And then he stripped everything from my body except for his earrings.

54

*S*everal hours later, I was walking across a room festooned in mirrors designed to match the vaulted French doors set across from them. The echoed light lent *la Galerie des Glaces* a brightness rivaling the Channels'.

Celeste clomped in her black boots beside me, alternately eyeing our tour guide—a historian with a puff of gray hair and a plethora of fascinating accounts about the palace—Amir who walked behind us like an overstretched shadow, and the opulent murals adorning the ceiling.

When I'd stopped by the guild to ask if she was free, Celeste had groused and slapped her pillow over her head, insisting she needed more sleep. But then, I'd mentioned it would be just the two of us, and she'd hopped out of bed like a kernel of corn in a hot pan.

"Asher told me one of the Seven had lived here," she whispered, as we trailed after the tour guide. "Before the Revolution. I'm not sure which one, though."

Even though I'd grown up around immortals—Ophan Mira had been born at the time of the Renaissance, and Ophan Greer in a wagon heading west on the Oregon Trail—it never ceased to amaze me that someone who looked youthful was in fact ancient.

"Do you ever wonder how different the world will be when you'll return in a century?" I murmured to Celeste.

She sighed. "Yeah, but then I bring these out"—her purple wings spilled from the back of her white ribbed tank top—"take a good look at them, and realize I should stick to thinking in decades instead of centuries."

"Celeste," I chided her softly. "Get rid of your pessimism. If you want this, you'll get it."

It dawned on me that by staying I could help both *her* and Jarod, and excitement teemed within my breastbone.

"I'll make sure you get there. I'll find you people to help and work with you on them." Mortality needn't equate the end of saving souls. I'd just be doing it without wings, without recompense.

The way it should be done.

"If you stay, I'll never talk to you again." Celeste's eyes blazed like the row of baroque, crystal chandeliers.

I wedged my lips together, hoping she'd said that because she was mad and not because she truly meant it.

The awe, which had filled Celeste when we'd started the tour, dwindled to paltry curiosity, as though the castle had dulled once we'd exited the Hall of Mirrors even though its grimiest nooks had been mesmerizing.

A picnic lunch was set out for us in the manicured gardens of the castle, complete with a white tent, a dressed-up table, and wooden chairs. Even though I was glad to hear more stories about the naughty courtiers of France, I sort of wished the historian would leave so I could speak to Celeste alone.

After coffee and a platter of petits fours ranging from miniature lemon tarts to bite-sized chocolate macarons, the historian finally bade us farewell. Amir peeled a crisp pink bill from a thick wad and handed it to the woman who blinked at it, then at him, then around her. She folded it, then furtively slid it inside the collar of her salmon-colored blouse and traipsed away on her kitten heels.

I sort of wished that Jarod's bodyguard would leave, too, but imagined he wouldn't take any orders from me, so I made do with the respectable distance he afforded us, hoping his sense of hearing wasn't too keen.

"Celeste, you can't hate me for a decision that affects only me."

"Only you?" She shook her head. "It doesn't affect only you. It affects . . . it affects *everyone*."

"Really? Name a single other person my *not ascending* will affect."

"Asher."

I sighed. "We've talked about this, honey. I'm not interested in Asher, and he—"

"He unblocked Jarod's score," she hissed. "For you! He did it for you."

"No, he did it for himself, to fix a mistake, and he did it for Jarod. My wings played no role in his decision."

A brave little sparrow landed on our table, hunting for crumbs.

Celeste peeled the crust off a tartlet and tossed it at the bird's outsized feet. "You're missing seven by the way. I checked two days ago. All you need is seven feathers."

"Eight. I lost another one last night."

"How? Did Jarod make you lie again?"

"No. And he never made me lie. I chose to do it."

Another brown sparrow perched on our table, emboldened by his friend, and Celeste fed it too.

"I love him, and if you gave him a chance, you'd understand why."

She folded her arms and eyed the thin white scar on my neck as though Jarod himself had put it there. "Then I hate him even more."

"Celeste . . ."

She raised her chin and shifted her gaze to the perpendicular hedges hemming in our tent.

I leaned toward her. "You know what he suggested?"

"That you ask Asher to burn the wings off your back before they fall off?"

I jerked, my spine hitting the wooden rungs of my chair. She really thought the worst of him. Not that I could truly blame her since there had been a time I had, too. "He suggested I sign off from him, so that you could take him on."

Her eyebrows dipped as she side-eyed me.

"To help you earn ninety-nine feathers, or whatever's he's worth these days." I prayed it wasn't a hundred.

"Ninety-six. That's what he was worth yesterday."

My pulse sprang at that news.

Her arms untightened but didn't untangle. "That was . . . *nice* of him, I guess."

I smiled at her euphemism.

"But I still don't like him."

"Your hatred is undeserved and misplaced." I dragged a fingertip over the condensation beading down my water glass. "He doesn't want me to stay. He keeps pushing me to earn my last feathers." I dried my finger on the white tablecloth. "But I don't want to. It's hard to explain, but it feels like . . . like my soul is going to rip in half if it leaves his."

"You've known him for two weeks, Leigh."

"I'm aware of that, but I'm also aware of how special he is and how special he makes me feel. I don't mean to sound patronizing, but until you meet someone who becomes more vital to you than air, I don't think you'll understand what I'm feeling. *All* I'm feeling."

Celeste finally unbound her arms. "What if in three years from now, or ten, you fall out of love with him. What then?"

"You don't fall out of love with your soul mate."

"There's no such thing."

"There is. And Jarod is mine."

Celeste's eyebrows bunched together. "I love you, Leigh, but I think you're crazy."

"Maybe a little." I smiled. "Can you promise to keep loving me whatever decision I make and however crazy I get?" I was still holding out hope that losing my wings wouldn't make me lose my sanity. Maybe I could seek out another Nephilim. But how would I find them? The Ophanim would probably blow a gasket and leak angel-smoke if I asked them for a contact.

She puffed air from the corner of her mouth, pushing a glossy chestnut lock off her forehead. "Like I could actually stop."

The intensity of my smile strengthened, melting her residual annoyance.

"I can't promise not to give you crap if you're still around next year, though."

"I'll take your crap, as long as it comes with your friendship."

Finally, she released a breath that seemed too large for her lungs. "I still don't believe in soul mates, though."

"Wait till you meet yours."

"I can't meet someone who doesn't exist." She filched the crustless lemon tartlet and stuffed it inside her mouth.

"He exists."

55

*A*fter dropping Celeste back off at the guild and making her promise to visit, I headed back to a place that was starting to feel like home, a place with blood-red doors and a dazzlingly dark sinner. When I arrived in the checkered marble foyer, I heard voices in the study. Raised voices. Tristan's. Jarod's. But also two unfamiliar gruff ones.

"You can't be serious, Jarod!" Tristan must've yelled at the top of his lungs, because the walls of this house, that usually gulped down all sound, let his words pass through the thick wood without obstruction.

The guard standing in the entryway eyed me as though urging me not to intrude. I wouldn't, of course, but had he not been there, I might've lingered to glean what Jarod "wasn't serious about."

Not wanting to be alone, I headed into the kitchen in search of Muriel and found her kneading a big ball of dough—brioche, she told me. As her hands pressed and pulled, I regaled her with stories of Versailles.

"You've probably heard them all already," I said, realizing I might've been boring her.

"*Non, ma chérie.* I didn't know any of them. Why don't you tell me more while you help me make dinner?"

I washed my hands, thrilled at the prospect of a cooking

lesson. Recounting anecdote after anecdote, I learned how to emulsify egg yolks, softened butter, and lemon juice to make a velvety hollandaise sauce to complement the stalky white asparagus she'd bought at the market.

"Thought I'd find you in here."

I twirled around at the sound of Jarod's voice, my heartbeats melting into one another like the butter and egg yolks earlier.

Muriel smiled. "Why do I sense you're about to steal my sous-chef?"

"Because I'm about to steal your sous-chef," Jarod said.

Already unknotting the apron tied around my waist, I walked over to where he stood in the entrance of the kitchen, filling the entire frame. "Thank you, Muriel."

"Thank *you*. I got a fantastic history lesson *and* extra help."

I shot her a grin as I slid my hand into Jarod's outstretched one.

"How was your tour?" he asked.

"Amazing. Beautiful. Enriching. Did you know that the king had a secret passageway inside his bedroom that led straight into his mistress's apartment?"

He pushed out of the pantry and tugged me up the stairs. "How convenient."

"And it took three thousand candles to light up the Hall of Mirrors."

"That's a lot of wax."

"And when there were guests in the palace, they were called in to witness the king's rising." Jarod opened his bedroom door. "That's why Louis the Fourteenth was called the Sun—"

He kissed me, stealing the last word from my mouth, then shut the door, and backed me up against it. "I want to hear all about it, but first"—he dropped to his knees in front of me and unbuttoned my slacks—"first, I want to do something that I've been fantasizing about all day."

When his stubble scraped the inside of my thigh, I flung a hand out to grasp something solid. My fingers closed around the sculpted bronze handle.

Jarod guided my thong down my legs, and every atom in my body contracted, then damn near snapped when his long fingers closed around my calves and tracked over my knees before spiraling up my thighs and easing my legs farther apart. My chest pumped in and out, fluttering the white fabric of my T-shirt.

After swiping one finger over my seam, Jarod's eyes flared. "Hmm . . . so wet."

The growl of his voice against my skin was almost enough to make me come; it was most definitely enough to make me begin to tremble.

He gripped my legs again, then dipped his head, and licked over the line he'd traced.

I gasped, clutching the handle tighter. He spread my legs wider and lapped at me again. The hand not keeping me upright came down on his head, my fingers tangling in his gelled locks, creating chaos where there was order.

His knuckles flexed white as he licked harder, quicker, before pulling away to murmur dirty words that sounded sweet against my tensing flesh. His lips closed over me in a languid kiss before his steel and silk tongue took over, lashing violently until it tore a scream from my lungs.

"So. Fucking. Sweet," he rasped.

He kept licking long after I'd drifted down from my high, as though on a mission to absorb every last ounce of my pleasure. Satisfied, he unfurled his imposing body and brought my eyes to his with the softest brush of his fingers under my chin. He didn't say anything, didn't kiss me, just drank from my eyes the same way he'd drank from my body.

Still trying to catch my breath, I murmured, "I'm not sure what I did to deserve that, but thank you. It was . . . extraordinary."

"First off, that was entirely for me." He licked his glistening lips, and the air that had been cooling my damp skin gained a dozen degrees. "And secondly, you deserve so much more than *that*. You deserve so much more than I have the means to give you."

I cupped his jaw, my heart feeling as though it would balloon right out of my chest. "You've already given me everything I want."

"No. I haven't." His pupils shrank, granting his irises more space. The effect lent his eyes an unusual brightness. "I haven't given you the words you gave me last night."

I frowned. "Which words?"

"The ones I told you not to feel for me."

Oh. I combed my hair back, my earring catching in a snarled lock. As I worked on freeing it, I said, "I'm not expecting you to say them back, Jarod. I know I'm important to you—you've shown me this in so many ways—and that's enough for me."

I climbed onto my tiptoes, needing more inches than my heels afforded to kiss the puckered ridge between his eyebrows.

"I'm trying to be a better man, Feather." His arms came around me, sealing us close. "I'm trying to be worthy of you."

I hadn't thought I could love him any more than I already did, but with that declaration, he conquered every last uncharted territory in my heart.

56

The following morning over breakfast, Jarod told Muriel to help me pack for a trip. When I asked him where we were going, he said it was a surprise. When I enquired as to how long we'd be gone, he repeated that it was a surprise.

As he left to attend to some business, I wondered why we were taking a trip. Was guilt fueling this impromptu escapade? Did he think he needed to give me an adventure to make up for being unable to say that he loved me?

I tried to worm the answer out of Muriel, but she was a tomb. So, I helped her fold the clothing she'd picked out, studying her selection, but it still didn't give me an inkling as to where we were going. Would we be driving or flying? I'd never been on an airplane, never had use for them because of our Channels.

Our angelic transport system made me think of the guild and the Ophanim. No one had come to check on me. Not that it surprised me all that much. As long as we had wings, they didn't worry about us.

Lunchtime rolled around, and Jarod still hadn't come home. Growing skittish and bored, I scoured his bookshelves even though I wasn't sure if reading any of his books was permitted considering the pages crinkled like tissue paper and the leather bindings were stamped in gold. I went down to ask Muriel. When she said yes, I scampered back up the stairs, moved aside the purple-stingray box Jarod used as a bookend, and grabbed *Cyrano de Bergerac*, placing it delicately inside my bag along with my cell phone before returning to the foyer.

"Where are you going?" Muriel asked, balancing a crystal vase filled with drooping callas on her hip.

"Just to the park across the street."

Her gaze flicked to Luc, the guard on duty today. "Jarod should be home soon, *ma chérie*. You know he doesn't like to be kept waiting."

"But I have my cell phone. So—"

"Leigh, he doesn't want you going outside the house today."

My insides seemed to melt away. "Why?"

"He didn't tell me why." Her attention slid to the two other guards discussing something beside the fountain in the courtyard.

Their anxious expressions made me think it wasn't weekend plans.

My excitement and nervousness turned into dread. *Jarod Adler, what are you doing that requires me to stay indoors and hidden from the world?* Did I even want to know?

On wooden legs, I climbed back up the stairs and let my bag drop to the floor. Here I'd thought he was taking me on a romantic getaway, but maybe it was just a getaway.

I turned on the news, hoping and yet despairing I would hear something that would explain why I had to stay locked up. I'm not sure how long I stood there, in the middle of Jarod's bedroom staring at the television screen, but I was pretty certain I'd heard all the national happenings at least twice.

The door snicked open, and I pirouetted. "What in the world is . . ." My voice trailed off when I saw it was Tristan and not Jarod.

His face was rife with a tension that echoed throughout his entire body.

Terror seized me. "Is Jarod okay?"

Tristan shut the door behind him, and my heart leaped into overdrive.

"Tristan, you're scaring me. Is he okay?"

"No, *Plume*." He flung my nickname at me as though it were a filthy word. "He's not."

My hand climbed up to my neck as the noose of fear tightened around it. *Ninety-six.* If he'd— My stomach heaved. I couldn't even think the word.

"He's completely lost it!" Tristan snapped, his long strides eating up the oriental rug, carrying him to where I stood. He poked me in the chest so hard I stumbled backward.

Lost it? "So, he's alive?"

"No thanks to you." He palmed his silvering strands. "Everything was fine before you showed up. More than fine. Fucking perfect. And then you come in here with your big ideas and big eyes and fill Jarod's head with ideas, and now we're all going to be fucked." He poked me again.

"Stop touching me," I said, trying to keep my tone calm, hoping it would calm him.

Although the Ophanim taught us basic self-defense in the guilds, they urged us to find peaceful ways to resolve conflict, insisting words were more dignified and beneficial than fists.

An ugly smile sprouted over Tristan's reedy lips, injecting a crazed gleam into his eyes. Jarod was convinced his walls could protect me from evil. He'd failed to see evil had already breached them.

"Get out of this room before I call for one of the guards," I warned.

"Those guards answer to *me*, not to you, you little whore." His hand lurched to my neck and cinched it, and my heart damn near exploded. "But go ahead, Feather." His manic smile grew and grew. "*Scream.*"

I tried to say his name, tried to say *stop*, but only threads of air slid through my parted lips. I clawed at his wrist. I mouthed *Stop*, again.

"Did you say something?"

Tears pricked my eyelids as his fingers reawakened an ache I'd thought had healed. I realized then that mended wounds were like hidden wings—invisible but ever-present. The thought made my feathers spill from my back.

If only I could flap them in his face.

A creak made my gaze fly toward the door. Jarod's home was old and often popped and groaned, but maybe . . . maybe someone was coming.

"Jarod's not done with the meeting he called to ruin our reputation." Still, Tristan's gaze flicked to the sealed doors. Had he locked them? I couldn't remember . . .

Using his fleeting lapse of attention against him, I shook my head hard and gasped as his fingers snapped off my neck. I was so startled I barely had time to scramble two feet away before he was on me again, collaring me with hands that felt like metal claws. I batted at his arms, but my strength was dwindling along with my supply of oxygen.

"Don't worry, you'll pass out before dying."

Dying? He wanted to kill me?

"By the time he gets home, you'll be gone. Without a trace. I'm good at making people vanish without a trace. One of my special talents."

My fingers scrabbled uselessly around his wrist. Since I couldn't speak, I implored him to release me with my wet gaze.

"Would've saved me a lot of trouble if you'd died back at the store, but I shouldn't really be surprised you didn't. Women are so fucking useless. You give them all the tools, put the fucking knife in their hands and the victim in their lap, and they still manage to botch the job."

Was he saying that . . . that he'd . . .?

"It's not like I told her to stab you in the heart. Ribs are fucking nuisances. No, I tell her to slit your throat." His thumb and index finger hardened around my neck, denting my aching flesh. "I even demonstrate on a waste-of-space hobo, and she messes up."

My vision grayed, frayed. In one last desperate attempt, my mouth formed the word *please*. I didn't want to pass out, afraid of what he was going to do with my body. What if he chained and tossed me into the Seine like he'd done with the woman's father? The woman *he'd* sent to kill me. My immortality would allow me to survive, but it wouldn't melt the chains. It wouldn't make me magically float up to the surface.

I searched his pale eyes for a glimmer of hope but found nothing but hatred and a coldness that iced my already clammy skin. His soul was soiled beyond repair.

Something moved over Tristan's shoulder. I imagined my oxygen-starved brain had conjured up the disturbance. The room swam, darkened. I fluttered my lashes, fighting the only way I knew how—quietly and steadfastly.

If I ever made it back to a guild, I would tell the Ophanim they needed to train us better, give us more adequate tools, because not every situation in the human world could be fixed with words and goodness.

"To think I brought you to him," Tristan mused.

I would've found my way to Jarod without his help.

The same way Jarod had just found his way to me.

Tristan's hand was wrenched off my body. I collapsed on the floor, and air streaked down my throat like scalding coffee. The *whooshing* in my ears distorted Jarod's shout and muffled Tristan's squeak of surprise.

Luc and Muriel rushed into the bedroom. Jarod yelled, and both lunged toward me. Muriel crouched, gathering my hands off my neck to witness the damage, while Luc shielded us, gun aimed at Tristan, who stood so close to Jarod that I was terrified a loosed bullet would injure the wrong man.

"No . . . gun," I croaked.

Jarod's fist flew into Tristan's jaw, snapping his head sideways and sending him stumbling backward through the gaping French windows and onto the balcony. Muriel helped me onto my feet, binding her arm harder around my rib cage when I teetered like a drunk.

For all his putrid intentions toward me, I didn't think Tristan would harm Jarod. I tried to reach over and draw the guard's arms down, but my trembling hand swiped air before uselessly tumbling back against my side.

Jarod backed Tristan against the limestone guardrail, hands fastened around his throat.

My heart was still banging too hard to hear any of the words they exchanged, but at least, my vision had cleared. Muriel pivoted my body away from the tussle and attempted to drag me out of the bedroom, but I dug my heels into the rug.

"Muriel, I need . . . to help . . ."

"There's nothing you can do, Leigh."

"But Jarod . . ."

"Jarod will be fine."

A thunderous grunt slashed the air, and I flipped around in Muriel's arms, my wing bones jostling her.

That sound had come from Jarod.

My pulse knifed through me, blighting the gasp tearing up my throat, transforming it into a frozen puff of air.

Only one man remained on the balcony.

I flung Muriel's arm off my body and sprinted toward Jarod, who was clutching the stone guardrail as though contemplating jumping.

"Get away from here, Feather," he growled between rasping pants.

His gaze was fused to the fountain, to Tristan's body that lay unmoving inside, legs sprawled and submerged, arms stretched over his head pillowed on the rim. Blood glistened on the gray stone, clouded the water like ink. I shuddered, bringing my attention back to Jarod.

"Get away from me, Leigh!"

A rib-cracking sob fractured the air, made his big body quake.

I placed my hand on his hunched spine. He spun and tossed my arm away, glaring down at me and my wings with a violence that stopped my heart.

I magicked them away.

"Go! Fucking go, Feather!"

He hated me. Even though I hadn't pushed Tristan over the railing, it was my fault he'd died.

"I'm sorry," I whispered.

"Sorry?" He grabbed his hair and yanked so hard I thought he'd come away with handfuls. "You're not the monster; I am!

Now, go before you end up like him." He gestured wildly below. "Like *her*!" The statue. Lifeless and wingless.

Jarod's men rushed to the fountain, belting the guns they must have raised to cover their boss. Amir pushed two fingers against Tristan's arched neck. He looked up and shook his head. Jarod let out an inhuman sound before seizing one of the sconces woven into the ivy and ripping it off the wall. He flung it over the railing where it smashed at the feet of one of his guards. The man hopped away to avoid the projectiles ricocheting off the cobblestones.

We all froze, all waited to see what Jarod would do next, what he would throw next, because the anger was only just beginning to well up inside of him. His fingers flexed into fists that seemed intent on pummeling someone else. From the way he still glared my way, I imagined that someone was me.

He yelled at Amir to get Tristan out. The big man curled his arms underneath Tristan's slumped shoulders and hoisted him out of the fountain, streaking the gray stones with blood. The tang of salt and copper filled the air until breathing became almost painful, but I labored through it, battling down the nausea, pushing away all signs of weakness.

I needed to stay strong for Jarod, because I feared Tristan's death might destroy my sinner's good intentions and scar his soul all over again.

Blood seeped from his knuckles, or was it from his palms? Had he broken his skin on the glass sconce or on Tristan's skin?

His feral eyes were still on mine, as though challenging me to look away first. Didn't he know I was more stubborn than he was?

Every tendon in his neck stood out as he panted. I took a step forward slowly, afraid that if I approached too fast he'd spook and run. But he didn't move. I took another step, and then another, until I was only a millimeter away. His body shook so hard I wrapped my arms around him. I waited for him to push me away. To yell at me to leave. To blame me.

Instead, his body melted over mine, his head sagging into the slope of my neck. His sobs tangled in my long hair, matting it to my bruised neck. Not thinking I could hold him up much longer, I guided him to the lounger and eased him down, then climbed onto his lap, and curled my body around his, tucking his head under my chin, letting his broken heart bleed over my writhing one.

Muriel stood beside the French doors, mouth tight, eyes bright. Was she grieving for Tristan or for Jarod? Heaving a sigh, she closed her eyes, and a tear glistened out.

Jarod spoke against my chest, but his words were garbled by the wet silk.

I pressed him away lightly. "What did you say?"

"Montparnasse. I need—to call—"

"I'll call the undertaker, Jarod," Muriel said, understanding.

"I promised him—a place in—" A cry lurched out of him. He banded his arms around my back and crushed me against him, screaming his pain into my chest.

"I'll take care of everything," Muriel said. She was about to retreat into the bedroom, but came toward us instead. She peeled his head off my chest and cupped his jaw. Her thumb stroked his cheekbone. "He brought this upon himself, Jarod. You are not to blame."

"I killed him, Mimi. My best friend," he wailed. "My brother."

"He was never your brother. He never had your best interest at heart. He never gave you an ounce of all you gave him."

"He saved me. So many times." Jarod's hoarse voice scraped the air.

"And I'll always be grateful for that, but he only saved you because he saw his own salvation within the walls of this house . . . within you." She stroked his cheek again. "He never allowed you to get close to people. Our relationship infuriated him. More than once, I feared he'd suggest firing me."

"He did suggest it."

She grunted. "Of course he did. I hope you know that even Amir with his big muscles and scary guns couldn't pry me away from you." Her gaze drifted to me then, and as though her eyes were connected to Jarod's, his moved to my face too. "I didn't want to speak out of line before, but that day in the shop . . . the way Tristan acted . . ." She let her voice trail off, but her accusation was loud and clear.

Jarod sketched the shape of my face with his fingers, dragging away a lock of hair and tucking it behind my shoulder with heart-breaking gentleness. "I figured that out too late."

Had he heard Tristan confess, or had he guessed this some other way? Not wanting to bring it up, not now, perhaps, not ever, I lowered my gaze to his Adam's apple that bobbed sharply, as though shoving down a bolt of grief.

"Doesn't make me less of a monster, though," he murmured.

I whipped my gaze back to his. "You're *not*."

"I just broke someone's spine, Feather. Someone, who in spite of everything, meant something to me."

"Saved me from committing a felony," Muriel muttered.

"Mimi!" Jarod gasped.

"What? You don't think I'd be capable of murder? Do you think your uncle hired me because I was good with baby bottles and whisks? He hired me because he'd heard I'd put a bullet through my abusive father's brains."

Jarod's body stilled beneath mine. "You never told me that."

"And I'll never tell either of you any more about it." Her lips pinched at the memory. "Now, I'll go call the undertaker. You two go back inside and get rid of your guilt. I won't have you moping around the house, Jarod. I raised a tough man. A *good* man. And I couldn't be prouder about what you did today, and I'm not talking about—" She cocked her head toward the courtyard.

Jarod gulped. "How did you hear?"

She tapped one finger over his scrunched brow. "You really think anything in this house escapes me?" She pressed a kiss where her finger had been, then turned and left.

Somewhere below us, the guards spoke in hushed tones but turned silent when Muriel started barking orders.

"And here I thought I was the big boss," Jarod mumbled.

Even though so many things about this moment were terrible, I smiled. "I better not get on her bad side, huh?" I bumped his nose with mine.

He grunted.

"Jarod, what was she talking about before?"

He gave a heavy sigh. "Evidence surfaced today. Enough to revive a cold case and destroy a political career." A muscle in his jaw ticked. "The prime minister"—his gaze set on the stone guardrail, and I knew he was thinking of Tristan—"he's going away for a long time. Forever, really. Tristan wasn't on board with my decision and stormed out of the meeting. I should've followed him sooner. Before . . ." His thick lashes swooped over his reddened eyes.

I kissed his temple.

For a long beat, neither of us spoke. Then, I sighed. "And I should've tried to help him."

His lashes lifted. "He wouldn't have accepted your help, Feather. He was much too proud to accept anyone's help. Especially a woman's." Jarod examined my throat, then caressed it, and although my skin felt raw, his touch was soothing. "They didn't come for him."

"Who?"

"The . . . what did you call them again? Malahim?"

"Malakim. Killing us . . . well, trying to, is a great sin."

"*Right* . . ." He was probably remembering how he'd earned his rank. "So, his soul is . . . lost?"

"I think so."

Jarod nodded slowly. "What about my uncle's?"

I tugged my lip inside my mouth, unwilling to answer him and add to his sorrow.

He looked up at the sky. "If I ever end up there, I'll know no one."

"Can we not talk about you ending up there? Please?"

He pulled in a big breath. "You're right. Enough." He pushed the air back out of his lungs as he stood, taking me up with him.

I didn't think he'd finished grieving for Tristan. You didn't get over someone who'd shared your life for so many years in the space of a few minutes, not even if you were used to death.

Jarod's grief was just beginning, and however tough Muriel had raised him to be, he'd break again, and I'd be there, and so would she. Together, we'd pick up the pieces of his guilty heart and glue them back until the day came when he'd stop blaming himself.

The following morning, we dressed in black and left at daybreak, not on our trip. At least, not any trip that required a suitcase. We drove to the Montparnasse Cemetery. Tailed by Luc, Amir, and two other bodyguards, we walked down a long road lined with gravestones, mausoleums, and lindens in full bloom.

Muriel held Jarod's arm, as though trying to lend him some strength. I walked alongside him, but our hands didn't so much as graze. Even though I wanted to be there for Jarod today, I'd been worried my presence would be an intrusion. Or worse, a reminder of why we were traveling through this repository of bones. I read the etchings on tombstones, grimacing when the years separating a birth from a death were too few. Human life was fragile and fleeting and, sometimes, unfair.

Without realizing it, my wings cascaded out of my back. It was Jarod's hand combing through my feathers that alerted me to their presence. "Thank you for coming," he whispered.

I threaded my fingers through his and pressed our palms together. "Always, Jarod."

He stared around us at the sea of gravestones that recorded human lives. "I'm afraid there's no such thing as always."

He was referring to Tristan, to his uncle, to his mother.

Wait . . . Did he know that his mother's soul hadn't been

collected? Had I told him? He raised our clasped hands and pressed a kiss to my knuckles.

When we finally arrived in front of a crypt that bore the name Adler, Jarod released my fingers to greet the undertaker. A black marble pillar bordered the crypt, inscribed with names: Isaac Adler, Jane Adler, Neil Adler, Mikaela Adler, Tristan Michel. I hadn't even known Tristan's last name, not that last names were important. After all, angels weren't born with any.

Gentle hands wrapped around my arm—Muriel's. "Last time we were here, he was eight." She sighed. "History's just an eternal cycle."

If only she knew.

"Was Jane Isaac's wife?"

"Yes."

"And Neil?"

"Jarod's father." After a quiet moment, she said, "When my name goes up on the stone, can you make sure they write Adler instead of my maiden name?"

I looked over at her, surprised by her request for so many reasons.

"Don't look so appalled. I've already told Jarod my wishes. I just wanted to share them with you in case he forgets."

Stunned to silence, I only managed to nod. Jarod came back toward us, eyes as black as the marble pillar mapping his family tree. He crossed his arms and kept them that way until the urn containing Tristan's ashes had been lowered inside the crypt and the undertaker presented him with a bowl and a spoon.

"Ashes to ashes, dust to dust, dirt to dirt." Muriel sighed, releasing me. Once Jarod had tossed two spoonfuls into the dark pit, Muriel took the spoon and tossed in some more. "May you finally find peace, Tristan."

I bit my lip, my teeth digging in so hard they almost drew blood.

Tristan's soul wouldn't find peace.

He'd died a Triple, and Triples had no souls.

59

*T*he days that ensued Tristan's burial were strange and peaceful.

Strangely peaceful.

I kept waiting for the other shoe to drop, for Jarod to break down, or for someone else to try and kill me, but nothing like that happened. Although there were moments when Jarod was contemplative, *La Cour des Démons* filled with chatter and laughter. Jarod and I spent hours meeting with people who needed help, and once we were done weighing in on the most pressing cases, we would seek out the privacy and stillness of his bedroom.

We spent hours together, exploring each other's bodies, watching movies, reading books, taking strolls through public gardens bursting with spring blooms before either returning to his home for Muriel's cooking or sampling new restaurants all over the French capital.

It was wonderful.

Too wonderful to last, even though I dared hope it would.

It was only when I erupted into Jarod's office one rainy afternoon, giggling with Celeste about how sodden we both were, and saw Asher sitting across from Jarod that reality knocked into me and dried up my laughter.

Once Jarod's guard closed the door behind us, I said, "What are you doing here, Seraph?"

Jarod smiled, and even though it was soft, I knew the shape of his smiles by heart, and there was something wrong about this one. "He stopped by to see how I was doing."

"Since when do archangels make social calls?" I asked.

Asher's turquoise feathers fluttered behind his back. "You're right. This isn't a social call. I stopped by to tell Jarod how impressed we were by his dwindling rank."

"Seventy-two, Feather," Jarod said, his voice catching on my nickname. "Almost there."

"Seventy-two?" I yelped, flouncing onto his lap and linking my arms around his neck. In spite of our audience, I kissed him.

And he kissed me back.

I used to think seventy-two was a terrible score, but that was when I evaluated scores starting at zero instead of at a hundred.

Asher cleared his throat and rose from the green velvet armchair. "I should—*We* should leave you two . . ."

Celeste was frowning, gaze skipping between Asher and Jarod.

Asher tipped his head toward the door. "Come on, Celeste. I'll give you a lift."

When she didn't move, the rainwater dripping down her body and absorbing into Jarod's rug, Asher touched her shoulder. Ungluing her boots from the rug, she turned and followed him out.

The second it was just Jarod and me, I clutched his face. "I'm so proud of you."

His smile strengthened but still didn't reach his eyes. "How was your day, my love?"

"Amazing. Muriel gave me a cooking lesson. Then I read some more of those old books you have upstairs—can we please buy some newer ones?—every time I flip a page, dust poofs off the paper and makes me sneeze. Plus, they're a little boring."

Jarod chuckled, but the sweet sound was faint, as though Asher's visit had caused his voice to lose power.

"After that, Celeste called, and we went to try out that éclair bakery Muriel told us about." I could still taste the rich coffee pastry cream on my tongue, the pliant shell, the glossy icing. "And then, as we ran home"—yes, *home* . . . the irony that an angel had made a home for herself inside the Court of Demons wasn't lost on me—"I thought up some new ways to salvage your soul."

He smiled, but it was still too tight for my liking. "What am I going to do once you're gone?" he murmured.

My suspicions that something was wrong worsened. "Once I'm gone? Where am I going?"

His Adam's apple jostled, and he cleared his throat. "Upstairs." He stood so abruptly I would've toppled right off his lap if he hadn't scooped me up. "In my bed. *Our* bed."

"I like the sound of that," I said, linking my arms around his neck.

"And I like the sound of you"—he trekked to the door—"when you moan my name."

My cheeks warmed as his elbow jammed against the handle to flick it open.

We bypassed Luc posted outside the study. Thankfully, he kept his gaze averted. How I wished there were no guards, no need for them, but unfortunately, Jarod could never live without people protecting him, especially now that his rank was decreasing. To rectify his wrongs, he was probably crucifying some of his clients.

"You know, I *can* walk," I said as he lunged up his stairs.

He pecked my lips. "But I can walk faster. Longer legs."

I laughed. "And we're in a hurry?"

"I might sprain a muscle."

I moved my mouth to his ear. "It's not a muscle."

He grunted. "Then why can I flex it?"

I rolled my eyes when he finally put me down to open his door. I shut it behind us. Before the latch even clicked, his mouth was on mine, his hands in my rain-slicked hair, then on my hips as we walk-stumbled toward the bed, bumping into one of the wooden posts.

"Let me see that muscle you're so proud of," I taunted him, pushing my hair off my face as I dropped on the bed, my head leveled with the erection tenting his pants.

When he smirked, the worry I'd felt down in his study began to fade.

I hummed. "It *is* pretty impressive."

"Pretty impressive?" He snorted. "I'm requesting the same size or larger when I get access to my elysian form."

Emotion fluttered beneath my ribs. Was that what Asher and Jarod had been discussing? *Elysium?*

To be together in the land of angels meant I would have to complete my wings, and he'd have to drop more points from his sinner score. Not to mention that he'd have to die.

"Jarod?"

"Yeah, Feather."

"You're only twenty-five."

"Your point?"

"You're too young to contemplate dying."

He blew some air from the corner of his mouth. "Because you think I'm going to leave you up there on your own? An angel like you? So beautiful, inside and out? I'm going to be joining you as soon as my rank drops under fifty."

"How about the day your rank drops under fifty, we discuss my ascension?"

He pressed his lips together, then held out his hand. "Come here."

I threaded my fingers through his and let him pull me up. Slowly he placed my hand over his heart, cementing it there.

"Feather," he murmured, his voice hoarse, "thank you for choosing me. For coming back to me again and again. For your patience and your smiles. For your laughter and even for your tears. Thank you for glittering for me and for kissing me. For allowing me to desecrate your body." His lips twitched, and I rolled my eyes. "For showing me that wings aren't always used for flying away."

"Jarod, I—"

"Wait. I'm not done."

I sealed my lips.

"This last month has been . . . it's been—" His pause was brutal, but I kept silent and waited, sensing that sharing emotion was still challenging for Jarod. "What I'm trying to say, and doing a crap job of, is that . . . it's that I love you, Feather."

My eyebrows jumped.

He pressed my palm harder against his chest, and it felt like I was touching the very organ beating there. "Can you always remember that, baby?"

"How about you just tell me every day?"

His dark eyes glittered even though my skin hadn't lit up. When his thick lashes lowered and a single tear coursed down his face, catching in his dark stubble, time slowed.

Stopped.

"Jarod?" I murmured his name across the slender expanse dividing us. "What's going on?"

"It was my turn to save you." His ragged tone made the expanse grow and grow.

Panic shortening my heartbeats, I curled my fingers to grip something solid. Since I couldn't reach his heart, I grabbed onto his shirt.

"I can't protect you down here, Leigh."

Beads of rainwater bled from my hair and trekked down my spine. "I can't die."

"For now!" His lids flipped up, his grief smearing into anger.

My eyes widened.

"I won't let anyone hurt you again, Feather."

His heart pounded into my clenched knuckles, the thunder in his body streaking into mine.

"So, what?" My voice wobbled. "You're breaking up with me?"

"No."

The rumbling in my chest quelled but didn't dissipate. "Then what's going on?"

"I know you want to wait for me, but you're going to ascend ahead of me."

"No!" I shook my head. "I'm not."

The anger drained out of Jarod so fast I thought it would puddle at his feet.

"We leave together or not at all," I said, still shaking my head like a madwoman.

Jarod's hands came up to my face, steadied it. "Shh."

"I'm not signing off from you, Jarod Adler. *Ever*." At least, no one could take that decision away from me.

His eyes gleamed again, and I scavenged their depths for the source of this pain so I could uproot it once and for all.

"I'll be right behind you," he said, after what felt like an eternity.

"Stop talking like I'm going somewhere, because I'm. Not. Leaving."

"Your wings are complete. They have been since last night."

I opened my mouth but no sound came out.

"After Tristan's funeral, Asher stopped by to see how I was doing. How *you* were doing. I've never been scared of anything. At least, not in a long time . . . But after Tristan tried to kill you, I was fucking frightened. Frightened that one day, when you had no more feathers to keep you safe, you'd succumb to my world the same way he did. The same way my mother did. And I shared my fear with Asher, asked him for his counsel. Feather, I thought up the worst scenarios"—he shuddered—"to make you hate me, but I was too much of a coward to enact any of them. When Asher handed me a solution, I took it."

"What . . . solution?" My voice trembled so hard the syllables knocked against each other as they tumbled out.

"Asher signed you off from me."

I gaped in horror at Jarod. "All those people we've been helping . . ."

The rain lashing his windows mirrored the pain lashing my chest.

"Please don't be mad at me, baby. It was the only way I could think of to keep you safe."

Tears pooled and distorted his beautiful face. "It wasn't your decision to make. It was *mine*."

The pads of his thumbs stroked over my cheeks, trying to catch the tears that fell too fast.

"I don't want to leave you," I sobbed.

He sighed, combed my hair back, then tracked his hands down my frozen body, and gathered it against his. "I know, baby." His chin settled on the top of my head.

"I hate you." I waited to feel the jab of a falling feather. Yearned for it. None came, cementing my dread to my marrow the same way Jarod and Asher had cemented my feathers to my wing bones.

His Adam's apple jutted against my throbbing forehead. "I hate myself more than you could ever hate me."

I closed my eyes and cinched my arms around him. "I won't go."

His palm skated over my hair. "Asher promised to come at the very last minute."

The lump that swelled inside my throat turned solid as rock. "Good. He can burn my wings off."

"He'll do no such thing."

"Jarod, I—"

His hands curled gently around my biceps and pressed me away. "Listen to me. You'll go up and make a home for yourself. For us. And no white quartz everywhere, all right?" His lips flexed but slackened almost as quickly as they'd bent.

I inhaled a long breath, trying to ease the cramping in my chest. "Is your rank really seventy-two?"

He nodded.

"I can't believe I'm about to say this, but you can't take your own life. People who commit suicide, their souls . . . they're not collected."

One of his hands drifted off my arm to set on my jaw. "Don't worry. There are plenty of people who'd line up to put a bullet through my skull."

I shuddered.

"Pardon, ma plume." Forgive me, my feather.

I swallowed, and my saliva slithered around the receding lump. He was going to make it. "Don't expect me to forgive you when you show up at my door. I'll let you in, but I might not talk to you for days. Months even."

"As long as you make love to me, I'll accept your silence."

I glowered at him. "I might make you wait for that."

His mouth softened into a smile. "You know I hate to be kept waiting."

I sighed, and the air in my lungs seemed to fill up the entire room. "I can't believe you did this."

His smile turned sheepish, then pained. "I can't believe I did it either."

I decided to push away my annoyance and anger. Fighting wasn't how I wanted to spend our last hours on Earth. "Kiss me, Jarod, and don't stop until Asher pries me out of your arms."

His face dropped toward mine heartbeat by heartbeat, so slowly I thought he'd never reach me before I would have to leave. When his mouth touched mine, my body sparked and smoldered. And my wings . . . they spilled out of my back unbidden the same way they'd sealed to my bones unbidden.

60

*W*hen Asher came to collect me, I wasn't ready.

Then again, who is ever ready to have their heart split in two?

I tried to stay strong but failed miserably. When my fingers slipped out of Jarod's for the last time in who knew how long, a cry tore from my lungs and filled his bedroom. He turned away right before Asher cloaked our bodies in angel-dust to make us invisible to the guards in the courtyard below.

The proud line of Jarod's shoulders slumped and then his body began to tremble like my own. I wanted to be angry again, because anger beat misery.

Asher's brow grooved, and I was glad for his guilt. Glad for his silence. I couldn't stomach talking to him right now.

Maybe I'd stay mute until Jarod ascended to show how violated I felt that the archangel had acted against my wishes. Since when did archangels listen to the wishes of sinners?

The archangel curled an arm around my waist and sprang into the dead sky that contained no moon or stars tonight, just steel clouds and needles of rain. I closed my eyes as we soared over Paris, as the wind and rain flogged my hair, turning it into an orange squall.

When we reached the guild, he set me down and drew the door open. I didn't look behind me as I entered. I neither possessed the will nor the desire to set my gaze on all I was leaving behind. As I forded through the Atrium, I pulled the scent of Jarod into my tender lungs—mineral, musky, and sweet. So very sweet. My heart—what was left of it—disintegrated further, the beats clattering to the floor like crumbs.

Crumbs to lead my sinner to me.

The Fletchings who'd been out and about stopped to watch, gazes wide with envy even though I felt like a prisoner being led to her execution. How I wished I could pull my wings off and offer them to one of my peers so I could run back out into the soaking streets.

When we approached the Channel, the Ophanim of Guild 7 were lined up. They congratulated me and wished me a good ascension. I didn't say anything and would've kept my vow of silence had Celeste not come tearing down the quartz hallways like a bowling ball. She flung her arms around me, and my rickety heart dropped another crumb, one for her this time.

"Oh, Leigh, I'm going to miss you so much," she wept.

I crushed her against me wishing I could take her with me at least. "Ditto, honey."

Our system was cruel—casting us out, making us grow up without parents in a world that wasn't always kind, and then, once we'd made a home for ourselves, once we'd woven bonds with humans and Fletchings, it called us back and expected us to sever the strings of our past so we could start braiding new ones.

"Leigh, we need to go," Asher said softly, the first words he'd spoken since leaving Jarod's study that morning when the world had still been a lustrous place.

"Grow those pretty purple feathers fast, okay?"

Celeste wiped her freckled cheeks.

I leaned toward her ear and whispered, "And watch over Jarod for me. Protect him until he gets to fifty." As I straightened, I added, "And Muriel!"

I hadn't even said goodbye to the woman who'd mothered me this past month. Hadn't hugged her. Hadn't expressed how grateful I was for her endless patience and tenderness.

Another crumb tumbled from my chest.

Celeste swallowed, her eyes so red her irises seemed more amber than brown.

"Love you, kiddo." I stamped a long kiss onto her brow, then turned, and entered the Channel.

Asher stepped in after me, and the sparkling smoke thickened as it lapped at our bodies. He extended his hand, and even though the only one I wanted to hold had been ripped from my fingers, I placed my palm over his.

As we rocketed upward, I thought I heard the archangel mumble that he was sorry, but perhaps, it was the wind *whooshing* in my ears and dancing in my hair that created the illusion of an apology.

*O*ur childhood had been filled with stories about Elysium —the arch made of mother-of-pearl that welcomed angels and souls into the quartz capital, the seven glittery waterfalls that coursed down the white stone walls and crashed melodically into a fountain broad as a lake, the floors of abodes and shops and restaurants carved into the glossy rock, the rainbow-colored creatures that frolicked through the balmy air, their scales, fur, and feathers glinting in both sunlight and starlight.

My broken heart pumped with hollow joy as the stone beneath my feet began to glow, the veins of angel-fire flickering to life as the elysian day dimmed. The glittery lavender smoke twined around my feet as I stepped out of the Channel, a cavity built right into the rock façade, too symmetrical and smooth to be natural.

"The Canyon of Reckoning," I whispered, spinning to take in the walls of solid white rock so tall they seemed to pierce the very sky.

Above me, a skein of birds—not birds . . . *angels*—flew around the arch, some swooping beneath it and others climbing higher before diving back down. I missed their landing because of the distance and the tall wall guarding the entrance to the fortified city.

I'd dreamed of this place; it outshone all of my dreams.

How I longed to hear Jarod carp about how everything was so tediously shiny and white, how I yearned to feel his fingers squeeze mine and twirl me so I could take everything in. But the man who stood beside me was blonde and winged and blue-eyed, not my dark sinner with his twisted sense of humor, ridiculously expensive suits, and smooth wingless shoulders.

"Is this how you imagined it?" Asher asked, and I sensed him trying to inject enthusiasm into his voice, enthusiasm he himself wasn't feeling.

"It's more beautiful."

His eyebrows quirked, probably surprised I was capable of finding splendor in anything.

"I can't wait for Jarod to see it," I murmured. "That's the Pearly Arch, isn't it?"

"The one and only." His timbre was low and gentle like the breeze that gusted through the square, carrying the scents of citrus and salt.

The arch's pearlescent surface refracted light and dappled the stone surrounding it. Two rainbow-winged sparrows swooped around me, greeting me with a melodious aria before flocking down the opposite end of the canyon.

"The Nirvana Sea," Asher explained even though I hadn't asked what lay on that end.

"And where is Abaddon?"

He lifted his chin toward the opposite wall and the identical hollow that graced the rock wall. "The entrance is through that Channel."

Dark, shimmery smoke slithered around the white rock, enticing and chilling.

"How long do you think it will take Jarod to get his score to fifty?" I asked, just as two Malakim materialized in the Channel behind us, golden orbs nestled in their palms—harvested souls.

"Evening, Seraph," both intoned.

"Good evening," Asher said.

"How long?" I asked again, one-track minded.

Asher cleared his throat. "Your parents are here." He nodded to the Abaddon Channel.

"My . . . parents?"

Two winged figures emerged from the steel smoke, draped in

black leather from neck to toe. They stopped in the middle of the canyon, shimmery wings tucked into their spines.

I pushed all thoughts of Jarod aside and concentrated on the angels who'd created me. I didn't run to them, the same way they didn't run to me—all of us strangers.

My mother's golden hair snapped in the breeze, wavy and long like mine. My father's was cut short but not short enough to hide the copper shade of it that shimmered in the glowing rocks confining us.

"Are you ready to meet them?" Asher asked, as another Malakim passed by us, leading his collected soul toward the dark entrance of purgatory.

Jarod's face flashed behind my swollen lids, and my hand rose to my heart. "No. But I wasn't ready for any of this."

I pressed my palm to my chest and shut my eyes, and for a second, I could almost imagine it was *his* pulse I was feeling instead of my own. I'd started to know the rhythm of his blood better than my own.

Soon, I told myself, inhaling the lingering scent of him.

When I opened my lids, the two angels were watching me, patient or unhurried, I wasn't sure. "What am I supposed to call them? Mom and Dad?"

"It's up to you."

"What do you call your parents, Seraph?"

"I call them by their names."

My gaze lingered on my father's wings, entirely silver as though tipped in a vat of liquid metal. Like mine. "What are my parents' names?"

"Raphael and Sofia."

I studied their features as I loomed closer, trying to spot other similarities.

"Hello, child," Raphael said.

Child? How old was my father? Since he was a pure Verity like myself, and I was the first to be born in several generations, I estimated he was quite ancient.

"How lovely you are," Sofia said, her gaze running over me the same way mine had raced over her. She broke away from my father to move closer and lifted her hand but hesitated. "May I?"

May she what? Touch me? I nodded, and the pads of her fingers landed gently on my cheekbone.

"You have my eyes and mouth, but your wings"—she turned to Raphael, her pale pink feathers tipped in silver swaying from the abrupt movement—"they're your father's. Pure Verity wings." She swung back around, green eyes glistening with amazement.

In the human world, she would've been considered my sister. Not my mother. Angels who remained in Elysium were untouched by time. Only those who traveled to Earth or lived in guilds aged, slowly but still their faces wrinkled and their skin softened.

"Why didn't you ever come to see me?" I hated how juvenile I sounded, especially since most parents didn't visit their offspring.

Sofia looked at Asher as though seeking help in how to answer my question. "It is hard to get away from Abaddon. Our workforce isn't very consequent in the nether region of our dimension."

Work had kept them away? "In twenty years, you couldn't get a single day off?"

My mother flinched.

My father's hand wrapped around her wrist and pulled her back toward him. "We could have traveled to Earth, but we chose not to make the trip, child."

"Why?"

"You are our third offspring," Raphael said.

Perhaps hearing that I had siblings should've been what stuck with me, but jealousy sprang up instead. "And what? You used all your vacation days on them?"

My father's eyes narrowed. I'd known him all of a minute, and he already disliked me. We were off to a great start. "Our two other Fletchings never completed their wings."

"And it destroyed us, because we'd traveled to the guilds, built relationships with them," Sofia said. "We couldn't go through that again, Leigh." She smiled, her hand moving toward my cheek again.

I sucked in a breath but allowed her palm to bond with my skin.

"We are so happy to meet you and so proud." My mother's

voice shook. "We heard you gave Seraph Claire's husband a run for his money. A Triple. Well done, my beautiful girl."

I bristled. Jarod wasn't a Triple, not anymore. And lowering his rank wasn't an achievement; it was justice.

"You'll get to meet him soon." I glanced toward Asher, who was staring at the Pearly Arch as though he'd never seen it before. "His rank's dropping fast. He'll reach Elysium in no time."

My mother nodded. My father didn't even twitch. Apparently, I hadn't inherited my effusiveness from him.

Silence billowed around us like the smoke from the Channels.

"How wonderful," my mother finally said.

The luminescent stone made Raphael's silver feathers glitter. "We should let her get settled, Sofia."

"But we just—"

"May we come visit you tomorrow, child?"

I wished he hadn't felt the need to ask for my permission, but I was as much a stranger to him as my parents were to me.

I sighed, tabling my unduly chilliness. They'd lost two kids. Even though I wished they'd visited, I understood their reticence. "You can come to see me anytime."

The set of my father's shoulders relaxed, and a smile breached his stiff expression.

It was strange to think of them as my parents since they both looked so young. I wondered if that incongruity would ever change. What if my trips to Earth—once I became a Malakim—left more traces on my face than existed on theirs?

I stared around me again, at this home I'd need to apprehend, and it reminded me of the first time I'd entered Jarod's realm. How lost I'd felt that night, and yet I would've given anything to turn the needles of time and go back to that day. I would've given anything for Jarod to find me all over again.

I glanced back at the lavender smoke curling from the portals and whispered, "Hurry."

*a*sher led me under the Pearly Arch that loomed breathtakingly high and glistened like the inside of an oyster shell in spite of the entrenching dusk. Did angel-fire also irrigate it or was some other magic making it glow?

I was about to ask Asher when I got distracted by a flock of angels gliding overhead, wings extended, feathers fluttering, voices crisscrossing the warm air. Their gazes arrowed to Asher, then to me, and their eyebrows rose, but they didn't land to greet me or salute the archangel.

"You can do that too, now." Asher's voice made me jump. "Want to try?"

"Um." The breeze tickled my feathers. No. Not the wind. They were twitching. "What if I fall?"

"Wings make you fly, Leigh. It is only their absence that make you fall."

He smiled an encouraging smile, the sort of smile the Ophanim offered us Fletchings when we doubted ourselves. *Us Fletchings . . .* I was no longer a Fletching. I'd graduated from the guilds, but since there'd been no celebration, the promotion went unnoticed. I'd celebrate when Jarod arrived. My chest squeezed for the trillionth time, dropping another invisible crumb.

I tucked my wings into my back, deciding I would wait for Jarod. I had no desire to soar without him. "Some other time."

Asher's brow crinkled, and his wings, which had started to spread, retracted a little. "Don't be scared, Leigh."

"Scared? Oh, Seraph, flying doesn't scare me."

"Then why don't you want to try?" His long golden hair frolicked around his face. He bound it with his fist to keep it out of his eyes.

"It's a big milestone for angels. One I'd like to share with Jarod."

Asher's pupils shrank, and he released his hold on his hair. "By foot, the way is longer, so we should get going."

His tone was edged with something . . . an emotion I couldn't put my finger on. Annoyance? Frustration?

"You're mad at me," I said.

"You stopped living the day you met Jarod; you stopped dreaming!"

"No, Seraph, I never stopped living or dreaming. I merely redesigned my life and dreams to fit with Jarod's. You can't open your heart to someone and expect things not to fall out or to slip in."

His turquoise eyes ground into mine, condemning. Just like Celeste, he thought I was crazy. I didn't hold it against them. Love needed to be experienced to be understood.

He huffed as we crossed beneath the Arch and came to a stop at the top of a knoll. He jabbed at the air, gesturing to the sunken center where gilt-edged smoke curled off the surface of a body of water so wide and round it seemed ridiculous to call it a fountain even though seven colossal angel statues rose in the middle and spurted water from their raised hands.

"The Lev—it's the heart of the city." Asher's tone was short.

He pointed to the horseshoe-shaped rock surrounding the fountain along which coursed the seven waterfalls. Openings were sculpted into the glowing rock, like bay windows. "Every layer of rock comprises a tier of elysian society. At the bottom you have the Neshamaya, where human souls reside and operate businesses open to all—restaurants, shops, clubs. Then the Hadashya, where the new angels live."

"My stop."

"Yes. Above that, there's the Yashanya where older angels reside until they elect to retire to the Nirvana Mountains."

"Where are the mountains?"

He pointed in the direction the sparrows had flown earlier. "Beyond the sea. You can't see them from down here."

I squinted toward the cleft in the rock, trying to spot what lay beyond, but the miles and narrowness of the opening hid the landscape, so I refocused on the city. "What's on the fourth tier?"

"The Emtsaya where you'll be sorted by calling and taught everything you'll need to know. And then at the top"—he pointed to the plateau from which flowed the waterfalls—"is where I live and work. The Shevaya. Angels and souls—or Neshamim in the celestial tongue—may wander everywhere. Erelim guard the capital and all the cities surrounding it but rarely have need to intervene."

I followed him down a staircase carved into the rock. Since the Neshamim floated and the angels flew, I doubted the stairs were put to much use.

The Arch cast dabs of color on the molten spread that filled the fountain basin and undulated like water but swelled like smoke. I crouched by the edge and dipped my hand inside, the substance licking my fingers like warm clouds.

"Our water is called *ayim*."

An iridescent water lily knocked gently into my knuckles, its petals falling open as though to welcome me, or was it the stars it welcomed? Did it bloom at night like the ones in the guilds?

As I rose from my crouch, I repeated the word, rolling it on my tongue, "*Ayim*."

"It also fills the Nirvana Sea."

"How very strange."

"One day, you'll find human water strange." Asher untensed a fraction. "Keeping you here a hundred years isn't simply to guard you from recognition in the human world. The law was primarily put in place to help you adjust to your new world."

It was still a cruel law.

He led me around the belt of quartz, feeding me more words from the celestial tongue. Angels and humans—not humans . . . souls cloaked in the human flesh of their choosing—stared at us as we passed. Well, at the Seraphim. It wasn't customary for new angels to be escorted into Elysium by one of the Seven. Usually, the Ophanim brought their students up. But not much about my ascension had been customary.

There were openings between the shops and restaurants that led to winding streets. I stopped next to one and took in the strip of sky that ran the length of it even though solid rock covered the passage.

"The sky is an illusion, the stone magicked to mirror the elysian firmament, just like in the guilds."

Mirror? It hadn't been a real sky I'd spent my childhood watching? Real stars I'd wished on? "The Ophanim lied to us, Seraph. They told us it was real."

"They told you what they were taught to say."

"They are taught to lie? What an example that sets for us."

He ground his teeth but didn't dispute my claim. I sensed his patience wearing thin, but I took my time exploring this new world. He'd forced me inside of it, so it was only fair he paid the price of my curiosity.

There were no street plaques or numbers. How was I supposed to find my way back if I wandered?

As we passed beneath one of the waterfalls, I reached out and glided my hand through the *ayim*. It slid through my fingers like Jarod's hair in the mornings when the gel relinquished its hold on his soft locks. "Are there no addresses?"

"How did you find your way to your dorm room in the guilds?"

I snatched my hand and dried it on my flowy black pants even though my fingers weren't wet. "With all due respect, Seraph, Elysium isn't the size of a guild."

"You have a century to map out the capital and surrounding cities and learn each street by heart." His boots lifted off the ground and he hovered. "Your floor is the next one up. There are no stairs."

I sensed he was waiting for me to flap my angel-given gift, but I didn't. "Will you help me up, Seraph?"

"How will you get down later?"

"I'll figure out some way." I'd probably have no choice but to fly and dreaded the prospect, but I'd cross that bridge when I got to it.

He offered a stiff hand, which I took. My fingers tightened

around his as he yanked me up. As soon as we landed, he let go and booked it down a road that was much wider than all the others we'd passed. "Behind each waterfall, you'll find the arteries of the Lev—our version of avenues."

I studied the curtain of *ayim* a moment longer, then the street below—*far* below—before gulping and trotting to catch up with him. Bronze doors and sparkling panes of glass lined the quartz walls, along which crawled vines heavy with blooms that fragranced the glowing white street.

I craned my neck to stare at the angelic trickery of sky, attempting to find fault in the illusion, but there was none, the same way there had been none in the guilds.

Oomph. Distracted by the fake sky, I bumped into Asher's coppery-turquoise feathers. He gripped my shoulders to keep me from flopping backward, then tucked his wings in, and let go.

Behind him, the glittery sea foamed and puffed. "Is that also an illusion?"

"No, the sea is real. And so are the Nirvana Mountains in the distance."

Tall peaks covered in glow-in-the-dark blooms crenellated the cobalt sky. I remembered Ophan Mira telling us the fluffy flowers were slippery like snow but warm like desert sand.

"Because you're a Verity, you have a sea view," he explained.

"I shouldn't get special treatment because of my origin."

"I didn't make the rules, Leigh."

"Perhaps not, but you're one of the Seven, so you have the power to change them."

He narrowed his eyes that glowed like the stars over my street.

"Just like you unblocked Jarod's score." My fingers curled into my palms. "Just like you signed me off from my mission."

His eyes hardened along with his voice. "Completing your wings was Jarod's idea, Leigh. Not mine."

"Leigh?"

The flow of blood in my veins stilled at the familiar sounding of my name. Slowly I spun, coming face to face with my past.

My present.

And I supposed, since both our wings were now complete, my future.

*E*ve landed on the edge of the avenue, her body haloed by her yellow-gold wings and the puffing sea at her back. "Good evening, Seraph."

Too stunned to utter a word, I simply stared. At her oval face, her hazel eyes, and the long swoop of dark hair that fell over a dress made of several layers of red chiffon accented with a gold leather belt.

"I just dined with Mother who told me you were ascending, Leigh." Eve was slightly flushed, as though she'd flown at wind speed to arrive before I did. "I didn't believe her, but here you are."

"Here I am," I said drily.

Asher cleared his throat. "You two are actually neighbors. We thought you'd appreciate having a friend close by."

Oh, the sweet torture. I supposed he hadn't been informed of our little spat back in Paris. Unless he had but deemed our bond too solid to be destroyed by barbed words.

Eve plucked a small bloom from the wall and twirled it beneath her nose. "Mother wanted a word with you, Seraph. At your convenience, of course. You can find her at Great Oak."

As he began retreating down the avenue, I called out, "Will I see you tomorrow, Seraph?"

He glanced over his shoulder at me. "If you want to."

What I wanted was to return to Earth and see Jarod, but that was impossible. Seconds ticked by as he waited for my response. One that never came, because I didn't want to give Asher the impression I desired anything more than his friendship. Until he got betrothed or Jarod arrived—whichever happened first—I'd keep my distance.

"Good night," he said in a tight voice that rumbled through the street, garnering more than a little attention from the angels passing by or watching from their windows.

Once he was gone, Eve said, "I didn't request this living arrangement."

"I imagined as much."

She dropped her hand to her side, bruising the small flower in her fist. "I apologized. What more do you want from me?"

"I'm not angry about Jarod. I was at first, but Jarod's the best thing that's ever happened to me, so thank you for him."

Her long, arched brows dipped low. "Then why did you blow up at me in Paris?"

"You mean, when you insulted Celeste?"

"She insulted me back."

"Eve, you think you're better than everyone else, and in many ways, you are, but don't expect to have real friends if you belittle them at every opportunity."

She gasped, the flower sliding from her fingers and drifting like a feather toward the buffed stone. "Belittle them? Who did I belittle?"

"Me." Even though I kept my voice low, the heat of it seared the air. "You've always disparaged me—my weight, my proclivity for romance novels, my deliberate slowness to accomplish missions. I'm far from perfect, and considering all that's happened to me in the last few days, this"—I gestured between us—"feels ridiculous, not to mention petty. I don't want to fight with you. I'm tired of fighting. I'm plain tired."

"You look exhausted."

I shut my eyes, annoyance threatening to boil over.

"But most of all, you look depressed."

My gummy lids opened. "Wow. Thanks. Criticism was exactly what I needed."

"I didn't mean it like that—" She squared her shoulders.

"Forget it. I'm the bad guy, and that's all I'll ever be to you." Her wings unfolded, and her sandaled feet lifted off the ground.

Before she could take off, I said, "I didn't want to ascend. Jarod and Asher took the choice away from me. The Seraphim signed me off so I could start earning feathers again. I'm trying not to be angry at either of them . . . or at you. I don't want this anger. I hate anger. It's toxic."

Eve turned toward me, eyes flashing with pity. "I'm sorry. What they did wasn't fair or right."

I lowered my gaze to the flower whose petals fluttered like ladybug wings. In so many ways, we shared the same fate—plucked, taken, and tossed, but where it would wither, I would live forever. Unless cut flowers didn't wilt here?

"I don't understand how he made it into the system in the first place," she said. "It ranks souls, and he has none."

The roots of my hair felt like they'd caught fire. "Just because he's done some bad things, it doesn't make him soulless."

"He's a Nephilim, and you know, as well as I do, that they don't have souls. That's why no Malakim goes to them upon their deaths."

My heart started to bang. "If that were true, he wouldn't be in the system."

"The Ophanim explained—"

"They also explained the sky in the guilds was real, so forgive me if I don't give a crap about what they've told us! If Jarod's in the system, then he has a soul!"

The street turned ghoulishly silent.

"His father was human," I added, voice shaking, "and *all* humans have souls."

Eve's pointy chin seemed to become pointier. "Nephilim blood poisons souls. Even if he's a hybrid—"

"He's the first of his kind!"

"My mother told me she knew another Nephilim hybrid—soulless like your Triple."

"Jarod's not a Triple. Not anymore!"

"It doesn't change—"

"Stop it!" I pressed my palms against my ears, and my aching heart stuttered to a halt, braking the flow of blood beneath my skin.

Eve's eyebrows pinched together as though in genuine regret.

Slowly, so *very* slowly, I lowered my hands. "I need—I need to talk—to talk to Asher. Where's—where's Great Oak?" My throat was so dry the words were brittle and hurt to push out.

Eve sighed. "Come. I'll take you." She started down the avenue, past wide-eyed angels.

When I didn't follow, she returned to my side and took my limp hand. I stumbled after her. She jumped off the ledge behind the waterfall, and I plummeted down with her, her spread wings decelerating our fall, then she tugged me past the waterfall and farther around the Lev, past groups of angels sharing laughs and drinks beside the fountain and couples dining by angel-fire.

I bumped into someone. "S-Sorry." If it weren't for Eve's firm grasp, I would've keeled right over from the impact.

The angel I'd collided with—a man with broad shoulders and an even broader smile—stared down at me, then at my wings. "You can bump into me whenever you want, Silver."

Eve rolled her eyes. "You're wasting your breath, not to mention your extraordinarily original pickup line, Jax."

I gaped dumbly up at him as Eve dragged me farther around the arc, stopping sometime after the fourth waterfall. Three angels dressed in white tunics stood shoulder to shoulder. As we approached, one of them raised a palm. "This restaurant is closed until further notice."

"Erelim aren't reputed for their intelligence," Eve muttered to me. Then to them, she said, "I was just here. Have you already forgotten who I am?"

One of them elbowed the other, then tipped his head toward the mirrored façade behind them. In perfect synchronicity, they parted, sanctioning our entry. Eve released me as she traipsed past them, head held high and gilded wingtips extended as though she were one of the Seven.

The inside of the restaurant—was it a restaurant?—was entirely made of copper from the mosaic floor to the hammered slabs paneling the wall to the copper-toned mirrored ceiling looming the equivalent of two stories high. The only thing not made of copper was the fat tree rooted at the center of the restaurant whose branches either supported slices of green marble or had been whittled into stumps to perch on.

A set of fuchsia wings tipped in platinum swayed from one of the uppermost branches where a wingless waiter deposited two slender flutes filled with something clear and bubbly.

"Do you want me to stay?" Eve asked quietly.

Before I could answer, my name rung out. Seraph Claire broke into a smile statelier than the circlet ringing her black hair. "What a splendid surprise. Seraph Asher was just informing me of your arrival. Join us for a drink. Now that you've ascended, you may finally sample something a little more grown-up than Angel Bubbles."

I had no desire to drink. Besides, I'd sampled plenty of grown-up drinks before my forced ascension. "I'm sorry to interrupt, but I have a pressing matter to discuss with Seraph Asher."

Claire tilted her head to the side. "If this concerns your sinner, then speak freely."

I ground my stilettos into the mosaic floor. "Will he ascend?"

Seraph Claire's eyebrows pinched. "He's a Nephilim, Leigh. Nephilim don't ascend."

I gripped my elbows. "He's only part Nephilim."

"His Nephilim half cancels his human half."

"Seraph Asher said his rank was dropping, which means he has a soul."

She pursed her lips.

"Right?" My question quivered through the air like the feathers at my back.

"We do not allow Nephilim souls to be harvested."

"They're not soulless, Mother?" Eve sputtered.

Claire fixed her emerald eyes on her daughter. "Every living creature possesses a soul, but Nephilim souls are toxic to our kind, and, thus, cannot be reaped."

Tears pricked my eyes, turned the tree into a gnarled giant. "That's not fair."

"What isn't fair? That we choose not to poison our realm with their noxious souls?" Claire's tone was as cold as the layer of ice enveloping my skin.

"Why did you tell Jarod he was going to ascend, Seraph Asher?"

His turquoise wings tensed at his back. "I didn't, Leigh. Jarod knows he cannot enter our world."

"But he said—he said . . ." *That he'd be right behind me.* His promise rang through my throbbing skull, turning the pounding at my temples agonizing.

Smears of yellow and red coagulated before me. I blinked to find Eve moving closer to me. She didn't reach out, just stood there, her arm touching mine, lending me a wisp of solidarity.

It was my turn to save you.

He'd tricked me so that I wouldn't sacrifice my wings.

"He's nobler than I gave him credit for," Claire admitted.

I swallowed, and it left a trail of fire inside my clenching throat.

Eve's arm slid around my hunched shoulders. "Mother, he saved Leigh, a Verity no less. That should grant his soul access to Elysium."

"The law is the law," Claire said.

Eve's jaw clenched. "You'd be dooming a deserving soul."

"A deserving soul? He is a *Nephilim*, Eve!"

"But he *has* a soul, Mother. At least, bring his case up with the Council."

"You may be my daughter, but this does not permit your tongue to run wild. Besides, Seraph Asher brought his case up already, and we voted. End of story."

I touched Eve's forearm, appreciating her unexpected support. "I don't want you to get in trouble because of me."

Her lips pressed into a hard line. "It's not right," she murmured.

"Seraph Asher," I said tonelessly, "please burn away my wings."

Color leached out of Asher's skin.

"Don't be ridiculous," Claire said. "No one's burning anyone's wings off."

I gripped my elbows tighter, my palms molding around the sharp bones. "They are mine to do as I wish, and I want them gone."

Eve's lids pulled up so high white surrounded her hazel irises. "Leigh, no!"

Asher pumped his great wings. A heartbeat later, he landed in front of me. "Jarod sent you away to protect you."

"It wasn't his decision to make. Or yours. It was mine!"

Claire flew down from her perch, her bright pink wings dappling the copper mosaic. "You are behaving like a petulant child."

My blood boiled in my veins as though angel-fire now irrigated my body. But it didn't. Not yet. Not ever. I turned toward Asher. "Burn. Them. Away."

Raking his hand through his long hair, Asher hissed, "He wouldn't want this."

"Again, they are *my* wings. Mine to keep or discard, and I choose to discard them."

I didn't think Asher could grow any paler but his skin turned alabaster. "Leigh, please take some time to reflect on this."

I stretched them out so his fire could have unobstructed access to each silvery barb. "Now."

"Fletching manners are deplorable," Claire huffed. "If we'd talked like this to our predecessors, they would've burned more than our wings."

I narrowed my eyes. "I apologize for being such a terrible disappointment to our race." I released my elbows. "On the upside, as soon as your fellow archangel removes my wings, you will be rid of me and my deplorable manners."

All of Claire's features tautened. "If she doesn't appreciate her gift, then by all means, remove them, Seraph."

Eve's arm stiffened around my shoulders.

"Leigh, please," Asher murmured raucously. "It'll break your parents' heart."

"My parents? You mean those angels who gave birth to me but never visited because they were too worried I would fail? Excuse me if I sound ungrateful, but I favor my heart over theirs."

"Leigh." My name fell from his lips, a hollow murmur.

Eve's wide eyes glistened. "Give yourself a few days to think about this. Please," she added in a tremulous whisper.

"Your heart may be broken," Asher said, "but it'll heal, and one day, you'll thank Jarod for the gift he gave you."

"I understand the consequences of my choice. I understand the pain will terminate my immortality and scar my mind, but my wish remains unchanged. I want to return to Earth and be with the man I love. Now, will you do it here, or must it be done in the Shevaya?"

"Have you even used your wings?" Asher asked.

I clamped my molars. "Here, or in the Shevaya?"

"Fly once, Leigh. Circle Elysium. Look our world in its face before you decide to forsake it." Did he really think that a gravity-free stroll would miraculously alter my will? "Once. And if after that, you still desire to renounce your heritage, I will strip you of it."

"I'll go with you," Eve volunteered.

"No." Claire eyed Asher. "Let them go alone." She probably considered me a terrible influence and wanted to keep her daughter away from me.

"You promise to burn them as soon as we're done with our promenade, Seraph?"

Asher seemed to reach deep for patience. "I promise."

"Let's go then."

A hand caught mine and reeled me back. And then a pair of thin, rigid arms came around me.

"I know I sent you away," Eve mumbled, "but I hated living without you. I hated our fighting. I want you back, and I swear that if you choose to stay, I will be the friend you deserve."

Slowly, I lifted my hands and hugged her back. "I can't stay, but I appreciate every word you just said. And you *have* been a good friend." I smiled. "Most of the time."

A strangled laugh leaped from her, followed by a sob. "Pick us, Leigh. Pick us."

I kissed her cheek, my lips coming away wet with the salt of her sorrow. In all the years I'd known Eve, her composure had never splintered. "You're going to be a great angel, but use that greatness to better our two worlds, okay?"

A new sob lurched out of her. She pressed her knuckles against her trembling lips.

I sighed. "I wish you didn't have to wait a century before returning to Earth."

Celeste was right. So much had to be changed, and however deeply I wanted to see this change come about, *help* it come about, I needed to get back to Jarod before he assumed I'd abandoned him forever.

"I'm ready for my tour, Seraph."

*A*sher stretched his great wings and pushed off the glowing quartz floor, then waited for me, suspended among the stars.

"Do you remember when we used to hop between our beds with our arms out and pretend to fly?" Eve called out.

I looked for her, found her standing beside the Erelim, eyes still shiny but face otherwise composed again.

"Well, it doesn't feel like that at all." She raised a smile.

I returned her smile with a quiet one, then rolled my shoulders, and eased my wings out.

If I had wings, they'd be stretched from one wall of this office to the other. Jarod's words tumbled through my mind, shortening each beat of my heart. I stared toward the Arch, toward the Channel that would soon take me home, then snapped my wings.

The ground vanished from beneath my feet, and then all of the angels staring up became no larger than ants. Gasping, I strained my feathers to brake my dizzying climb, then retracted my wings, and plummeted as quickly as I'd risen. An arm caught me around the waist, kept me afloat.

"It's all right. I got you," Asher said, as anguish battered my ribs. He angled my body so that my stomach was parallel to the ground. "Stretch your wings back out but don't flap them."

I followed his instructions, the fluid fabric of my pants twisting around my legs.

"I'm going to let go now."

Every muscle in my body spasmed with fear. I was about to plead with the archangel not to let go, but it didn't feel right to let him hold me, so I bit my tongue and steeled my spine.

His arm unwound slowly, then completely.

And I didn't fall.

We remained suspended in midair, our feathers fluttering in the balmy breeze.

He studied the taut lines of my body before shifting his gaze to the top of the plateau from which rose a seven-pointed stone edifice nestled in the smoky *ayim* that raged toward the sides of the cliff and tumbled down the rock façade in seven powerful waterfalls. At first, I thought the pointy structure was an island, but then, I realized it moved, floated, like a star discarded from the sky.

"Is that the Shevaya, Seraph?"

"It is."

I observed the glowing, unmoored star, then the land wreathing it—the crenellated mountains in the distance dappled with phosphorescent blooms and the dozens of other white islands that rose from the billowing *ayim* like Muriel's soufflés.

Once I'd drunk my fill of this strange land, I turned toward Asher. "So, how do I maneuver these things?"

"Flex them once, then glide. The more you flap, the faster you'll go. The key is finding the right balance."

I moved my wings up and down. When my body lurched forward, I flung my arms out, trying to balance on the breeze. Somehow, I managed.

"That's it," Asher said encouragingly.

My speed slowed, so I pumped my wings again, and although I bobbed a little, I managed to make my way across the sky without falling. Other angels flitted around us, keeping their distance as though not wanting to disrupt my lesson.

"Should I land beside the Channel?"

Asher frowned.

"I imagined that's where you'll burn my wings?" Could I still travel through the Channel wingless? "Unless you have to do it back on Earth?"

His confusion turned to fury. "You hardly flew at all!"

The wind twisted my hair, tossed it into my eyes. "Have you ever been in love, Seraph?"

"No, and I hope I'll never be."

"Why do you say that?"

He flicked his hand toward me. "Look at what it did to you."

I blinked but then sighed as I realized he was lashing out because he didn't understand what it was to share a heart and soul with another person. "Look at what it did to Jarod," I countered.

His jaw sharpened. "Another reason you shouldn't give them up. Imagine how many human souls you'll be able to touch with your patience and love."

I smiled sadly.

"Sacrificing your life for a few years on Earth"—he shook his head—"it's not worth it."

"Change the law and allow his soul to ascend, or allow me to return to Earth with my wings intact now."

He wrenched his hair off his face. "You don't understand what you're asking! I can't just snap my fingers and amend laws that were established to keep our kind safe."

"I think you're capable of a lot more than you give yourself credit for, Seraph."

"If I take you back to Earth, I'll lose my place on the Council, not to mention the other archangels will probably char my wings right off my back."

"Better mine than yours, then."

"Leigh," he growled, slapping the air.

"I'm sorry if my decision angers you, Seraph, but I don't want to live in a world ruled by laws I find outdated and senseless."

"You think the human world is so much greater?"

"No. But the human world has Jarod."

He fixed me with his turquoise eyes. "Marry me and change the laws."

A wave of sadness lapped against my ribs. "I'm sorry, Seraph, but I can't. I'd be a terrible partner, because I'd never be able to give you my heart."

"I don't need your heart, just your voice."

"You'd want to spend an eternity with a person who loves another?"

"It's a sacrifice I'm willing to make to save your life."

I smiled at his brusque and unromantic gesture. "As much as I appreciate your selflessness, I cannot accept. And one day, you'll thank me for having turned you down."

His gaze hardened. "Thank you?" He snorted. "Your death—because without wings, you *will* die—will forever be on my conscience, so I don't see how I'll be *thanking* you."

I dragged my gaze off his face and stared at the wisps of lavender smoke puffing from the white canyon beyond the Arch. "Please take me home."

"You *are* home." The pain in his voice made me want to reach out, but I didn't.

"This is your home, Seraph, not mine."

"Have you considered how seeing you wingless will make Jarod feel?"

Jarod's words swelled inside, filled the void he'd left when he'd sent me away: *I want you here. With me. I need you here.*

I smiled. "Angry. He'll be terribly angry that I disregarded his wishes. *Again.*"

Asher stared at me as though I'd already lost a piece of my mind.

"Celeste, too. She'll bite my head off."

Asher kept staring, dumbfounded by my eagerness to feel their wrath, not understanding that some furies were fueled by love. "Let's get it over with then," he said gruffly.

My heart lightened as though it, too, were made of feathers.

He dove, his massive wings creating a current that pushed me higher. My wings strained to keep me in place, and then they, too, pumped the air, sending me hurtling toward the Arch and the future that awaited me beyond it.

"*I* can make it quick but not painless," Asher said, as I dusted myself off after landing a tad brutally.

I nodded.

"There is no reversing this once it's done."

Thin ropes of lavender smoke twined around my ankles, as though trying to carry me home. "I understand."

He shut his eyes, and his nostrils flared.

I stared around me one last time. Perhaps I hadn't given this world a fair chance, but how could I when it wouldn't give Jarod one?

"Stretch your wings out and kneel." Asher's deep voice drifted to me on the breeze. "I don't want you to fall and hurt yourself."

I was touched by his concern. "You're a kind man, Seraph."

He grunted. "My kindness cost you your wings."

I frowned.

"If I hadn't listened to Jarod . . ." He let his voice trail off, but I heard all the unsaid words.

I would still have lost them, but their demise wouldn't have weighed on his conscience. "I'm sorry you got tangled up in our story, but please don't blame yourself. None of this was your fault."

"*All* of it was my fault." He squeezed the bridge of his nose.

"If I hadn't entered Jarod into the system, you wouldn't be begging me to burn off your wings."

"If you hadn't entered him into the system, I would've missed out on meeting my soul mate."

His hand arced toward his thigh, smacking the brown leather ensconcing it. "There is no such thing as soul mates!"

I didn't want to waste any more time fighting with Asher over our diverging beliefs, so I chose silence and knelt, pressing my palms into the warm stone and offering the archangel my back.

For several heartbeats, nothing happened, and I thought he was going to go back on his word. But then, the reek of burnt feathers filled my nostrils, followed by a bolt of scorching pain. I gritted my teeth as tongues of fire lacerated my back, excruciating and insistent, like slashes from a serrated blade. White dots danced at the edge of my vision.

I would ask if all angels are as beautiful as you are, but I've seen them, and fuck if any hold a single feather to you.

Fighting to stay conscious, I dug my palms and knees into the stone, perspiration dripping from my scrunched brow. Another wave of fire streaked over me, so violent I thought my entire body would go up in smoke.

To Abaddon and the magnificent angel who'll be sharing my cell.

Another brutal wave of pain sank into my spine. Even though I clamped my jaw together, a muted sob lurched out. The world grayed, and Jarod's face, the one which had danced out of my holo-ranker, shimmered behind my closed lids.

You are blinding me to the surrounding world, Feather.

More gray dappled my vision, and I clawed at the hot stone to stay upright, but my elbows bent, and the ground rushed toward me. The world darkened, then came into focus. Clumps of silvery ash fell around me like fresh snow.

The temperature dropped, and I shivered, the frost that replaced the fire burning just as fiercely.

"Is it . . . is it over?" Sweat and tears ran into the corners of my mouth.

"Yes."

I closed my eyes, letting air whisper through my cracked lips and across my scourged skin. Slowly, my heartbeats spaced out, my breaths, too. I tried to push myself up, but my muscles convulsed, and my bones rattled. My cheek smacked the hard stone.

"Don't move, Leigh," Asher commanded.

My fingers twitched as I pressed them into the stone. The archangel lifted my limp body, and I gasped from the pain of his arm pressing against my back.

Like peeling paint, the world flaked away, strip by strip, until only starless blackness remained.

6 6

*P*ale light filtered through my clasped lids. Slowly, I pried them open. The bluest, brightest sky streamed through a large window. I stretched my body that felt like it had gotten trampled during the night.

I'd ascended, and then I'd . . . then I'd . . . I tried to move to check over my shoulder for feathers, but a face appeared over mine, and I froze.

"How could you do this?" Celeste's eyes were redder than when I'd left her.

The last few hours trickled into my mind, feeling like both a dream and a nightmare. *Had* it been real? Had I flown over Elysium? Had Asher burned my wings?

"Can't believe you got rid of your wings," Celeste said, her voice breaking over a sob.

Apparently, it had been real.

I lifted my hand and touched her narrow jaw. Her tears ran over my fingers.

"When Asher carried you through the guild last night, I thought . . . I thought you were dead."

I breathed in deep, and it reawakened the leftover agony of the archangel's fire, so I held my breath instead, and that eased the pain. "Where are we?"

"A hotel. You're not allowed inside guilds anymore."

I stared at the unfamiliar room done up in heavy brocades and buttery yellow paint. "I need to get to—"

"Why?" Celeste's voice sounded as raw as my back.

"Why what?"

"Why did you do it? Why did you get rid of them?"

"Because they weren't going to let him ascend."

"What?"

"Jarod is part Nephilim, and they won't allow Nephilim souls to be harvested."

"Nephilim have souls?"

I stole a breath, then retained it until the pain eased. "They do."

Her large eyes grew larger.

"You were right, Celeste. Our laws—*your* laws . . ." They were no longer mine. "They need to be reassessed and reformed."

Her pupils swelled in disbelief.

"Will you help me sit?"

She wrapped her fingers around my shoulders and began to lift me but let go when I winced.

"No. Go on."

She hooked her fingers around my shoulders and peeled me off the downy pillow.

My bones felt as though they were being broken, one after the other, as though Asher's fire had welded my vertebrae together and they were popping apart. The hotel room vacillated and vanished.

When it reappeared, it was cloaked in darkness, and Celeste was nestled beside me, her soft snores filling the quiet space. I shifted underneath the sheets, taking inventory of my body. The flesh on my back still tingled, but there were no fiery jolts of pain.

I edged away from Celeste, then eased my legs off the bed. The room spun but eventually settled. I pushed up and stood, one hand clasped around the headboard in case gravity stole my equilibrium. When several minutes passed, and my body hadn't collapsed, I walked to the bathroom. I shut myself in, then felt the wall for a switch. I flicked it up, temporarily blinded by the sconces beside the mirror. I blinked, and peach marble—not white quartz—filled my vision.

Peach suddenly became my favorite color.

I turned on the tap, splashed cold water over my face, then stared at my reflection. My eyes looked sunken, and one of my sickly pale cheeks was marbled by a bruise. I lowered the straps of the navy nightie Celeste must've salvaged from my closet in the guild, tucked my hair over one shoulder, then let the silk slide down and turned.

Two purple angular crescents marred the skin over my shoulder blades—a reminder of what I'd given up to return to Jarod.

Although I didn't regret my sacrifice, proclaiming their absence didn't weigh on my heart would've been a lie. If only I could've kept them *and* Jarod.

But that hadn't been an option.

Readjusting my nightie, I tiptoed back inside the bedroom and opened the closet, but it was empty except for Celeste's black boots, a pair of terry slippers, and a bathrobe. I slid the slippers on and pressed a kiss as light as icing sugar to my friend's brow before leaving.

When I reached the lobby, I realized I had no money. No cell phone either.

Oh well . . . I'd sort this out once I reached Jarod's home.

I passed by the hotel lobby, thankfully deserted at this late hour. The concierge manning the night desk looked up at me, then down at my slippers, his brow furrowing.

"Bonsoir," I said, blustering past him and out through the revolving doors.

The valet attendant blinked at me.

"Can you get me a cab please, sir?"

After another quick sweep of my odd outfit, he raised his gloved hand and whistled, and a cab glided beside the curb.

"Where to?" the woman driver asked once I'd settled in.

"Place des Vosges."

She glanced into the rearview mirror several times during the drive. "I don't know how close I'll be able to get to it. It's been a circus around there."

I frowned.

"That mobster, Jarod Adler, well, he leaked names and documents detailing crimes to every paper in the country. The press is calling it the Demon Files. You haven't heard about them?"

Alarm skipped down my spine. "I've been away."

"Hasn't been this crazy in Paris since the bombings a couple years back."

I looked out the window, wishing the hotel Celeste or Asher had picked had been closer to Jarod's home.

The radio blustered to life, and as the cab rolled slowly across the dark city, I heard Jarod's name being spoken over and over as the late-night hosts speculated about what could have triggered the mob boss's change of heart. I heard them mention Tristan's death and then venture another hypothesis—*secret agent of the DGSI.*

I'm trying to be a better man, Feather. I'm trying to be worthy of you.

All at once proud and frightened by his reveals, I worked the lace hem of my silk shift between my fingers, my pulse drumming quicker and quicker until it drowned out the sound of the radio.

I'm almost home, my love.

When the iron fence framing the manicured square appeared, I almost ripped the handle off the car door. News vans and police barricades clogged Jarod's street, and bright beams slashed the darkness. The thunder in my ears grew so loud I thought it would slit my eardrums. As soon as the car slowed, I leaped out.

The cabdriver lowered her window. "Hey. You forgot to pay me!"

"I'll send someone out with money."

A police officer stepped in front of me. "This road has been shut down."

The cabdriver was still hollering.

"I need to see Jarod Adler," I said, desperation shaking my voice.

"Sorry, but I can't let you through."

I calculated how I could get around him, and in doing so, my gaze landed on Amir, who was arguing with a man shouldering a huge camera.

"Amir!" I yelled, waving my hands.

The bodyguard with the smashed face looked up, and his eyes, which were as bruised as my cheek, widened. "Mademoiselle Leigh?" He shoved past the cameraman. "Jarod said you'd left."

"I'd never leave."

Someone tapped my shoulder, and I twirled.

"*Mon argent.*" The cabbie stuck out her hand.

"I'll take care of it." Amir shoved the police barricade aside so I could slide through, then peeled a green bill from his pocket, and handed it to the woman.

Is that the girl from the opera? What's with the hotel slippers? What happened to her? Questions were flung left and right. Flashes from camera bulbs went off brightening the darkness before blackening it further.

Amir draped his jacket around my shoulders as he walked me to the porte-cochère. Even though the fabric smelled of sweat, I tugged it around me, thankful for the extra bit of warmth and privacy it afforded me.

There was no familiar click tonight. The door just gave way when Amir pressed his fingers into the lacquered wood.

"Jarod broke the lock," he explained, the bones in his face straining his skin. "The boy has had a death wish since you—since you left."

Even though I'd been removed from this house against my will, guilt washed over me. "I'm back. For good."

I stepped over the raised threshold, looking toward Jarod's balcony. I wanted to shout his name, tell him I was home, but my violent pulse made the measly act of breathing an exploit.

I quickened my footsteps, almost colliding into a bodyguard. As we glided past each other, a bitter, gray scent wafted off the man's bushy, wiry beard—gun smoke? Had the man fired his weapon? Had someone tried to harm Jarod?

He peered down at me, and his eyes went as wide as Amir's. I surmised Jarod's staff hadn't put much stock in me returning.

Running a hand over his bald head that reflected the glow of the sconces, he nodded to me before scuttling across the courtyard, probably to go guard the doors that no longer kept Jarod safe.

I shot my gaze to the balcony. All was calm inside the house yet I sped up.

I finally found my voice in the checkered foyer. "Jarod!"

A door snicked open, and I readied to launch myself into his arms.

"Leigh?" Muriel's eyes were smudged with so much black

makeup and worry. "*Ma chérie!*" In three quick strides, her arms encased me, banding against the scars on my shoulders.

I crushed my lips together to avoid yelping.

"Oh, *ma chérie*. He said you left him, but I knew you wouldn't."

I hugged her back, hard. "I'm so sorry I left, Muriel." And not just Jarod, but her, too. "I'm so sorry," I whispered, emotion threatening to spill over. "I had to do something, and it's done. And I'll never leave again."

She pressed me away, her palms skating over my cheeks as though to make sure I was real. She narrowed her eyes on my bruise. "What happened? Who—"

"Where's Jarod?"

"Upstairs." She tucked a lock of snarled hair behind my ear and sighed. "Thank goodness you're home."

"Amir said he broke the lock on the front doors."

"He did. And then he fired everyone. *All* of his bodyguards. *Everyone.* Including me and Amir."

"But you stayed." So had Amir and the other guard I'd passed in the courtyard.

"Like I would ever leave him." Her mouth curved into a sad smile, which she pressed against my forehead. "I'm so glad you're home, *ma chérie*. Now, go to him."

I spun away from her and tore up the stairs, kicking off the slippers after tripping twice.

His door was already gaping, so I pushed it wider, my entire body skittering back to life as though it had lain dormant since being torn away from Jarod.

"My love, I'm home!"

He lay still on the cowhide recliner.

"Jarod?"

His head lolled toward me, and then his lids pulled up, and his dark, radiant eyes locked on mine.

6 7

I shut the door and raced toward him, about to throw myself over his prostrate form and kiss him senseless when the upturned, purple-stingray box beside the recliner startled me to a stop. Amir's jacket tumbled noiselessly off my shoulders, pooling at my feet. Silver feathers littered the oriental rug, seesawing from my brusque arrival.

Were those the ones I'd lost the night I'd spouted lies like exhales? I'd never asked what had become of them, but now, I knew. Jarod had kept them.

All this time, he'd stored them like treasure.

At least, until tonight. Had replaying one of my memories angered him so much he'd tossed the box?

"Feather?" Jarod's deep timbre made my gaze leap back to his.

I sidestepped the box, careful not to touch a feather—I didn't have the heart to revisit my past.

"Asher said you wouldn't be . . . allowed to return . . . in my lifetime." His quiet speech was laborious, punctuated by long intakes of air. "But you made them . . . change the rules." The awe burning in his eyes sent goose bumps scurrying over my skin. "That's my girl."

The tiny bumps on my skin hardened, and I swallowed. He thought the Seven had allowed me out of Elysium with my wings intact? I kneeled beside him and gathered the hand dangling off the edge of the recliner, pressing it against my cheek.

His twitching fingers felt like ice. "Did they also . . . change the law . . . on Fallen souls? Have you come . . . to collect mine?" His lips parted around the shortest, quietest breath, and then his heavy eyelashes dragged over his eyes.

I stared at him, perplexed. "Collect yours?"

Something plopped against my bare thigh.

Something warm and wet and—

"Jarod!" I gasped as blood dripped off the edge of the cowhide and onto my lap.

He heaved his lids up, then shifted his body as though trying to roll onto his side, but his jaw clenched, and he grunted. I released his hand and shoved his jacket open, then his shirt, the buttons popping off.

Right below his ribs, a depression in his skin oozed blood.

A bullet hole!

As I prodded it, his lungs spasmed, and his stomach muscles contracted. I snatched my hand back. I wanted to yell for help, but my voice was rooted to my throat the same way my knees were rooted to the rug that was slowly darkening with blood.

"I gave my enemies every chance to get their revenge . . . because I didn't want to live"—he lifted his hand toward my face, but it flopped back down without making contact—"without you." His chest rose and fell sluggishly. Too sluggishly.

I finally located my voice, and it shredded my throat as it soared out of me. "Muriel!"

Would she hear me? I'd shut the bedroom door, and the walls in this house were so damn thick. I twisted around to eye the door, then twisted back toward Jarod, who seemed to have lost more color during the fleeting second I'd looked away.

Useless. I felt so useless.

When his eyes closed, I lifted off my knees to lean over him and cocoon his sallow cheeks with my palms, running my thumbs over his proud cheekbones.

"Stay with me, Jarod," I pleaded before screaming Muriel's name again, praying the thick wood wouldn't swallow my shout. As I waited for someone to arrive, I asked, "Who did this, my love?" I had every intention of finding the culprit and putting a bullet through their putrid heart.

"The former prime minister's"—his features crinkled in pain —"guard."

His guard?

Horror struck me. The bearded man I'd passed! He'd looked familiar. I'd assumed it was because he worked for Jarod. My stomach seized as rage swished inside. I yelled for Muriel again, then for Amir, and then, although my voice wouldn't carry into Elysium, I screamed for Asher.

Jarod lifted his hand and curled it around my wrist, his shiny eyes losing some of their luster. "Show me your wings."

My throat rolled with a swallow. I wanted to lie, tell him Asher warned me to keep them hidden while on Earth, but Jarod was as familiar with my expressions as I was with his. He saw the truth before I could bury it.

"Feather, you didn't . . ." His Adam's apple juddered angrily.

My wild pulse battered the crescents seared into my back. "I couldn't live without you either."

He shut his eyes as though the sight of me was unbearable.

"Look at me, Jarod. Open your eyes and look at me. I'm not going anywhere, and you're not either. I'm going to get help."

"It's too late."

I leaned closer to his mouth, stroked his high cheekbones faster. "No, it's not. It's not. I'm going to fix you."

He grunted.

"Don't hate me, please," I croaked.

His eyes opened, hardened by grief. "I love you too . . . *fucking*"—he hissed in pain—"much to hate you."

Why was no one coming? I tried to extricate myself from his grasp to wrangle the phone off the nightstand, but Jarod's grip tightened.

"Since you can't give me forever . . . then at least, give me now." His low, stricken tone made tears swell behind my lids.

I ripped one of my hands off his jaw and pressed it over his chest, clawing through the dark curls desperate to breach skin and reach the failing organ.

His thumb caressed the inside of my wrist. "Kiss me, Feather. I want to end my life . . . with your taste on my lips."

I shook my head. "This is not the end. It's not. It can't be."

He smiled so sadly my disintegrating heart crumbled like a wasted feather. "If it's not . . . then you can bet . . . that I'll find you again."

I whimpered, dragging my gaze to the bullet wound. Maybe, I could plug it with fabric, or—

Jarod sputtered, and my eyes snapped back to his. When his forehead grooved, I pressed my trembling lips to his to swallow his pain and make it mine.

"Don't leave me, Jarod. Please, don't leave me," I spoke against his mouth.

His thumb stroked my wrist with heartbreaking tenderness, and then his mouth whispered over mine as soft and chilled as an autumn breeze. I wedged our bodies closer, welding my skin to his, my pulse to his.

"I love you," I murmured, nudging his mouth open.

His thumb stilled, and then his grip slackened.

My ears began to ring. "Jarod?" I dug my palm against his chest. Either my skin was growing numb, or I was missing *every* beat of his heart. "Nononono. You can't leave me."

His fingers fell away from my wrist, banging against the recliner before spreading open like a night-blooming lily.

"*Nononononono.*" My cries bled into one another.

I kissed him again, willing his lips to move over mine, willing his lungs to expand, willing his heart to spring back into motion.

Tears streamed off my chin and bled into his unmoving mouth. I prayed for a miracle, prayed my kiss would magick this incredible man back to life. But his mouth didn't prod mine, his hands didn't tangle inside my hair, his thick eyelashes didn't flutter against my cheek.

Was this my punishment for giving up my wings?

How cruel fate was!

My lips slid off his but didn't leave his face. I kissed his stubble-roughened jaw before keening my agony against the cooling skin of his neck.

The scent that had intoxicated and seduced me night after night curled into my lungs like spiny velvet—soft yet shredding.

I understood, then, why his mother had put an end to her

days. How could one go on with a deadened heart? How had she lasted four years when four seconds already felt too long?

I rocked back onto my heels, scrubbing the tears out of my eyes as I scanned Jarod's bookshelves. When the letter opener glinted back at me, I rose, crossed the room, and clutched the cold metal, curling my anesthetized fingers around the hilt.

I'd already committed the gravest sin of all. What was another?

The angel was now a sinner.

I returned to the recliner and climbed over Jarod, nestling in the cradle of his body, remembering a time when he'd held me so close I didn't think he would ever let go.

I stared at the knife, caught sight of my swollen green eyes in the blade. I tried to muster the courage to plunge it into my chest. I pressed the tip into my skin, but metal met bone. How had Mikaela done it?

A bead of blood bloomed and trickled between my breasts. I'd need to deepen the cut to join Jarod.

I'd known we'd end, both of us Nephilim, but not so soon.

Not like this.

I licked the tears off my chapped lips.

Butchering my skin was so brutal, but it wasn't the pain I feared. It was the time. The time it would take my soul to meet Jarod's, wherever it was Nephilim souls went.

Perhaps they drifted around the world together . . . forever.

I lifted my wrist and studied the web of blue veins, focused on the thickest one, and then slashed the sharpened letter opener over it until the blade broke the skin and blood spurted, streaming out like the wine Jarod had forced upon me to prove there existed more to life than rules and regulations.

How I'd hated him that night. But how I'd adored him every ensuing night.

I reached for his jaw, trailing crimson ribbons over his rigid chest. "I'm coming, my love. Wait for me this time."

As Jarod's jewel-toned world began to fade, I trapped his cheek and angled his face toward mine, then pressed my leaden lips to his.

Into his mouth, I poured my slowing heartbeats and softening breaths until my body released my ruined soul from its cage of flesh and blood.

EPILOGUE

ASHER

*D*eath.

In my world, dying wasn't a notion that instilled sadness or anger. It was merely an essential stage in the cycle of souls.

Until tonight.

Until the Ishim came to alert me that two Nephilim had passed away in Paris.

The word devoured me then.

I strapped on my leathers and shot from Elysium to Earth in a single heartbeat.

I thought of Celeste, of how devastated she would be once she learned that Leigh was gone.

Eternally gone.

Fuck!

Fuck.

I should never have burned her wings.

I should have forced her to keep them.

Leigh believed love was a vital part of life, but vital things didn't lead to annihilation.

I thudded onto Jarod's balcony and hunted the darkness for their bodies, found them entwined on the recliner.

Bloodied.

Marbled.

Peaceful.

I shoved the glass doors, but they were closed. I punched in one of the panes, thrust my arm through, and twisted the cool handle. Cloaked by angel-dust, I was invisible, not that anyone guarded his courtyard.

Where were all his guards?

Where was that lady who cared for him more fiercely than a lioness?

Losing him would kill her. Unless she was already dead. I hoped she hadn't taken her life, because her pristine soul merited another round but wouldn't be granted one if she'd ended her days.

How I loathed death tonight.

And our system. It, too, deserved my rage.

I stalked toward the recliner and stared down at the lovers, balling my fingers into fists. Growling, I pummeled the wall next to me, splintering both wood and skin.

Door hinges groaned a floor below me, followed by a feminine voice that echoed against the marble walls of this lavish tomb. "Amir?"

Muriel. At least, she was still alive. But for how long?

I returned my gaze to the bodies, itching to throw them over my shoulders and carry them into the night to spare the woman the cruel sight.

But the blood.

There was so much blood.

I could burn it away, but it would take time.

Time I didn't have.

I shut my eyes, my wings flaring as I battled a dangerous consideration, one that would cost me my title, my feathers, and quite possibly, my life.

Muttering an oath, I splayed one palm against Jarod's rib cage, the other against Leigh's chest, and coaxed both their souls to the surface.

As the gold threads of Leigh's being lapped against my fingers and bound to my skin, pliant and warm, palpitating with calm energy, its virtue and beauty struck me anew, blinding me as formidably as her silver feathers had the afternoon we'd collided in the guild hallway.

Back then, I'd sensed the potential for prodigious change contained within her soul.

Tonight, I finally understood just how deeply it was about to alter the celestial world.

Or, at the very least, *my* world.

ACKNOWLEDGMENTS

I'd like to start this letter by apologizing for having killed off Jarod and Leigh. Until the very end, I wanted to save them, give them the happily ever after they so deserved, but I would've done so for the wrong reasons, for selfish reasons, to preserve your heart and mine.

This book was the hardest and most painful book I've written in my four-year career. I loved and loathed every second of it, because I knew where the story was going. Most of the time, my plots take unexpected turns, but not this time. This time, it all unfolded according to plan.

My tremendously sad plan.

However, I offered you a silver lining at the end. That *wasn't* planned. *Feather* was supposed to be a standalone, but I fell into my world too deep to surface. I won't tell you all I have designed for Asher and Celeste and the celestial gang, but I will admit you'll get that Happily Ever After.

For *everyone*.

What I will tell you is that the story takes place four years later and that the clock is ticking for Celeste who's lost all motivation to ascend.

Now onto the acknowledgments' part.

First of all, thank *you*. I am so grateful you picked up my book and read all of my words. I hope you've enjoyed the journey and will come on others with me.

Next, I'd like to thank the members in my Facebook reader group *Olivia's Darling Readers* for their input, enthusiasm, and constant love. If you enjoyed the setting, you have them to thank for it—they picked Paris. From this wonderful group, I want to send an extra big hug to Kate Anderson for her astounding proofing skills, and Kalli Bunch and Maria Silk for reading an early copy of *Feather* and giving me such helpful feedback. Slipping in a big thank you to the woman who edited my angel romance, Kelly Hartigan.

Thirdly, Astrid, Katie, Theresea. My dream team. My work colleagues. My besties. I heart you three so darn much. Thank you for always making time for me and my books.

Fourthly, my husband. This story was about soul mates. If you had any doubts, Jon, you are mine, so you are *not* allowed to go anywhere, because there is no version of my life that would be worth living without you in it. When we met, you told me it was love at first sight, that you knew I would be it for you. Your unwavering conviction and gifts baring our entwined initials just about scared me right back to New York, but in retrospect, I was immature and selfish, and hadn't yet understood that I'd won the love lottery. Every single day, I grow a little more in love with you, which is frightening, because I'm aware forever doesn't exist, although I'd like to think there's something after this life. You can be certain of something, though. If there is an afterlife, I *will* find you. It's no longer just our initials that are entwined, but our very souls.

And our blood. Hope you appreciated my gory transition to the fifth people I wanted to thank: my children. My wonderful, loud (oh, *so* loud), vibrant children, Adam, Gabrielle, and Estée. Thank you for making my life so colorful and vanquishing boredom before it could ever take root. You might not own all of my time, but you do own all of my heart.

To the family I was born into, I wish there was no geographical distance between us. I wish we could still all live in the same city. Not in the same house, though . . . Don't think I could survive my father's need to close every gaping door or my little sister's hording tendencies. Sorry for singling you two out. Next time, I'll target the others. ;)

To the family I married into, I love you and our lively chat group very much. What luck to have been adopted by such an extraordinary and united clan.

LOVE ALWAYS,

Olivia

ALSO BY OLIVIA WILDENSTEIN

YA PARANORMAL ROMANCE

The Lost Clan series
ROSE PETAL GRAVES
ROWAN WOOD LEGENDS
RISING SILVER MIST
RAGING RIVAL HEARTS
RECKLESS CRUEL HEIRS

The Boulder Wolves series
A PACK OF BLOOD AND LIES
A PACK OF VOWS AND TEARS
A PACK OF LOVE AND HATE
A PACK OF STORMS AND STARS

Angels of Elysium series
FEATHER
CELESTIAL

The Quatrefoil Chronicles series
OF WICKED BLOOD
OF TAINTED HEART

YA CONTEMPORARY ROMANCE
GHOSTBOY, CHAMELEON & THE DUKE OF GRAFFITI

NOT ANOTHER LOVE SONG

YA ROMANTIC SUSPENSE

Masterful series

THE MASTERKEY

THE MASTERPIECERS

THE MASTERMINDS

ABOUT THE AUTHOR

USA TODAY bestselling author Olivia Wildenstein grew up in New York City and earned her bachelor's in comparative literature from Brown University. After designing jewelry for a few years, Wildenstein traded in her tools for the writing life, which made more sense considering her college degree.

When she's not sitting at her computer, she's psychoanalyzing everyone she meets (Yes. Everyone), eavesdropping on conversations to gather material for her next book, and attempting not to forget one of her kids in school.

She has a slight obsession with romance, which might be the reason why she writes it. She's a hybrid author of over a dozen Young Adult love stories.

oliviawildenstein.com
press@oliviawildenstein.com

Made in the USA
Las Vegas, NV
03 January 2021

15228147R00243